THE JANE AUSTEN MARRIAGE MANUAL

Kim Izzo

WINDSOR
PARAGON

First published 2012
by Hodder & Stoughton
This Large Print edition published 2013
by AudioGO Ltd
by arrangement with
Hodder & Stoughton

Hardcover   ISBN: 978 1 4713 2508 3
Softcover   ISBN: 978 1 4713 2509 0

British Library Cataloguing in Publication Data available

Printed and bound in Great Britain by
MPG Books Group Limited

THE JANE AUSTEN
MARRIAGE MANUAL

For my mother, Carolynne. And my beloved grandmother, Muriel, you are greatly missed.

Happiness in marriage is entirely a matter of chance.

—*Jane Austen,* Pride and Prejudice

Introducing Me

It's my wedding day. The skies open up and sheets of rain and hail pelt the stone terrace where the ceremony is to take place. I suppose that any other bride would be in hysterics by now. But I don't have time to fret over the weather, because I'm wanted elsewhere. Or I think I am. I walk stealthily down an unending hallway inside an English country manor as the rain and hailstones strike the windowpanes in a savage rhythm. My heart is pounding from nerves and exhaustion. Wedding jitters? I'm just thankful I chose a simple bias-cut gown instead of one of those corseted numbers. Besides, as a woman of forty, a corset would make me look like I was trying too hard, or worse, like some desperate reality show contestant.

I glance over my shoulder to see if anyone has noticed me, but the hall is empty. Down the grand staircase I glide, managing to move past wedding guests stuffed inside the enormous ballroom without detection and fling open the doors to the driveway. I hate getting wet, but not today—today the rain is liberating, so out I go, my bare feet making muffled, crunching sounds on the gravel as I start to walk faster. And I think that only six months ago everything was normal. I knew who I was. I had a job, a home, friends . . . a life that made me happy. Who knew turning forty would be so fraught? It wasn't supposed to be this way, it was supposed to be just another birthday, just another number. But that's not what happened.

A huge thundercloud rolls overhead, threatening

1

to let loose. I can't see through the rain. Not far enough to catch even a glimpse of what I came to see. Of who I came to see. I take it as a sign. I pause and take another look at the stately mansion that's now behind me. It is a beautiful estate deep in the English countryside. I should go back. There's still time. A menacing clap of thunder shakes the ground. The storm isn't letting up. Good or bad omen? The wind picks up and lifts the edge of my soaked dress, revealing my bare legs. I must decide. No one knows I'm here. I can dry my dress. Redo my hair. Going back isn't exactly a hardship. After all, what woman in her right mind would try to escape a Jane Austen fantasy come true?

BOOK 1

THIRTY-NINE
AND COUNTING

1

With Child

Vanity working on a weak head produces every sort of mischief.

—*Emma*

Six Months Earlier

'It is a truth universally acknowledged that a single woman of thirty-nine and in possession of a good complexion must be in want of a husband. And a baby. Unless you are me.' My personalized version of that famous line from *Pride and Prejudice* was a mantra of sorts for me—a self-professed Jane Austen addict and an exception to this truth. Not that it mattered. I was as swept up in other women's pregnancies and new-mothering dramas as if I did want those things.

Modern life as we know it is divided into two camps: the haves and the have-nots. The haves being those with children and the have-nots those without. As a have-not it was up to me to be as supportive and understanding of the haves as possible; after all, I had more disposable time and income than they did. At least that's how it was in the beginning. 'Get closer, all of you!' Gavin, a South Asian man of slight build and large personality yelled at us. 'Us' being the entire staff of *Haute*—fashion magazine du jour—gathered in the staff's overly stylish kitchen, chattering away,

5

jobs forgotten. The occasion? Babies shower. The plural being necessary given that five women on staff were about to pop. To save catering costs the editor-in-chief, Marianne—one of the five, eight months' pregnant and my best friend since college—decided to do an all-in-one shower. At least there were cupcakes.

'Closer!' Gavin shrieked. He's our fashion director and a complete scream. 'Don't just stand there! Squeeze in as tight as you can to Kate.'

That would be me. Kate. The one minus the baby bump. The one perched on the wooden stool surrounded by pregnant bellies swathed in all-black designer maternity wear and teetering on four-inch platform pumps. The women did as they were told and moved closer. Too close. As they turned to check one another's hair and makeup, their five swollen tummies, hard as basketballs, knocked my head in rapid-fire succession. I fought to keep my balance on the stool and tightened my grasp on the precious cargo in my hands.

'Don't get those out of order, Kate,' snapped Ellie. She was seven months along and also one of the smuggest pregnancy snobs I'd ever met. Ellie routinely boasted about getting in the family way after only one attempt, even when she knew others on the staff were up to their ovaries in IVF treatments. Still, I smiled reassuringly, recalling my duty to be supportive of all pregnant women no matter how unruly their hormones made them.

'They're irreplaceable, you know,' she barked.

'They' are the five-part series of ultrasound images I held in my hands. For some inexplicable reason the mothers-to-be had decided to bring their collection of ultrasounds to the party for

6

comparison. Somehow I was given the task of holding them before they were to be pinned to the inspiration board that was normally reserved for fashion tears and layouts. I wanted to ask if we could play a game of pin the tail on the baby, but thought better of it.

'Say "cheesy,"' Gavin called. We did. He snapped away as if we were supermodels striding down a Paris runway. 'Perfection!'

That task complete, the women went back to sharing their child-birthing anxieties and thrusting baby bumps in my face as though I were invisible. I stood up to avoid the line of fire—which made all the difference because I'm five ten in bare feet, six two in my four-inch Mary Janes—and that's when I spotted Jennifer, twenty-seven, stick thin, bottle blonde, drop-dead gorgeous, and the new features editor at *Haute*. She was munching a celery stick and rolling her eyes at me in sympathy. She had a reputation for being ruthless and had written articles about how to network with winners and avoid losers; how to be a good frenemy to those who count; and how to rise above your colleagues even if they're better at the job than you are. She had even complained about having to ante up cash for other people's unborn children and their toys. I smiled slightly and moved away.

'The fetus has turned,' Ellie gleamed to Marianne and glared at me for daring to listen in on a story that I couldn't possibly relate to. Now that I think back, Ellie was a bitch long before the invasion of the hormonal body snatcher.

I wanted to say 'so has the worm,' but bit my tongue.

7

'I think the fetus is actually bigger than normal for this stage,' she said proudly. 'At least the doctor says the fetus is bigger.'

How many times can one person say 'fetus'? Whatever happened to 'baby'? Now don't misunderstand me, or my tongue, which sometimes speaks like it has acid reflux. I have nothing against babies or pregnant women, and I offer my support whenever possible. That may mean choosing the perfect gift or baking the perfect lasagna—my signature dish—for when a new mother arrives home with the baby and can't bear the thought of cooking.

I get along just fine with pregnant women. And pregnant women, especially of a certain age (those closer to forty than thirty) were everywhere. Which was all right with me because my livelihood depended on them. You see, I am hired to fill in for women on maternity leave at fashion magazines. I work contract to contract, so I even keep a journal of who is newlywed, who is trying desperately to get pregnant, and which of the slutty girls at the various magazines around town had a drunken weekend.

I had found my niche as a beauty editor, which means I spend my days writing about the latest mascara innovation, lipstick shade, and antiaging procedure. Or, more accurately, I'm an acting beauty editor, emphasis on 'acting,' making me the ideal solution for every pregnant woman who still worried about her career before the birth, the sleepless nights, and diaper changes hit. Most women who have kids later in life view their career as their firstborn, and so they panic when faced with the prospect of handing the reins over to a stranger.

That's where I come in. I'm a career contract player and I like it that way because each contract comes with an end date and that comes with freedom: freedom from office politics, freedom to frequently change scene, freedom to freelance, and freedom to travel at a moment's notice. That I hadn't traveled or freelanced or even changed scene as much as I had envisioned was beside the point. I could if I wanted to. But none of that mattered now because my pattern of short-term employment was about to change. Darlene, whom I replaced three pregnancy contracts ago at *StyleView*, a sister magazine of *Haute*, had resigned to be a full-time mom. The magazine had to hire someone to fill the vacancy. And that someone would be me. I had turned down permanent offers in the past, so I knew the company wanted me. Just thinking about it made me smile. This is where all those years of playing hard to get would pay off in an above-average salary, private office, and—I was convinced—a signing bonus. An injection of cash that I needed desperately because I was broke. Through no fault of my own. Or at least not entirely. Put it this way: I had misjudged a man, but more on that later. Besides, there comes a time in every woman's life, even a self-described intrepid one such as me, where stability is as sexy as adventure. This job would give me what I needed to be happy.

Right now, though, I was hungry. Still clutching the ultrasound images I spied the Magnolia cupcakes on the table and was about to pounce when I felt a hand on my arm. It was Marianne. Wearing an empire-waist tunic and leggings, she rocked maternity wear better than anyone.

'I can't believe I got the stroller I wanted,' she

9

beamed. 'You must have told them.'

'Maybe,' I admitted. Marianne had her eye on this very posh stroller from Germany that wasn't available in America yet. But the magazine had loads of European contributors so I had made a few phone calls and raised the appropriate funds from the staff—Marianne was the boss, after all.

'Are you sure you could afford it?' she asked softly. She guessed, correctly, that whatever we were short I had topped up. But that was before the incident, the error in judgment that had made me broke.

'Don't even think about it,' I said reassuringly, still eyeing the cupcakes, narrowing my choice down to a red velvet one with vanilla frosting.

'Have you heard from him?' she said, bringing up the incident.

'Not a word, and not a penny,' I answered gamely.

Here's what happened. I was living with a guy named Chris on the Upper West Side for three years. We were content, sometimes even happy, with how things were. I never wanted the big ring, the fluffy wedding or, even worse, the marriage, so cohabitation was for me. For us. I believed that we were as committed as any married couple. I believed this so firmly that when Chris was laid off from his graphic design job and wanted to pursue his lifelong dream of becoming a film editor I offered to put him through film school. After all, we were a couple and I'd amassed enough savings to make his dream possible. He was ecstatic and we made room in the apartment for the state-of-the-art edit suite he needed to practice on.

It was perfect.

10

Until he met a sexy postproduction coordinator. He moved out almost immediately, swearing to pay me back the more than fifteen thousand dollars I'd loaned him, not to mention the debt he'd run up on my credit cards when his own were maxed out and he needed new software or whatnot. Well, that was over six months ago and I've not seen a penny. Just excuse after excuse about the low wages of an apprentice editor and could I try being a little more patient? Sigh. I was a first-class sucker and now, along with my patience, all I had left was my own retirement savings plan—mutual funds and the like.

I needed Darlene's job. Badly.

'Really, I'm fine,' I insisted.

'I'm glad,' Marianne said sweetly and rubbed her stomach. 'And I'm looking forward to having this baby and eating some of your famous lasagna.'

I smiled. 'The secret family recipe,' I said furtively. 'You might get more than one.'

'Kate, can I speak with you a moment?'

We turned around to see Gloria, the executive publisher of the entire company, and Marianne's boss, walking toward us. This must be it. My job offer had arrived. I practically floated out of the kitchen and into Gloria's office.

'Sit down,' she said. I smoothed my hair and dress as I sat in the gray guest chair. I wondered if I could order a red one for my office. 'You obviously know the economy is in a slump,' she began.

Of course I knew. It was September 2008 and the economy was big news. The words 'financial crisis' were everywhere. So maybe I'd have to forego the signing bonus.

'We're anticipating a heavy loss in advertising

11

revenue,' she continued. 'Not just *Haute*, but across the entire company. We have to make cutbacks. I know you're substituting for Claire but she's back next week.'

'And you have to find Darlene's replacement,' I interjected with a knowing smile. 'My salary requirements are negotiable.'

She stared at me and shook her head. Maybe I'd spoken too soon. 'Not anymore,' she said and averted her eyes. 'We're no longer filling her position.'

I couldn't decipher what Gloria meant because of a sudden sensation I might faint.

'Her assistant will be promoted and she'll have to do both jobs herself,' Gloria explained. Then seeing my blank expression, she continued. 'We've also made the decision not to fill maternity leaves. Existing staff will make up the slack. To be clear, once Claire returns next week, you're not needed here any longer. I'm sorry.'

I swallowed. 'I'm fired?'

'No, not at all,' she corrected me. 'You were never an employee, just a contract worker. We're simply not renewing your contract.'

It was suddenly very hot in Gloria's office. I thought back to the kitchen full of my now former colleagues. The Ellie types, the Jennifer types, and all those in between. 'Does everyone know?'

'No, not even Marianne,' she said. 'I wanted to tell you first.'

I marched to my cubicle, my Mary Janes clipping and clopping so loudly on the hardwood floor I felt like a cavalry officer or his horse. My plan was to slip away without having anyone see me. I was no longer in the mood for cupcakes.

12

'Kate, darling!'

I nearly tumbled over when Claire appeared and threw her arms around me.

'I brought a new photo of Peanut,' she said smugly and plopped down a glossy five-by-seven of her son. 'I hope you don't mind. I'm back next week and, well, it's not like you have photos to put up.'

She hovered, opening packages of makeup, rifling through my in-tray. There went my plan.

'I'll be right back,' I said and trounced off to the ladies' room in the hope that Claire would be at the shower by the time I came back.

I shut the stall door and leaned against the metal partition. That's when I realized I was still clutching the ultrasound photos. Fuck. This meant I would have to return to the party. At that moment I heard two women walk in and begin to preen in front of the mirror.

'Why was Kate in the photo?'

Did she mean me?

'It's like she wants to be one of them,' the other voice chimed in. 'All she does is cover maternity leaves. It's weird.' They were definitely talking about me.

'Why doesn't she have kids of her own?'

'Instead of hanging around all the pregnant women? I heard her boyfriend dumped her.'

'Really? Why?'

'He met someone else after Kate put him through school! He left her with a big, empty apartment and loads of debt. She had to move back home to Scarsdale,' one of them said with a snicker.

I sat there gripping the toilet. Should I remain silent and keep my dignity? Or confront the cows then and there? I chose option two. I stood up,

13

opened the door, calmly walked out, and washed my hands. Seeing me, one of them grabbed on to the counter as though she were about to topple over. I refused to make eye contact but I recognized them; they worked down the hall in ad sales. What was obvious was that they were both pregnant, but forget Yummy Mummies. These two were Monster Mamas. They had been at the shower but were too early in their pregnancy to be included in the actual celebration. I wiped my hands dry, tossed the paper towel into the bin, turned and faced them, and, making a show of staring at their swollen bellies, I smiled warmly.

'Did you know that half of all men start an affair during their wives' final trimester?' I lied pleasantly.

I went back to my desk, grabbed my things, and ran, but not before stomping back into the baby shower to find Ellie. I didn't do it on purpose but as I stuffed the ultrasounds into her hand, the images flew onto the floor like a deck of cards, scattering in all directions. I heard the surprised shrieks from the women but I didn't stop to help. Maybe I was crying.

Marianne tried to chase after me. But that's the thing about pregnant women, they're easy to outrun, even in four-inch Mary Janes.

14

2

A Male Perspective

Those who have not more must be satisfied with what they have.

—Mansfield Park

'That's rough,' Brandon admitted after listening to me recount my lousy day. 'But those girls in the bathroom? They're jealous.'

I looked at Brandon, who had just emptied a martini glass in three slurps, clearly skeptical.

'Jealous of what? They have everything they want. They're married and pregnant.'

Brandon gnawed on a helpless olive. 'Katharine Billington Shaw'—he always said my full name when he wanted to make a point—'you're tall, thin, gorgeous, and single,' he said, as though that explained everything. 'They're married to men who bore them, who they don't want to have sex with except to get knocked up. And now they're scared witless that their lives are no longer going to be glamorous—no more cocktail parties, free trips to Paris on the magazine's dime, or squeezing into sample sizes. But you . . . you're free.'

Let me explain Brandon. He's my other best friend, alongside Marianne. Super cute, super smart, and super sweet, Brandon. We were madly in love in sophomore year at college. Naturally I dumped him. But he was devastated. It took the entire junior year for Brandon to forgive me

15

and then one day he was my friend again. Every once in a while in between boyfriends I wonder if I should get back with Brandon. But we're so like brother and sister that the ick factor outweighs any short-term benefits. He makes his living directing television commercials, not exactly his Hollywood dream, but he was always one of those people who could adapt to anything thrown their way.

'I wonder if Gloria was making excuses and they just don't like my work,' I said feebly. 'When is this slump going to ease up?'

'It's not, Kate. It's very bad,' he said with sudden urgency. 'You should be squirreling away every penny.'

I glared at him.

'Oh God, sorry Kate, but you know what I mean. Be careful with the money you have. It's really important.' Frankly I hadn't seen Brandon so worked up since George Lucas refused to release the original *Star Wars* on DVD.

'Have you been reading your investment statements?'

'Not lately,' I answered glibly. 'Can't bring myself to open the envelopes now that it's all I've got.'

'You'd better,' he explained seriously. 'Stocks, mutual funds, your retirement fund, are all worth much less than they were.'

I flinched. I had been contributing to my retirement plan steadily—well, not steadily—for about a decade. I had saved nearly thirty thousand dollars. I was relying on it in case I couldn't find new work fast.

'What do you mean, 'worth much less'? How much less?'

'There's something in the air, Kate,' he

16

said grimly. 'We may be headed for another Depression.'

I sighed. He was being overly dramatic. This sometimes happened with Brandon; after four years of film school he saw life in epic movie proportion.

'I thought I'd find you here.'

We turned to see Marianne lumbering up the small steps toward our table by the window. We were at my favorite bar, an elegant space called Avenue, which was in a luxury hotel. I always imagined that I would meet the man of my dreams in a hotel. But so far I'd only ever met my two best friends here. Marianne sat down and ordered a pinot grigio, ignoring the glare from the waitress. She allowed herself the occasional glass of wine, which she'd sip and, more often than not, I would finish.

'Are you okay?' she asked me gently. Her tone was a bit too babying, like she was practicing her mommy voice on me.

'Quit asking me if I'm okay,' I said firmly. 'Why wouldn't I be?'

'Oh, I don't know, because you didn't get the job you thought you were a shoo-in for. Because the publisher isn't renewing your contract. Because of what happened in the washroom,' she answered. 'Belinda and Rosalie confessed.'

I squirmed at their names. As if sensing my discomfort, Brandon piped up to change the subject. 'We have to make plans for your birthday, Kate,' he said gleefully. 'Forty and fabulous!'

I rolled my eyes and gulped my wine. I was the first of the three of us to turn forty, and in less than two months. 'You know how I feel about parties.'

17

There are two things I have always felt strongly about: I don't celebrate my birthday and I don't fret about my age. Even as a child I dreaded having a party. Too much attention and fuss for what seemed, even then, to be a minor accomplishment. After all, there is little achievement in being born; everyone I know has done it. And as my grandmother would say, 'age is only a number.'

'But this time we *are* doing something,' Marianne insisted. 'Why not a forties film theme? Those are all your favorite movie stars!'

I stuck my finger in my mouth. They were treating me like a child.

'You can dress up as Katharine Hepburn,' she added.

'You mean as the other unmarried, childless Kate?' I snapped.

'You don't want to be married with kids. That's why you've avoided the altar—remember?' she reminded me. Not that I needed reminding. 'Or have you changed your mind?'

I wrinkled my nose at her to indicate my mind remained unchanged.

'What about Jane Austen then?' Brandon jumped in swiftly. 'You never get sick of her stories.'

There you have it. What I'm known for: a love of 1940s movies and Jane Austen. All I needed was a house full of cats and I was ready to age gracefully into spinsterhood.

I sipped my wine in silence. They took the hint. I had a theory about where my determination and confidence to skip my birthday came from. Forty wouldn't bother me as long as I was in a good place—in a home of my own, a job I enjoyed, with

18

family and loved ones around me. In other words, being perfectly fine with forty depended on where I was when it hit. But after today one of those prerequisites—the job—had vanished.

'So how is the quest for fatherhood going?' Marianne asked Brandon. Our conversations always diverted back to pregnancy when Marianne was around. She had a rather militant approach to the process.

'Fine,' he said uncomfortably. 'I'm having sex on demand.'

'How arousing,' I said sympathetically. Brandon's live-in girlfriend, Lucy, was desperate to get pregnant. They had been trying for a year with no luck. I didn't like Lucy. If a woman could be described as a package wrapped in brown paper and tied with string, this was she: plain, sturdy, and tightly wound. But Brandon was nuts about her. I never understood the appeal: Lucy was one of those girls that men drooled over but women couldn't stand. Marianne's theory was that Lucy wasn't a girl's girl—she didn't like the company of women and that was why we disliked her so much.

'It's how babies happen,' Marianne said patiently.

'With a temperature reading and a command performance?' I asked sarcastically. She glared at me. I was the only woman on Brandon's side.

'It's a bit of pressure,' he admitted softly. 'I do want a baby, but she's obsessed. I feel like I'm not really involved, except in the obvious way.'

Marianne rolled her eyes.

'Maybe I'd like to get a girl pregnant the old-fashioned way,' Brandon confessed sheepishly. 'Lust.'

19

'Don't be silly,' Marianne snapped.

Brandon shrugged and proceeded to choke on an olive. Coughing, he said, 'But forget about my issues. Poor Kate!'

'Yes, I know.' Marianne's voice had softened once again. 'I'm so sorry about the job. I had no idea. I'll make sure we have loads of freelance writing for you.'

'Maybe I could get a job outside of publishing?' I suggested. After I'd stormed out of the office I had called around every magazine editor I knew and got the same resounding response: there were no jobs, not even maternity leave contracts, available anytime soon.

'You could be a wardrobe mistress again!' Marianne said happily. I had spent my twenties on independent film sets sewing buttons and steaming period costumes. I shuddered at the thought of the eighteen-hour days and minuscule pay.

'Or you could try bartending again,' Brandon added, smiling. I had been a bartender for one horrifying day back in the nineties. I still can't open a wine bottle or mix a cocktail without having a panic attack.

'I could temp,' I said meekly.

We sat in silence for a few moments, trying to think of what I could do for money.

'Too bad you couldn't teach classes on Jane Austen.' Brandon smiled.

'Too bad I wasn't one of her young heroines, then my mother would marry me off and I wouldn't have to bother with all this work crap.' I shrugged. 'Women had it easier when all they had to do was find a husband.'

'That would have been a challenge for you

20

considering your aversion to becoming a bride,' quipped Brandon. 'You're too independent for that anyway.'

'Touché!' Marianne said and clinked my glass. I rolled my eyes and took a slow, deep sip. As the wine coated my tongue a disturbing thought crept into my mind, so unnerving that I shivered.

'Do you think I'm too old to marry well?' I asked cautiously. Marianne and Brandon chuckled. They thought I was joking. Maybe it was the wine or all our talk about birthdays and money but as they laughed the reality hit me square on the jaw. Soon I would be forty. A middle-aged woman. Maybe it *was* too late to make what Austen called an 'eligible match.' Maybe marrying a wealthy man had an expiry date, and I had reached it. I was past due. I was best before. I shook myself free of the thought. It was silly to worry about *that*. My love of Jane Austen aside, I had never aspired to marry, let alone marry *well*. I was in a bad spot financially, but otherwise I was just fine, thank you very much.

'I'm ready to go,' I announced. 'I've had a hell of a day.'

3

The Misses Shaw

There are few people whom I really love, and still fewer of whom I think well. The more I see of the world, the more am I dissatisfied with it . . .

—Pride and Prejudice

I lived in Scarsdale in a house I shared with my grandmother and mother. After the Chris debacle left me with no money and no roommate to split the rent I had to give up the fifth-floor walk-up on West Ninety-first Street I had called home. 'Give up' is generous. 'Eviction' is more accurate. Still, the commute by train into Manhattan each morning didn't bother me one bit; after all, I'd grown up doing it. And in a stroke of genius my family had kept an old beater just in case, a black Chevy, which made the trip from train station to home passable.

The asphalt on our driveway was warped and cracked from years of snow and salt but we never had the money to repave. The tires rolled comfortably to a full stop in their familiar sunken grooves and I switched off the engine and sat staring straight ahead.

I was out of work. I looked up at my family home with its pale blue paint and white shutters and trim. It was always a pretty little house kept neat and tidy due to my grandmother's handiwork. What a relief its existence didn't depend on me. It was paid off

22

thanks to my grandparents' diligence and frugality back in the day. I felt the corners of my mouth turn up into an involuntary smile. Our home was no Mansfield Park, but at least I would always have a roof over my head. With this happy thought I got out of the car.

I opened the front door and tossed my handbag onto the floor. My mother, Iris, was sitting on the sofa checking her lottery tickets. At the kitchen table was my grandmother, who preferred that everyone call her Nana ('Grandmother' sounded too old), calmly sipping a gin and tonic.

'Hi, love,' Nana said with a smile.

'Hi, Kate,' Iris chimed in. 'We won a free ticket.'

My mother and grandmother were dedicated lottery people. Winning anything, even a free ticket, justified their obsession.

'How was your day?' Nana asked me with a look that seemed to sense my day hadn't been all that good. I didn't want to worry her and decided to keep my situation to myself for now. I could still head to the city every morning; they didn't have to know.

'It was fine. Here, Nana, I brought you this,' I said and handed over an elegant gold compact with translucent powder in it that I'd taken from the beauty closet. I would miss this particular job perk, free products, very much.

'What's that for?' Iris asked jealously. 'Why do *you* get a present?'

Iris hated to be left out. Of course I had a gift for her, too, but her childish reaction took away any pleasure in giving it to her. Iris's fits of jealousy were legendary and something I'd grown up with but had never grown fond of. It was a trait we all

23

endured, except for my father, who couldn't take it and left when I was four, never to be heard from again. Though according to Nana and my older sister, Ann, Iris had plenty of reasons to be jealous: reasons like Debbie, Sandy, and Suzie, for starters. Apparently my father could charm the pants off of anyone and that was the problem.

'Thanks, love. I needed this so badly.' Nana smiled at me, revealing the gap between her front teeth. She ignored my mother and busied herself by swiping the fresh puff across her skin. 'It's for my nose,' she answered.

'You don't use that on your nose,' snapped Iris. 'You use that Pan-Stik makeup.'

'I use this, too.' Nana turned her head side-to-side examining her reflection in the tiny mirror. I could tell she wasn't happy about her wrinkles but at ninety-three, even an exceptionally spry and mentally sharp ninety-three, there had to be some. 'Can't you get me something to fix all these lines?'

'Not without surgery.' I grinned. We always had this conversation. I told her the truth once more; that the tiny vertical lines above her lip were from years of smoking. But she never bought it.

'I've seen you use the Pan-Stik,' Iris insisted.

Nana rolled her eyes. 'I use the Pan-Stik, then I put powder on top.'

'I was right,' Iris said triumphantly. 'You do use the Pan-Stik.'

'Iris, just drop it,' I snapped and picked up the packaging for the recycling bin.

'No one ever lets me be right!' she snapped back as she headed to her bedroom to sulk.

This was my home life. Our family legacy was

24

to get knocked up, make a bad marriage, divorce, then move in with your mother. This was how it had been for my great-grandmother, grandmother, and mother. I'd managed to avoid the marriage and baby, but somehow I still ended up living with my mother. Unlike Ann, who lived in a two-bedroom rental in Park Slope and eked out a living as a legal assistant. She's divorced.

Her marriage had been one of those starter types—two years, no kids—to a regular guy named Matthew. To hear her tell it Matthew was the nice guy, the one good guy she let slip through her fingers. She left him because he wasn't exciting enough and fifteen years and as many jerks later, she regretted it.

I consoled myself with the fact that even if I was back living at home I wasn't one of those freeloading kids who never contribute. Every month I gave Iris a check and she made sure the bills were paid—I paid half the taxes, utilities, and food. She was retired now, but had spent her working life as a civil servant at the Department of Motor Vehicles.

A half hour had passed when Iris came back into the kitchen, her sulk session over. I pulled a lipstick out of my handbag and held it out to her. Iris loved lipstick and never left home without it. She practically snatched it from my hand and tore at the box like a child at Christmas. That was it: Iris was like a child in her reactions and her tantrums. She was unable to handle adult responsibilities beyond her mundane job so Nana took over and raised Ann and me. She was the only true mother I knew and I loved her dearly. Unlike me, Nana had great sympathy for Iris and indulged her in ways I

25

never understood. Even Ann, who was six years older than me, had a fondness for our mother that allowed her to be supportive of her whims. Maybe because Ann saw her as a true 'mom' before our father left, a side I never saw. Iris's troubles were the reason the house would belong to Ann and me after our grandmother passed away, with the provision that Iris could live out her days here.

She slicked the new lipstick across her mouth and preened in front of the hall mirror like she was a movie star. Then, satisfied with her appearance, she sat down on the sofa once again and furiously scratched the play area of a lottery ticket with a quarter.

'Did you win?' Nana asked warmly.

'Not a thing,' Iris said dejectedly. 'Kate, the Lotto is twenty-five million dollars this weekend, you should get a ticket.'

'No thanks,' I answered. I flatly refused to waste money gambling on the lottery.

'You can't win if you haven't got a ticket,' my grandmother added.

'I don't win anyways.' I smiled. 'Neither do you.'

They both shrugged; it didn't matter that they'd never won more than a couple of hundred dollars, they'd still play, no matter the odds. That they believed winning millions was a real possibility always struck me as slightly crazy. No one I knew was ever that lucky, certainly no one in my family.

'I'm starving,' Iris announced and grabbed some leftovers out of the fridge. Popping off the lid of the plastic container she began to eat furiously.

I crossed over to the fridge and grabbed a bottle of barbecue sauce.

'At least put some of Ann's sauce on it,' I

26

said flatly. As sort of a side business Ann made sauces—pasta, barbeque, you name it, all very fancy and gourmet. Cooking was her passion—our grandmother's, too—and together they had come up with these 'secret' recipes.

Confession time: my signature lasagna? All Nana and Ann, no Kate. Although I do help layer the thing in its casserole pan. Iris and I just weren't cooks; it was the one thing we had in common. Ann was convinced she could make a living selling the sauces, but so far only a few friends had forked over the cash for them. My mother, however, wasn't a fan.

'No thank you,' Iris said firmly.

I shrugged and put the bottle down. Then I noticed that my grandmother had barely touched her dinner—leftover roast chicken and vegetables that Ann had brought over the night before.

'Why aren't you eating?' I asked.

'My mouth is still sore,' she answered quietly. Nana was never sick but she'd been experiencing pain in her jaw and having trouble eating for the past month. She had finally agreed to see a doctor and had an appointment today. In all the drama at *Haute* I had forgotten all about it.

'What did Dr. James say?' I asked, trying not to sound worried.

'He doesn't know,' she responded wearily. 'He's sending me to an ears, nose, and throat specialist.'

'An ENT? Is it anything to worry about?' I asked, feeling my stomach lurch.

'Only the good die young.' She grinned.

I smiled weakly.

'We've got an appointment next Monday,' Iris said.

27

'I'll go with you, too,' I said firmly.

Nana stood and took her plate to the dishwasher. As she shuffled along, slightly hunched from her arthritic back, I saw how thin she'd become, too thin. Why hadn't I noticed how frail she was? And as I watched her move slowly toward the sofa so she could watch *Jeopardy!*, the fact that I was turning forty hit me again. My grandmother was more than double my age and I found myself wondering if she considered herself happy. Had life turned out like she'd wanted? It had been decades since she was able to realistically imagine leading a different life. I tried to envision what it must be like when you are forced by old age to stop chasing dreams. I supposed contented reflection replaced striving ambition. A pang of doubt that my life would turn out any differently hung in the air and it occurred to me that I may never amount to anything other than an acting beauty editor and I wasn't even that anymore.

'I'm off,' Iris announced, shaking me from thoughts of doom and gloom. There was only one place that my mother ever went on a weeknight. Bingo.

'Not again?' I said, though I didn't really care. It was her money. If she wanted to spend it sitting on a folding chair, drinking Sprite and gnawing on Doritos, waiting for someone to yell 'N35,' so be it.

'Don't wait up for me,' she said tartly.

*   *   *

By 10:30 I was ready for bed. I walked down the hallway toward my bedroom and as was the norm, my grandmother was propped up in bed, her

28

eyeglasses still on, her book clutched to her chest, softly snoring. I tiptoed into her room, gently removed her glasses, and tugged the book from her hands. 'Good night,' I whispered. She stirred gently but didn't open her eyes; instead, she rolled over and answered sleepily, 'Good night, love.' I switched off her bedside lamp and kissed her on the forehead.

I padded down the hall to my room. When I was little I fantasized that I lived on a great estate. On weekends, Nana would drive us around leafy neighborhoods we could never afford. We'd point out houses we wanted to live in, and I'd daydream about becoming rich enough to one day own one.

Although our house was no great estate, it was home. And even though my room was the smallest, I adored it. The window overlooked our yard. The houses next door and across the street were completely obscured by a tall blue spruce and crabapple tree so I could imagine we were in the countryside. My bed was a mahogany four-poster with a giant feather duvet and the most expensive, high-thread-count sheets I could afford. The whole effect was finished with two antique side tables and a vintage lamp. For the walls I had splurged on Farrow & Ball and the color was called Smoked Trout, which I loved as much for its name as its rich taupe shade. It was supposedly a perfect match to a color found in the library of an English manor house, and was dated to approximately 1813, the same year that *Pride and Prejudice* was published. Yes, I was that much of an Austen fan. Where Ann and Nana bonded over a hot stove, Nana and I would read Austen together and take turns playing the heroines. I was ten when Nana first read *P&P* to me. Austen was my comfort food.

So needless to say that when I climbed into bed and my mind raced back to the reality of unemployment, only one thing could rescue me. I picked up *Pride and Prejudice*.

4

Assigning Women

So many fine ladies were going to the devil nowadays that way, that there was no answering for anybody.

—Mansfield Park

I'd spent my final days at *Haute* tidying up loose ends. On Friday I had unceremoniously handed in my security pass. Now here it was, the very next Monday at 9:30 a.m., and I was standing in my former cubicle. I had come to meet with Marianne about freelance assignments and to double-check that I hadn't left anything behind. It was odd being back so soon, odder still to see how quickly Claire had rearranged the desk. Then Claire was suddenly at my side. 'Hiya,' she said and flashed her veneers.

As Claire droned on about how tough it was for her to reorganize her desk and the beauty closet, something caught my eye. Lying on top of a pile of file folders was a blush pink envelope with my name written in gold calligraphy. I knew immediately what it was: an invitation to a beauty event. If I were right, then it would be my last beauty trip for the foreseeable future. But I knew Claire; she lived for beauty junkets and all the free travel, luxury hotels, and expensive meals they entailed. 'Did you see how I refiled the press kits?' I asked with mock solemnity and pointed to her desk. If she would just turn around for a few seconds I could grab the envelope without her seeing. Gotcha. I snatched the envelope and attempted to stuff it into my handbag but I wasn't fast enough.

'What is that?' Claire's head whipped around like a cobra.

'It's mine,' I responded firmly and held it up so she could see my name plainly spelled out.

'Is that an invite?'

'I don't know.' I shrugged, trying to act as if it didn't matter in the least. But Claire's steely eyes bore into me.

'Open it,' she ordered and held out a silver-plated letter opener.

I don't know why I listened to her. It did have my name on it but, as she would point out, it was really an invite for *Haute*, not for me. I quickly sliced open the envelope and pried out the heavy card stock invitation. I was right, it was a beauty trip and a really good one: a first-class flight to London for a perfume launch. I savored the moment as long as I could, knowing every second was killing Claire. Never one for subtlety she grabbed it from my hands and read it for herself.

'Ooooh,' she purred. 'I fucking love London!'

Clearly she wanted the trip. But so did I.

'It does have *my* name on it,' I pointed out bluntly.

Claire squinted at me. 'It's *my* job, Kate.'

31

No one liked to be put on the spot, least of all a thirty-nine-year-old woman who is eight months pregnant, but that's what happened next. Claire and I marched over to Marianne's office and sat down. It would be Marianne's decision.

'It would be my perfect return to *Haute*,' Claire said tearfully, as though she were a long-forgotten movie star begging for a comeback role. 'It would make returning full-time less daunting, exciting even. You'll understand, when you have your baby, you'll want the same compassion.'

Wench. Pulling out the baby card was cheating.

'I'm almost forty,' I blurted out pathetically. But it was no use. What seemed like hours passed in silence. Then, satisfied she'd put us in our places using only her psychic ability, at last she spoke.

'I think Kate should go,' Marianne said icily. 'She's more up to speed on the perfume and she was invited specifically. This is your first week back, Claire, and you should spend it getting caught up.'

I avoided looking directly at Claire, but I was sure I could feel hot steam spewing from her head.

'Fine,' Claire snapped and stamped her foot. 'What time is it?' She looked at her Cartier watch, then stood up as if the building was on fire. 'I have to go home to breast-feed,' she announced before storming off.

Once we were alone, Marianne's features softened.

'What a drama queen,' she said, not unkindly. 'Now there's something else I want to talk to you about. It's the perfect assignment. It has *you* written all over it.'

I sat up, intrigued. 'Let me call in Jennifer,' she said and picked up her phone.

Moments later Jennifer sat down beside me and I could see in her hands one of *Haute*'s standard freelance writing contracts.

'It was really Jennifer's idea so I'll let her explain,' Marianne said.

Jennifer was practically bouncing in her chair with excitement. 'I want you to write a big, juicy feature on how to make a good marriage in today's social and economic climate,' she breathed. My heart sank; I was the last person who should write about getting married, but she continued excitedly as though she were giving me a fabulous present. 'Everyone around here knows you're the resident Jane Austen expert, so naturally your name came up.'

'Naturally,' I repeated dryly.

Jennifer's expression turned serious, as though the article could save humanity. 'The economy isn't getting any better, some of my female friends in the financial sector have lost their jobs already,' she said grimly. 'But we don't know how bad the situation will get or how long it will last. Job prospects could slow for years. It made me think that making a good marriage will become far more vital to a girl's future than it has been for generations. It was *the* issue in Jane Austen's time, and women today are back in the same situation she was in. I'm sure of it.'

'So, you think women will start behaving like an Austen character and marry for money because they can't find a job?' I summarized bluntly, and stole a glance at Marianne. This was starting to sound an awful lot like the chat we had at Avenue with Brandon. She refused to make eye contact.

'Exactly.' Jennifer smiled, clearly pleased that I

33

was so astute.

'Isn't that a bit mercenary?' I understated, clearly less pleased. 'I admit that some women *do* marry for money, and we have a word for that: gold digger.'

'This is different. With the current job market the choice between a high-powered career or a high-powered husband just got easier,' she explained without irony. 'Having it all by doing as little as possible is the new American Dream.'

'What happened to the old American Dream of hard work and pulling yourself up by your bootstraps?' I asked coolly.

'It's 2008 and we live in Manhattan. Our boots are Italian made and designed in Paris. Besides, who says it's not hard work landing a billionaire? Didn't the Dashwoods and Bennets work at it?' Jennifer said in an ominous tone. 'You're almost forty, Kate, and unmarried; has it been easy for you?'

Before I could respond with the thump of my boots and their straps on her behind, Marianne coughed. 'It got me thinking about your joke the other night about whether you were too old to find a good husband,' she added.

'I had a hunch,' I said tersely.

'Yes, you can write it in the first person,' Jennifer continued. She stopped talking and stared at me. I shifted in the chair.

'Let me get this straight. I'm to write about finding a rich husband, at forty, as a guide for women, as though nothing's changed since *Pride and Prejudice* was published?'

'You'll make it modern. Women from twenty-five to fifty-five will love it,' Jennifer offered

34

confidently.

'You do know that Jane Austen never married, right?' I pointed out and locked eyes with her.

'Reaaaally?' Jennifer drew the word out slowly, then shrugged her shoulders. 'I still think women will like the Austen angle, even if she was more of an armchair expert on marriage.'

'As you pointed out, I'm almost forty,' I said tautly. 'Faking like I'm on the hunt for a husband won't be easy. Won't these legions of rich men prefer much younger women?'

'Don't worry, you look great,' Jennifer said reassuringly and placed her hand on my knee in a show of support. 'No one would think you were a day over thirty. Seriously. I mean that.' Then she stared for a second longer before adding, 'Maybe thirty-two.'

'It's part of the process,' Marianne explained. 'You can answer your own question. Is there such a thing as being too old to marry well? That's your angle.'

My first reaction was to run screaming. Why would I want to write about being too old for anything, even if it turned out I wasn't too old? Yet I couldn't escape the harrowing fact that I was broke and this was a paying gig I couldn't turn down.

'We'll pay you two-fifty a word, so about five thousand dollars,' she explained and lifted the contract up for me to see.

'Sounds good,' I choked. 'Plus London?'

Marianne nodded. Maybe I could make a living at this freelance business. I left Marianne and Jennifer and smiled as my thoughts returned to my upcoming excursion to London—a much easier task than a marriage guide. But my satisfaction quickly evaporated as I remembered my promise to take my grandmother to the specialist the same week as the press trip. I thought briefly of giving in to Claire, but changed my mind. My grandmother was fine. I didn't really need to be there, Iris could handle it. I knew Nana would understand my need to go, she always did. Who could turn down a free trip to London and get paid for it?

5

Perfume and Englishmen

One half of the world cannot understand the pleasures of the other.

—Emma

That's how I happened to find myself a week later, along with what seemed like hundreds of other beauty editors, crushed inside a tent in a London park to witness the launch of a new fragrance called Intuition, which was described in the press release as having 'the most delicate notes of amber, jasmine, and musk' but actually smelled like gin. In a rush of excitement, the spokesmodel, a famous English actress, swanned into the tent wearing a flowing gown of tulle and made her contractual sixty-second speech about the honor of being chosen as the face of Intuition and how it smelled exactly as she wanted to smell.

Like an alcoholic, I thought as I strained to see the

actress, but my table was so far from the podium that her famous features were indiscernible. She was just a blonde speck on the horizon. And that was all she was to remain, as the next day, which was supposed to be my interview, she had woken up ill, no doubt from inhaling too much Intuition, and canceled. I called the only person I knew in London, my dear friend, Emma.

*   *   *

Emma was an English girl that I had met one summer during my stint working as a wardrobe assistant. We had bonded over the grueling hours, the crap pay, and the icky advances of the perpetually drunken leading actor. That was years ago but we had remained close friends. She had moved back to London to become a film composer; instead, she'd fallen in love with a man named Clive who worked in the City as a hedge fund manager (whatever that is). He was loaded and had bought them a town house in Notting Hill, which I had yet to see. It was high time for a visit.

A snapshot of Emma: she was thirty-seven, tall like me, pencil thin, and always kept her hair supershort in a pixie cut circa Twiggy from the 1960s. She spoke in one of those lovely, lyrical English accents that was considered posh, but not mannered like the queen. Did I mention that she liked to drink?

We began our reunion with a glass of white wine at her place, which was airy and bright with high ceilings and white walls, and outlandish white shag rugs over dark hardwood. We sat perched on snow white leather sofas flanked by white accent tables. It must be Clive's taste; Emma could never be this neat on her own, or by choice. I for one was thankful that the wine was white.

From there we moved on to a succession of pubs and many more glasses of wine before meeting up with Clive at his private club in Soho. We were seated at a table close to the fireplace, which had two large leather club chairs facing it.

'I'm very drunk,' I announced.

'I'm bloody drunk, too,' Emma yelped.

As we descended into a fit of giggles a very pregnant woman glowered at us before taking up residence in one of the club chairs.

'Everywhere I turn there's a pregnant woman,' I said, exasperated. 'Does no one use birth control anymore?'

'She's jealous that she can't drink,' Emma offered, then went silent. 'I should tell you,' she gulped. 'I'm trying to get pregnant.'

'Not you, too!' I said accusingly. Catching myself, I quickly added, 'That's awesome! But should you be drinking?'

'The whole bloody thing terrifies me,' she said seriously. 'I reckon getting drunk is the only way to cope.'

I was happy for my friend, but to be honest I was sick of baby talk. The conversation soon went down the familiar road of how long she'd been trying, what she and Clive had done to try, and the usual assortment of tricks, herbs, and science that had brought nothing but worry, tension, and no baby. I listened and gave her tips that I had gleaned from Marianne and every other woman I knew. I was immensely relieved when Clive showed up.

Clive was the picture postcard Englishman. He wore a Savile Row pinstripe suit and bold striped

38

shirt, a silk tie, and pocket square. His face was clean-shaven, with a ruddy complexion and his hair appropriately tousled. His manners were refined, his wit pitch perfect, and his bank account flush.

'I see you two have had a few,' he noted gravely. 'Let's get some water.'

'Oh, come on, luv,' Emma teased. 'Have a pint or five.'

'I need it,' he answered and slumped into the chair and loosened his tie. I didn't know Clive very well, but I sensed his dark mood.

'Something wrong?' I asked.

'The stock market is about to go tits up,' he said bluntly, then continued in a tone that said he was making an obvious understatement. 'No big deal, really. Just a few American mortgage companies are filing for bankruptcy, investment firms are losing billions.'

'Boring!' Emma pronounced.

'You won't think that when we're flat broke,' he snapped.

'Don't be alarmist,' she teased, then turned to me. 'He always thinks we're headed for the poor house.'

I didn't know what to say. I hadn't gotten around to telling her that I'd already fallen victim to the recession and that this trip was my swan song as an acting beauty editor. And I had no idea what their financial situation was. I didn't think of Emma as a big-ticket shopper but their house looked expensive. A woman could get used to that style of living very easily.

'Are things really that bad?' I asked sympathetically, remembering Brandon's warning to me.

39

'It's not good,' Clive answered glumly. 'I'm not sure I'll get my bonus this year.'

'Is that all?' Emma chided him. 'We can get by without your bloody bonus.'

But the look on Clive's face made me doubt that was true.

We let the subject drop and ordered more wine. As we drank and chatted about nonfinancial matters, like where all those shag rugs came from, Clive spotted someone he knew.

'Excuse me,' he said and left the table. I watched as he stood talking to a man who was about our age.

'Who's that?' I asked nonchalantly.

Emma looked over, a bit bleary-eyed, and smiled. 'He's a childhood mate of Clive's,' she explained. 'They went to school together. He lives in the country near Clive's mum. I've only met him once or twice.'

'Well, he's on his way over,' I said and sipped my pinot grigio.

As the two men got closer I was struck by how different he was from Clive. For one thing, he was far less stylish, dressed in a baggy pale blue cotton button-down, faded blue jeans with frayed hems, and scuffed brown loafers. He was tall and skinny, and I mean really skinny, like rock star skinny. But once he was stood at our table I could see his physical attributes trumped his taste in clothing. His complexion was pale like ivory, skin a supermodel would die for. And then there were his eyes. They were oversized and pale blue, the color of antifreeze poured over ice. All this white and blue was made more extreme by his thick jet-black hair. He was quirky looking but strikingly handsome all

40

at once. Suddenly scruffy jeans didn't seem such a fashion crime.

'Kate, I'd like you to meet Griffith Saunderson,' Clive said.

Was Clive so drunk he was lisping? Griffith?

The man held out his hand, and a wide smile slowly unfurled across his face, revealing a set of straight, white teeth.

'Grifter?' I said carefully so as not to lisp like Clive had. 'With a name like that I hope you're not in banking, too.'

'Griffith,' he repeated impatiently. 'Not Grifter. People call me Griff. And no, I'm not in banking. I manage a country estate in Dorset.'

'Oh, you're from the country,' I slurred. 'That explains it.'

'Explains what?' he asked suspiciously.

'Your clothes. You're a kind of farmer?' I smiled up at him.

Emma burst out laughing.

'No, I manage a bed and breakfast,' Griff repeated, clearly offended. I shrugged; maybe it was all the wine but I couldn't fathom that what I'd said was insulting. At least it wasn't intentional.

But Clive, positively horrified, glared at me. 'What precisely is wrong with Griff's clothes?' he asked icily.

'I didn't say anything was wrong,' I protested but it was too late. Emma burst out laughing and answered on my behalf.

'Griff, you are dressed a bit scruffily,' Emma sputtered. 'Kate works at a fashion magazine in New York. She's accustomed to men swanning around in Armani.'

Before I could disagree, Griff rolled his blue

41

eyes to the rafters and sneered at me. 'Well, I wouldn't want to insult such a discerning eye as yours,' he said seriously. His tone was so solemn and condescending that I, too, burst out laughing and felt compelled to defend my innocent, albeit drunken, farmer observation.

'I'm sorry. It's just that your shirt is practically worn through! And those jeans are frayed at the hem; when you said 'country' I assumed you worked outside. Maybe you've got to get yourself some new things,' I said simply. My remark sent Emma into another fit of laughter and I wasn't far behind.

'Kate!' Clive snapped and loomed over us, seething with embarrassment. Griff, not amused in the least, sniffed and looked away.

'Don't bother,' Griff said dismissively. 'I've got to catch the train back to Dorset.'

'Kate's about to turn forty,' Clive said in an attempt to get even.

'Clive!' said Emma through her laughter.

'Really?' Griff mocked me. 'I would have thought you were much older.'

The following morning brought the worst hangover of my life and little memory of the night before. I crawled to the bathroom and forced myself to stand in the shower, clinging to the wall for support. I felt very sorry for myself. But as I stood there, my head pounding, my body sweating, I had a memory flash of Clive's friend and of being slightly rude to him. Was I rude? What was his name? Biff?

Eventually I managed to make my way to the living room, where Clive was cooking a fry-up for Emma.

'God, you look as bad as I feel!' she blurted as I

42

collapsed on the sofa.

'What were we thinking?' I groaned.

'You both ought to be ashamed,' Clive said. 'You behaved like . . . what do you call it in America? Trailer park trash.'

'What do you mean?' I asked, offended.

'He'll get over it,' Emma said dismissively.

'Who?' I asked. 'Biff?'

'Griff,' Clive corrected me sternly. 'You two made such severe fun of his fashion sense that he left, quite embarrassed I'm sure.'

'He has no fashion sense, that was Kate's point.' Emma smirked.

It all flooded back to me. I had told a complete stranger he was a fashion disaster, and worse, I had done so in public. I was a horrible person.

'Christ,' I groaned again. 'I'm sorry, Clive. Should I e-mail an apology?'

'I already have,' he explained.

'Bollocks,' Emma said. 'You did no such thing.'

'I do feel awful,' I admitted. I turned to Clive and pronounced, 'I vow that if I ever see him again I will be polite, complimentary, and sweet.'

Of course the fact that I would never see him again made my vow extremely easy to keep.

As Clive served up the bacon and eggs, my BlackBerry went off.

'Sorry,' I said, and rummaged in my purse for the offending PDA. But my mood changed when I saw it was my grandmother calling. She never called when I was on a business trip. It was a rule we had made long ago; no phone calls unless it was urgent. Seeing her name on the display terrified me.

'Hello?' I answered, panic in my voice. What I

43

heard was the unmistakable, and disturbing, sound of my ninety-three-year-old grandmother crying.

'Kate?' she asked faintly.

Suddenly my hangover cleared and I sat bolt upright.

'Are you okay?' I demanded. 'What happened?'

Hearing the urgency in my voice, Clive switched off the radio in the background.

'My mouth hurts,' Nana answered through tears. 'I can't chew, I can barely put my teeth together.'

It was at that moment I remembered yesterday's ENT appointment. I had completely forgotten.

'Did you take the liquid Tylenol?' I asked desperate to help. 'What did the specialist say?'

'He found a tumor and he did a biopsy,' she explained. Her crying had stopped. She relied on me for comfort as much as I did her.

'He did?' I asked, choking on the fear I felt swelling in my throat. A wave of guilt washed over me. I should have been there. 'I'm coming home,' I said. 'I'll be there as soon as I can catch a plane.'

I hung up and realized that I was shaking, partly from the hangover, but mostly out of fear. I was suddenly very afraid.

'Everything okay?' Emma asked.

'No,' I answered. 'I don't think so.'

6

House Hunting

There, I will stake my last like a woman of spirit . . . I am not born to sit still and do nothing. If I lose the game, it shall not be from not striving for it.

—*Mansfield Park*

On a bright Friday morning my cell phone rang. I was in my bedroom and instinctively knew to sit down when I answered. When I'd flown home I'd arranged with the doctor to call me directly, and not my grandmother, as was her wish because if there was anything complicated she wanted me to understand and explain it to her. But the call came faster than I'd expected.

'It's cancer,' the doctor said without hesitation. 'I'm sorry. I've made your grandmother an appointment with an oncologist on Monday and he'll explain the options to her. But where the tumor is, it's very difficult to treat, especially at her age.'

I don't remember what I said to him. I simply sat on my bed, half-dressed, and looked out my window at the trees blowing lightly in the breeze. I thought what a beautiful sunny day it was and I suddenly despised the perfect weather. I knew what I had to do. Nana, Iris, even my sister, Ann, didn't need to know the truth, not right away. I wanted to give them one last weekend of believing there was hope.

When I came downstairs there was my

45

grandmother on the sofa with her cookbook, plotting the weekend menus, which she now made solely for us since the pain in her mouth had made eating anything but soups and mashed potatoes impossible. Iris was sitting in the kitchen checking her lottery numbers yet again, still chasing a life of luxury. Right now the only luxury I wanted was time, time to spend every precious second with my grandmother.

'The jackpot is thirty-nine million dollars,' Iris announced as I came into the room and sat beside Nana. I held her hand; her skin was soft and warm. I'd always admired her hands, she had long thin fingers, 'piano hands,' she would call them. But what I loved most was how elegant they looked. Even to dust or stir a pot, her hands were ladylike.

'Did you buy a ticket?' Iris asked.

'You know I didn't,' I said but forced the irritation out of my voice. Now was not the time. 'Do you want me to get you a ticket, Nana?'

'I've got mine, love,' she said sweetly and squeezed my hand. I squeezed back.

'Do you want to come for a drive with me while I buy one?' I asked.

She looked up from her cookbook and gave me a puzzled look. Buying lottery tickets was out of character for me. But the great thing about my grandmother was she never asked questions. She always said that if I wanted to tell her something, I would.

It took all of five minutes to drive to the corner store and buy a ticket for the lottery. But I had another destination in mind.

'Want to go house hunting?' I asked, using our shorthand for driving around and picking out our 'what if' homes.

'Yes!' she answered and clasped her hands together in excitement. I got behind the wheel and we were off. The weather was so oppressively lovely, we rolled down the windows and hung our elbows out as we cruised through neighborhood after neighborhood, street after street. We noted sale signs. We criticized poor taste. We discussed what we'd do if we won the lottery. We acted like there was a future with both of us in it.

'This is so nice,' she said wistfully. Her beautiful wrinkled face turned to the window, with a pensive expression that clouded her features. Was she worrying about her biopsy results? I wondered if she was afraid, like me, or if at ninety-three she was prepared for this. I wasn't going to ask, there were too many beautiful homes for us to dream about.

Our drive took us into the countryside and onto a meandering dirt road. We passed farms with grazing cattle but eventually the road turned up a steep hill and ended at the driveway of a large Georgian-style mansion surrounded by fir trees. I stopped the car at the bottom of the drive. The rich red brick and black shutters were so welcoming. It looked lived in, it looked loved, the sort of house you'd want to spend your life in and you'd want to die in.

'Now, that's what I call a home!' I said, grinning.

My grandmother nodded and pointed to the house. 'You'll have to marry a very rich man to live in a place like that.'

I chuckled, thinking of the article I had yet to start. 'Nana, I think it's too late for that. Rich men don't want women my age.'

She turned to me, her expression serious. 'It's

47

never too late, my love.' She smiled, her eyes never leaving mine. 'Promise me, should anything happen to me, you'll take care of yourself.'

'Don't be silly,' I began but she cut me off.

'Promise me!'

'Fine, Nana,' I teased, desperate to lighten the mood. 'I promise to marry a rich man and live in a mansion.'

'Good girl,' she said with a laugh. 'I just want to know you'll be happy, that's all the promise I need.'

* * *

Monday came abruptly and suddenly I was staring blankly as the cancer specialist sat perched on his black leather stool and gave my grandmother her prognosis. 'You have tongue and throat cancer,' Dr. Wexler spoke succinctly. 'We can't operate.'

Nana sat facing Dr. Wexler like she was a prisoner in an interrogation room. Iris, Ann, and I stood against the wall and listened, our arms folded, our backs stiff, like we were police backup. But there was no good cop, bad cop, just a conviction and a death sentence.

'Are there any options?' Ann asked, her voice shaking as she spoke. 'Treatment or something?'

He nodded. 'We can do radiation. But it will be very painful,' he said solemnly. 'And it will only prolong your grandmother's life by maybe six months or a year.'

After he'd finished speaking my grandmother did what I had never seen her do in my nearly forty years—she cried in front of a stranger.

When she gathered herself, she said quietly, 'I don't want radiation. I want this to be over.'

48

I wanted to interrupt and force the doctor to convince her otherwise; even an extra six months would mean the world to me. But he listened to her, and he sympathized. I had known she was in pain but the extent of her suffering was only now clear. The tumor was torture and it hurt so much she wanted to die. Her mind was made up.

'I've had enough,' my grandmother repeated.

'I understand,' he said and put his hand on her knee. 'You're very brave.'

'Can you get rid of the pain?' Nana asked and rested her hand on his.

'We can give you morphine,' he explained.

I don't remember the drive home from the hospital. I recall only a blur of passing scenery, each red light punctuating the reality as it sunk in. My grandmother was going to die. I had kept the secret to preserve my family's hope for one last weekend. But I soon understood that by withholding the truth, by not saying 'cancer' out loud, I had also given myself two more days of denial. We were in shock, all of us, but somehow my family picked up that it wasn't as much of a shock to me.

'Did you know?' Nana asked me point blank.

'Friday, when the hospital called,' I confessed.

'You kept it to yourself?' Ann asked incredulously.

'I wanted you all to have one last weekend thinking everything was all right,' I admitted quietly.

Nana patted my thigh. 'Thank you.' And that was the last we spoke of it.

We pulled into the driveway but no one got out of the car. We were frozen to our seats with no clue what to do next. After several minutes Nana sighed.

'I need to lie down.'

'Why don't I go and get your prescription?' Ann offered.

'Thanks, love,' Nana said softly. Glad to have a task to perform, Ann darted to the pharmacy. Her slamming of the car door jolted the rest of us into action. As if on cue, we unfastened our seat belts, the *click, click, click, slam, slam, slam,* providing the soundtrack to our slow march to the front door.

Once inside, Iris's mood shifted. She shuffled through the day's mail and, tucking an envelope under her arm, practically ran upstairs.

'What's that about?' I asked when she was out of earshot.

'Your mother is having money troubles,' Nana explained as she tried to make herself comfortable on the sofa.

This revelation wasn't exactly news. Iris had been known to splurge. Often it was a wardrobe binge that would take two years to pay off. Once it was kitchen gadgets and stainless-steel appliances, though she never cooked. Another time it was running up long-distance charges calling Tasmania to speak with a man she'd met online. A small part of me was curious as to what bills she'd run up this time, but before I could ask, Ann returned with the morphine.

'This should help,' she said as she held the full dropper up to my grandmother. Nana opened her mouth, letting the tiny droplets fall onto her tongue.

'I'm going to my room to lie down,' she said softly and went upstairs for a nap.

Ann and I sat in the living room listening to each

50

muffled step. When her door closed, Ann burst into tears. We were not an affectionate family by any means. We greet each other with the requisite hug and kiss but otherwise we aren't big on physical displays. So when Ann collapsed on the sofa in sobs, I just sat there and watched.

'I know, this sucks,' I said, obviously. 'I was a wreck all weekend. Still am.'

When at last Ann wiped away her tears, I sat down and put my arm around her. That's when Iris came into the room, her purse over her shoulder; from her eyes I could see that she, too, had spent the past half hour crying.

'I'm going out,' she said and left without even looking at us.

'Bingo?' Ann asked after Iris had gone.

'What else,' I said. 'At least *she* has some distraction. Maybe we should all take up Bingo.'

'I couldn't afford it,' Ann said matter-of-factly. 'Not the way Mom plays.'

'What do you mean?'

'I went with her once and she spent close to a thousand dollars in one sitting.'

I was taken aback.

'Do you think she spends that much every time she goes?' I asked.

'I have no idea, why?'

'Nana said she was having money trouble,' I admitted. 'What else does she spend money on but Bingo?'

'And slot machines,' Ann reminded me.

Iris also took regular bus excursions to local casinos. I had thought it was just a good way for her to get out of the house.

'Do you think she has a gambling problem?' I

asked, suddenly horrified.

Ann shrugged and changed the subject. 'I brought over a new marinade to try,' she said and crossed the room to her overnight bag. She pulled out a mason jar containing a thick greenish substance with flecks of herbs in it.

'You're doing marinades, too?' I said, part of me relieved to be discussing something else besides my grandmother's cancer and my mother's mysterious debt.

'Why not? Everyone is marinading now,' she said with authority. 'Besides, I want five products to take to the National Food Fair in Chicago.'

I vaguely recalled this goal of Ann's. It was supposedly a big deal for food producers because lots of grocery chains and specialty food store buyers showed up.

'When is it again?'

'January,' she said quietly. Neither of us spoke but I'm sure we were both thinking the same thing. Would our grandmother be alive then?

'Marianne is going to have her baby soon and I'll need another lasagna,' I said sadly. It was strange the way things pop into your head during a crisis. Who cared about lasagna? Yet it was suddenly an insurmountable problem and I wondered how I'd cope trying to make one on my own. Ann touched my shoulder, understanding what I was saying.

'Don't worry, there's lots of sauce around here,' she said and opened one of the kitchen cupboards to illustrate her point. It was stacked with jars of the stuff. 'I can help you.'

Ann moved in with us and the extra pair of hands was needed far sooner than anyone imagined. The cancer seemed to have a life of its own, a parasite with a schedule. We had found Nana a palliative-care doctor who made house calls, which had become necessary because she became so incredibly thin and much too weak to travel. It was as if the diagnosis had slashed away every ounce of will she had. She accepted her impending death stoically, telling us that everyone's time came and that after ninety-three years she was ready.

I wasn't so ready. Every night before I went to bed, I kissed my grandmother's forehead and turned off her light, but she no longer had a book in her hands. The morphine had seen to it that she didn't need to read to fall asleep.

I buried myself in *Pride and Prejudice*, but even Austen held little solace for me. I found myself reading the same page ten times before giving up and instead, staring at the Smoked Trout walls until the color became a pinkish-gray blur, I switched off my light.

7

Self-Help

What wild imaginations one forms where dear self is concerned! How sure to be mistaken.

—Persuasion

I had filed the perfume story to *Haute* but had neglected to even think about the Jane Austen story. In one week I would be forty, my grandmother was quickly slipping away, and yet I had to continue working. So on the Saturday night before my birthday I opened my laptop and just stared at the blank screen. And kept staring. All my knowledge and love of Austen's novels and I had nothing to say.

I lay my head on the table, closed my eyes and sighed, thinking of how in the end Elizabeth Bennet married Mr. Darcy out of love. The article's premise wasn't right. It was a happy coincidence Darcy was rich. Then again, rich is relative. Given my current state even Mr. Collins—moderately secure, but unattractive and socially inept—looked good. I opened my eyes and sat up, stunned by my sudden clarity. Maybe Jennifer's ruthless approach to life and love wasn't so off base. Times had changed. I wondered if, unlike in the novel, a modern-day Elizabeth Bennet would turn down a Mr. Collins? I picked up my cell phone. It was Saturday night and that meant the answer would be holding up in a bar somewhere in Manhattan.

*   *   *

'I'm so glad you called!' Jennifer shouted at me above the loud music. We were in a hipper-than-thou club called Condo 11 in the Meat Packing District. As I looked around I realized that I was one of the oldest people in the room. The crowd was stacked with young women, some dressed very well, others in very little, and the young and not-as-young men appeared aloof and disinterested. In other words the situation was desperate. Jennifer wore a slinky minidress covered in shimmering silver paillettes with equally shiny Gucci stilettos

54

from a few seasons back. She waved into the crowd and two girls galloped over. One was blonder than Jennifer and was squeezed into a purple velvet dress so tight that the only thing she could possibly be wearing underneath was a Brazilian wax job. The other was brunette and more conservative, slightly, in her choice of a little black dress that gave her cleavage plenty of fresh air.

They stuffed themselves into our booth and Jennifer pointed to each one. 'This is Tina,' she said and the blonde smiled at me. 'And this is Arianna,' to which the brunette stuck out her hand. 'And this is Kate.' Jennifer finished off her introductions with, 'You three have a lot in common.'

I looked at her blankly, given that I was wearing a knee-length skirt and a cashmere turtleneck.

'You are all victims of the economic downturn,' she said nonchalantly. Turns out that Tina and Arianna had both lost their jobs at investment firms and were on the lookout for a solution to their personal financial crisis. Several minutes of sympathetic small talk later Tina sat up and smiled brightly.

'Well, at least we're young enough to bounce back,' she chirped.

'Kate's almost forty,' Jennifer said darkly.

'No!' Tina exclaimed in disbelief.

'You're so well preserved,' Arianna added kindly. I wanted to be flattered but the truth was I was horrified. I immediately slipped into journalist mode and asked them what they thought their solution was. As predicted they wanted an easy out, one that came fully equipped with a wedding band.

'Why else get married except for money?' Tina asked rhetorically.

'I'm living off my savings but that will run out soon,' Arianna explained with an expression of grave seriousness she once reserved for trading stocks. 'So we're here to meet potential husbands.'

'Here? In a bar?' I asked astonished. 'Wearing that?'

They looked more puzzled than offended. 'Men like how we dress,' Tina said.

'Yeah, we get noticed,' Arianna added.

'I'm sure you do but you're not taken seriously,' I said, trying to soften my tone.

'We aren't applying for a job,' Tina said as though I was the fool in this conversation.

'Yes you are,' I said. 'If what you really want is a marriage, then men need to take you seriously as a potential wife.'

'We read *Forbes* and *The Wall Street Journal*,' Arianna shot back. 'We'll land our billionaires, we speak their language.'

At that, the two of them slid out of the booth and back into the crowd. I felt my jaw go slack. I couldn't help thinking that if these two were considered high rollers on Wall Street, no wonder it crashed. I looked at Jennifer and saw that she was grinning slyly.

'I see what you mean,' I said, referring to her out-of-work friends.

'Yup. Dumb as posts in certain areas, right?' she said. 'They can decipher the most complex financial systems but old-fashioned romance is too high-tech for them.'

'They do need help,' I admitted, realizing that I had lots of opinions on the topic. I knew then I *was* the perfect writer for the story.

'When is the article due?' I asked, raring to start.

'We want to run it in our June issue. You know, wedding season,' she said. 'So I'll need it by the end of March.'

'Is there a travel budget?' I asked, suddenly inspired.

'I'd have to check,' she said and cocked an eyebrow. 'Why? I thought there'd be plenty of material here in New York.'

'I'm just thinking,' I said and tapped my pen on the table. Then I added wryly, 'If I'm trying to be a social anthropologist and observe the mating rituals of tycoons, my chances are better if they're away from the doom and gloom.'

Jennifer nodded thoughtfully. 'You probably have loads of frequent-flier miles from your beauty editor days.'

'I do,' I agreed, thinking on my feet. 'And I can write up reviews of hotels and restaurants for the magazine to keep costs down.' That was the pleasure of writing for a top magazine like *Haute*. With advertising budgets slashed, luxury properties fell over themselves for editorial coverage, so all-inclusive complimentary stays were a slam dunk.

She grinned knowingly. 'I like how you think. Let me clear the rest with Marianne and our travel editor.'

*   *   *

The trip home seemed endless but it gave me time to reflect. My predicament was the same as the other girls and perhaps the solution was, too. How easy my life would be if I could fall in love with, and marry, a rich man. I fantasized about having all my needs taken care of, the lack of stress, and the

57

joy of being the spoiled bride of a man who could afford such a luxury. The thought made me giggle. I felt very young again and that pleased me. Why shouldn't I marry a man who would take care of me the old-fashioned way? Maybe Jennifer's friends were right.

Then the same question I had posed to Marianne and Brandon threatened the fantasy. *Is it too late to find a good husband?* Was forty too old? Tina and Arianna had the advantage of youth, but after tonight I wasn't convinced that was all it took. My added experience gave me an advantage. I told myself I was more sophisticated and elegant. There was nothing stopping me from getting out there and charming an eligible man. Even my grandmother said it wasn't too late. Why should younger women have all the fun? Surely I had a few more seductions left in me? Suddenly this Jane Austen article wasn't so ridiculous. Jennifer was right. I had found a third subject to make marrying well a trend. Me. And I vowed to do it in style.

8

Maybe I Was Crazy

Be honest and poor, by all means—but
I shall not envy you; I do not much think
I shall even respect you. I have a much
greater respect for those that are honest
and rich.

—Mansfield Park

'Are you joking?' Marianne said as if waiting for the punchline.

'Not one bit,' I said and forced a confident smile. We were seated by the window in Avenue. Brandon shook his head. It was clear by his dour expression that he wasn't fond of my plan to find a rich husband, either.

'Don't you need a job?' he asked.

'That's kind of the point,' I said flatly. 'I can't find a job. I've looked. Called everyone I know. Apparently I won't find a job. Besides, it was Marianne's idea.'

'What?' Marianne shouted.

'Okay, it was Jennifer's, but you agreed to it,' I pointed out.

'Hold on, what?' Brandon asked and gave Marianne a scathing look.

'I've been assigned a story about making an eligible match,' I explained. 'To see if Austen's strategies still hold up. I'm writing it in the first

59

person.'

'Define "eligible,"' Brandon commanded.

'Successful, confident, worldly,' I rattled off, intentionally avoiding the word 'billionaire.' 'I'm going to be forty. If not now, when? This is my last chance to marry well.'

Marianne and Brandon stared at me in silence. I didn't know where to look or what to do, so I began to fiddle with the cocktail napkin on the table. But twisting it around my fingers didn't calm me. Instead, as I watched the white paper scrunch and tear, I was struck by how prominent the veins in my hands had become, my knuckles looked bigger, the skin more lined. They say a woman's hands were the first to go.

'The sooner you stop believing your life is a Jane Austen novel, the better,' Marianne stated bluntly.

I ripped the napkin in half and sat on my hands.

'The older women in her books don't fare so well. You have to be one and fucking twenty to have a happy ending. Not one and forty,' she continued on her tirade. 'You're not Elizabeth Bennet, you're her mother.'

Ouch. The pregnancy hormones sure kept her moody.

'I agree with Marianne. You've read one too many novels, watched one too many movies, my love,' Brandon cooed at me as though I were an infant. 'You're upset about your grandmother and you're out of work. It's natural to feel mixed up about your life, what it all means.'

'You're having a midlife crisis,' added Marianne.

'I'm *not* having a midlife crisis,' I retorted.

'It's classic,' Marianne disagreed. 'Only instead of a convertible sports car you want the man who can buy you one. It's a phase.'

'And you can't just dump your life and take off,' Brandon insisted. 'Especially now, your family needs you.'

'I didn't dump my life,' I answered grimly. 'My life dumped me. And I'm not talking about leaving now. The article isn't due until the end of March. By then . . .' My voice trailed off, thinking that my grandmother would be gone long before spring.

'You've avoided marriage this long,' Marianne continued. 'If you're going to be married, why not marry for love and be happy?'

'Who says I can't fall in love with a rich man?' I asked, but Marianne just screwed up her nose.

'I'll see you next week at your birthday,' Marianne answered with a forced smile and gathered her things to leave. Clearly she was angry.

I pointed to her stomach in an attempt to lighten the mood. 'With that?'

'He's not due for two more weeks,' she reminded me. Marianne was a control freak. No kid of hers would arrive before she allowed it to.

9

Sense of Entitlement

One man's ways may be as good as another's, but we all like our own best.

—Persuasion

It was on an absurdly and unseasonably hot October Sunday that my birthday, at long last, arrived. I woke up with a gentle breeze wafting through my open window, the sheer cream drapes blowing across my toes. When I was little we called this Indian summer; I'm sure it's not politically correct anymore, but it's what I remember and the only term I know for it. One thing for certain, it was the kind of autumn day that makes you want to leap out of bed and get outside to soak up those final drops of sunlight before the damp chill of November steals all the warmth away. Throughout the day I walked into my grandmother's room to check in on her until finally, in the late afternoon, she opened her eyes and held out her hand to me.

'Hi, love,' she said and smiled weakly.

'I'm going out for dinner,' I said and brushed her hair with my palm. 'Will you be okay?'

'I'm fine,' she said. 'You have a nice time.'

As I dressed for dinner I tried to remind myself that I had no reason to expect my grandmother to remember my birthday. Not with the frequent doses of morphine clouding her mind.

When I arrived at Marianne's condo I found the

door slightly ajar, so I snuck inside. There were Marianne and Lucy, pouring over fertility charts. I scanned the room and spotted the men, Frank and Brandon, Marianne and Lucy's respective spouses, out on the deck drinking.

'You must be so relieved that you got pregnant without all this,' Lucy said with a hint of envy.

'It will happen,' Marianne told her encouragingly.

I coughed but no one heard me.

'Your baby is going to be gorgeous,' Lucy gushed.

'I heard the word "gorgeous,"' you must be talking about me,' I joked, realizing how hopeless it was for a forty-year-old to divert attention from a baby, even an unborn one.

'Hey, happy birthday!' Marianne shouted and threw her arms around me. Brandon and Frank came in when they saw me.

'Have some pink Veuve,' Brandon said cheerfully and popped open a bottle. Drinks in hand we raised our glasses.

'Happy fortieth birthday to our beautiful Kate,' Brandon toasted.

They repeated it in unison and I blushed. But I was also very grateful. Being surrounded by my friends made me feel normal again.

'Thanks, all of you,' I gushed. 'This means a lot to me.'

For dinner, Marianne had outdone herself with a homemade beef Wellington. I was plied with pink Veuve in lieu of the cabernet someone had brought to go with the beef. But it was getting late and I wanted to spend the last few hours of my birthday with my grandmother.

'I think it's time to call a cab,' I suggested.

'You can't leave without your present,' Marianne chimed in. 'It's got a theme to match your Jane Austen story.'

I perked up at this.

'While we think this finding a rich man scheme of yours is a bit nutty,' Brandon explained, 'we do think you need to get away, go someplace warm, have an adventure . . . and if you find love along the way, even better.'

'We love you,' Marianne said softly.

'I love you guys, too,' I said, feeling very loved indeed, but not at all convinced I'd find love in the true sense of the word.

'We got you this,' Brandon said, and handed me an envelope. I opened it, removed the paper inside, and unfolded it. It was a fake flight itinerary made on Brandon's computer with the destination left blank.

'Oh my God!' I squealed. 'Thank you!'

'We thought you could use a ticket somewhere, so you just name the locale and we'll make it happen,' he said.

'I love it!' I announced with a smile.

'Great, because you needed the ticket to go with part two of your gift,' Brandon stated matter-of-factly.

'And I'm afraid we couldn't find a tiara in our budget,' Marianne said with a sly smile. 'Hope you like this present. It's meant to be fun.'

Brandon pulled out a dark green leather folder from a large manila envelope that I hadn't noticed before.

'Happy birthday, kiddo,' he said with a cheeky grin.

On the folder, embossed in gold was the name

'Loch Broom Highland Estates.' I opened the folder and inside was a parchment document handwritten in calligraphy with a giant red seal in the bottom-right corner. In large letters it read:

This title Deed is made at Tulloch, in the Braes o' Loch Broom, on this day of October 2008 between Loch Broom Highland Estates and Lady Katharine Billington Shaw.

'What the?' I asked and turned to my friends for explanation. They just sat there grinning. The letter read like this:

Dear Lady Katharine:

According to the letter I was the owner of a one-square-foot plot of land on a Scottish estate. I had never been to Scotland. I was stumped. But then I read the rest of the letter and it said it all:

You may also wish to know that by ancient tradition, the ownership of land in Scotland may allow you to style yourself with title Laird (Lord) or Lady. We hope you enjoy your highland estate.

'Oh my God! You bought me a title!' I shouted. If it was true, it was possibly the best gift I'd ever received.

'Yes,' Marianne said excitedly. 'Brandon found it. We thought it might help you in your quest to live out the Jane Austen fantasy life if you were a lady. Will make for interesting stuff in the article, too.'

I looked at Brandon. I could tell he wanted to

65

behave modestly but he was beaming at his own cleverness.

'As part of a conservation project to raise money, this park in Scotland sold off one-foot plots, and all Scottish landowners have a title. We figured you deserved to be an aristocrat.'

'You'll have to call me "lady,"' I teased.

'Your name screamed out for a title. Now you sound like you should be in the pages of *Tatler*,' Marianne explained, faking a posh English accent to say my name in full, 'Lady Katharine Billington Shaw.'

'I love it,' I said.

I had to hand it to them. They had ensured that my fortieth birthday wasn't only about grief.

'Would Her Ladyship like another glass of Veuve?' Brandon asked gleefully.

'And cake!' Marianne exclaimed and rose from the table to get dessert.

I was now Lady Katharine Billington Shaw, what else did I need besides a steady diet of cake and champagne?

*   *   *

The light was on in the kitchen when I tiptoed into my house just after eleven. It was Ann. She had stayed up for me and had a small vanilla cupcake on a plate, complete with lit candle.

'I heard the cab pull away,' she explained. 'Make a wish.'

'Is Nana asleep?' I asked, feeling horrible that I'd been gone so long.

'Yes, but she wants you to wake her,' she said. 'Don't feel bad. It is your birthday and forty is a big deal.'

'So everyone keeps telling me,' I answered, not liking the reminder.

I closed my eyes and wished for the one thing that was impossible: I wished my grandmother would get better. I blew out the candle and we were in darkness. My sister turned on the dimmer switch so that the kitchen glowed. I shared the cupcake with Ann in silence. Then I crept upstairs and was surprised to see my grandmother awake in bed, waiting for me.

'Hey!' I said happily and sat down beside her.

'Happy birthday to you,' she sang in her once-perfect voice that was rapidly being snuffed out by the tumor. When she finished singing I saw she was crying and as I leaned forward and held her I realized I was crying, too. She held out a birthday card in a mauve envelope.

I opened the card; it was an illustration of a very fashionable brunette who was carrying tons of shopping bags; inside, the printed greeting was a simple 'Have a Fabulous Day,' but Nana had written several lines to me in her distinctive handwriting. I tried as hard as I could to decipher her message, but the morphine had muddled with her mind so that she had written birthday with six 'B's and so on. Most of the letters and words ran together in one long squiggle. It was illegible. Then there was the 'love, Nana' and a row of XOXOXO's. I stared hard at it, knowing it was the last written words I'd ever receive from her and yet I couldn't read it.

'Do you like what I wrote?' she asked proudly. 'I meant it all.'

'I love it,' I answered softly.

67

10

A Matter of Life & Death

There are people, who the more you do for them, the less they will do for themselves.

—Emma

Exactly thirty-seven hours and thirty-three minutes after my birthday, Marianne gave birth to a boy, Thomas Andrew. He was a breech and the obstetrician recommended the one thing that Marianne had dreaded above all else—a C-section. It wasn't just the bikini-line scar that got her; it was the thought of being wide awake as she was sliced open.

'I felt like a Ziploc bag,' she confessed to me after it was over. But of course by the time I got through to her, and little Thomas was in her arms, the horror seemed worth it.

'You have to meet him!' she squealed proudly.

'I will as soon as I can,' I promised. 'I'm so happy for you! I bet he's gorgeous.'

'He is,' she cooed. 'Oh, and I want my lasagna as soon as I'm home!'

'You got it.' I laughed.

Three days later, Marianne was home and I realized that I didn't have any real clue how to make it. Of course I'd watched my grandmother and Ann dozens of times. They even let me layer ingredients. But what those ingredients were was beyond me. Downstairs to the kitchen I went. How hard could it be?

I grabbed what seemed like logical ingredients—ground beef, lasagna noodles, cheese, herbs, and the crowning glory, the pasta sauce. I ran over to the cupboard and snatched a giant jar of tomato sauce off the shelf. Easy.

The two deliciously gooey lasagnas cooling on the kitchen counter proved it. I had to admit I was proud of how they turned out. Maybe Nana and Ann's cooking expertise had rubbed off on me.

*   *   *

'Come on in,' Frank whispered when I arrived. He took the two casserole dishes from me and I entered as quietly as I could. 'Thomas is asleep.'

I tiptoed into the living room and there was Marianne, a bit tired looking but still beautiful and a pinkish baby in her arms swathed in a fluffy gray blanket.

'He's so handsome!' I said. I was never sure what to say to new moms. New babies always looked kind of funny to me.

'I'd ask if you'd like to hold him but I know better.' Marianne grinned.

I've got a bit of a reputation for being antibaby. It's not that I dislike babies. They simply terrify me. Newborns are so fragile that the thought of holding one and worse, holding one incorrectly, sends me into fits of anxiety. Maybe it was because I never wanted children of my own. I had zero maternal instincts. Even as a teenager I never baby-sat. Instead, I walked dogs for extra cash.

When I was an adult I made an attempt to be more baby friendly by watching a colleague's eight-month-old son at a Christmas party. She had left me with the baby to go grab herself a cocktail. While she was out of sight I noticed her son trying to pull himself up onto his feet by grabbing my fingers. He stood there, holding on lightly but steadily. He seemed really good at it. Extremely good. So good, in fact, I was convinced that some magical combination of his balance and my skill at baby-watching was the reason for his success. When his mother returned I was excited to show her his trick.

'He can stand!' I exclaimed.

She looked at me doubtfully. But before she could answer, her son had grabbed onto my fingers and was once again up on his feet. Determined to show off his skills I decided to pull my fingers away so that he could stand on his own. Only he didn't. He crashed immediately to the floor and burst into tears.

'He's too young to stand on his own!' his mother shrieked and picked him up.

No one ever asked me to watch a baby again after that. I was stuck with giving the gift of lasagna.

'I can't wait to have a bite!' Marianne said as she dove her fork into the dish. It was steaming hot, thanks to their microwave. Frank sat down and they sank their teeth into a gooey mouthful. But then they made a face.

'What's wrong?' I asked, worried I'd poisoned them. 'Is the cheese off?'

'It's not the cheese,' Marianne said gingerly, spitting the food into a napkin. 'Did you make this the regular way?'

Trick question. I tried to come up with a reasonable answer, considering I'd never made it

70

regularly or irregularly ever before. 'Yes, I think so.'

'It's the sauce,' Frank offered. 'It's sweet.'

'Sweet? Is that bad?' I asked and went to the kitchen to try for myself.

'And spicy,' he continued. 'Kind of sticky.'

I shoved a fork into the lasagna and took a bite. Right away I knew. I love Ann, but if she wanted to make a living cooking she should learn how to label things better.

'It's barbecue sauce,' I announced grimly. 'I grabbed the wrong jar.'

'That's okay.' Marianne smiled. 'I've never had barbecue lasagna before. Maybe it will catch on.'

'Yes, like barbecue chicken pizza,' Frank offered helpfully and bravely took another bite, then grimaced. 'Or maybe not.'

11

Chanel Slut

I am only resolved to act in that manner, which will, in my own opinion, constitute my happiness . . .

—*Pride and Prejudice*

Exactly seven days and six hours after my birthday my grandmother died. She lay in her own bed, Iris, Ann, and me at her side, and she slipped away.

My grandmother and I had only argued once in our forty years together. I was twenty-two years old

71

and we were on vacation in Los Angeles. When it came to me, my grandmother's indulgence knew no bounds. Which is how we found ourselves in the Chanel boutique on Rodeo Drive having a little black dress hemmed. Nana had bought it for me as a graduation gift, which was how she justified the cost. The dress was demure. Sophisticated. Grown-up. Its skirt and waist were made of wool crepe that gave way to a pleated chiffon bodice. It was a classic sleeveless sheath, the very picture of tasteful chic.

The only trouble was that the length was below my knees and that just wouldn't do. I wanted to rock it up a bit.

My grandmother had agreed to a slight adjustment, but how high the hem could go was up for debate.

The seamstress seemed to read my mind and pinned the skirt four inches above my knee. I loved it. Nana despised it.

'That's too short!' she snapped. Now my grandmother was not a conservative woman; I had plenty of miniskirts that she encouraged me to wear. 'If you've got it, flaunt it,' she liked to say, beaming with pride at my long legs. So when she objected to the Chanel going micro, I was perplexed, but assumed she'd be won over easily.

'No it's not,' I said with youthful confidence.

The poor seamstress, unaware of who she was defying, came to my defense.

'It's the fashion,' she said sweetly. 'She's young and the dress should be young.'

'You're both wrong,' Nana said bluntly. 'This is a classic dress; it's not for going to nightclubs. It's not meant to be sexy in *that* way. You'll ruin its lines.'

I sighed and rolled my eyes, hoping to catch the seamstress's sympathetic glance. But my grandmother caught my eye roll and it made her livid.

'Kate,' Nana spoke through clenched teeth. 'This is a ladylike dress. You can't have everything you wear slit up to there.'

And with that, she rose from the pink-and-gold-upholstered chair and marched to the dressing-room door. I felt the seamstress shrink away in fear and hide behind my skirt.

'I don't get why you're so angry,' I said flatly, still refusing to give in.

'Fine,' Nana said icily. 'You shorten it as much as you want, but you'll look like a slut in Chanel.'

She stormed away. I was speechless, but my shock didn't stop the tears of humiliation from running down my cheeks. I wiped them away before the seamstress could see.

'What do you want to do, miss?' she asked gently.

'Keep it short,' I said defiantly. 'Right where we have it pinned.'

*   *   *

We never spoke about the Chanel dress again. It was easy to avoid because I never wore it; every time I slipped it on it never looked quite right. I convinced myself I was too young for it, or that it wasn't trendy enough, or that it just wasn't my style. I avoided the obvious: that it was too short. It hung in my closet, its garment bag with the famous logo gathering dust, untouched and unworn for more than a decade, as a symbol of my poor judgment.

It wasn't until I was thirty-five and Marianne had

made editor-in-chief at *Haute* that the dress found its place in my life. As a sort of congratulatory gesture, the House of Chanel invited Marianne to Paris to see the couture show. We were both ecstatic and spent an entire Saturday looking for the perfect outfit to sit in the front row. But somehow we came up empty-handed.

'What about the purple Marc Jacobs?' I suggested as we shared a cab back to her condo. She had bought the purple cocktail dress for an arts charity ball and had only worn it once and no one in Paris would have seen it. She didn't respond; instead, she shuffled around on the seat and cleared her throat.

'I was wondering,' she paused. 'Would you consider loaning me your Chanel dress?'

I recoiled. I didn't answer right away, but the uncomfortable silence screamed loud and clear. I didn't want to loan her the dress, but I didn't really have a reason to say no. I'd never worn it. Marianne knew that I'd never worn it. Yet I felt very possessive, even jealous at the thought of someone else in my dress. It was as though she'd asked to sleep with my boyfriend. Well, maybe not quite, but close.

'Um,' I hesitated.

'I'll take good care of it,' she pleaded.

*   *   *

At home, with the dress held up in front of me, I stared at my reflection in a full-length mirror. I was being silly. What difference did it make if Marianne wore the dress before I did? She was my best friend. We always swapped clothing. But the fact that Marianne realized the value of the dress more than

I did caught me off guard. I had learned to dismiss it as conservative and fussy. Clearly Marianne didn't think so. My grandmother didn't think so. That meant I was wrong.

I stepped into the little black dress. The zipper was in the back and it took me several attempts and acrobatic moves to get it done up. Before I allowed myself even a glance, I slipped on a pair of black velvet open-toe shoes. There wasn't a dress made that wasn't improved with a pair of strappy heels. At last I was ready and turned to face the mirror. The cut was perfect and hit every curve of my body at just the right angle. It didn't pull or gape anywhere. Without a doubt it was an elegant dress. But it still didn't suit me and that made me very angry. I practically tore the zipper in my haste to get the dress off, nearly falling over in a fit of rage as it became entangled around my heels. Marianne could have the damn thing. I was breaking up with my Chanel dress for good.

Marianne took the dress to Paris but didn't wear it. The Chanel people loaned her something from the current collection instead. When she brought it back, neatly folded and still remarkably unworn, I was relieved to touch it again. I had missed it after all. But I didn't hang it back in its garment bag. Instead, I made an appointment at the Chanel boutique. When I came out of the dressing room the seamstress stood at the ready, pincushion in hand, tape measure around her neck like a boa. I stepped onto the circular platform and dropped my arms to my sides.

'Let the hem down four inches,' I said determinedly.

'I have to see if there's enough fabric ...' she

began, but I cut her off. 'There is,' I stated with authority. I would not be swayed from my mission by doubt. 'I had it taken up years ago. Now I want it restored so I can wear it like it was meant to be worn.'

This time when I stood before the mirror I didn't avoid looking. The skirt now grazed my knee, giving the dress the sexy silhouette of the pencil skirts that I had started to wear almost as my uniform. I also couldn't deny that in my mid-thirties I had grown into the dress. It was finally mine.

The first time I wore it my grandmother clapped her hands together and gushed, 'You look beautiful!' as if it were the first time she'd ever laid eyes on the dress. There was no, 'I told you so.' That wasn't her style.

'I'm finally old enough to do it justice,' I said wryly. 'You were right, this is the length it should be. Just at the knee.'

Nana nodded graciously. 'It really shows off your figure.'

It quickly became our favorite dress. I wore it only occasionally so that I would never tire of it. It was that special. We never spoke of the Chanel boutique incident. But that was so like my grandmother and me, we could forgive and forget without having to blare it out on a loudspeaker.

*   *   *

On the morning of her funeral I zipped up the Chanel dress as though it were a suit of armor. It wasn't a large gathering—mostly family and a smattering of neighbors and friends. All day I was terrified I'd faint, even though I'd never fainted before. Yet

76

somehow I got through the service and the kind words from everyone that kept me on the verge of tears. Afterwards, everyone came back to our house and we fed them little tea sandwiches and served sidecars. There was much laughter and plenty of 'do you remember when?' but eventually the inevitable happened: the mourners went home. Even Ann had moved back to her apartment, and I was left with Iris.

'I'm going to go to bed. I'm exhausted,' I said and pulled myself up from the couch.

She nodded. I could hear her clanking dishes in the kitchen as I dragged myself up the stairs. Despite my exhaustion, I sat on the edge of my bed, staring out my window at the treetops.

12

Your Money or My Life

My conduct shall speak for me; absence, distance, time shall speak for me.

—*Mansfield Park*

I stood in my bra and underwear and stared at my closet. Inside was an unchartered expanse of black with a few gray and chocolate brown patches scattered in the sea of darkness like deserted islands. I grabbed random pieces and pulled them on, shoving fists through armholes and stepping into a skirt, nearly falling over in the process. I was already late and I was in no mood for a meeting.

My grandmother's lawyer had contacted me a

couple of days after the funeral to discuss the will. There was the house that needed to be signed over to Ann and me, but my sister had to work, so the plan was for me to go alone and bring the documents home for her to co-sign.

The law office was in a small pre-war house that had recently been given a stucco facelift. It was dove gray with black shutters. The lawyer was a woman named Nelly Lemmon, who my grandmother had used for years. She must be ancient now.

I stepped out of the car, my heels twisting dangerously on the gravel drive, my delicate velvet shoes no match for the pebbles and small rocks that gave way under each step. Ungracefully, I stumbled to the porch, straightened my skirt, and knocked.

'Come in!' a woman's voice shouted from inside.

I twisted the doorknob and felt the latch click open. Inside the vestibule were stacks of files mixed in with old newspapers and magazines.

'Is that you, Kate?' the same voice cracked.

'Yes it is,' I yelped and followed the voice down a narrow hallway strewn with files piled high atop battered steel filing cabinets.

'I'm back here!' came the voice again.

I turned a corner and nearly crashed into a goblin of a woman who stood five feet, if that. Her hair was a mass of red corkscrew curls with strands of white poking through like steel wool. She wore mascara and a pale pink lipstick, but otherwise she was deathly pale, as though she hadn't stepped outdoors in decades. Her face, with chubby cheeks like an overweight cat, was remarkably unlined, no doubt due to a dearth of sunlight. She reached out a hand. 'Glad you could come so soon.'

We sat down. Her desk was shockingly clutter-free except for one legal-size gray file lying centered on the smooth glossy wood with her arms folded on top of it. Nelly leaned forward, her soft fleshy arms jiggling as though boneless, her stubby legs tapping the floor beneath her desk in some imagined rhythm.

'The will is simple,' she began calmly enough. 'You and your sister get the house. But I need to know how you plan to deal with the bank.'

'Bank?' I repeated blankly. 'What bank?'

She sat back, practically disappearing into her armchair so I had to lean forward to maintain eye contact. 'The bank that holds the mortgage,' she said, giving me an odd look.

'We don't have a mortgage,' I answered, puzzled.

She rocked in her chair. We stared at each other; neither of us seemed prepared to speak. She was obviously confused.

'You mean Alice never told you or Ann?' she said at last.

'Told us what?' I demanded, anger nipping at my voice.

'About a year ago Alice and Iris came to me for help,' she explained reluctantly. I sensed she didn't want to be a rat, but she had no choice. 'I take it your mother likes to gamble.'

My stomach lurched.

'She plays Bingo,' I answered somewhat defensively.

'A lot,' Nelly said firmly. 'She ran up over a hundred thousand dollars in debts. Alice tried to bail her out by getting a mortgage on the house. But your mom never made the payments.'

I was silent.

'It's gone into default.'

Still silent.

'The bank is about to foreclose,' she said slowly, as though English were my second language. 'You're to be evicted in thirty days.'

My silence filled the room. Could this be true? I couldn't imagine Nana agreeing to this and not telling me. But the reality of Iris and all her trips to the Bingo hall and the casinos told me that Nelly wasn't making this up. My mother had become more secretive and anxious in the months before Nana was diagnosed, but her behavior had gotten stranger recently. I'd assumed it was the strain of caring for her dying mother. But there was clearly more to it; there was massive debt and now Ann and I had to deal with it.

'The bank will put the house up for sale, "power of sale," they call it,' she continued robotically.

'We don't want to sell,' I snapped.

'Then I'm hoping you have assets of some kind? If you could throw some cash down, say about twenty-five thousand dollars, then that would keep the bank at bay.'

Of course, my savings! All those mutual funds had to be worth something, even in this damn recession. I always forgot about my investments because they weren't meant to be touched until I retired. Thanks to the recession I was retired. 'I have about thirty thousand. I'll have to ask Ann what she has.'

'Thirty would go a long way,' she smiled encouragingly.

*   *   *

I drove home in a fog, replaying every last word of Nelly's explanation. She had given me copies of all the foreclosure notices; the evil slips of paper that Iris had been hiding. I had to come up with at least a quarter of the money.

Stuffed under my bed was a box where I kept all my bank statements. I tore off the lid and dumped the contents out. There were statements from March 2008. I ripped into the envelope: $30,000. According to Nelly I needed only twenty-five thousand to stave off the foreclosure for another month, in which time I could maybe find a job. But March was a long time ago. I found more statements and tore them open. June: $27,000; July: $24,000 . . . I was becoming more alarmed. I opened my September statement: $19,800. Finally, I found November and I unfolded the statement and just stared at it: $14,890.34. I had lost half of my savings in less than a year. I grabbed my BlackBerry. Ann answered and I told her everything. She was as in the dark as I was. And worse, she had even less money than me because she'd been using her savings for night school, ingredients, and a website and logo designer for her sauce idea. I stuffed my statements back into the box.

Then I heard my mother come in and I froze.

'Kate?' Iris called out. Her breezy tone irritated me. I didn't answer her. All I wanted to do was leave the house and figure out what to do. I grabbed my purse and marched downstairs.

'Everything all right?' she asked with an innocent smile.

I swiveled around to face her. The tears came back. God, why couldn't I stop crying? I had lost my grandmother and now, thanks to my mother, I was

81

losing my home.

'No, Iris,' I said shakily. 'Nothing is all right. I just came from seeing Nelly Lemmon.'

My mother's lower lip began to tremble.

'I know about the mortgage,' I snapped. 'And the foreclosure. How could you do it?'

I realized I was shouting. Iris was mouthing something. Probably that she was sorry. But I wasn't able to hear over my shouts.

'How you tricked Nana into doing this I'll never know! But we're going to lose the house. Our home!'

'I told Nana to tell you, she wouldn't let me,' Iris sputtered. 'We thought we'd win the lottery and pay it off.'

'Don't try and blame Nana for this!' I snapped again.

I needed to calm down. I gulped for air, then turned and walked out the door.

*   *   *

I drove around for more than an hour and somehow all roads led back to that same country house I'd seen with my grandmother the weekend before she found out she was dying. I turned off the engine and watched the house as though I were a prowler staking out a target. Then I realized I did know what to do. There was only one option now. The article was no longer just a writing assignment worth five thousand dollars. Nor was it an escape from my problems or a guide to help other women; it was my only hope of getting any semblance of a life back. Unemployed, single, and homeless, I was a modern Austen character, only instead of having a mother determined to introduce me to the right sort of man, I had to rely on my own smarts. I was desperate. I had to do more than write the story. I had to live it.

13

Family Matters

They gave themselves up wholly to their sorrow, seeking increase of wretchedness in every reflection that could afford it, and resolved against ever admitting consolation in future.

—Sense & Sensibility

I once read that when you leave a place you love you should say good-bye to it. After our belongings had been packed and shipped into storage and the foreclosure sign had been hammered into the lawn, I walked through my house room to room to have a final look inside my past. I lingered in every doorframe, opened each closet, their emptiness a mirror of my own. Like my belongings, my feelings had been stuffed into boxes, their contents to be revealed one day in an as yet undisclosed location. At the end of my tour I came to my bedroom. The smoked trout walls were bare and scuffed from the movers. Without the cream sheers the window resembled a giant gaping mouth and the hardwood floors were peppered with dust bunnies. My room looked lonely and abandoned. I'm not sure how long I sat there, but eventually Ann arrived to coax me out of my cover as a pointer does a pheasant before the hunter opens fire.

'I know you're sad,' she observed unnecessarily. 'Mom is sad, too. We all are.'

My eyes remained fixed on the open window and the trees outside, their leafless branches twisting and bending in the bitter November wind, the same wind that now lashed my tears dry.

'I don't know how I'm ever going to forgive Iris,' I said after what seemed an eternity. I turned and met my sister's gaze. I could see the pain in her eyes, sympathy for me, for Iris, her own grief mashed up in between. 'How are you able to be so nice to her? Knowing what she did?'

Ann was always the sweet sister, she was softer in every sense, even physically her features were rounder.

'We still have each other. Houses can be replaced,' she answered. 'We all make mistakes and bad decisions. She gave into a weakness. I can't carry anger around.'

'Unlike me, you mean?' I asked.

'It's time to go now,' she said softly.

Ann retreated downstairs. Alone once more, I leaned my head against the wall, closed my eyes, and wept. But as I cried yet again, it occurred to me that I hadn't *not* wept for weeks. I was sick of it.

A strong gust of wind blew in through the open window, but the cold was muted by a sudden streak of sunlight that stretched across the room, blinding me for a split second, its heat a welcome surge of energy. I looked directly into the light and as I did, something somewhere inside me snapped. I dried my eyes and took in a gulp of air. Better.

84

I'm done crying.

I repeated the words over and over and in a final farewell gesture slapped my hand on the wall and walked away.

*   *   *

We drove toward Ann's Park Slope apartment, just the two of us. It was all arranged. Iris had the spare room. I had the sofa. My laptop would live on Ann's teak coffee table that would now double as my desk. Privacy would occur only in the bathroom.

'Mom is seeing a trustee tomorrow,' Ann went on, her eyes focused on the highway.

'What she needs is therapy,' I said, watching the leafy neighborhood I called home for my entire life flit by with no fanfare. 'She has an addiction.'

'You're right about that,' she agreed. 'But first we have to help her get the debts under control. The house may not sell.'

'One can hope,' I said. I wondered what Ann would think of my turning the marrying well article into reality. She was always so practical.

'I have an idea,' she said, preempting me. 'Why don't you become my partner in the sauce thing? Fifty-fifty. You're living with me anyway and you have more free time now. We can double production because you can keep cooking when I'm at work.'

'I don't know what to say,' I said. I did know that I wasn't going anywhere near the kitchen. Ann's sauce business had been floating around for years and hadn't even touched success. Compared to sauce, my eligible bachelor idea was solid gold. Still, I didn't want to hurt her feelings. 'Thanks, that's

85

very generous,' I began. 'Can I think about it?'

'Sure,' she said, sounding clearly disappointed. 'We could have a blast at the National Food Fair in Chicago.'

The idea of having a blast anywhere seemed impossible. But I kept quiet as we left Scarsdale behind.

*　　　*　　　*

Dinner that night was pizza and soggy Caesar salad with a side of silent resentment. I avoided looking at my mother, choosing to let Ann carry the conversation. But after chasing a final crouton around my plate as they prattled on about their favorite television commercials, I could no longer take the small talk.

'I have to write an article for *Haute*,' I announced and got up from the table and walked to my 'office' on the sofa three feet away. As if on cue, my mother and Ann dispersed into their respective bedrooms, the double click of shutting doors my signal that I was alone at last. But the solitude didn't help. The screen was still blank and I hadn't a clue what the first line of the story should be. Instead, I sat there and began to Google gambling addiction centers for my mother. Not a cheap therapy as it turned out; ironically, it would take thousands in winnings to afford to go to one. Then there were her debts. My grandmother would have wanted Ann and I to do everything in our power to take care of Iris. My plan had to work. It was late but what I had to say couldn't wait. I knocked on Ann's door and sat down on her bed and explained what I was going to do. She listened, bleary-eyed, and said nothing until

86

I was finished.

'It sounds like a fun article,' she said carefully. 'But the world doesn't work like that.'

'Like what?' I asked defensively. This from a woman who thought her fortune was in a mixture of ketchup and spices?

'I know you love those books. So did Nana,' she went on. 'But marriage isn't going to solve our problems.'

'But you're missing my point. It will if I choose a good husband. I don't need a Mrs. Bennet to do it for me.'

'By good you mean rich?' Ann asked derisively. 'Oh, Kate. Have some sense. Write the article, take the money, and let's find a real way to put this whole bad episode behind us.'

She crawled back under the covers and switched off her light, leaving me to make my way to the sofa in the dark. She was wrong. I knew she was. My plan would succeed and when it did, none of us would be poor, my mother would get the help she needed, and we'd have our home back. All I had to do was make it happen.

14

A Ticket to Ride

She must escape . . . as soon as possible, and find consolation in fortune and consequence, bustle and the world, for a wounded spirit. Her mind was quite determined, and varied not.

—*Mansfield Park*

When it comes to stumbling upon dozens of wealthy men, there was only one leisure activity that mattered: polo. Even kings and princes played polo. I had read that West Palm Beach had a vibrant polo scene and Florida was an easy flight; I would start there. I e-mailed Jennifer at the magazine. She thought I was brilliant and arranged for a hotel to put me up. There was just one tiny glitch. I was terrified of horses. But, I told myself over and over, I didn't have to ride one, I just had to get close enough to a horse to get close to its owner. At least the airfare was taken care of.

'You two are the best friends ever,' I gushed when they handed me the ticket over champagne at Avenue, as a sort of impromptu bon voyage party.

'Actually, that may be true.' Marianne laughed. 'Look more closely.'

I raised an eyebrow and examined the ticket more carefully. It was first class.

'First class! So fabulous!'

'You can't meet a rich guy in coach,' Brandon teased. 'Hope that will do.'

'Does it ever!'

'She hasn't even noticed,' Marianne sulked and sank into the sofa with her champagne.

'Noticed what?' I asked.

'The name on the ticket, stupid,' Marianne joked. 'It's all about your name.'

I examined the itinerary again. There was no missing it this time. The ticket was issued to Lady Katharine Billington Shaw.

'You can travel under your title, too,' Marianne said. 'Lady Katharine.'

'Really?' I asked doubtfully.

'It's true,' Brandon continued. 'I triple-checked. You're a real lady.'

'It's all aboveboard!' Marianne howled with delight.

I couldn't take my eyes off my name; seeing it in print was surreal. On my birthday it had been a cute joke, but now, it seemed official.

'It will be our little secret,' Marianne said and poured more champagne all around.

'Absolutely,' I agreed. 'It's not as if I'm going to announce it to the world.'

BOOK 2

FREE TO A
GOOD HOME

15

VIP

Now there will be a great match and of course that will throw the girls into the path of other rich men.

—*Pride and Prejudice*

'How long is this press junket?' Ann asked as she stood watching me pack a second large suitcase to the brim. She was well versed in the last-minute travel whirlwind that had been my life as an acting beauty editor. But she was accustomed to my jetting off for three or four days with only a carry-on.

'It's not just one press trip, it's several,' I explained vaguely, wanting to avoid any details about putting my plan into action. 'I'm not sure when I'm coming back.'

She nodded. 'Kate, I'm sorry we argued. You and I just have different ideas on how to solve our problems. I love you and just want you to be happy.'

Her words made me feel lousy. Guilty, even. I could see from my sister's face that she was hurt and I couldn't do that to her.

'Remember what Nana used to say about finding the right man?' I paused and smiled. 'It's as easy to fall in love with a rich man as a poor one.'

'Of course I do.' She smiled back.

'I'm going to Palm Beach to meet a man,' I admitted at last.

'Aaah, now I get why you're taking your entire

wardrobe. I'll assume he's rich, but who is he and how did you meet him?'

'I haven't met him yet,' I said reluctantly. Ann looked at me blankly.

'Trust me, I know what I'm doing,' I said, although part of me was convincing myself as much as Ann.

'Will you be back in time to go to Chicago with me?' she asked. She was still holding out hope that the Food Fair in January would be the solution to everything.

'I'll try,' I said gamely, although I think we both knew the real answer. 'It will depend on who I meet.'

I smiled at this last bit, hoping Ann would smile, too. She didn't. She simply nodded.

'Then you'd better take this,' she said and went to my closet and removed a garment bag. Folding it gingerly, she laid it on top of my suitcase. It was my Chanel dress.

'Thank you,' was all I could think to say. 'I was leaving it for the end. But I'm done.'

'What time is your flight?'

'In a couple of hours,' I said. 'The cab is coming for me.'

She shook her head. 'Let me drive you.'

'That would be great. But I have one favor to ask. Don't say anything to Iris about what I'm doing?'

'It will be between us,' she answered. 'Now promise me one thing.'

'Anything.'

'Make sure your rich guy has an older brother.' She grinned.

'Is there any way I can switch my window seat to an aisle seat?' I asked the hostess manning the desk in the first-class lounge at La Guardia.

With a sourpuss expression she snatched my ticket away. I'd never had any success getting an airline to change anything for me, not even peanuts for a cookie, but for some mysterious reason she suddenly stood straighter, smiled warmly, and began typing furiously at the computer.

'Yes, of course we can do that,' she said, overly polite. 'If you'd like to make yourself comfortable in the lounge, I'll page you when I have your new boarding pass.'

She handed my ticket back to me. I was dumbfounded.

'Thank you,' I said and picked up my carry-on.

'Thank you for choosing our airline, Lady Katharine,' she called after me.

I stopped dead. I'd completely forgotten about Brandon and Marianne's little joke. Oh well, if it got me an aisle seat, I was happy. No one else had to know.

I found an empty sofa near the window and staked my claim. For a first-class lounge it was in dire need of a design overhaul. The tables were black lacquer with glass tabletops, each with a chrome lamp; the sofas and armchairs were black leather. All in all, it was very 1980s but without irony. It was also mostly deserted. There were only a handful of people and of all of them, less than half were men, and all of *them* appeared to be attached to wives.

Not a productive start to my mission. I sighed

and began reading the newspaper when a flood of footsteps marched past me. I peeked over the top of my paper like a spy in an old movie, as a dozen new arrivals filed into the lounge and, to my delight, many of them were men. That's more like it! A quick scan revealed that a least three of them appeared to be traveling alone. It was time to get to work.

Businessman Number One, fifty-something, had reddish hair with wisps of gray and gold wire-rim glasses. He wore a navy suit, no tie, his jacket unbuttoned so that his bloated girth was on display.

Businessman Number Two, mid-forties, was tall with a receding hairline. He, too, sported glasses but of the horn-rimmed variety. He was reading *The New Yorker*, always a good sign. He wore a charcoal suit with pink shirt and purple tie, very chic. But, big sigh, he also wore a wedding band.

That left Businessman Number Three, who was short and stubby with light brown hair that swept across his forehead. It was the kind of hair that wouldn't move in a hurricane. He had a bulbous nose that was red and shiny. He also had what my grandmother called 'duck's disease.' An ass that was close to the ground, perched on short legs with a round belly in front—a build that gave him a waddle when he walked. Even his protruding lips reminded me of a duck. His face was pale but glowing and he kept sweeping a tissue across his forehead to remove beads of sweat. He was not a man I would normally look at twice. But that was then.

The new me, the me in search of a rich husband, would find out what he did, where he lived, and where he was going. I stood up, smoothed my hair, and was about to step forward when I heard myself being paged. Only it wasn't exactly me.

'Lady Katharine Billington Shaw,' the hostess called over the loudspeaker. 'Lady Katharine Billington Shaw, please come to the front desk.'

Eyes darted in all directions as everyone in the lounge tried to see who had the fancy title. My feet felt stuck to the floor.

'Lady Katharine Billington Shaw!' this time the girl shouted.

It couldn't be helped; I had to get my boarding pass. I tossed my head, flicked my hair, and marched to the desk with all the self-confidence I could muster. The hostess smiled and handed me my new boarding pass.

'Thank you,' I practically whispered, hoping not to draw attention to myself.

'Thank *you*, Lady Katharine.'

I nodded, not wanting to draw more attention, but as I turned around I practically fell over a white-haired woman with a glaringly obvious fake tan.

'I'm so sorry!' I stammered and was about to step to the side when she put her hand on my arm.

'Oh, but it's you I want to meet,' she purred. 'My name is Orietta del Bianco.'

'Have we met before?' I asked. I had a bad memory and on more than one occasion had offended a person by not remembering them. For all I knew, this woman worked for a cosmetics company and knew me in my former life.

'Oh no,' she cooed. 'I'm on my way back home to Palm Beach. My husband and I were visiting his sister in England.'

I nodded and smiled, not sure where Orietta was

97

going with this.

'We dined with others of your class,' she said a little smugly. 'Even spent a weekend in a *stately*, as you like to call mansions over there.'

'How nice,' I said. 'But I'm not English. I'm American.'

She frowned. 'But you're a lady,' she said as though I must be mistaken. Then she nodded as if she had an unspoken understanding of my situation. 'You got your title from your husband.'

She grabbed my left hand, but seeing no wedding band added, 'Your ex-husband? Oh, but I shouldn't be so thoughtless, you could be a widow.'

I desperately wanted to escape Orietta. Clearly, she was some kind of aristocrat groupie.

'I'm afraid I'm neither,' I said forcefully. But I sensed she wasn't going to give up so easily. All I wanted was to make a break for it and go back and find the duck man, but she had yet to let go of my arm. Trapped, I told a white lie. 'I inherited an estate in Scotland.'

She clapped her hands together gleefully, like a child who had found the missing piece of the jigsaw. 'How fabulous for you!'

I was relieved she was satisfied, although I wasn't entirely comfortable with the white lie I had told. Who would have thought that a birthday gag could get so out of hand and that I could be mistaken for actual aristocracy? I attempted to walk away but Orietta, my new best friend, seemed hell-bent on sticking close by.

'I have to go sit by my carry-on,' I explained. Lame excuse, I know, and yet she didn't take the hint. Despite my being five foot ten with a gangly stride, all five feet, two inches of Orietta, who had to be in her mid-sixties, kept pace.

'You have to meet my husband, Anthony,' she went on. 'And you must come for dinner at our house in Palm Beach. There is a ton of people I'd like you to meet.'

That got my attention. One thing I couldn't afford to do was turn down an invitation, especially not at a home in Palm Beach, and Orietta might have rich, single men friends.

'That would be lovely,' I said, now reasonably enthused. As we walked across the lounge, Orietta nipping at my heels, it occurred to me that my title could help me quite a bit. No one would know me in Palm Beach; I could be whoever I wanted to be, and it was certainly a good time for reinvention. Good-bye, acting beauty editor, hello, acting Lady Katharine.

We reached my carry-on and I sat down, hoping that now she'd secured me as dinner guest she'd leave me in peace. But Orietta was one of those social butterfly types that lived to play hostess at every opportunity, even airport VIP lounges.

'There's someone I want you to meet,' she exclaimed with excitement. 'I met him on the flight from London. He's English,' she added unnecessarily. 'Perhaps you know him, what with your being a Scottish landowner and everything.'

Before I could utter a single vowel of objection, she vanished. I considered abandoning the VIP lounge for the uncomfortable chairs at the gate when Orietta returned with the Englishman.

'Lady Katharine, I'd like you to meet . . .' Orietta began with the polished grin of someone who thinks they are giving you a coveted gift.

But introductions weren't necessary, for I found

myself standing face-to-face with Clive's old school chum.

'Griffith Saunderson.' Orietta breathed his name like he was a prince. 'This is Lady Katharine,' she erupted gleefully.

My mind raced back to that drunken slosh of a night when my worst problem was too much pinot grigio and a vow that I had made to Clive about his friend with the unusual name. What was it? I remembered how impossibly rude I'd been and vowed that the next time I saw him, and who thought there'd be a next time, I'd be polite, complimentary, and sweet.

'Lady, is it?' Griff said slyly and with a smirk that screamed revenge for my rudeness. 'I had no idea.'

Skip polite, complimentary, and sweet, then.

'It's just Kate,' I corrected her, desperate to end the charade then and there.

'Oops, my mistake,' Orietta chirped. 'Griffith, this is Lady Kate.'

'Please call me Griff,' he suggested gently.

We stood in silence. The man hadn't changed since the last time I'd seen him. Seriously, he looked as though he was wearing the same clothes, all with that slept-in look and messy hair. In other words, he was still sexy. I caught myself staring at him but got the feeling that he liked me staring at him, so I stared at the floor instead. But dear old Griff Saunderson, clearly amused by my predicament, refused to budge. I was afraid he'd out me as a fake or find some witty English way to socially skewer me. What did he know about me anyway? For all he knew I was a lady. Though why I was so afraid to come off as an imposter to a badly dressed Englishman, I'll never know.

100

'We've met,' I said politely.

'I thought you must have!' Orietta said, clearly pleased with herself.

'But I can't remember where, it was so long ago,' I began.

'And you'd had quite a bit to drink, if I recall,' he finished snootily.

My face turned red.

Satisfied he'd embarrassed me enough, he bowed, 'Have a safe flight, Your *Ladyship*.'

I heard him stifle a laugh as he turned and walked back to his lounge seat. Bloody Brits! Who did he think he was?

'Come with me, Lady Kate,' Orietta said and pulled me along. 'I want you to meet the gang we have going down for the polo. Are you free Sunday? I'd love you to be our guest at the IPC.'

I hesitated at first. I had no idea what Orietta was talking about. Not that I wanted to appear ignorant, but I had to ask. 'IPC?' I tossed off casually, making like I didn't really care.

Orietta giggled as though I had said something witty. 'Forgive me, I should have told you. IPC is the International Polo Club, very exclusive. I hope you can join us.'

'Of course it is,' I pretended. 'I would love to come.'

I smiled as warmly as I could—this was going to be easier than I thought. My title was making entry into Palm Beach society positively seamless. Still, I couldn't help feeling uneasy about Griff. A fear swept over me that Orietta had also invited him to polo. He was obviously still angry with me, not that I blamed him entirely, but it gave him a motive to embarrass me publicly, as well. I had to find out.

'How do you know Griff?' I asked, trying to sound nonchalant.

'Oh, I don't know anything about him. I met him on the flight from London,' she said vaguely. 'He's coming down for some horse show, for the show jumping. He works with horses, or runs a stable.'

'I think he manages a bed and breakfast,' I corrected her.

'I'm not sure how he got into first class. These days you get all sorts, what with frequent-flyer miles and all that nonsense.'

I sighed with relief. That was that. He was out of my life forever.

'They let *anyone* in these days,' I agreed.

16

Up Chukka

How very acceptable it must be, at Miss Taylor's time of life, to be settled in a home of her own, and how important to her to be secure of a comfortable provision . . .

—Emma

I had been wrong to try and avoid Orietta. It turned out she was quite the respected hostess in Palm Beach. She took such a liking to me, and I felt so comfortable with her, that during the flight I made a subtle admission that I was single and looking for romance. This seemed to thrill her; she was obviously one of those older women who lived to matchmake—a must-have for Austenesque success—and she assured me that there would be a slew of eligible men at the polo tournament fit for a lady. She would pick me up at my hotel on Sunday in time for brunch.

Jennifer had ensured I would look the part and had booked me into The Breakers in Palm Beach. A hotel dripping in history, it looked like a museum with giant stone columns and ancient tapestries brought over from Europe at the beginning of the twentieth century. It was gorgeous and regal, but the owners wanted to change its stuffy image to appeal to hipsters. That's where I came in and why I was given a free room for a week so I could write a story and blog for *Haute*. To be honest, it was my kind of place. I loved the old-world opulence, the architecture, and the fussy decor; it made me feel like I was in Europe. In particular, I loved their homemade strawberry daiquiri. What would Florida be without a pink cocktail in a curvy glass complete with straw? As I strolled the grounds sipping away, I stopped dead in my tracks beside a hotel shop window. On a mannequin was a white halter dress with an eyelet overlay and a full skirt, very 1950s, and very sexy. It was perfect for polo watching. Within minutes, I was standing in front of the dressing-room mirror in the dress. It was perfect. I didn't even look at the price tag. Before I left home I had cashed in all my investments, which were now sitting prettily in my bank account for just such an emergency. I only hoped that my new dress would pay better dividends than my stocks had.

*   *   *

'What an adorable dress!' Orietta exclaimed when she arrived to pick me up. 'The men won't be able to take their eyes off you.'

That was the idea.

I smiled innocently. 'I'm not exactly twenty,' I pointed out, though not daring to divulge my actual age. Orietta brushed my worries aside.

'You're gorgeous, that's all men will notice,' she grinned.

We walked to the circular driveway of The Breakers where Orietta's husband, Anthony, was idling his Bentley. It was the color of vanilla and that made me want to lick it. The valet opened the rear door for me and I slid gracefully, I hoped, inside the ivory leather backseat.

'Hi, Anthony,' I said cheerfully.

Anthony caught my eye in the rearview mirror and nodded. He was obviously the strong, silent type. Orietta got in beside him and we were off.

*　　*　　*

When we arrived at the IPC we left the car with the valet and walked along a brick path to the clubhouse. The brunch buffet was enormous; table after table was laden with platters of oysters, shrimp, bacon and eggs, you name it, even custom-made ice-cream sundaes. The clubhouse had a bar and a swimming pool, but we were led through the clubhouse and outside to a giant shaded patio overlooking the playing field. The field was such a bright green it looked like it had been painted. Maintenance crews were busy dashing up and down the field, putting on finishing touches. There were no signs of horses yet, but I took deep breaths to

104

calm myself in anticipation. It was ridiculous. I was at a polo match—of course there were horses. And there was no need that I would ever have to get within touching distance.

Let me explain. I have had exactly one firsthand experience with a horse and it didn't go well. I was twelve years old and at a friend's birthday party, a party that included trail riding. I envied the birthday girl's pretty pinto pony. In fact, all the girls were given ponies except me. When it was my turn I was given a giant to ride, because even at twelve I was at least five foot eight and leggy. I'm not sure why, but Pebbles, that was his name, took an instant dislike to me. I hauled myself up onto the saddle and the first thing he did was whip his head around to take a bite out of my foot. The handler yanked the reins down and Pebbles threw his head up in the air and snorted. Not a good start.

We meandered through meadows and forests with Pebbles and me bringing up the rear but I don't think he liked being last in line for he kept crowding the pony in front. I yanked on the reins as I'd been instructed but that seemed to piss Pebbles off even more because when we rode onto an open field he yanked the reins from my hands and took off at a gallop. I heard the trail guide scream to pull back on the reins but I no longer had the reins. I clung on to his neck for dear life until he'd have no choice but to pull up. When we reached the edge of a thick forest I was proven right. Within inches of hitting the tree line Pebbles slammed the brakes so hard that I flew over his head and landed face-first in a thorny bush. I lay there for I don't know how long, unsure if I should move. I don't even remember the guide lifting me out, bruised and scratched, but otherwise okay. My fall had terrorized the rest of the girls who had all begun to cry and were begging to dismount their ponies. The birthday girl whined that I had ruined her party and I went home in a huff and without cake. I've been terrified of horses ever since.

* * *

Orietta ordered a bottle of champagne, but after our glasses had been filled Anthony abandoned us and disappeared into the crowd. I was beginning to think Anthony didn't like me and wondered if, as a rich man himself, he could sniff out my ulterior motive. Orietta didn't seem to notice he was gone; she was busy scanning the room.

'When does the polo start?' I asked.

'At three o'clock,' she said, finishing off her second helping of eggs Benedict with a side of steamed mussels.

'That long?' I wondered what we were to do since it was only one o'clock.

'Don't worry,' she said as though reading my mind. 'I'll make sure you meet people.'

But I wasn't sure how I was going to meet anyone with us sitting at the table like two wallflowers. The only people who popped by were septuagenarian couples and the wait staff. I watched as the grandstand adjacent to the clubhouse filled with spectators and across the polo field private tailgate parties were in full swing. Everyone was having a grand time but me. I kept myself busy by eating too much from the buffet. My excuse was I needed to soak up all the champagne; the truth was I hadn't eaten much since I'd been here. The hotel didn't

106

comp my food and I didn't want to spend more than I had to unless I was out with people I needed to impress, so I'd made do with granola bars and apples. If I filled up now I wouldn't need dinner.

When eventually the polo began, it proved to be more exciting than I expected. Watching as men on galloping horses swung mallets and smashed into each other to score a goal was thrilling and I found myself cheering on the local team. Orietta explained that a polo game consisted of six chukkas of seven minutes and thirty seconds. But like in football, the referee would call timeouts so the first three chukkas took more than an hour to finish. When the clock ran out signaling halftime, Orietta stood up at last.

'Lady Kate,' she said with a slight burp, 'this is our chance to mingle.'

I stood up and followed her to the edge of the patio. 'Where shall we go?' I asked, scanning the grandstand. I was surprised to see a mass exodus as the crowd made their way down the steps.

'We go get a glass of champagne,' Orietta said with a smile as she teetered on the edge of the patio for a moment before stepping onto the field, her heels sinking into the grass with each step. I followed, determined to make a show of it. But as we progressed toward the champagne truck, I realized that Orietta was in her element. She introduced me to everyone and anyone. 'Please just call me Kate, so nice to meet you,' I found myself repeating over and over.

There must have been over a hundred people on the field, all vying for a glass of free champagne. Eventually we made it to the source and I was shocked to see a pickup truck full of crates of Moët, with a man standing on its flatbed, free pouring the champagne as dozens of men and women swarmed him, holding their plastic flutes aloft to catch the drippings.

'It's like a UN relief truck for the rich,' I said to no one in particular. But someone heard me and laughed. Out of the corner of my eye, I spotted a fine-boned blonde woman wearing a dove gray cocktail dress and a matching gray fascinator with feathers that swirled around her head. Her eyes were hidden under oversize sunglasses, her full lips painted a brilliant red. She raised her glass to me and swanned off. She had to be at least fifty, older even, but she was one of those mature women who seemed ageless, the kind of older woman I wanted to grow into, the kind who could age gracefully and still be hot.

'Who is that?' I asked Orietta. She followed my gaze and smiled. 'That's Fawn Chamberlain. She was a beauty queen when she was a teenager, from the South, Tennessee, I believe. Never had a penny growing up. Now she's fabulously wealthy and has been married three times. Would you like to meet her?'

I nodded. Fawn Chamberlain looked like a former beauty queen, all right. I had the gut instinct that Fawn knew all too well how to snag a rich man. As we made our way through the crowd Orietta halted abruptly and whispered in my ear.

'Oh, look,' she breathed. 'It's that English friend of yours, Griffith Saunderson.'

'Griff,' I corrected her.

Sure enough, Griff stood not five feet from us with an empty champagne flute in his hand. When he looked in my direction, I smiled and took a

108

step toward him, but instead of acknowledging me he turned away. Was that a snub? Giving him the benefit of the doubt—maybe he hadn't seen me—I walked up to him and tapped him on the shoulder. He turned around and with what seemed a disappointed half smile, muttered, 'Oh, it's you.'

'Didn't you recognize me?' I asked, ignoring his rudeness.

He looked perplexed. 'Yes, of course,' he said in a tone that implied I was an idiot.

I didn't know what to say next. Luckily Orietta jumped in.

'How lovely to see you, Griff,' she said, beaming. 'I didn't know you were interested in polo.'

'Always like the horse sports,' he said and turning his gaze to me, he stared intensely—was he sizing me up or did I detect derision? I felt the need to cover up only I didn't have anything to cover up with.

'So how's it going with the B and B?' I asked. Despite my discomfort, I was determined to make conversation. After all, he was a familiar face and we had mutual friends, why shouldn't we hang out together?

'Fine,' he answered brusquely and raised his eyebrow. Clearly, he didn't feel the same about me. 'Now if you'll excuse me, I have to find someone.'

And with that, he disappeared into the champagne-mad crowd. I felt my face turn red, which only added to the embarrassment. I shouldn't let him get to me, what did I care if Griff was rude? I gulped my Moët so quickly I felt ill. Not that it stopped me from fighting my way back to the truck for a second glass. As I stood with Orietta in the crush of people, the alcohol soothing my anxiety,

I couldn't help noticing how young everyone was. Many were in their twenties, including quite a few very tanned, coltish girls squeezed into tiny dresses. These were the very girls my article was aimed at, and more importantly, they were also my competition. It was disheartening. There was no mistaking the allure of young skin, a carefree disposition, and a body that was perky everywhere. I felt the anxiety rise again. What was I doing here? I should be in New York writing this article from the safety and sanity of my life, such as it was, on Ann's sofa. I needed a third flute of champagne to give me courage. I stepped toward the truck and that's when I saw Griff, smiling and flirting with a pretty blonde half his age. At least I had my answer as to why he had no time for me. What little remained of my confidence sank as quickly as my third champagne flute emptied. Then I spotted Fawn in the distance, laughing in a small group of men—the unchallenged center of attention. She didn't seem to mind being the older woman.

'I know what you'd enjoy,' squeaked Orietta, snapping me out of my self-pity. 'I'll introduce you to a friend of mine who owns one of the teams. He's very fetching.' She led me off the field and I followed rather unsteadily from both the grassy terrain and my bubbly binge, but instead of returning to the clubhouse we went in the direction of the sand rings where a couple of teams seemed to be practicing. I froze. This was what I'd been dreading—being up close and personal with horses.

'I'm not so sure,' I said, trying to think of an excuse fast. 'Won't we get dirty?'

'Don't be silly.' She laughed. 'We're not going to *ride* the horses. Besides, the owner is handsome,

110

freshly divorced, and *well-to-do*.'

I sighed. This was what I was here to accomplish, meeting rich men, yet I felt as enthusiastic as I would about getting a root canal.

We walked past rows of horse vans with polo ponies hitched up to them as grooms darted about with buckets and tack. Orietta stopped abruptly when we came to a trailer that had 'Team Madewell' painted on its side.

'Hello! Hello! Is Scott in there?' she called out.

We could hear rustling from inside the dark trailer and within moments, one of the most beautiful men I have ever seen stepped out into the sunlight. He was tall and lithe and wore a navy polo shirt with a crest over his heart; his biceps bulged as he held a bridle in one hand and a large bucket full of soapy water in another. He was swarthy with wavy black hair and equally dark eyes. He smiled at us. His teeth were bright white but naturally so; there was nothing fake about him. 'Manly' was the only word I could think to describe him. I was beginning to understand why there were so many young women around this sport.

'Scott is in the warmup ring.' He spoke in a thick but entirely discernable Portuguese accent. I felt his eyes on me and blushed.

'Okay, we'll find him.' Orietta turned and led me away.

'Who is he?' I demanded.

'Bernardo?' she asked as though she couldn't imagine why anyone would want to know. 'He's Scott's pony manager. Such a cutie pie.'

'I like pie,' I teased.

'Careful,' she warned me. 'He's just a boy, only twenty-five years old.'

111

I shrugged and followed her to the sand ring. I tried to hang back, not wanting to approach the fence, worried that a sudden breeze would coat my white dress in dust, but Orietta wouldn't hear of it. Instead, she grabbed my arm and marched me up to the gate where four horsemen were careening around the ring, practicing their swing and defensive maneuvers. We were so close to the horses that I could smell them.

'Is one of these riders your friend?' I asked fretfully. I was desperate to be back at the clubhouse with the champagne and smoked salmon instead of standing here with the flies and manure piles.

'He's the one on the white pony. Wait until you see him up close,' she gushed. 'He looks exactly like that James Bond actor.'

'Daniel Craig?' I asked, suddenly very interested.

'No, no, not that *blond* man,' she sniffed. 'The really handsome one before him. Pierce Brosnan.'

At that, she proceeded to jump up and down and wave until the riders couldn't help but notice. Terrified that her flailing arms would spook the horses, I took a step back and felt my heel squelch and sink into something soft. Manure. Mortified, I surreptitiously wiped my heel on a patch of grass and moved back to Orietta's side as the man on the white pony trotted over to us. As he got closer I felt a wave of anxiety wash over me. Polo *pony* my ass, the horse was huge, and it was breathing hard, red nostrils flaring, veins popping all over its body, it looked like it belonged to one of the Four Horsemen of the Apocalypse.

The rider removed his helmet and I felt a smile spread across my face. He really did look like

112

Pierce Brosnan. My odds of falling in love with a rich man just improved.

'Hello, Orietta, it's been ages,' he beamed. 'How have you been? Anthony well?'

'We're both divine. Scott Madewell, this is Lady Katharine Shaw,' she said proudly. 'But she prefers Lady Kate.'

I smiled up at him. One thing was for sure; he was handsome and very sexy. He managed to be masculine even in a yellow polo shirt and tight white riding pants. I guessed he was in his late fifties, older even; I'd never been attracted to a man his age before and wondered briefly what sex with a man his age would be like. Not that it mattered. Scott was indisputably attractive—I could picture him in a tuxedo ordering a martini, shaken, not stirred all right. My confidence began to rise. To him I was still a pretty young thing.

'Lady Kate, it's such an honor to have you in our little corner of the world,' he said graciously. Our eyes met and lingered. *Ding, ding, ding.* I felt a definite spark flare up between us. This day wasn't a dud after all. Screw New York and Ann's sofa! To heck with Griff and his blonde friend! I was in the presence of a true gentleman.

'Lovely to meet you, but please just call me Kate,' I said with a note of flirtatiousness. What sort of compliment do you give a polo player? 'Good riding,' I said as poised as I could. Then immediately second-guessed if that was a dumb thing to say. Apparently not. He jumped down from his horse—in my opinion a clear signal that he was interested—so I continued my horsey-set small talk.

'How often do you play?'

'Not nearly enough to beat the Argentineans

today,' he said with mock solemnity, then asked me. 'Do you play?'

'No,' I answered quickly, then immediately regretted it. I needed to find common ground. Thinking fast, I added with as much authenticity as I could muster; 'I mean, my family used to. But we haven't kept horses on the estate since granddaddy had a bad fall years ago, after the war.'

Orietta beamed at me, overjoyed that she'd brought an aristocrat into her inner circle.

'You sound American. Where's your estate?' Scott asked, eyes still locked on mine, a playful grin on his worldly face.

'I live in New York,' I answered. 'But I inherited the estate from my Scottish side.'

'A Scottish lass? No wonder you're so beautiful,' he said with a naughty look. We were definitely getting somewhere, and fast. Then he asked something that tripped me up completely. 'What sort of game do you keep there?'

I didn't know what to say, I was much better at flirting than discussing my fake past. My mind raced for an answer. 'Croquet,' I said at last. But from his puzzled expression I knew it was the wrong answer. 'We play cricket, too, but only during summer,' I continued hopefully. He seemed to be stifling a laugh.

Orietta cleared her throat. 'That's very nice, Lady Kate, but I think what Scott meant was what shooting birds are on your estate, such as grouse.'

Now it was my eyes that widened, only in horror.

'Oh, you mean animals!' I laughed as if it were Scott who had made the error. 'No birds, unless you count peacocks.' But that sounded dumb, too, so I quickly added, 'We have cattle. We keep

Highland cattle.' Good God, what had gotten into me? I knew nothing about cattle. But Scotland had highlands didn't it? Wasn't that a good place for cows? He smiled politely but I couldn't tell by his expression if he was impressed or more confused.

'So, is this your first polo match?' he asked, wisely changing the subject.

'Yes it is,' I admitted. 'I loved it. I would definitely watch another match.'

'But there is still half a game left to see.' The voice came from over my shoulder with an accent that packed a sultry European punch. I watched as a young woman looked straight through me and beamed her assets at Scott. She had long blonde hair, which, as she got closer, I could see were extensions. She had large breasts that were corseted inside a push-up bra, and bee-stung lips painted a dewy pink. Her dress was pale lavender and she wore silver gladiator sandals. She couldn't be older than twenty-one, if that. She glided up to Scott and curled herself around him. I felt invisible.

'This is Tatiana,' Scott announced. 'She's visiting from Slovenia. Aren't you, my dear?'

'I am,' she purred and kissed his cheek.

Well, that's that, I thought. So typical that all the interesting men were taken and by girls young enough to be their daughters. What an idiot I was assuming that at forty, I would be young enough! I sized up Tatiana. She would be tough to beat. I felt my confidence sinking once more. She could write the damn article better than me!

'This is Orietta del Bianco, she's Palm Beach's most elegant hostess,' he said making pitch-perfect introductions. 'And this is her friend Kate.'

115

Tatiana gave me a critical up-and-down gaze, but laid on the charm when she spoke.

'Nice to meet you, I hope you enjoy your visit here.' Then she sniffed dismissively and turned her eyes back to Scott. I instantly despised her. Just then Orietta's cell phone blared.

'Hi, Anthony,' she squeaked. 'Oh, all right, I'm on my way.' She snapped her phone shut. 'I have to race back to the clubhouse, one of my husband's business partners just showed up with his new girlfriend and his ex-wife is livid and has thrown vodka in the poor girl's face.'

'How awful!' I said.

'I can take you in my golf cart,' Scott offered generously.

But Orietta wouldn't hear of it. And she flatly refused my offer to walk back with her. 'You stay here and learn about polo,' she said with an obvious wink and darted away, leaving me alone with the happy couple.

'Do you play polo?' I asked Tatiana.

'I can ride,' she said, tearing her eyes off Scott just long enough to answer. 'But I do dressage. It's much harder than polo.'

'That's not true,' I corrected her, even though I hadn't a fucking clue what dressage was, but I did have a clue how men liked to be defended.

'Oh, do you ride, too?' she asked me with a raised eyebrow.

'Whenever I can,' I lied. Then I turned my attention to the animal in front of us. 'Very beautiful horse. What's his name?'

'Jackson,' Scott said proudly. 'You can give him a pat, if you like.'

I froze, not expecting such an invitation.

116

'I don't want to get dirty,' I said with a smile, using the white dress as an excuse for the third time that day, but Tatiana wasn't buying it. Is was as though she could smell my fear and wanted to go in for the kill.

'Oh, come on,' she said, taunting me. 'Don't worry about your dress. Scott keeps his horses very clean.'

Damn her. I had no choice but to step forward and touch the horse. I could feel their eyes on me as I inched toward Jackson. I was just within reach, my heart pounding, trying to steady my hand to stroke him, when he suddenly shook his head like a wet dog, sending sweat flying everywhere, followed by a huge roaring sneeze that sounded like an elephant. I felt the spray hit my face, my chest, and arms. If you think horse sweat is bad, you haven't seen the amount of snot that comes out of a horse's nostrils. I couldn't help it, I screamed and leapt backward, but instead of hitting solid ground my heel slipped in and I fell toward the moist, soft earth that wasn't earth, but manure. I landed with a squishy thud and felt the dampness soak through my dress. If sitting in fresh manure wasn't bad enough, try doing it with a gorgeous billionaire and his catty girlfriend watching. I tried not to squirm but couldn't get my heels to grip in the soft ground. As any gallant gent would, Scott rushed to my side and helped me up. But it was too late for the white cotton eyelet; the skirt was stained greenish brown, the bodice strewn with green and white goo.

'I'm so sorry,' he fussed. 'Your dress.'

'It will be fine,' I said swiftly, desperate to appear unflustered. He handed me a towel and I wiped off my chest and arms, but there was no denying the dress was ruined.

'You should go home,' Tatiana chirped. She was holding Jackson and trying not to laugh, but not trying too hard. 'Get some cold water and baking soda.'

'Yes, I have to get changed,' I agreed. 'But I'll be back.'

'Let me drive you,' Scott offered firmly. 'I can take you to your car in the golf cart.'

I contemplated his offer. It would mean time alone with him. But under such embarrassing circumstances I couldn't do it.

'Thank you, but I'll be fine.' I smiled through gritted teeth. 'Please go back to your polo game.'

I had no choice but to turn my stained backside to them and march away as though everything was perfectly normal and I did not have manure smeared across my bum.

* * *

As I slunk toward the clubhouse someone with an accent called out to me. And no, it wasn't Bernardo.

'What the bloody hell happened to you?'

It was Griff again. Why I didn't just keep moving I have no idea; instead, I stopped in my tracks, huffing and puffing, as he emerged from a horse trailer.

'It's not blood. It's horse shit,' I retorted sarcastically, feeling no need to be polite after how he'd treated me. 'I fell into a pile of manure.'

I could see Griff trying to contain his laughter. My temperature rose.

'Look, we started off on the wrong foot,' he said with sudden kindness. 'Let me take you back to

118

your hotel, you can get changed and we'll see if we can't cheer you up over drinks.'

As if I would spend time with him—after how he'd treated me. If Austen's books taught me anything, it was how to spot the wrong sort of man! I looked him up and down. He didn't even know how to dress for a polo tournament. Definitely not a gentleman. His charm was all in the accent anyway. He could fool younger girls, like that blonde, but he couldn't fool me. I swept my hair from my face and said coolly, 'No thank you. I have other plans.'

'Very well,' he said, clearly amused.

I stomped away determined to prove that I could land in shit and come out smelling like a rose.

17

Hitchhiking

I doubt that you will ever have to make a choice between marrying for love and marrying for more material considerations.

—*Pride and Prejudice*

It wasn't only the dress that was ruined. My hair had managed of its own volition to do what no hair product could—be limp and straight, yet soap opera big, due to the humidity and the various tangled clumps jutting out in all directions, all with added shine gleaned from being dampened by sweat. Then there was my face. My skin was greasy, as though I

119

had emerged from a pot of boiling water, and what makeup remained was either smeared across my cheeks or caked in the tiny creases around my eyes and mouth. One thing was certain; there was no way I could set foot inside *that* clubhouse looking like this. I cowered behind the limousine and tried desperately to recall Orietta's cell phone number when a woman's voice called out to me.

'Hello there!'

I raised my head reluctantly, embarrassed at being caught crouching behind a limo, to see the lady in gray, Fawn Chamberlain, in the next parking space gazing down from the sunroof of a gray Rolls-Royce. The car was the same gray as her dress and fascinator, she held a glass of champagne in one hand, and eyeglasses in the other, which she put on to examine me in more detail. I expected an admonishment, but her tone was sympathetic and right then I needed any help I could get.

'Have you had an accident?' she asked, clearly searching for a plausible explanation for my state of dress.

'You might say that,' I admitted and slunk toward her, my hands clasping my skirt behind me to hide the manure stains. 'I ran into some trouble on the polo field.'

'Sat in trouble, is more like it.' She grinned. 'Need a lift back home?'

'That would be awesome,' I said and chided myself for sounding like a schoolgirl. 'But don't you want to watch the rest of the game?'

'Don't be silly,' she said, as if astounded by my suggestion. 'I always leave after the fifth chukka, otherwise it's hell getting out of the parking lot.'

'I'm staying at The Breakers,' I added in the

hopes she wouldn't think me a total loser. She nodded and disappeared into the car as if she'd fallen through a trapdoor, then the passenger door opened and she waved me toward her.

'Are you sure it's all right?' I hesitated, seeing the polished leather seats.

'Of course, why wouldn't it be?'

I gestured to her pristine automobile. 'That's an expensive car and my dress has seen better days.'

'Oh, I see,' she responded with a burst of laughter. She had a robust laugh, not at all ladylike but like a woman who spent her days in pool halls with hard-drinking men. 'I have something you can sit on.'

Fawn spread a beach towel out on the passenger seat and I sat down gingerly, fastening my seat belt tightly, determined not to move an inch. The car was enormous, more like a yacht than an automobile, but that seemed the norm in Palm Beach. I was certainly getting around, first a Bentley, now a Rolls, and in between a pile of horseshit.

'Breakers, you said?' she asked and hit the accelerator. I braced myself, anticipating a mighty lurch, but the Rolls glided forward as though it were a warm knife slicing through butter.

'I love your dress,' I said simply. Orietta had said that Fawn was a southern belle and her accent confirmed it, which probably went a long way to explain why she was friendly and helpful to a total stranger—southern hospitality. I wanted to prove that I was worth knowing, too. Summoning my inner aristocrat I introduced myself, 'My name is Kate Shaw.'

'Fawn Chamberlain,' she said and held out her

hand without taking her eyes off the road. 'Are you Lady Kate? Orietta's new friend?'

Word spread fast in Palm Beach.

'Yes, but please just call me Kate,' I said quietly and took the opportunity to examine Fawn as she drove. She definitely had had work done, but it was good work. The acting beauty editor inside me wanted to ask her which doctor she'd seen, but thought better of it; women like Fawn didn't reveal beauty secrets.

'Orietta mentioned that she'd met you on the flight from New York,' Fawn continued. She kept glancing over at me as she spoke although I couldn't help wondering if she weren't sizing me up, trying to determine if I was a fake. 'Your accent isn't European,' she added suspiciously.

'I'm American, from New York. I inherited some land in Scotland,' I answered confidently; telling my new story was getting easier all the time. 'I own Highland cattle, but wanted to escape the cold for a week or two.'

'A Yankee? That explains it. But with cattle, now I am impressed,' she said with a grin. 'My pappy had Herefords on his farm. I love cows and their big eyes, don't you?'

Yikes. Of all the things for us to have in common: cows. 'Yes, especially during calf season,' I said, then quickly changed the subject. 'Are you going to Orietta's dinner party tonight?'

'Of course.' She grinned. 'I never miss one of her dinners when I'm in town. Someone is bound to get drunk and make a fool of him or herself. And by that I mean ending up in bed with another guest's spouse during the cheese course.'

'Really?'

122

'Happens all the time.' She laughed. 'It's a buffet so it's easy to slip away. Although people have been known to wait until coffee.'

I nodded and smiled. I wondered who else would be at the party. As I fondled the hem of my dress my mind went back to Scott and Tatiana.

'Do you know Scott Madewell?' I asked nonchalantly.

'Scott!' she practically shrieked. 'Scott and I go way back. He was a business partner of my second husband. And my first, come to think of it. He's single now. Handsome, isn't he?'

'I met him and this young girl today.' I tried to sound vague but truth was I couldn't bring myself to utter her name.

'Tatiana?' Fawn said it for me. 'That little gold digger has got her talons sunk into him. I'm determined to rescue him from her.'

'She didn't seem his type,' I said, as if I knew what his type was.

'She's a sexy young girl. She's every man's type,' she retorted. 'My first husband married me when I was Tatiana's age. A girl can get a lot of mileage out of her youth. Mileage and millions, I always say.' She smiled and winked.

When we stopped at a red light, Fawn turned to me and smiled but didn't look away.

'Are *you* looking for a husband?'

I never knew that southern belles could be so blunt. 'Of course not!' I said forcefully and stared out the window as my hands grasped the skirt of my dress and twisted it. 'It's all right if you are,' she continued. 'In this economy, women have to be creative. But I suppose with you having a title and an estate to go with it, you don't need to think of

123

those things.'

I kept silent, unsure how to answer. 'Even a girl with a title needs a man,' I said, attempting humor. 'It's cold in Scotland.'

To my relief Fawn laughed very hard. 'And you've set your sights on Scott Madewell?' she stated matter-of-factly.

'Not at all,' I protested but to no avail. She immediately let out another of her pool-hall laughs.

'He's a catch, all right, worth billions, enough to keep you warm for life! He's a whiz in the market, or so people say,' she went on. 'We don't have any of our money with him, but tons of people around here do. He handles billions of dollars in investment portfolios. But he's just one man. There are plenty of others like him, depending on what you want out of it,' she said slyly.

'What do you mean?' I asked, my curiosity piqued. Who knew there were options?

'If you're content for a high-end affair with some travel and trinkets, there are loads of men who will do,' she explained with the same tone one would have when giving out the recipe for apple pie. 'If you want a permanent arrangement, if what you want is to be married, well, then you have two ways.'

I sat up straighter, the article was writing itself! And who better to get advice from than a woman who has had three rich husbands?

'You get the man to fall in love with you and become his mistress and pray he leaves his wife, but that rarely happens. But it was the case with my first husband,' she added with a wink. 'Or you find a single, newly divorced man—like Scott—and fight tooth and nail for him. How old

124

are you?'

I recoiled. Fawn noticed my reaction and grinned. 'You look like early thirties, but from your reaction I'd say older?'

'I just turned forty,' I confessed.

She pursed her lips as though my age were some problem that could be solved.

'No matter, you're still a gorgeous girl. But getting pregnant to snag a husband isn't so easy for you,' she said flatly. I was amazed how she could broach the topic so coolly.

'Does that even work nowadays?' I snapped dismissively. It seemed so 1960.

'Not as much as when I did it,' she said breezily. 'Husband number two.' She held up two fingers for emphasis. 'But a baby would at least guarantee child support payments, and a child of a billionaire has to live in the lifestyle into which he or she was born.'

I was speechless. And depressed. Maybe I was too old to marry for money. Maybe I would end up like Miss Bates in *Emma*, an aged spinster living with her mother for the rest of her life, only minus the sunny disposition. For a brief moment it occurred to me that while it may be too late to marry for money, I could still fall in love. Be less mercenary. Be happier. But with my track record, who was I kidding? I had to stay the course.

'There's no shame in marrying for comfort and security,' she continued with the first note of seriousness I'd heard from her. 'Especially at our age. You're forty. I'll be fifty-six next month. If you haven't got it all saved up by now, what are you supposed to do? Live on the street? Tough it out in some tiny rental? No thanks. While we still have our looks, faded or not, we have to use them to earn our way. My mother always said, "That's how a beautiful girl uses her head."˜' Fawn poked her forehead with her index finger. 'Have you ever had a job?'

I wasn't sure how to answer, but I needed some semblance of truth in case she asked for details.

'I dabble in writing,' I explained. 'I've worked as a beauty editor, just for fun. I love makeup.'

'What name do you write under?'

'My own, Katharine Shaw,' I said. 'I don't use my title in my byline, seemed too pompous, and I'm not.'

'Of course you aren't!' she agreed wholeheartedly. 'I adore fashion magazines! I read a ton of them. Which one did you work at?'

'*Haute.*'

'Oh, I love it!' she exclaimed excitedly. 'The photography is just divine! And of course the writing is too, dear.'

She seemed very pleased with this new piece of information and she dropped the inquisition for the remainder of the drive. When at last we pulled up to the front entrance she turned to me.

'I'll see you tonight. Don't you worry, Scott will be there, too.' She beamed. 'I'm going to try and find you on Google.'

I smiled back. To be honest, it wasn't that unusual for women who didn't work at fashion magazines to be overly impressed by women who did. The job did reek of glamour, even if the truth was a disappointment. But my revelation seemed to make us instant best friends, which was fine by me; I needed one, and if my girl crush on Fawn was reciprocated, even better. Traveling alone makes

126

for strange bedfellows, so why not a journalist working undercover as a fake aristocrat and a three-times divorced southern belle?

'See you tonight,' she said and drove away.

A long shower soon put to rest my disastrous first go at mingling with the rich. It was abundantly clear that polo season and me didn't mix but Orietta's dinner party was an entirely different matter. I excelled at this type of event. And I had just the dress.

18

Look the Part

A large income is the best recipe for happiness I ever heard of.

—Mansfield Park

'It doesn't work like that,' Emma chided me over the phone from London. 'Referring to yourself as "*Lady* Kate" all the time is a dead giveaway you aren't one.'

Emma should know, being English and all that. But the real reason I called her was to discuss Griff. I quickly ran through the ordeal of the day. She listened carefully, clucking in disapproval at his behavior.

'He's very snobby,' I observed. 'And then the next minute he's trying to be my friend. I don't get him.'

'I'm sorry he did that to you,' she apologized.

127

'Clive insists he's a good person. He is painfully shy apparently.'

'He showed no sign of shyness with the young babe he was chatting up,' I reminded her. 'Strange he's in Florida, don't you think?'

'I think he travels a lot during the winter and does a sort of marketing campaign for the estate,' she explained. 'He's run ragged.'

'Yes, tough life, Palm Beach,' I joked. 'There are tons of rich men here. Throw a stick and you hit ten.'

'Kate,' Emma began in a tone that implied a warning was coming. 'Be careful. You're not like those people. I don't want some rich man eating you alive and tossing you in the rubbish bin.'

'I'm a grown-up, forty, remember? I can take care of myself,' I answered breezily.

We hung up and I immediately felt better despite her concerns. I was ready to put on my game face and meet my new social circle.

'What a lovely dress!' Orietta called out when I arrived, her words felt like déjà vu from my doomed polo outfit. 'Is it vintage?'

'1991,' I said with a nod and stroked my Chanel dress. 'It's almost twenty years old.'

'Just a year younger than me,' came Tatiana's purr as she slunk out from behind a bamboo screen and with a smile disappeared into the house.

'Such a child,' Orietta said sweetly as though Tatiana were a precocious five-year-old instead of a slinky twenty-one-year-old. It wasn't fair. Austen never had to contend with sluts! But I wasn't about to give up hope. I'd find a way of outshining her. Orietta grabbed my arm and led me in the direction that she had gone.

128

'As a special treat,' Orietta told me. 'I've managed to dig up one of your kind.'

I was taken aback. 'Another New Yorker?'

'No, silly,' she said with a sweet smile. 'I invited Colonel Stuart MacKay to dinner. He's a Scotsman like you've never seen! He even wore his kilt in honor of you.'

'What?' I stopped dead.

'I told him all about you. I mean, how else to get him here?'

'Orietta, you shouldn't have,' I said, horrified. A real Scotsman would see through my act in minutes, I was sure of it. I had to think fast.

'It's nothing, dear,' she answered and continued to lead the way. I tried to regain my composure and formulate a plan. But as we walked through the house I was distracted by its decor. I had never seen anything quite like Orietta's mansion. The foyer was pink marble complete with statues of nudes that looked authentic, as in ancient, not cheap copies like you see at garden centers. From there we entered a long hallway that was like a museum gallery with African masks, sculptures, and spears lining both sides of the wall, then we descended a small flight of slate steps and came to a sliding screen door.

'Your home is breathtaking,' I gushed.

'Oh, thank you,' she muttered. 'This is the garden. My favorite place in the world.' With that she slid open the door and we stepped into a lush tropical forest of palms, ferns, and all sorts of frothy greenery that framed hundreds of exotic flowers. Tiki torches illuminated the slate pathway that led us through the forest and into a clearing where a giant fire pit roared and what looked like fifty people milled about sipping

129

cocktails.

I suddenly felt very nervous. There was Scott sucking on another cigar and Tatiana gazing at him as if no one else could smoke a cigar like he could. Too bad he didn't know he was supposed to be falling for me right about now.

Then I saw Colonel MacKay. He was round and short with red hair, a beard, and yes, a blue-and-green tartan kilt. I swallowed. Fortunately, I also noticed Bernardo, the gorgeous, sexy Brazilian stable boy, leaning against a trellis. He smiled at me. I felt my face go red.

'Everyone, I'd like you to welcome my new friend, Lady Katharine Billington Shaw,' Orietta announced solemnly.

I waved to the room and felt idiotic doing so; after all, I wasn't the queen. But what else should I do? Curtsy? 'Just call me Kate,' I said and smiled.

Colonel MacKay took the opportunity to introduce himself to me.

'So you're the famous Lady Katharine?' he said with a thick burr. 'A pleasure to meet you.'

'And you,' I said with a sweet smile plastered across my face. I felt my blood pressure rise as Scott and Tatiana joined us. Just what I needed, an audience to witness my act, and what an audience!

'Kate, a pleasure to see you again.' Scott smiled and kissed my cheek, his lips resting longer than a casual greeting should entail. *Ding, ding,* and more *ding.* I swallowed. Tatiana and I air-kissed like two boxers touching gloves before a match.

'So nice to see you again. Was your dress ruined?' Tatiana asked with forced grace. Faker. As if she was happy to see me.

'So, what part of Scotland are you from?'

MacKay interrupted. Fair question, but one I was loath to answer.

'North,' I said simply. I saw MacKay flinch.

'She has cattle,' Scott interjected. 'And peacocks.'

'Peacocks?' MacKay said, looking as if he were about to spit. 'Where in the north?'

'Near Loch Broom,' I said, deciding to go as close to the truth as possible. 'Great fishing up there.'

'You fish?' MacKay asked dubiously. Orietta appeared with a drink. I gulped it down.

'Doesn't everyone?' I laughed; everyone laughed with me. 'And what do you do?'

'I'm retired,' MacKay answered. 'It's nice of Orietta to invite me, I don't accept many invitations these days. But I wanted to meet you, Kate.'

'So sweet,' I said uncomfortably. 'So, Scott, are you playing tomorrow?'

Before he could answer, MacKay blurted out, 'But tell me, Kate, what kind of Scottish name is Shaw?'

I took a deep breath. I could sense Scott, Tatiana, and Orietta fixing their eyes on me. 'It's my mother's name,' I said. 'The estate is from my father's side.'

'What name did he have?' MacKay insisted.

'Have you no manners?' Scott came to my defense. 'Kate needs a refill. What are you drinking?'

I smiled at Scott and he gave me what I thought was a knowing look. 'Pinot grigio.'

'I'll be right back,' he said with a nod.

As though reading my mind, Tatiana took the opportunity to tell me I wasn't in the least special.

'He is always this way. Scott is very classy.'

Wish I could say the same for you, I thought bitterly.

'Are we ready to eat now?' Anthony del Bianco snapped to the gathering.

'We're still waiting for Fawn,' Orietta answered impatiently. 'She's always at least thirty minutes late.'

'Oh no, I'm not!' Fawn shouted breathlessly as she loped into the clearing. 'That's how rumors get started!'

'Where's William?' Anthony asked.

Fawn scowled, looked over her shoulder, and shrugged. 'I must have forgot him at home.' She giggled and grabbed a cocktail from the waiter's tray.

Anthony shook his head and muttered to another man standing nearby, who looked familiar to me but I couldn't place him.

Fawn grabbed me excitedly. 'I Googled you and I *have* read your work,' she said loudly.

The rest of the party went silent. MacKay perked up.

'Your work?' Scott asked, handing me my wine. 'Are you a novelist?'

'Better!' Fawn shrieked. 'Kate wrote the best article I've ever read on the history of face powder!'

I felt the room let out a collective gasp.

It was true. I had written an article about a makeup trend that used pale face powder to reinvent the look of eighteenth-century European aristocracy.

'Since I discovered you're not just Katharine but *Lady* Katharine, I read it under a whole new light,' Fawn gushed. 'All of you should know that we have

132

a fashion celebrity with us tonight.'

There were polite murmurs but thankfully no one asked anything further.

'Dinner is served,' Anthony said flatly.

As we moved toward a table glowing with lanterns Fawn grabbed my arm, leaned in, and whispered. 'Lovely dress, by the way. So classic. Look, I've been thinking,' she said softly. 'You'd be perfect for Scott. He needs a creative woman, someone who understands how the world works. We just have to get him away from Tatiana and closer to you.'

*   *   *

'I'm sick of getting divorced,' Fawn said with mock exasperation. 'For once, can't one of my husbands just die? A widow is so much more sympathetic, so much easier to remarry.'

Dinner was over and we were lying side-by-side on lounge chairs by Orietta's pool. We were very drunk. Fawn had told me that her third husband was about to leave her for a younger woman. I had been horrified but she had waved me off. 'It's what men do,' she scoffed. 'I'll be fine. I'll have plenty of money to get by until I find husband number four.'

I doubted she was as sanguine as she acted but didn't want to push, either; after all, we'd only just met. Besides I had other things on my mind. Colonel MacKay had kept his distance but I had a feeling I hadn't heard the last from him. And even more unnerving, Scott and Tatiana were off in a dark corner snuggled up together on a lounger. He had been completely charming throughout dinner, regaling the group with stories of sailing

133

and how he'd ridden a motorcycle across Malaysia to raise money for a children's charity. He even built a school while he was there. Not by himself, of course, but he did real labor. He was first class all the way and I don't just mean money. He cared about the world. I'd always imagined that one day in between maternity leave contracts, I would do similar work. Travel to Africa or Asia and get my hands dirty building hospitals or something of value. Make a difference. I never did any of these things because I was always too busy; it was always 'after the next contract is over.' But if I was married to Scott we could do them together. I could imagine riding behind him on his motorbike, building schools and drilling wells . . .

Then there was Bernardo. He kept looking over, trying to catch my eye. He had tried to make conversation over dinner but Fawn had chased him away each time. She was certainly in my corner when it came to my landing Scott. To her, Bernardo was a side dish, not the main course. And so the evening passed pleasantly, if not with any real progress. I was perfectly content, fantasizing on my future life with Scott when, inevitably, Colonel MacKay was at my side.

'We didn't get to finish our chat,' he bellowed, his voice so loud even Scott and Tatiana sat up to listen.

'Hadn't we?' I asked innocently.

'I've been thinking hard,' he continued. 'And I can't for the life of me remember any estates of note in Loch Broom. What did you say it was called?'

'I didn't,' I said dryly. 'I like to keep my life private.'

He rolled his eyes. 'What kind of rot is that?' He was obviously as drunk as I was. 'If Shaw's not the name, then what is it?'

By now everyone was watching and listening. I sensed Orietta's horror as she raced to my side.

'None of your business,' I said bluntly, hoping he'd go away. But he stood there, not moving an inch of his heft from my side. Fawn put her hand on my arm.

'Go away, MacKay,' she slurred. 'We aren't buying any.'

'Lady Kate,' he sputtered. 'Lady Kate of Loch Broom? That's shite!'

The patio was deathly silent. I had to do something before MacKay called my bluff any further. I didn't know much about Scotsmen, but I had seen *Braveheart*; they had a violent history and they had short tempers.

'Orietta,' I began and stood up. It was my only chance. 'I'm so sorry but I have to leave.'

'Lady Kate, no!' she cried out.

'It's this man,' I stammered. MacKay rolled back and forth on his heels, his stubby legs and fat knees all pink from hours in the Florida sunshine. 'I didn't want to say anything but I have no choice. The MacKays are the sworn enemy of my family.'

There was a huge gasp from Orietta and a louder one from MacKay. His eyes widened in shock, but I continued. 'Colonel MacKay's ancestors murdered members of my family on the battlefield, burned down our house, and stole our cattle.' I pretended to stifle tears and quickly scanned the faces of those within earshot. Miraculously, despite my pouring on the melodrama and pushing every stereotype I could think of, everyone appeared to believe me. So

135

I went for it. 'For two hundred years my family has despised the MacKay clan. We can't be in the same city, never mind the same room as them.'

'What are you saying?' MacKay yelped in horror, but the other guests had turned on him as though he had attacked me. 'Bugger that! Do you know how many MacKay families there are? I doubt we're the same ones who killed your family.'

'Where are you from?' I asked pointedly, not knowing a thing about the map of Scotland.

'The Highlands, near Wick,' he said sternly.

'That's them,' I gasped. 'You're one of those MacKays.'

The others gasped with me.

'I tried to be civil,' I said, my voice shaking.

'That's the stupidest thing I've ever heard!' he snapped but it was too late.

'Sorry, Colonel, you must leave at once.' Orietta had her arm on his and was leading him away. 'My goodness, what a discovery. Poor child!'

'Poor child!' he exclaimed in disbelief.

'Good night, Colonel,' Orietta said and left her husband to finish leading him out of the house. She rushed back to my side.

'I'm so sorry, can you ever forgive me?' she asked. I dabbed my eyes with a cocktail napkin.

'You couldn't have known,' I said.

'What a scary encounter,' Fawn said. 'Thank God you told us. You have to be honest about the past or else it can bite you in the ass.'

'So true,' I nodded and wondered just when my past might take an entire mouthful out of mine. By then the party had resumed but my heart was still racing as I gulped more champagne, trying to recover from my close call.

Not that it mattered how well I'd handled things with MacKay. For the rest of the evening Scott barely noticed me, preferring Tatiana's company. As I lay there, eyes shut to avoid the happy couple, I heard someone occupy the lounger next to mine. I opened my eyes only to be met with the protruding lips of the duck man from the VIP lounge, aka Businessman Number Three.

'Hello there,' he said and proceeded to use a toothpick with a vigor normally reserved for spearing fish.

I sat up and blinked a few times. But it was no use. The duck man was still there. I turned to Fawn for defense but she had vanished.

'I'm sorry, I've forgotten your name,' I said with a half smile.

'My name is Timothy Binkford, but special friends call me Binky,' he oozed, toothpick stuck in a back molar. 'And I'd like you to start calling me Binky right about now.'

'I'm Kate,' I said politely, and wondered if he'd made up his nickname to appear suave in a retro 1950s way, sort of like Bogie, but had missed the mark.

'I know who you are, *my lady*,' he said and winked. I didn't like the way he said 'my lady,' but chose to ignore it. 'I'm glad you got rid of that nasty colonel. He was very rude to you. The nerve of him! When he must have known what his family had done.'

'Yes, he should have known better,' I agreed and examined him more closely as he lay with his head resting on his arms. He was no Scott Madewell, that was for certain. But he was rich. I had overheard him discussing his tech company with Anthony. Maybe

137

he was nice? I bet Jennifer's finance friends wouldn't hesitate for a New York minute to bed and wed him despite his lack of physical charm. No one said that marrying well was easy. I'd see photos of beautiful wives and gnomish but rich husbands at parties and swishy events and wonder how the women did it, how did they fall for men who weren't obviously attractive. Were the men just so smart, witty, and successful it made up for the lack of sex appeal? That must be it. Power is an aphrodisiac, or so the saying goes. Maybe I had to prove once and for all that I could sleep with a man with a fat wallet, even if he was unattractive. Yet another modern dilemma that Austen never had to contend with! Perhaps Binky was outlandishly smart and witty. I would speak with him longer and let his intellect lure me into seeing him in another light.

Then something happened that changed everything. He touched me. I looked down and there it was, his hand on my thigh, his giant sausage fingers squeezing my flesh. I gulped.

'I like you,' he said and suddenly kissed me hard on the mouth. His duck lips were so soft and flabby I felt as though a rubber chicken had slapped me. But it was now or never. I had to know if I could be one of those other women. Closing my eyes, I leaned forward for a real kiss. Binky wasted no time. I felt his chubby arm encircle my neck and pull me in tight, his lips flapped over mine and his tongue flicked inside my mouth. Within seconds his hand was fondling my breast. But the sensation of Binky's greasy palms touching my Chanel dress was too much to take. I pushed him away and we sat staring at each other. He was panting. I wiped his drool from my face.

'You're a hot one,' he breathed.

I watched his chest heave and knew what had to happen next. It was time to go to bed.

19

The Full Brazilian

Varnish and gilding hide many stains.

—*Mansfield Park*

There are no words to describe what sex with a twenty-five-year-old Brazilian stable boy is like. It's as good as it sounds, better even. I woke up beside Bernardo. Naked. I wish I didn't remember how it happened but that would be a lie.

I had intended to go home with Binky to prove that I could sleep with a man I wasn't physically attracted to just because he was rich. But I never found out because I decided that in order to sleep with Binky, what I needed was one final glass of pink champagne. So there I was at the tiki torch-lit bar in Orietta's garden having just poured a glass, fully prepared to chug it in one gulp, when Bernardo appeared at my side.

'You should never drink champagne alone,' he said and leaned over me to grab a clean flute, his bicep brushing my breasts as he did so. 'You are a beautiful woman, Lady Katie.'

I laughed at his accidental near-rhyme, which offended him.

'You are making fun of my accent?' he asked,

perplexed that any woman would do such a thing.

'God no!' I squealed. 'I was giggling at being called "Lady Katie."'

'That's not right?'

'It is when you say it,' I flirted blatantly. As I gazed into the beautiful eyes of the stable boy I felt the hair on my neck stand up. I turned and saw Binky swaying on his little duck legs, his eyes red from drink, his forehead beaded with sweat, and knew then and there that I couldn't leave with him.

'Are you ready, Kate?' Binky blurted out and grabbed the bar with one hand to steady himself.

I couldn't bring myself to look at Bernardo. But I needn't have worried. Bernardo leaned into my neck and whispered.

'Are you with him?'

'Please get me out of this,' I whispered back helplessly.

'Don't worry, I'll take care of it.'

'Lady Katie is not well,' Bernardo said to Binky. 'I'm taking her back to her hotel.'

'I thought she was coming with me,' Binky argued hopelessly. 'I can drive her.'

'You've had too much to drink, sir,' Bernardo said politely. He was obviously accustomed to dealing with the massive egos of the very rich. 'You should stay here. I will see she gets home.'

Bernardo grabbed my hand and, giving Binky a reassuring pat on the shoulder, led me away. Sure, Bernardo wasn't rich but it proved one thing. I may be homeless, broke, and unemployed, but I wasn't desperate. I still wanted the whole package—and so far that meant one man: Scott Madewell. But until I could wrestle him away from Tatiana, Bernardo was a nice distraction.

140

I spent the next three nights with my Brazilian. Fawn was exasperated and couldn't fathom why I would waste time on a fling when I should be focusing on Scott.

'But he's with Tatiana,' I whined.

'And he's going to stay with Tatiana unless you start showing your face more,' Fawn scolded me. 'Really, besides sex, what could you possible have in common with Bernardo?'

It was true, Bernardo and I had nothing in common, but the sex was unbelievable. Although we also talked a lot; in fact, I learned about Brazil, about the village he came from and how poor his family was. His father had been a racehorse trainer and had taught him everything he knew about horses, but then his father was killed in a car accident and Bernardo had quit high school to provide for his family. He loved horses and polo and was apparently a great player, but lacked the money to own ponies, so had accepted this job to be close to the animals he loved. I told him nothing of my situation. He was the one person in Palm Beach who I didn't have to impress.

The Breakers, however, was impressed with my blog for *Haute*. It was going so well that the hotel not only offered to extend my stay an extra week, they moved me to my own private beach bungalow. Jennifer loved the blog, too. I simply avoided answering any direct questions about how my experiment in finding a wealthy bachelor was going. The fewer people who knew about Bernardo the better.

It was our fourth night together and as the smell of Brazilian steak wafted in from the patio, I gathered up the appetizers Bernardo had made and carried them outside. He stood there in his white tank top and dark denim jeans and poured us two glasses of pinot grigio from a frosty green bottle.

'You like my new digs?' I asked proudly.

'Dig?' he repeated.

I waved my arms around, taking in the bungalow and the view. 'My bungalow.'

'You bought it?'

'The hotel gave it to me,' I said. 'Because I was a good girl.'

He grabbed me by the waist and pulled me inside his massive arms. 'And why shouldn't the hotel treat you this way? They are lucky to have someone of your class here. This is how it should be.'

I grinned. 'I suppose you're right. Lady Katie deserves a house of her own.' We burst out laughing.

Later that night the sex was as great as ever, but when we were finished Bernardo sat up and stared out the patio door into the darkness. I wanted to cuddle, so I reached for his arm and tried to make him hold me but he wouldn't touch me.

'Are you okay?' I asked, wide awake with concern. 'What's wrong?'

'I shouldn't say,' he spoke softly. 'It's hard to discuss with a woman like you.'

My curiosity went into overdrive. There's nothing more titillating than a gorgeous naked man with a secret.

'You can tell me anything,' I prodded.

'I want to ask you something but I'm afraid of your answer,' he said without looking at me.

I turned his head toward me so that I could see into his eyes. He looked longingly at me and

142

we kissed. But as his lips pressed mine I had a horrible sinking feeling that I was about to receive a marriage proposal.

He pulled away and smiled. 'I shouldn't be ashamed to ask, we are practically in love.'

Ashamed? In love? What the fuck was 'practically'? I decided to try and stop him before it became embarrassing. I could only imagine Fawn's reaction.

'Bernardo, look,' I said warmly and touched his thigh. 'I've loved our time together but I'm not looking for a commitment.'

Without missing a beat he smiled and said, 'Neither am I. I need money.'

I snatched my hand from his thigh as if it were on fire. 'Money?' I stammered. 'How much money?'

'Not much for you, Lady Katie,' he said swiftly, beaming those white teeth at me the way he did that night at Orietta's dinner party. 'I want to buy a string of polo ponies, I know of an Argentinean player who needs money and will sell to me dirt cheap. You can be a sponsor, if you like.'

'If I like?' I snapped. 'What makes you think I have enough money to buy a string of horses? I don't even *like* horses!'

'But Lady Katie,' he continued. 'You don't understand because you are rich. When you are rich and an aristocrat people give you things, like this bungalow. But when you are poor, people try and keep you that way. I want to be a player and I deserve it.'

The tables had turned. I was sleeping with a man who was a gold digger. He wasn't interested in me. He wanted my money. He had taken me literally when I said the hotel had *given* me the bungalow.

This stable boy was better at gold digging than I was. I was suddenly horrified by the thought that maybe he was sleeping with someone he didn't find attractive because he needed the money and that someone was *me*. Just the possibility felt a whole lot worse than when Chris left me for that other, younger woman. I'd never felt so used. I was hurt and livid, and yes, a hypocrite.

'I can't help you,' I said at last.

His demeanor changed at once and he got up from the bed and began dressing in the dark, muttering in Portuguese.

'What are you saying?' I asked, knowing as I watched him dress it would be the last time I'd ever see him.

'You don't want to know!' he shouted.

'I wish you weren't angry,' I said quietly. There was no way I was going to confess my situation to him. I couldn't risk it.

'Don't tell me how to feel!' he continued to shout. 'You used me!'

I laughed out loud. 'You're the one who wants the cash!' But I stopped myself there. I wanted cash, too. 'Bernardo, I can't explain, but trust me I don't have the money you want.'

'Trust me,' he growled, now fully dressed and poised in the doorframe. 'You are no lady.'

And with that he stormed off.

'Ain't that the truth,' I said to the empty room.

With a deep breath, I climbed out of bed and stood staring at the ocean for what seemed like forever. I had wasted precious time on a fling. Enough was enough. I had to get serious. No more Bernardos. I strolled onto the veranda and poured the leftover pinot grigio into my glass. It was no

144

longer chilled so I tossed in a fading ice cube for good measure and took a sip, feeling as leftover and lukewarm as the wine, alone and forgotten, waiting to be tossed out after the party was over.

20

Holiday Shopping

Give a girl an education, and introduce her properly into the world, and ten to one but she has the means of settling well, without further expense to anybody.

—*Mansfield Park*

Christmas came and went exactly as I had imagined. I had flown back from Palm Beach on Christmas Eve and spent the night tossing about on Ann's blue sofa, missing my king-size bed at The Breakers.

In the morning we opened presents, a ritual that no longer seemed right without my grandmother. But we tried to keep our spirits up. I had splurged on Ann and picked up a beautiful gold-and-turquoise silk beach caftan on Worth Avenue. She adored it and immediately pulled it over her flannel nightgown.

'It's gorgeous! It looks like it was spun from turquoise and gold dust.' She beamed and twirled around like a music box dancer. 'I'm wearing it all day.'

'Over your flannel nightie? That's a look I've never seen before,' Iris cracked.

'I don't care,' Ann retorted. 'It's mine and I'll wear it anyway I please.'

'Exactly,' I said, slightly irritated by my mother's tone. She had avoided me since I'd come home. Ann said she'd caught Iris at a bingo hall more than once since I'd left. I would talk to her about it later but Christmas morning was not the time.

Ann handed me a thin, gold rectangular box tied with a green grosgrain ribbon. I gently untied the ribbon and tore the gold wrapping as neatly as I could, too neatly, for Ann rolled her eyes impatiently.

'Good God, Kate, you used to rips gifts to shreds,' she said playfully.

I laughed and yanked off the paper, revealing a blue box. I held it to my ear and gently gave it a shake. As children we had done this with all our presents, hoping that a muffled rattle would reveal all. It rarely did. I heard nothing, which made Ann giggle.

'Knew you'd do that,' she said, remembering our childhood game. 'It's shake proof.'

The box had a hinge; I opened the lid slowly until it snapped back. What was inside made me gasp. It was a string of pearls the size of marbles in shades of pink, black, sand, and white, each pearl separated by a couple of inches of fine gold chain.

'Ann,' I spoke softly. 'These are unbelievable.'

'Try them on,' she coaxed.

'How did you afford those?' Iris asked jealously.

'They're not new,' Ann explained. 'I got them at a pawn shop. This recession has them hopping. The owner said that tons of people come to him for a quick loan instead of a bank. No one claimed these so I picked them up. I thought you might need them . . .'

We exchanged knowing glances. A string of real pearls would add luster to my role as Lady Kate. I stood barefoot in front of Ann's full-length mirror in the black slip I always slept in and did up the clasp. They really were exquisite. For a brief moment, I felt sympathy for the woman out there who was spending Christmas missing her pearls, having lost them through circumstances beyond her control. But only briefly did I entertain such thoughts because whatever misfortune had befallen its previous owner, the strand of pearls looked made for me, a muted rainbow of gumballs that I hoped would lead to a pot of gold.

'Isn't that your grandmother's slip?' Iris asked suddenly as if I'd stolen it. 'It is,' I answered solemnly. Nana had bought it in the 1940s and had given it to me because she knew how much I loved vintage clothes.

'Ann, these are stunning. You have awesome taste.' I grinned, ignoring Iris's glare. 'I never thought I'd own real pearls. And such large ones!'

'Your grandmother used to say that pearls meant tears,' Iris muttered loudly enough for all to hear.

'Nana was very superstitious,' I snapped.

'Pearls mean tears?' Ann repeated softly, a hint of anxiety in her voice. She had always followed my grandmother's superstitions to the letter.

Acting blissfully unaware of Iris's warning, I stroked my pearls as if they were a Himalayan cat.

'Just like you can't give a knife as a gift because it cuts the friendship,' my mother continued. 'Or leave a hat on the table.'

'Hat on a *bed*,' I corrected her and then felt a fool for letting myself fall into her trap. 'Never

147

leave *shoes* on a table.' Then I spun around and, as joyously as I could, glided across the parquet floor twirling my pearls.

'You don't have to keep them,' Ann offered shakily. 'I can take them back.'

I halted my dance abruptly at the edge of the Christmas tree, my arm accidentally brushing its branches, causing the glass ornaments to rattle and twinkle. It sounded like music, but as it faded I turned back to my mother.

'Not on your life!' I answered defiantly. 'I don't believe in superstitions.'

'The woman who owned them before must have had bad luck to lose them,' Ann pointed out cryptically.

'Ann's right,' Iris announced triumphantly at having ruined my gift.

'You can't be serious?' I continued, my voice rattling like the shaken ornaments. 'If you think that I could cry any more than I have these past few months, you're mistaken.' As I spoke, I wound the strand of pearls tighter and tighter around my wrist until I felt the sting of the chain cutting into my flesh. 'And you know what else? I cried all of those tears without a single pearl in my possession.'

'So, you're keeping them, then?' Iris said sarcastically.

'I am,' I answered and forced a smile even though I was shaking. 'Ann is going to wear her caftan over her flannel all day, I will wear my pearls over my slip all day.'

'And what am I going to wear?' Iris asked sulkily.

'Try this,' I said and grabbed a large pink box from under the tree. It was from Florida. I knew Iris and my grandmother had always longed to

148

winter there, but it was the best I could manage for now. She opened the box and unfolded the pink tissue paper to reveal the long pink-and-white sarong with matching one-piece swimsuit beneath it. Her eyes widened in excitement and tears swelled up momentarily, but she was quick to wipe them away.

'I love it!' she gushed. 'Straight from Florida.'

'From Palm Beach,' I corrected. 'The best part of the state.'

'I'm going to try it on,' she shouted and fled the room.

Ann looked up at me and smiled. 'That was nice of you.'

I shrugged. 'We all have to have some sun and warmth in our lives.'

*   *   *

I used to love Christmas. I had always been able to look past the tacky shop decor and the bombardment of ads hawking giant televisions. I loved the spirit of the holiday, albeit not in a religious way. Baking, decorating the tree, roasting turkey, my grandmother had taught me everything, but this year I didn't have it in me. For Ann's sake, I put on my best game face as she struggled to keep the mood light. The three of us stayed indoors all day wearing our presents. Iris had not bought us anything. We had asked her to save her money for her debt. Instead, she had made us gingerbread cookies. This being Iris, they were a bit burned, but we ate them anyway. I knew I had to discuss the gambling with Iris, but it was tough to talk seriously about anything when she was wearing only a swimsuit and sarong.

'Ann said you were still gambling?' I asked pointedly.

'No!' she snapped. 'Bingo is all. I haven't gone once to the casino since your grandmother died.'

'Bingo is still spending money you don't have,' I pointed out.

She didn't answer me. Instead, her chin dropped and she stared down at her lap and played with the knot on the sarong.

'It's okay, Mom,' I said, struggling to use the term instead of the usual 'Iris.' 'We'll figure it out. Ann and I both have plans.'

'I've been helping Ann with the sauce,' Iris said, shifting her mood instantly. 'We have all the samples ready for Chicago. I've always wanted to see the Windy City.'

'Oh, are you going?' I asked, a bit surprised. The sauces were always a project for Ann and Nana. Iris had never shown interest until now.

'I needed the help,' Ann explained, having re-entered the room from the kitchen where she was preparing dinner. She didn't meet my eyes. I felt bad. She had asked for my help but I had said no to chase men in Palm Beach, for what good it did the family.

When we sat down at last for dinner, the conversation returned to the usual source of obsession for our mother. The lottery.

'It's fifty million this week,' she said, beaming.

'You still playing?' I asked even though I knew the answer.

'Yes, of course,' she said and brightened. 'It's frustrating how they've changed it. I used to play five lines for five dollars, now to play five lines it's

150

sixteen dollars. So I only play two lines for five dollars.'

I tried to listen but my mind wandered and I was thankful when dinner was over and I was officially released. I got dressed and went for a walk so I could call Marianne. Since I'd been home we'd only exchanged text messages. I was anxious to hear her voice and have a sympathetic ear. But I should have known better. Thomas had taken over her life and his first Christmas was an occasion not to be disrupted by my crisis.

'Merry Christmas!' I strained to sound upbeat.

'How did it go? Are you married?' Marianne answered happily. It was nice to hear someone sound sincerely happy.

'No,' I answered, sounding sincerely unhappy.

'Engaged?'

'No.'

'Going steady?'

'No.'

'Don't tell me you're a mistress.'

'No such luck.'

'Suntanned?'

'I'm a former acting beauty editor,' I teased. 'Of course I'm not tanned.'

'Please tell me at the very least you've got a story!' She laughed.

'Plenty!' I laughed back.

Marianne's voice was a tonic to me and I felt a small chip of my dark mood fall away as we spoke. She went on at length about how difficult the transition was between running the magazine and new motherhood. She was exhausted. There were all these new baby pressures she hadn't anticipated. I gave her a pep talk, even though I

151

knew nothing about what she was going through, but it reassured her just the same. I was dying to tell her all about Scott but Thomas had other plans.

'So, how are you really?' Marianne asked. As I began to tell her the truth, that my mission had failed miserably, Thomas wailed with such hysteria that it was impossible to squeeze in a full word, never mind a sentence.

'He's having a fit,' she said at last, giving up on adult conversation. 'Are we still on tomorrow with Brandon?'

'As far as I know,' I said, pleased she wasn't canceling. I decided to risk new mother ire by asking if Thomas was coming, too. In truth, I hoped he would stay at home; if he were to join our merry group, all cute bundle in his stroller, inevitably he'd steal the show.

'Frank is taking him,' she cooed to Thomas, not to me. 'That way we can talk.'

'Great,' I said, then quickly added, 'Of course I want to see him. He must have really grown.'

'He has. You can see him after our tea,' she said. *Whaaaaa!*

'I'd better go, he's really losing it now.'

The shrieks reached a fevered pitch as Marianne hung up.

*　　　*　　　*

I shoved my hands in my pockets. It was icy cold; maybe my blood had thinned after Florida. I walked back to Ann's feeling more lonely than I'd ever felt before. My grandmother was gone, my mother showed no sign of recovering from the

152

habit that had lost us the family home, and now a gurgling baby had hijacked my best friend. Being away hadn't made me miss my life here, or what was left of it; instead, it had cemented the fact that I needed a new life. But I was running out of time and money. My backup friend had also vanished. I had text messaged Fawn a few times over the holiday but she never answered. I began to fear that I'd been dumped. After all, she had her real society friends, her real mansions, and her real millions to keep her warm at night. The possibility that I was just an amusement to her had slowly begun to sink in and the thought depressed me. Then there was my continuing obsession with Scott Madewell. If only he had gotten to know me. If only I had gotten within three feet of him. He would feel the same connection I felt and we'd be off. I was convinced that if he gave me half a chance he'd realize that Tatiana was just a sexy, young thing with a sultry accent and big breasts. I wondered what they were doing for Christmas, if they were together or if he had packed her off to Slovenia.

No matter who was where, the fact of the matter was I missed my new life, my fake Florida life as Lady Katharine Billington Shaw. I even missed Orietta and her bright orange spray tan.

*   *   *

My cell rang the next day as I drove down to Avenue to have tea with Brandon and Marianne. It was a Florida number.

'Hello?'

'Kate?' the woman's voice whispered.

'Yes.'

153

All I heard were sobs.

'He . . . he . . . he left.' It was the drawling out of 'left' that made me recognize Fawn's voice and she was as hysterical as Thomas.

'What? When?'

'Today. He said he didn't want to ruin my Christmas!' She began to bawl full tilt. I now had the reason why she hadn't returned my text messages.

'But didn't you know he was leaving?' I dared to ask and suddenly wished I hadn't.

'How can you say that at a time like this?' she wailed. 'He dropped her and asked me to forgive him.'

I listened to Fawn explain what happened. The gist of it was this: Fawn's husband number three got dumped by his college sophomore and came crawling back to his wife. But as Christmas approached, said sophomore decided she missed her sugar daddy and had shown up at his office when she knew he'd be there alone, wearing a Santa hat, belt, boots, and not much else. That did the trick and now Fawn was alone again.

'So, what are you going to do now?' I asked as I parked my car at Avenue.

'That's why I'm calling,' she said, her crying subsided. 'Can you meet me in St. Moritz?'

My mind raced wildly for a minute. St. Moritz? Was that France? Italy? Think. Think. Got it. 'I haven't been to Switzerland in years,' I lied. I'd never been to Switzerland.

'Great, come with me, the season is just starting,' she gushed. I could tell that the thought of gallivanting in a luxury ski town had cheered her. 'I'm leaving tomorrow. I'll e-mail you my flight and

154

hotel itinerary. And you should know, Scott will be there, too. See you soonest.'

She hung up before I could ask any details. Scott was going to be there? What about Tatiana? I had failed to capture his heart in Palm Beach but a second chance to win him was irresistible. A last-minute flight to Switzerland wouldn't be cheap. I only had thirty-five hundred dollars left and hardly any room on my Visa. *Haute* had been paying me for the blog but it was barely pocket money. I thought about asking Jennifer for an advance on my Austen story but she'd want to see a draft and I'd been too depressed to write. Florida had cost me more than I had planned. I had spent a small fortune on entertaining Bernardo. But if I could get the ticket for less than thirty-five hundred, I could go. I'd be flat broke, but I'd be with Scott again. He had all the charm, elegance, and goodness I wanted in a husband, and the sizeable fortune to make Austen proud.

'Are you serious?' Marianne snapped half in exasperation, half in shocked disbelief. 'You just got home! Isn't it time to stop this charade?'

'Or at least find some part-time work so you can think things through,' added Brandon less angrily.

'Why go halfway 'round the world to chase after this Scott man? He's got a girlfriend so I highly doubt he'll be falling in love and whisking you off your feet anytime soon, then,' Marianne added pointedly.

I had given them all the details of my Florida trip, including meeting Scott and how I believed there was some real romantic potential between us. Then I came clean with Fawn's invitation to St. Moritz, thinking it would make complete sense. Yet

155

somehow, despite my telling them that there would be no stopping Fawn and me, neither Marianne nor Brandon thought that spending my last dime on a plane ticket would result in a fairy-tale ending. Truth was, I couldn't argue the point; spending my final dime on another jaunt in search of a rich man seemed reckless even to me, even with a specific target, even if it meant love and happily ever after. Still, I wasn't ready to give in. Not yet. Scott would be there, which meant I had to be there, too.

'Are there any contracts available at *Haute* or any of the other magazines?' I asked haughtily.

'Have you finished your story for Jennifer?' Marianne asked, avoiding answering my question.

'That's another reason to go to Switzerland,' I said triumphantly. 'I can't possibly finish the story without this trip.'

'Bullshit,' Marianne snapped. 'We're a fashion magazine, not a travel magazine. You can get all you need here in New York.'

'My offer to get you some PA work on a commercial still stands,' Brandon suggested mildly.

I rolled my eyes, which was the wrong move.

'What, are you too good to work for a living?' It was his turn to snap at me. 'Jesus Christ, Kate! You can't go on like this. You've had your adventure, it's time to—'

He stopped midsentence. 'Time to?' I egged him on, knowing full well what came next.

'It's time to grow up.'

'And do what?' I shot back. 'Work at WalMart? Temp?'

'If need be,' he said with a straight face.

I looked to Marianne for help but she nodded in agreement. 'Times are tough, Kate. You can't

156

spend your last dime chasing after men who don't want you. The article won't pay enough to cover your expenses. Fawn is rich and she can afford to fly around entertaining herself to forget about her troubles. You can't. You have to face your troubles head on, here, at home. I know you're grieving. Let yourself be sad, don't just take off thinking that if you run far enough and fast enough you won't have to cope.'

That did it.

'I'm sorry if my pathetic life has been a burden to you both,' I said defensively.

'Don't be crazy,' Brandon said desperately. 'You're never a burden.'

I swear I saw Marianne give him a look that said I was in fact very much a burden.

'You're not acting like yourself, Kate,' she said, clearly upset. 'This desperate, mercenary woman you've become isn't my best friend. I want the old Kate back.'

Her words stung but I was defiant. 'I'm still the old Kate, I'm just using my head for the first time in my life.'

Marianne shook her head.

'But look at what you're saying. You've whipped through more than half of what was left of your life savings to chase rich men.' Brandon threw his hand in the air for added punctuation. 'You passed yourself off as aristocracy, though I admit we had a hand in that.'

Spoken out loud, my life did have a whiff of the ridiculous, but what was the alternative?

'It's not ideal,' Marianne said soothingly, taking my silence for acquiescence. 'But stick it out with Ann and your mom and something will turn up.

157

Finish the article. Your adventures in Florida will make excellent copy. And I'm sure there's more freelance at *Haute*.'

* * *

On my way back to Ann's I stopped at a convenience store for milk. Maybe it was the fluorescent lights or the half-empty shelves of processed food but there was something about the atmosphere that depressed me. I marched to the refrigerated section and grabbed the milk, anxious to leave, but once at the checkout I hesitated. Everywhere were huge signs for the new lottery my mother had told me about in agonizing detail. I wondered what my chances of winning would be if I bought thirty-five hundred dollars worth of tickets? 'You can't win if you don't have a ticket,' my grandmother's voice echoed in my mind.

'Just the milk?' the cashier, a large, brown-skinned man in a yellow shirt asked. He was reading a newspaper and didn't even look at me.

I could do it—spend all my money on the lottery—or, I could just get one ticket. It only takes one. It could be mine. If I won the lottery my troubles would be over. I probably had more chance of winning the lottery than getting Scott to marry me. I grabbed a pencil and began to fill out the little circles beside the numbers. I filled in 4, 7, 40, 11, 19, and then the pencil broke. As a rule, I don't believe in signs, unless the sign points in the direction I want to take.

'Just the milk . . .' I finally answered.

I quickly scanned the confection counter and grabbed a milk chocolate bar. 'And this.'

158

He rang it in. On my way to Ann's I ate the chocolate slowly, letting it melt on my tongue until, impatient, I bit down and chewed it. I had to get in the mood; after all, I was going to Switzerland. What better way to prepare than eating Swiss milk chocolate?

21

Private Parts

As far as fortune goes it is an eligible match.

—Pride and Prejudice

When I was fifteen years old my grandmother told me the truth about my grandfather. Before her confession, all I knew was that they had been married during the Great Depression, my mother was born, and then sometime after World War II, their marriage became unbearable. They separated in the early 1950s, never laying eyes on each other again until years later, in the 1970s, when they finally decided to divorce. When the divorce papers arrived I was six, Ann was twelve. I'd be lying if I said I had any recollection whatsoever of the event. All I remember was that sometime afterward a strange man took my grandmother out on a date. Quite a few dates. What I do recall is being upset because I was left with Iris. What does a child know of rekindled romance? Or romance of any kind? My grandmother was gone entire weekends and I had to make do watching hockey on television with my mother and Ann.

Before my seventh birthday, Ann and I were told that we were moving with my grandmother into a house to live with her and this stranger so that my mother could have more time to herself to get over my father. The stranger turned out to be our grandfather. Apparently, though it made no sense to me, after the divorce was final, he called my grandmother. Turns out he was still in love with her. Always had been. He'd made mistakes, or so he said, and he wanted to make it up to her. They got back together. And we went with them.

My grandfather, Edward Shaw, was a short and stocky man with a pot belly that hung over his belt. He had thinning gray hair and green eyes, his nose was crooked as if it had been broken and not set properly. But what I remember most were his hands. He had giant hands that looked like they were several sizes too big for him and that could rip apart an apple and yet be delicate enough to tie a necktie. He wore a suit and a hat every day and was the sort of gentleman people called dapper.

He drove a big car; a baby blue Cadillac convertible with white leather seats and a giant steering wheel to match. Whenever we drove home at night with the top down I would lie across the backseat and stare up at the stars, an eight-track of Frank Sinatra, 'Old Blue Eyes,' Grandpa would call him, playing on the stereo.

Edward ran a business importing televisions, stereos, and eventually VCRs. He was a successful man by all accounts; the Cadillac, the house, and car he bought for my grandmother stood as testaments to his business acumen. When I was nine I had my own color television in my bedroom, much to the envy of my friends and the dismay of my other relatives. I adapted quickly to this new world order. Edward was especially pleased the first time I reached out to take his hand, my tiny paw swallowed whole by his giant palm.

But as I got older I noticed things. Like that Edward and my grandmother had separate bedrooms. And they argued. The arguments sometimes were so loud, and they were so mean to each other that I would walk outside and sit on the curb of our driveway until they were finished. I barely remember what they fought over except once, on their anniversary. Edward had sent my grandmother a dozen long-stem roses. I'll never forget the excitement when she received the long pink cardboard box from the deliveryman. She cut open the ribbon and dove fists first into the pink tissue. But her expression changed from excited anticipation to shock, her face flushed. Inside the box were a dozen silk red roses. Artificial flowers weren't what my grandmother had expected. She seemed embarrassed. My grandfather thought it was a good thing; they'd last forever. My grandmother didn't think it was so good; fake flowers were an insult.

'Gee, thanks,' she'd said, her voice shaking with hurt and disappointment.

'I thought you'd like them, Alice,' Edward said, equally offended that his artificial roses hadn't been a hit. Then he took her out to dinner in a very fancy restaurant.

The fancy dinner lightened the mood that night but the fights continued and worsened, year after

161

year, right up until two weeks before my fifteenth birthday when my grandfather had a heart attack and died. He was seventy-two.

It was a month or so after the funeral when she told me, although I'm not sure she would have if I hadn't asked one simple question.

'Do you miss him?'

She paused a long while before answering me. 'I miss him,' she said at last, 'but not as much as I should.'

Her words struck me as cruel. He had taken good care of us and he loved her and I told her as much.

'I didn't get back together with Edward because of love,' she admitted, not caring or even noticing my reaction. 'I never had much money in my life. I was tired of just getting by. You don't know how tough it was to raise Iris alone. We never had money for anything. So when Edward called after the divorce and told me how well he'd done with his business, I thought I deserved a piece of it. After all, we had been married. Your grandfather was a success. He could buy us a house, a car, which he did, and his money could make sure you and Ann got an education. I was determined things would be different for you.'

We were silent for a time. I didn't know what to say, I loved my grandfather, but Nana's confession made it seem that our life with him was a lie.

'So, you were with him just for the money?' I said, as though I needed to confirm what was glaringly obvious.

'You could say that, but it sounds so awful when you do,' she said, softening. 'Of course I cared for him, too. But he was also a pain in the ass.' She

162

smiled, hoping I'd understand. I didn't. 'He was my last chance to have some security.'

We never spoke of it again and I never told Iris or Ann what Nana had said. But my grandmother's plan hadn't worked out as she'd hoped. In the end there was no great inheritance, Edward's business was heavily in debt, and after the company was sold off and bills were paid my grandmother had a few thousand plus the house and her car, which we hid in a neighbor's garage to avoid the debt collectors seeing it. As it was, they later confiscated his baby blue Cadillac. They towed it away one morning as I left for school; it was hooked up to the tow truck before I had a chance to take out the Sinatra tape. I cried all the way to class.

*   *   *

'Do you ever wonder why the women in our family are so unlucky with men?' I asked Ann as she watched me pack for Switzerland. 'Our grandparents, Mom and Dad, me and you, and . . .'

'I ask myself the same question over and over.' She laughed. 'I never have an answer.'

'At least you've been married,' I pointed out. 'No one will ever call you a spinster.'

'People don't use that word anymore, do they?' she asked doubtfully.

'Only to be mean,' I said. 'Besides, it's better to be alone and a spinster than in an unhappy marriage.' I thought back to how my grandmother's master plan hadn't brought her the windfall she'd counted on. I vowed to have more financial certainty in my choice of husband. There was no way I would make the same mistake. 'In fact,

163

there's no reason to get married at our age except for money.'

'Money isn't the be all, end all,' she answered flatly.

'Next thing you'll be telling me it doesn't buy happiness, either,' I answered, trying to make light of the situation. I had finished packing, taking cold weather clothes, boots, and scarves and, of course, my Chanel dress.

'It doesn't,' she insisted. 'You're not happy.'

'I'm not rich,' I huffed. 'Money may not buy happiness, but it buys a hell of a lot of distraction from unhappiness.'

'Money couldn't have saved Nana,' Ann pointed out, unfairly.

'No, it couldn't,' I said slowly, refusing to meet her gaze.

'Kate, I don't like what's happened to you since we lost the house,' she said earnestly. 'You're obsessed with money and finding a man who has money. Writing a story about it is one thing, but you're trying to do it. It's not like you.'

'Maybe I've been wrong all these years, trying to find love and only love,' I countered. 'What do I have to show for it? Heartbreak and a deadbeat ex-boyfriend who can't, or won't, pay me back. No strong shoulder to cry on when I lose my job or lose my grandmother. Men and women should marry for more than love and passion, we need each other to survive in this world, just like in Austen's. So you're wrong, Ann. This *is* me. I've just woken up, is all. And I love you and I love Mom and I want to make sure none of us is ever without a home or money ever again.'

I dragged my suitcases out to the front door of

164

her apartment where an airline limousine was idling. Ann followed me out.

'Good luck in Chicago,' I said and meant it.

'I wish you were coming with me,' Ann said flatly. I knew I'd disappointed her. But Chicago was her dream, not mine. Mine was in Switzerland, or so I hoped.

'You'll do fine with Iris,' I said encouragingly. 'Maybe this will do the trick for her, too.'

Ann nodded and forced a smile. 'Did you remember to pack your pearls?'

'I did one better,' I answered and pulled the necklace out from under my turtleneck. 'They'll keep the evil spirits away.'

*   *   *

I had planned on taking a train from Zurich to St. Moritz but Fawn had insisted I wait for her at the airport before buying a train ticket. Her flight was delayed and I sat in the spotless airport terminal flipping through the latest issue of *Haute*. I needed a few copies to show the hotel manager in St. Moritz because she had never heard of it, but had agreed to give me three free nights in exchange for a story. I had the slight problem of not having cleared the story with Jennifer because I knew Marianne, whose decision it ultimately was, was dead against my going. But I had a plan; I would just keep filing to Jennifer and the travel editor and tell them that Marianne had approved it. None of them would dare disturb her while she was on maternity leave, especially not to check up on her best friend's antics. If Palm Beach was fine with Marianne, why would anyone doubt Switzerland?

165

By the time the story got printed and Marianne saw it, well, put it this way, I hoped to no longer be in need of freelance work.

'Darling!'

I turned in the direction of the familiar voice and was immediately smothered inside a giant fur coat.

'Hi, Fawn,' I said through a mouthful of mink.

'Cute jacket,' Fawn said, giving me the once over. I admit that I looked good. I had bought a sexy black ski outfit that was sixty percent off. The jacket had a faux-fur collar and I'd splurged on the matching hat and mittens, as well as a pair of black oversize sunglasses. The whole effect was very Audrey Hepburn in *Charade*.

'If the ski pants are as fitted, you'll certainly grab attention. Though I know there's only one man's attention you want.'

'He's still coming, isn't he?' He'd better, I thought, having spent my last penny for a final attempt.

'He'll be here.' Fawn grinned.

By now a porter had joined us, his trolley laden with suitcases.

'I know where we pick up the shuttle to the train station,' I offered helpfully.

Fawn laughed loudly as though I'd said the most amusing thing. 'Kate, you slay me! As if you had the slightest idea to take the train!' Then she suddenly looked at me doubtfully. 'Or maybe I neglected to mention?'

'Mention what?' I asked, feeling like a dope for acting anything less than a rich aristocrat, but surely some of them took trains?

'I'm keeping Mona,' she said with a sly grin and marched off at such a fast pace that the porter and

I had to practically jog to keep up with her. 'It's part of my divorce settlement.'

'Is Mona a dog?' I asked, scurrying after her.

'Don't be silly,' Fawn scolded me. 'Mona is a plane.'

With that she came to an abrupt standstill outside the terminal.

'We're taking Mona to St. Moritz,' she explained matter-of-factly, and gave me a puzzled look. 'I'm surprised you don't have a private jet.'

I was silent, unsure how to explain such a void in my life. She stood waiting for an answer and for a split second I had a suspicion that she wasn't buying into my act.

'I've never felt the need,' I said quickly. 'I happen to prefer trains, they're better for the environment.'

My answer seemed to satisfy her for she nodded silently.

'Yes, that whole green movement has ruined PJs for everyone,' she scoffed. 'I for one value comfort.' With that, we were bundled into the back of a limo and driven to the private airstrip.

Mona was parked on the tarmac awaiting our arrival with a supercute young pilot standing in the doorway to greet us.

'Hello, Johann.' Fawn beamed at him, then turned to me. 'Come along, Kate. Make yourself at home, it's only a short hop, but there's time for a cocktail or two if we drink quickly.'

I had never been inside a private plane before so I have no basis for comparison, but Mona was decked out in a level of luxury that I hadn't imagined possible, even though I'd seen plenty of PJs in photos. The walls were polished walnut, smoothed to such a glossy shine they almost looked

167

wet. There were leather seats and silky couches that turned into beds. A mahogany kitchen with stainless-steel appliances gleamed at the far end where a handsome steward stood awaiting Fawn's command.

'This is beautiful,' I said, trying not to be overly gushy.

'It's a Gulfstream IV,' Fawn stated proudly. 'It seats thirteen and sleeps six. I picked out the fabric myself. It's all fully custom.'

The handsome steward came by with a tray of four martinis. Fawn grabbed one and after I had taken mine, she gestured for the steward to place the tray on the table in front of us. Clearly, Fawn was determined to have fun and fast.

'Mona is lovely,' I said as we clinked glasses. 'I should look into one of these.'

'You really should. This was a bargain at thirty-three million dollars.'

I nearly spit out my martini. 'That's a lot of money.'

Fawn shrugged. 'In this economy, I'm sure you can get one for a song. Drink up. The flight is only half an hour.'

She took a big gulp of her drink and picked up a magazine.

My martini was deliciously dry; the right mix of vermouth and gin. As I sipped away I picked up a travel brochure that was lying on a side table next to me. On the cover was a photograph of an English country mansion that according to the caption was called Penwick Manor; it looked like something out of an Austen novel. Naturally, I fell in love with it.

'This house is stunning!' I gushed and showed it to Fawn. She glanced at it and sniffed.

168

'I picked that up at the Palm Beach polo,' she said with a bored yawn and returned to her magazine. 'Some Englishman had a stack of them. He was kind of good looking in that fey British way, so I took one. Although I can't abide a bed and breakfast! They expect you to sit at the same table and chat with the owner and other guests over your morning coffee like you were family. Hideous.'

She shuddered, but she wasn't the only one. I stared at the photo of Penwick Manor. It couldn't be . . .

'Englishman?' I asked, hoping to be proven wrong. 'What did he look like?'

Fawn cast her eyes away from her magazine, straining to remember.

'Hmmm. Black hair, giant blue eyes, very skinny.' She shrugged.

'I think I know who you mean,' I admitted sourly. There was little doubt that Penwick Manor was the very same B and B that Griff managed. I wish he'd been friendlier in Palm Beach as I'm sure he could get me a few free nights in exchange for a travel story. It was the perfect place to finish writing the article. I stared at the photo of Penwick Manor once again. I had to admit it was glorious, the kind of place I fantasized about as a girl, and still did, come to think of it.

'It's hard to imagine the owners would rent out rooms,' I said casually. 'I wouldn't want strangers touring about.'

'Well, as you would know, being a landowner yourself,' Fawn said, peering at me above her eyeglass frames. 'Large estates get rundown in the blink of an eye and the upkeep is crazy. Many of these aristocratic families open up their houses a

169

few times a year to allow the rest of us to get a taste of their upper crust. And they charge a fortune and people pay it, for the privilege of a room with a draft and no central heat, just to say they stayed in a castle or whatever they call them. We Americans are suckers for it.'

I nodded. 'Of course.'

'What about yours?' she asked flatly.

'My what?' I answered, forgetting for a moment that I supposedly owned an estate. 'Oh, you mean my land in Scotland? The house is barely habitable anymore. As a matter of fact, while I'm in Europe, I plan to go antiquing. I have the entire library to redo.' Good save, I congratulated myself. It seemed to satisfy Fawn.

'Then you know how it is.'

'Absolutely. But I love this Penwick Manor,' I repeated and thumbed through the brochure some more.

'Prepare for landing,' the pilot announced over the intercom.

I cinched up my seat belt. I had barely touched my martini, but Fawn had downed both of hers.

As we stepped down the metal staircase onto the tarmac I felt a shiver. It wasn't just the crisp winter air; it was the sudden reality check that I had spent nearly all my money and I had three nights, *only* three nights, before I would be penniless and stranded in Switzerland without a place to stay.

'I'm glad you got a room at Badrutt's Palace.' Fawn smiled, swaying on her four-inch high-heel boots. 'It's the best joint in town.'

And the only one who'd give me a complimentary room, I thought. As we started to walk toward the small terminal, I glimpsed an eerily familiar-looking couple descending the steps from a much smaller aircraft. It was Scott, all right, puffing on one of his cigars, but he wasn't alone; *she* was still on his arm. I stopped dead and grabbed Fawn's furry elbow so hard that she nearly toppled over backward.

'There's Scott.' I gasped. 'And Tatiana.'

She removed her sunglasses and pulling her eyeglasses out of her bag, stole a peek. 'Damn it,' she said. 'Never you mind, you'll steal him away.' Then she tossed her eyeglasses into the bottomless pit that was her handbag and, shoving the sunglasses on her head, continued on. She gestured for me to keep up and I trotted along beside her as she whispered in my ear. 'Did you see how they got here?'

'A plane?' I answered stupidly.

'It was a Citation,' she explained with a look of mild shock. 'It only seats eight.'

'So?' I asked, thinking that an eight-seat private jet was no reason to give up on a man. 'Maybe he likes smaller planes.'

'It's not just that,' she breathed. 'It's a *charter*. He used to *own* a Gulfstream.'

'Maybe it's in the garage, or hangar, or whatever you call it,' I suggested.

'Perhaps,' Fawn smiled unconvincingly.

'Or maybe he doesn't care about planes if all he wants to do is ski.'

'Ski? Scott Madewell? Don't be absurd! That's not why he came. Isn't it obvious why he's here?'

'Not to me,' I answered, feeling annoyed.

'Polo,' she said with a dismissive wave of her hand.

I felt my jaw drop. 'In January?' I asked as if I

hadn't heard correctly.

'Yes, silly,' she continued. 'Every January in St. Moritz they hold the World Cup Polo Tournament on Snow. It's a huge event. People come from all over the world to see it.'

Just my luck, more horses. As I continued to walk toward the terminal, surrounded by majestic snow-peaked mountains and tall evergreens that spread across the steep inclines like a shag rug, I took a long gulp of frosty air. It was a cool and clean breath of oxygen and I desperately needed the energy it provided. After all, I only had three days to change Scott's reason for being in St. Moritz.

22

Swiss Miss

But there certainly are not so many men
of large fortune in the world as there are
pretty women to deserve them.

—Mansfield Park

Badrutt's Palace sprouted out of the mountainside like a castle in a Grimm's fairy tale or EuroDisney. I half expected to find yodelers in the lobby. It looked ancient to me, but considering it opened in 1896, it was modern by European standards. When you're on a press trip the hotel tends to make a fuss, but not in a subtle way; Badrutt's was no exception.

'Welcome to Badrutt's Palace,' the manager,

a tall, blonde, angular woman greeted me enthusiastically. Her name was Helga. 'I can give you a complete tour in the morning if you'd like,' she explained as a bellboy followed us to my room. It wasn't a suite but a deluxe room overlooking St. Moritz and the Engadine Mountains. As long as it had a minibar I was happy. 'Let me know if you need anything,' she said and left me in peace. I flopped on the bed and had nearly fallen asleep when Fawn came calling, dressed to hit the slopes.

'Is this all they had?' Fawn stood at my window, outraged that my room wasn't as fabulous as hers. 'You should write a nasty article on them now.'

'Really, Fawn,' I said trying to be persuasive. 'It's fine.' I had admitted that my hotel was paid for in exchange for a travel series I was writing for *Haute*, and of course she found that exciting. I wasn't sure I should trust her with the truth about the Austen article, the timing wasn't right.

'You should see my suite,' she went on. 'It's enormous! Two bedrooms miles from each other, and the fireplace!'

'I'm glad you're happy,' I said as I changed into my full ski suit complete with slim-cut pants. I loved it because it was fitted; none of that puffy Michelin Man aesthetic for me. I wanted to look glamorous, not fat. And better yet, with everyone wearing a getup like this, no one could tell how old anyone was; unlike Florida with its beaches and bikinis, skiwear was age camouflage. Take that, Tatiana.

'I'm ready,' I announced and swanned out of the dressing room, ready to make my St. Moritz debut.

'Very nice,' Fawn said faintly and plopped on my bed, looking like she would burst into tears at any moment. 'Next to you I look like a buttered

173

crumpet.'

Her outfit was in fact pale yellow and puffy. 'You do not,' I lied. I headed for the door but was stopped short by Fawn's outburst of tears.

'I've . . . I've,' she cried. 'I've lost it . . .'

I wasn't sure what she'd lost because she was crying so hard. I had no choice but to sit there and wait it out.

'What have you lost?' I asked softly when her tears had subsided.

'May I have a tissue?' she asked like a little girl. I quickly ran to the bathroom and brought back the entire box. She blew her nose and forced a smile.

'That's better.'

'I'm glad. Can I help somehow?'

'No one can. What I lost I can never get back—my youth.'

I removed my ski jacket and sat down. Lost youth was no five-minute chat; this could take a while.

'When I saw how sexy you looked in your little black ski suit, I was jealous. I feel ugly and old in this buttery mess of a thing. No wonder my husband left me for a younger model. Who'd want this?' She held out her arms encased in yellow marshmallow sleeves. 'But look at you, Kate. You're exciting, glamorous, sexy, smart, and younger than me. With you zipping around in that ski suit, what chance does an old woman like me have? I'm no longer desirable. I've come to the end of my beauty.'

I didn't like her berating herself like this. I looked at her, sitting on the bed, vulnerable and sad; the sultry and confident woman I'd met in Palm Beach just weeks before had vanished. When I had met her she had been the picture of rich wife glamour, but now she reminded me of a broken

174

champagne flute, jagged, fragile, and discarded. I felt sorry for her and that made me angry. I cleared my throat and spoke honestly. 'You are one of the most elegant and beautiful women I've ever met,' I said, which made her smile. 'We are going to go out there and you're going to have dozens of eligible men fall head over heels in love with you! And better, they'll all be rich.'

I got up and pointed to the door. She smiled weakly.

'Ha! Or is it LOL?' She laughed artificially. 'It's not money I'm after.'

'What do you mean?'

She looked at me as though I had three heads.

'I don't want to grow old alone,' she growled. 'I want a man who loves me. Money doesn't keep you warm at night or hold your hand when you're sick.'

'But you always act like money is all that matters,' I explained. 'I for one would rather be rich and alone than poor and alone.'

'That may be,' she said, examining me through her bleary eyes. 'But neither of us are poor. Just alone.'

I felt her eyes focusing on mine as she spoke, scrutinizing me. Or at least it felt that way.

I wanted to tell her the truth and not just to make her feel better; it would be a relief to drop the act.

'I'm poor,' I admitted at last and waited for the fallout.

'Well, I assumed you weren't rolling in it, but poor? Define poor.'

'Empty bank account and maxed-out credit cards. No house. No job.'

'Just your land in Scotland?' she asked

175

sympathetically. I could tell she didn't believe me.

'The truth is my estate in Scotland encompasses exactly one square foot of conservation land.'

'I don't understand.'

Then I spilled the entire thing: my mother's gambling, my house, the genesis of my aristocratic title and, of course, my grandmother's death. Fawn took it all in, nodding patiently and giving my shoulder a sympathetic pat during the parts about my grandmother. Then I knew the timing was impeccable. So I told her about the article . . .

'I'm trying to see if Austen's approach to act like a lady and put yourself in the path of rich men will bag a billionaire,' I said with a sigh. 'Though it's gone far beyond research, after everything that happened I must do it for real. Making a good marriage is my only chance to have a decent life. Then I met Scott and I knew he was the right man for the job, so to speak. I know I could fall in love with him and he could fall for me if given half a chance. So you might say I'm a middle-aged woman trying to see if I can win the lottery, but instead of playing numbers I'm playing romance.'

'You know what this little adventure of yours reminds me of?' she asked with a twinkle in her eye. 'One of my favorite movies of all time, *How to Marry a Millionaire*, have you seen it?'

I had. It starred Lauren Bacall, Marilyn Monroe, and Betty Grable as three down-on-their-luck models who try and pass themselves off as society women in order to lure rich husbands. I hadn't seen it in years. Fawn was right on target.

'You're right, somewhere between Austen's books and that film is my life,' I admitted.

'That movie was practically my instruction

176

manual,' she confessed. 'How else could a small-town beauty queen become somebody who everyone respects, who everyone wants to be friends with, and who has more money than most everyone?'

'So, you don't think less of me?' I asked cautiously. 'I mean Scott is a friend of yours.'

'Think less of you? How can I? Honey, I *was* you back in the day. I went after my husband exactly as you're going after Scott. Who am I to judge? Now, does anyone else know your secret?' she asked. She had moved to my powder room to reapply her makeup and with a final stroke of red lipstick Fawn Chamberlain, the millionaire hunter, was back with a vengeance.

'You're it,' I admitted reluctantly. 'Please don't tell anyone.'

'Why would I do that?' she asked innocently. She was smiling again as if we'd never had the conversation, but she kept looking at me as though she had something on her mind. At last, and with a dead serious expression she said, 'I want to help you.'

'Help me?' I said, taken aback.

'What you need is a mentor.' She tapped my shoulder. 'Otherwise you'll be strutting around like a runner-up in a beauty pageant, sleeping with the judges, hoping they'll vote for you next time. I can teach you how to win and first prize is a billionaire. Wait until you get a load of the tiara!'

This was either a really great or a really terrible idea. Then again, I had three days to advance my plan or I would be out on the streets. I decided it was really great. 'Then consider me your pupil.'

She clapped her hands together gleefully. 'I love

177

having new projects!' she declared. 'I always try to set up my daughter but she flatly refuses, and is determined to never marry. I'm starting to think she's a lesbian.'

I giggled. I was sure that Fawn's daughter wasn't gay, just independent, and besides, she was an heiress. What did she need a rich husband for?

'Let's start by hitting the slopes,' Fawn suggested. 'Men love an active woman.'

Big confession; I don't know how to ski. Like tennis and equestrian, skiing is a sport with an outfit I admire but will only wear to sip pinot grigio. Fawn was amused by my lack of skiing abilities but didn't see any point in attempting a lesson on the bunny hill. Apparently the sort of men I needed to meet were strictly black diamond types. So instead of hitting the slopes, we hit the bar.

As it turned out, Badrutt's Palace had a rather splendid one called the Davidoff Lounge, so there we sat by a large picture window with an unobstructed view of the lake, skipping the ski portion of après-ski and enjoying a lovely white wine, when three men sat down at the table beside us. They were boisterous, but we didn't pay an iota of attention to them, which was made easier by the fact that they were speaking Russian, or so Fawn said. Our afternoon would have passed pleasantly, if unremarkably, if it hadn't been for one of the men lighting a cigar. Fawn was immediately indignant and began to sputter and shift in her chair. I did my best to ignore it but it was impossible. The smell was putrid, as was the thick layer of green smog that drifted to our table, encircled our heads, and crept into our nostrils as if it were on legs. I made a face. Fawn coughed and waved at the smoke. Scott smoked cigars but always outside, and with far more finesse than this lout. We waited, fully expecting him to head for the nearest exit, but he stayed put. 'I can't take it anymore,' I muttered to Fawn. 'Let's move to another table.'

'Not on your life,' she said sternly and spun around in her chair and tapped the shoulder of the man closest to us.

'Excuse me,' she said brightly. They all abruptly stopped talking, clearly shocked that someone dared to disturb them. The man she poked turned to face us. I caught my breath. He was extremely handsome. He had large, wide-set eyes the color of a ninety percent cocoa chocolate bar. I couldn't even make out the pupils, they were so dark. His hair was nearly as dark and it was long, past his jutting chin, and wavy with a center part. He wore a black leather jacket with a purple shirt underneath, the collar was a floral pattern and it looked custom made. With a pair of charcoal gray jeans and brogues, I assumed he wasn't much of a skier himself. He looked like a rock star.

'Can I help you?' he said in a heavy Russian accent and with a note of extreme seriousness.

Fawn, unaffected by his brooding sex appeal, smiled sweetly and spoke in her most ladylike southern accent. 'I hope you can. My friend and I can't abide that gentleman's cigar smoke. Would you mind asking him to take it outside?'

Then she waited, determined not to waver. Fawn was a badass when she wanted to be.

'Why don't you move table?' he said rudely.

Fawn bristled for a moment, then turned and pointed to me. 'Do you know who this is?' she

179

said as I recoiled into the safety of my wingback chair. 'This is Lady Katharine Billington Shaw of Scotland.'

I was horrified. Fawn grabbed her wineglass and took a swig like she was a biker chugging bourbon. He didn't answer straightaway; instead, he stared at me as though examining every detail; no emotion showed on his face. I stared back, which, to tell you the truth, was no easy feat. You try staring down a drop-dead handsome stranger who is either mentally undressing you or plotting an assassination attempt. I grabbed my glass of wine and, taking my cue from Fawn, took a massive swig to prove I wasn't afraid, only instead of exuding biker chick toughness I gagged. Fawn rolled her eyes as the wine dribbled down my chin.

'What are you drinking?' he asked.

'Pinot grigio,' I sputtered in feigned defiance. God, how wimpy did pinot grigio sound! I regretted not ordering whiskey.

He was still staring, and I was seconds from blurting that grade school idiom, 'Shake your head, your eyes are stuck,' when he suddenly turned to his companions and barked at them. His comrades, including Puff, quickly removed themselves from the table and took up residence at the bar. Fawn nodded her approval just as a waiter swooped in.

'Another vodka,' he said to the waiter in a less scary tone. 'And the women will have more pinot grigio.'

Hmmm. Not so wimpy when spoken with a Russian accent and looks to kill.

'That's much better,' Fawn said coolly. 'But I can't stay.'

As she got up to leave I grabbed her arm, or

180

clung to it, was more like it.

'Don't leave me,' I pleaded under my breath.

'This one is flush, I can smell it,' she whispered. 'Rule number one, always see where an encounter can lead. You can always say no, but you can't say yes if they don't have an opportunity to ask the question.'

'But what about Scott?' I muttered fitfully.

'He's not the only man who can make your dreams come true.' She winked. 'Consider it research, at the very least.'

With that, she disappeared and I was left with the sullen Russian. I smiled awkwardly at him and clutched my wineglass to my chest.

'Who are you exactly?' he blurted.

I nearly spilled the wine I was so stunned by his blunt question. He must have noticed for his features softened for the first time into a smile. 'My apologies. I'm Russian and sometimes my English isn't so good or so polite. What I wanted to know was where are you from?'

'I'm American, if you must know,' I said, trying to affect a regal air and hoping what I was about to say would be a 'do' on Fawn's list of ensnaring a billionaire. 'But my estate is in Scotland.'

He nodded. The waiter was back with our drinks. It was clear from the waiter's deferment that this grumpy Russian was a very important person.

'Enjoy your drink, Mr. Mihailov,' he said.

Mr. Mihailov picked up his vodka. I quickly picked up my fresh wineglass in anticipation of some fancy toast, but watched in astonishment as he took a drink without so much as making eye contact. It was anticlimactic but I took his cue and sipped my wine and waited for him to speak again.

'You like it here?' he said at last.

'So far,' I answered breezily. 'But this is my first day. Ask me tomorrow.' Then out of fear of more awkward silence, I asked, 'Where are you from?'

'I live in Moscow, and London mostly,' he said, checking his BlackBerry. 'But I'm from St. Petersburg. I came here for the polo.'

Not another one, I thought, but never mind that; according to my rich man calculations, homes in Moscow and London added up to one thing: Russian oligarch. Fawn was a genius.

'What do you do in Moscow and London?' I asked, feeling more at ease, so much so I was practically batting my eyelashes at the man.

'I run companies, mining, lumber, some oil,' he listed off his assets like a shopping list. 'What do you do in Scotland?'

'Whatever I want,' I said flirtatiously.

'And what is it you want?' he asked with a fixed glare.

This threw me off, so I laughed artificially to give myself some time to think of a witty answer.

'That depends.' I continued to laugh. 'On who is with me.'

'Do you have sheep?' he asked, blatantly ignoring my flirtatious remark. What a strange question. How odd that both Scott and Mihailov were so interested in what I *had* on my fake estate. It must be a male thing, like their bizarre fascination with Home Depot. I thought it best to ensure my lies had a certain continuity and that meant no sheep.

'I have the finest herd of Highland cattle in Scotland,' I boasted, slightly unnerved by how easy lying had become. It was nearly second nature.

182

'My cousin has cattle in Wales,' he said.

'What a coincidence. What kind are they?' I asked, hoping they weren't Highland cows, too. Thankfully Mihailov shrugged.

'They are just cows.'

I was relieved. It would have been complicated had he known one end of a Highland steer from the other.

'What do you do for fun?' I asked, much more relaxed. 'Do you ski?'

'I buy pretty women pinot grigio and then take them to dinner,' he said, still unsmiling.

I didn't know what to say, so reverted to my foolproof fallback position for these very situations; I drank more wine.

He was staring again. This time I didn't stare back. I turned to the window and tried to distract myself by the lake and mountains.

'It's beautiful here,' I said, and it was.

'You are beautiful,' he said. His compliment meant I had to look at him. My, was he gorgeous.

'Thank you.'

'Will you allow me to buy you dinner tonight?' he asked with a faint smile.

'Yes,' I said and smiled broadly. If Scott could be with Tatiana, then I could have a date with someone else, too. And Fawn was right, I had to keep my options open in case I couldn't pry him away. Day one was over and I had a date with a Russian oligarch. I loved the words so much I kept repeating them in the elevator as I rode up to my room to change. Thankfully I was the only person in the lift.

*　　*　　*

183

'Whatever you do, don't sleep with him,' instructed Fawn, lounging comfortably on the bed. I was in the process of dressing for my date, having settled on my Chanel dress and string of pearls. I rolled my eyes.

'You're just saying that because of Bernardo,' I said indignantly.

'Absolutely not,' she countered. 'Bernardo didn't have a dime; that's what you do with men like that, enjoy them for sex. Wealthy men who are also attractive are far more dangerous because women sleep with them on the first date, mistakenly believing that the man is falling in love and not just satisfying his lust. These women don't understand that a wealthy man does this all the time. If you want to marry the millionaire, save the sex for later.'

'That seems like very old-fashioned thinking,' I said cautiously, not wanting to offend Fawn.

'They are called old-fashioned rules because they withstood the test of time. And for a reason,' she continued. 'They work. Appearing aloof and untouchable drives them crazy and makes them want more.'

'Well, I have no intention of sleeping with Mihailov,' I insisted and slipped on my black velvet slingbacks. 'Besides, he scares me.'

'Precisely why you might,' she said with a tone that implied she didn't believe me. 'Where is he taking you?'

'Someplace called Chesa Veglia.'

'*Verrry* nice.'

'Why, what is it?'

'It's only the finest place to eat and be seen in

184

St. Moritz. There are three restaurants inside, I hope he takes you to The Grill; if he takes you to the Pizzeria he's not serious about you. Oh, and there are two bars; one is called the Polo Bar, it's only open during the winter season. You might run across Scott there.'

I waved away the suggestion.

'Look at you! Not caring about Scott.'

'He doesn't care about me,' I corrected her. 'Besides, he's still with Tatiana. And Mihailov is at least fifteen years younger, so at least if I ever do see him naked his body will be in fine shape.'

I regretted the words as soon as they left my mouth and saw Fawn recoil at the references to youth. 'Maybe you can join us later for a nightcap,' I said quickly to change the subject.

'I'm staying in tonight and watching dirty movies,' Fawn said with a laugh. 'I'll wait up for you.'

'Like a chaperone?' I teased.

'Exactly. Only I chaperone from the comfort of my luxury suite.' She laughed. 'Stick with me and you'll land your rich man.'

I intended to do just that. Picking up my evening bag, I glided across the floor and twirled in front of the mirror.

'How do I look?' I asked. Fawn gave me a nod of approval.

'Like a million dollars,' she said proudly.

'That's a good thing,' I answered solemnly. 'Because that's what I need to get.'

But as I headed toward the elevator I was hit smack on the head by a brick of self-doubt. Where did *this* Kate come from? My whole life I had never been more mercenary than taking the last cupcake off the dessert tray, and here was the so-called new and improved Kate, off on a date whose purpose was to attract a man solely for his money. I didn't really know *who* this Kate was that got in the elevator and strutted across the lobby, and I wasn't entirely sure I liked her any more than Marianne did.

23

Russian Doll

Our pleasures in this world are always to be paid for . . .

—Northanger Abbey

Chesa Veglia was definitely old, circa 1658, which made it the oldest building in St. Moritz. As Mihailov and I settled into our dining chairs in The Grill, I saw that Fawn was right; it was a scene. There was a heady mix of ages, tables of young studs on the make, dozens of pretty young things and the gray-haired men who loved them. The common denominator wasn't a passion for skiing; it was the patina of wealth, the clothes and accessories, the entitled tilting of heads, the flagrant consumption of rare vintage wine. In all my years as an acting beauty editor I'd never seen so much glossy hair; the room was a sea of expertly coiffed brown, auburn, and blonde manes that swayed and bobbed like flying carpets, all accompanied by flawless complexions that only money could buy.

We might have been in the midst of a worldwide recession but clearly the rich were alive and well and hiding out in Switzerland, maybe to keep watch on those fabled Swiss bank accounts. I spotted a few quasicelebrities, too; a former tennis champ and his Spanish girlfriend leaned in tightly toward each other and whispered, and a faded French film actress who, judging by her swollen figure and sun-damaged skin, had given up any possibility of returning to the big screen.

The room was pleasant enough, although the same couldn't be said about Mihailov's company. The old saying, Handsome is as handsome does, was never truer than on this night. He turned out to be one of those men who insist on ordering for his date. I hated that. I was more than capable of choosing on my own. Not bothering to ask what sort of wine I wanted, even though he'd bought me a pinot grigio that afternoon, he scanned the wine list and ordered a bottle of cabernet. He took the same control over the food. Lucky for him I liked lamb.

I struggled to think of something to say, any icebreaker would do, although I had a feeling I would need a very long, very sharp ice *pick* to thaw him. I decided to begin the conversation with a question, one that was easy to answer, a no-brainer.

'What is your first name?' I asked in what I thought was a friendly manner.

'Vlad,' he barked. Make that ice *prick*.

'Nice to meet you, Vlad,' I said, hoping the conversation would improve. 'That's a very traditional Russian name, isn't it?'

'Do you always talk so much?' he asked flatly as the sommelier arrived with the wine. As he had at

Davidoff's, Vlad began to drink without a toast of any kind. Disheartened, I followed suit. He was a surly man and I began to question why he wanted me there at all. He had neglected to say anything nice or to compliment me. Scott probably said nice things to Tatiana all the time, I was sure of it. I sighed quietly and allowed my mind to wander to Scott. He was the reason I got on that plane—I should be focusing on him, not wasting time with Vlad. I contemplated faking a migraine when all of a sudden he smiled like a normal human being.

'Do I scare you?' he asked and winked like a naughty schoolboy.

'Not at all,' I lied.

'What are you thinking?' he said in a tone that made me doubt he really wanted to know and I was definitely keeping visions of Scott to myself.

'I'm contemplating the use of mime,' I said coolly. 'Since I talk too much and I don't know sign language, I can't think of any other way to communicate. And while I despise miming, particularly when it's pronounced 'meem,' it will have to substitute for lively banter.'

He stared at me so intensely that I shifted in my seat, when, without warning, he burst out laughing. I was stunned, but there it was; a raucous laugh at my mime joke. Maybe miming *was* funny.

'I would like to see you mime.' He grinned. 'Naked.'

Nude miming had never been on my agenda. Tonight was no exception. Maybe if Scott had said it I would have found it sexy. Instead, coming from Vlad, the word reduced all his good looks down to Binky-size proportions. He was clearly just after sex and I, equally clear, was not. We were at an impasse. Marrying well was going to be much tougher than I thought. Even a *handsome* rich man could turn me off with a few choice words. After rejecting Binky I accepted that I could only be with a man I felt was physically attractive; now it seemed I needed a good personality, too. I was doomed. Fawn's fear that I was a middle-aged slut was completely unfounded.

Still, it was early and I had to eat. I was determined to give Vlad another try. There was a language barrier, after all. Maybe he didn't mean it the way it sounded.

'Do you have children?' he asked.

'No,' I said. 'I've never wanted them.'

He flinched. 'Women *should* have babies,' he practically growled.

I recoiled. 'Why *should* women have babies?' I asked defensively.

'Babies are God's way of letting women age gracefully,' he said self-righteously. 'When women age and lose their looks, babies give them another reason to live other than attracting men. How sexy you are is less important when you have children to occupy your time.'

I stared at him, not believing what I was hearing. But he wasn't finished.

'Women who don't have children, by the time they hit forty-five, they lose their role in life, they aren't the pretty young things men want, and they aren't the nurturing creatures children need. They are nothing. Invisible,' he continued with a chug of cabernet. 'But of course, that's your choice nowadays. Do you like hot tub?'

That was the extent of our conversation, how was I to respond to any of it? The remainder of the

189

meal was eaten in silence except for the occasional sexual innuendo, provided by him, of course. When dinner was over I attempted to say good night in the lobby but he insisted we stop in at Kings Club, an all-night dance club in Badrutt's Palace.

He marched into the club and found us two barstools facing the dance floor, depositing me there while he went to get drinks.

To say that Kings Club was not my scene would be an understatement. The dance floor throbbed as an undulating mass of youth flailed and bounced to remixed versions of eighties pop songs. All the Pretty Young Things had cascaded down from The Grill and were bumping and grinding with each other, the men who brought them, or some combination of the two. I have always avoided nightclubs; they were too loud, too smoky, and had too many barely clothed drunks falling all over the place. In a word: tacky. I hated tacky. Kings Club, despite its posh setting, was no exception; it took the term 'Eurotrash' to new heights.

'Enjoying the view?' It was a voice I'd been hearing in my fantasies for over a month now, only the extended techno mix of 'Like a Virgin' wasn't part of the fantasy.

I turned and spoke above the music, 'Scott, it's so nice to see you again!'

'What are you doing, sitting here alone?' he asked and smiled at me as if we were old friends.

'I have a date,' I admitted, wishing I were alone.

'He's a fool to let a beautiful woman sit by herself,' he said, his eyes scanning the dance floor as he spoke. He does think I'm beautiful! I couldn't help smiling. Sitting there with him next to me felt natural, comfortable, like we were already a couple.

Why couldn't *he* be my date?

'Have you seen Tatiana?'

Oh yes, that's why. I gazed up at him. I had tried so hard to put him out of my mind today, but seeing him again, so close, and for the first time alone, okay, alone with a hundred half-naked twenty-year-olds gyrating on the dance floor a foot away, made me realize how much I wanted to get to know him better. He didn't think I spoke too much. He was a man of conviction and passion. Again, the image of me clinging to his waist as we drove across Malaysia on a motorcycle came flooding back. We were meant to be. And he called me beautiful. I was right to spend every last dime coming to Switzerland.

'Sorry, who?' I said, pretending that I didn't know who he was talking about.

He grinned. 'Tatiana, my *girlfriend*.'

I shook my head innocently and tried to imagine how 'She is probably having sex with the bartender' would translate into mime. But I didn't get the chance to act it out because Tatiana bounded over, her breasts pouring out of a leopard print minidress like two flesh-colored Jell-O molds dumped on a platter.

'Yes?' I said tartly.

She nodded and smirked.

'You like that dress.'

'I do,' I replied, leaning on the edge of my barstool, desperate to wipe the smirk off her face.

'You wear it a lot.'

Scott cleared his throat.

'I want to dance!' Tatiana whined and tugged at his arm.

'You go ahead,' he smiled indulgently. She pouted mildly, then shimmied off into the darkness.

I caught the occasional glimpse of animal print beneath the strobe lights as she flitted about.

'I'm way too old for this place,' I said, much more loudly than I had intended.

'Me, too,' Scott agreed.

Finally, a connection! Though I wasn't so sure that bonding over the aging process was going to win me any points. Still, I wanted to make the most of my few stolen moments with Scott before Tatiana whirled back.

'I prefer a glass of wine, a fireplace, and good conversation,' I said with a sigh.

'I'm with you.' He nodded.

Okay, he's with me. But only until his young girlfriend returned all hot and bothered from her dance. Perhaps it was the wine I'd had at dinner, or the setting, but a sudden audaciousness came over me.

'So, what do you and Tatiana talk about?' I asked boldly, then realized as I said it that I really wanted to know.

Scott didn't shrink from the question. He simply smiled knowingly as if I wasn't the first person to ask. 'What do we have in common?' he asked.

I knew I was being rude, so I cut him off. 'It's none of my business. Forget I asked.'

'It's okay,' he said with a serious expression. 'It's a good question. She is nearly forty years younger than me. So there's that.'

'There's what?' I pushed forward fearlessly. 'I mean, there's the obvious: she's gorgeous.'

'Thank you,' he said as though I were complimenting him. 'I won't lie to you, Kate, young, firm skin is attractive. But that's not the whole of it. Tatiana has a naïveté that's very sweet

192

but she also possesses a boundless energy and enthusiasm for new things. She's not bitter or jaded. And through her eyes I get to experience life all over again.' I absorbed this information and hated that on some level I understood where he was coming from. It was so easy to become jaded and bitter with life's disappointments and it would be appealing to be with someone who saw the world through fresh eyes. But life as a series of firsts, of explorations, and possessing a faith that the universe would unfold as it should was the exclusive domain of youth. It was an intoxicating trait.

'Maybe if I'd had children, particularly a daughter, I would have received the sort of reverence from her I so obviously crave,' Scott continued. 'The admiration of a young girl keeps a man young. I suppose at a certain age all men feel we've earned the right to be respected and esteemed for our accomplishments, even if our accomplishments are as uninspiring as merely accumulating wealth and property rather than saving the planet or ending poverty or curing disease.'

'But with your money you can fund all of those things,' I countered, not wanting Scott to beat himself up. 'That motorcycle trip through Malaysia, you built a school!'

'Of course, you're right,' he smiled halfheartedly. 'I suppose what I'm saying is the trouble with money is that it's never enough. So here I am. Look who I'm talking to! You know how it is, Kate.'

I swallowed. 'A bit,' I muttered under my breath.

Our conversation was cut short when Vlad returned without drinks and looked at Scott suspiciously. Scott, being a gentleman, held out his hand and introduced himself. Vlad gave in and shook his hand.

'I want to leave now,' Vlad said abruptly, turning his back to Scott.

'Me, too,' I agreed as I watched Tatiana slink across the crowded dance floor toward us, mopping her brow. I couldn't bear to watch her wrap her limbs around Scott one more time.

'Good night, Scott.' I smiled.

'Good night,' he said giving the Russian the once-over.

Vlad insisted on escorting me to my room, only I didn't go to my room, I went to Fawn's suite. It was obvious that he wanted to have sex with me but that wasn't going to happen, with or without my 'chaperone.' When we got to the door I lifted my hand up to shake his at the precise moment he grabbed my shoulders and pulled me in for a kiss. I quickly turned my head so his lips struck my cheek. He bounced off me like a racquetball in-play, clearly shocked and, judging by his expression, unhappy with my maneuver.

'Good night, Vlad. Thank you so much for dinner.' I smiled warmly and smoothed my hair.

He was dumbfounded and clearly unaccustomed to women turning him down. It made me giggle.

'Good night,' he said icily before marching away in a huff.

Once inside the suite I burst out laughing. Fawn switched off the television and raced over eagerly.

'Well?'

'Put it this way. I'm terrible at gold digging,' I said. 'How did you do it?'

'Do what?' she asked.

194

'Have sex with men you didn't find attractive,' I said in a flurry. 'Because I'm clearly not up to the job.'

Fawn shook her head. 'I never said I did that. You have to like the man,' she said softly. 'There's the old saying, Mingle with the rich and marry for love, I never married a man I didn't find interesting or sweet. Marrying for money is like marrying for honesty. It's just a trait on your wish list. It can't be the only one, as you've discovered on your own, but it's in the top three. Heck, even those Austen girls got more out of them aristocrats than money. Mr. Darcy for sure was hot in bed!'

We burst out laughing. But Fawn had a point. And I had the distinct impression that Scott would also be hot in bed. And I liked him. I imagined long conversations about the problems of the world and how we'd help. It was much easier to imagine marrying a wealthy man if you also enjoyed his company. If love was as important as money, as Fawn said it was, then Scott was it.

'Let's order hot chocolate!' Fawn suggested, knocking me from my thoughts. She listened rapturously as I told her about the disaster date and bumping into Scott and Tatiana and of my heart-to-heart with him.

'I have to find a way to get Scott away from her,' I said in frustration. 'I know in my heart that she doesn't deserve him. But she's practically glued to him.'

'We'll get rid of her,' Fawn said confidently, then added, 'I think you need to arrange another date with Vlad.'

I balked. 'No way, not on your life,' I said firmly.

'Don't toss the baby out with the bathwater,'

195

Fawn said calmly. 'I have a plan.'

I wasn't sure I wanted any part of a plan that involved more time with Vlad the pervert but agreed to listen.

'Arrange to meet Vlad at the Polo Bar tomorrow night; if he wants to have sex with you he'll show up. I will invite Scott, who will of course bring Tatiana,' explained Fawn, but I stopped her from going further with a wave of my hand.

'I can't face Tatiana anymore,' I said, but Fawn was not deterred.

'We will all have drinks together and let nature take its course,' she said with finality.

'What are you talking about?' I asked, bemused.

'Vlad is a very rich man, possibly richer than Scott,' she explained as if the plan was obvious. 'He is, as you pointed out, much younger and to some eyes, much sexier. Tatiana is young and beautiful; deep down, she may prefer someone closer to her age. Both are from former Soviet bloc countries, so we can assume they have lots in common.'

'And?' I asked, still not getting it.

She threw her hands in the air. 'Vlad will want Tatiana and Tatiana will easily cross over from Scott to Vlad. It's a slam-dunk.'

I let her plan sink in. She was onto something. If all Tatiana was after was money and she could have money and a sexy younger man, why wouldn't she want Vlad? And what man could resist a twenty-one-year-old sexpot like Tatiana?

'You might be brilliant,' I admitted with a sly grin.

Fawn leapt up and went to the minibar and popped open a small bottle of Veuve.

'We're celebrating,' she said and poured out the

196

champagne. 'Here's to the happy couple, Vlad and Tatiana.'

'To Vlad and Tatiana,' I repeated and took a long sip of champagne.

* * *

By the next morning it was all set. Vlad didn't even hesitate when I called and invited him to have drinks with some friends. Fawn extended the invite to Scott, insisting he bring his charming girlfriend along. The plan was unfolding nicely until the subject of what I should wear came up.

'You can't keep wearing your Chanel,' Fawn pointed out.

I remembered Tatiana's derisive comment about my dress. 'I do need something new,' I admitted.

'I could lend you the money,' she offered kindly.

I shook my head. 'Never lend a friend money,' I said. 'Besides, I don't need *money* for a dress.'

I decided it was time to demonstrate to Fawn firsthand the clout a fashion magazine had, particularly during a recession. We marched into the hotel boutique and I proceeded to pull any dress that was suitable off the racks.

'The first thing that businesses do in a recession is cut advertising budgets,' I explained. 'But stores still want to promote their stuff. Getting editorial coverage is worth way more because editors like me endorse the products, readers listen to editors. So I can get almost anything I want without paying for it.'

'Is that what that new word 'recessionista' means?' Fawn asked, impressed.

'Not quite. But I *am* staying at the hotel for free,'

I admitted. 'This dress?' I held up a gorgeous black Balenciaga cocktail number that was by far the priciest frock in the shop. 'They may not give it to me, but they'll loan it to me to 'test drive' for the article.'

'Honey, if you've got all this, you don't need to marry for money,' she said and giggled as I signed for the dress.

'Oh, but I do,' I said seriously. 'I'm sick of borrowing my so-called life of luxury. I want to own it. I want to know its mine and no one can take it away.'

'My dear,' Fawn said sadly, 'none of us ever get that security, not from marriage, and as this recession proves, not from money.'

'I will,' I stated firmly, clutching the Balenciaga tightly to my chest.

24

Skip to the Loo

My good opinion once lost is lost forever.

—*Pride and Prejudice*

The Polo Bar was swarming but with a different crowd than had filled The Grill and the disco the previous night. As Fawn and I followed the maître d' to the table, I saw that the room had been decked out with Cartier banners trumpeting the start of tomorrow's snow polo tournament— that's what was different, this was the polo set. The men wore double-breasted jackets; the women wore tasteful dresses and Latin polo players mingled about, adding an air of sex to the room. I saw from a distance that Scott and Tatiana had already arrived, but for the first time since I'd met them, she wasn't draped over his body like a pashmina. She sat across from him, a sullen look on her face, sipping champagne as he focused on his BlackBerry. I was suddenly hopeful. After our talk maybe he realized he didn't need as much admiration as he thought. But as we drew closer to the table I saw that the Polo Bar also had one thing in it I hadn't expected.

'You certainly get around,' spoke the familiar silky accent.

The Polo Bar had Griff Saunderson.

Fawn and I stopped.

'Fancy meeting you here,' I said tartly. I thought back to my last conversation with Emma and her words, that Griff was a good sort of man, echoed in my mind. I would try yet again to be friendly.

'I guess Palm Beach made a polo fan of you, after all, despite your close encounter with manure?' he said with a half smile.

'I'm here for the skiing,' I answered coolly. He was making friendly a tall order.

'I wouldn't have taken you for a skier,' he said matter-of-factly.

'Why is that?' I asked, dreading his answer.

Before he could answer, Fawn coughed.

'Pardon me, Griffith Saunderson, I'd like you to meet Fawn Chamberlain,' I said, trying to contain my irritation. 'He prefers to be called "Griff."'

'We met once before,' she cooed and shook hands with him. I noticed she held onto his

199

hand longer than necessary. 'You gave me the brochure on that darling manor house.'

'Yes, it's lovely,' I agreed. Surely he was capable of normal chatter. 'So, are you here alone?'

'I am.'

'I wasn't sure if that girl I saw you with in Florida was your girlfriend,' I asked and immediately wished I hadn't.

'Girl?' he looked at me blankly. 'What girl?'

'Some blonde I saw you speaking with at the polo,' I said, flustered. The last thing I wanted was Griff to misunderstand and think I liked him *that* way.

'They're all blonde at the polo.' He laughed. 'You can spend all your time counting the number of bottle blondes versus natural ones. What about you?'

'Me?' I asked, puzzled.

'Ever been a blonde?'

'Never,' I said defiantly, with an involuntary toss of my head (at least it felt involuntary).

'Good to hear,' he said firmly. 'Brunettes are much more dangerous.'

'And you like danger?' I asked and realized with a shock that we were flirting. How did that happen?

'Not at all, I always go for redheads.' He smirked. Maybe we weren't flirting.

'As the token blonde in the conversation,' Fawn cut in, 'I prefer male-pattern baldness. Not that either of you asked my opinion.'

'Sorry, Fawn.' I blushed.

'Yes, Kate is in the habit of saying whatever is on her mind with little regard for whoever is in the room,' he said teasingly. 'I've borne the brunt of her comments myself.'

'Griff, that's not true,' I said, desperate to dispel his words.

'Perhaps I'm wrong,' he said with a faint grin. 'Clive and Emma tell me you have excellent taste, so what you say must be right.'

I wanted the ground to swallow me then and there.

'I love your accent,' Fawn gushed. 'Do you follow the polo around?'

'I go to as many tournaments as I can,' he explained. 'How long have you known, um, *Lady Kate*?'

'We met in Palm Beach,' Fawn answered and smiled flirtatiously at Griff. It was obvious she found him attractive. I admit those huge blue eyes were hard not to stare at, and his thick black hair seemed to beg my hands to run through it. Even his clothing was passable; crisp dark gray jeans and a gray chunky-knit sweater with a cowl-neck instead of his usual faded blue button-down. He didn't look anywhere near as scruffy as he usually did. But I didn't have time to critique Griff's wardrobe or fret about what he thought about me. A quick glance at our table told me time was of the essence; Vlad had arrived and was fixated on his BlackBerry, sitting as far away from Tatiana as a table for six could provide and no one was talking to each other.

'We have to go,' I said with sudden urgency and grabbed Fawn. She looked at the table and a sly smile spread across her face; she had other plans.

'Yes we do,' she agreed and turned to Griff. 'We have an empty seat at our table, would you care to join us for a drink?'

I bit my lip. Griff looked at me, no doubt to gauge my reaction. I stared at the floor. He would take my silence as a definitive no.

'I would love to,' he said and gave Fawn his arm, leaving me to follow as though I were an afterthought.

When we got to the table I whispered in her ear, 'This wasn't a good idea.'

'What party wasn't improved with a dashing Englishman?' she asked as if it were obvious. 'Don't tell me you're attracted to him?'

I shook my head furiously. 'Hardly.'

'Good. Keep your mind on the others and leave Griff to me,' she said confidently. 'Southern women know how to host.'

As it turned out, southern hospitality meant insisting on a boy-girl, boy-girl, boy-girl seating plan. To make matters worse, my reluctance to do as Fawn asked left me as the last man standing, which left me with the last empty seat. Seeing no way out, I reluctantly sat down sandwiched between Griff and Vlad with Scott across from me. There went any hopes of an intimate chat.

After that, nothing went to plan and I blamed Griff, or rather Fawn's impulsive invitation. Instead of stealing Scott's attention and Vlad and Tatiana falling for each other, the majority of the conversation was about polo. The three men discussed it with a zealousness usually reserved for soccer hooligans. Tatiana continued to sulk in silence while Fawn listened intently to the men and laughed at their polo inside jokes and debates about the skills of various players. I didn't know Fawn knew that much about polo. I was bored stiff and had begun to make origami with my napkin when my BlackBerry vibrated. I know it's rude to check one's text messages at a restaurant but no one was paying any attention to me. Stashing it under the table I saw the message was from Fawn. I shot her a look. She nodded. I read, 'Act interested. Laugh. Make eye contact with Scott but flirt with the other men, too.'

I was irritated and typed back furiously, 'Unlike you, I know zero about polo.'

I watched her read my message, shake her head, and type something back with equal fury. My device vibrated and I looked down. 'Do you think I do? Fake it.'

I looked up again and saw her laughing and patting Scott's arm. I laughed, trying not to sound too artificial, and turned to Vlad.

'Are you going to the game tomorrow?' I asked in my attempt to seem interested. 'Of course, that is why we are all here,' he said as if I were an idiot.

'Kate is not a fan of horses,' Griff announced. All eyes turned to me as if I had sprouted a third arm. If this was his idea of coming to my rescue, he was vastly mistaken.

'But I thought you rode?' said Tatiana, taking this moment to finally speak. 'You said in Palm Beach you rode horses.'

I froze, unsure what to say. I began to stutter something about once riding but Griff piped up.

'I meant she's not a fan of polo,' Griff said. 'Am I right?'

'Absolutely,' I agreed gratefully. 'I adore horses and riding. But polo isn't my thing.'

'That's too bad,' said Scott, his disappointment palpable. I had to do something.

'I would love it, Scott, if you could explain it to me tomorrow,' I suggested hopefully. 'I'm sure I'd appreciate it if I knew more about it.'

This seemed to brighten him up, although Tatiana and Vlad shot me a dirty look.

'I would be happy to,' he said.

That seemed to do the trick for the conversation picked up again. Then Griff stood up and excused himself. I knew I had to talk to him alone before he revealed anything else about me.

'I'm going to the ladies' room,' I announced and left the table. I caught up with him at the restroom entrance and pulled him aside, out of sight of the others.

'Can you keep your insights into my character to yourself for the rest of the evening?' I said angrily.

'Keep your voice down, Kate,' he said calmly. 'Sorry about that, I had no idea you were playacting, I mean beyond the title bit.'

'I may have said I rode,' I whispered back sharply.

'What are you up to anyway?' he asked. 'If you expect me to play a part, then I should know the plot.'

'Long story,' I said unhelpfully.

'I have time,' he said with a smirk.

'If you must know, I'm here to find a husband,' I said huffily, then toned it down when I saw his stunned expression. 'What I mean is, it's finally time to settle down and get married.'

He didn't react at first but then had the nerve to laugh. 'Well, if it's a rich man you're after, then you've come to the right place.'

My stomach lurched. Was I that transparent? 'What makes you say that?' I asked, astonished he'd guessed.

'Why else would a single woman travel to St. Moritz for the polo except to meet a wealthy bloke?' he asked.

'You make it sound so cheap and ugly,' I said unhappily.

'So it's true? I was only joking!'

This made me furious. 'So was I!' I lied.

'I don't think you were,' he said. 'But you can't be serious.'

I stood there, unsure how to answer. He held my life in his hands. I couldn't risk him telling anyone the truth, that I wasn't a lady in the real sense of the word. The silence drew on uncomfortably, seconds felt like minutes.

'Good God, Kate, money can't buy happiness,' he said at last. 'I hoped you were smarter than that.'

'This is being smart,' I insisted. 'I have my reasons for being here.'

'I understand money woes; when my parents died their affairs weren't in order and I'm still reeling from it.'

I bit my lip. Maybe Griff *did* get my problem even if I didn't tell him everything.

'I'm sorry about your parents,' I said gently.

'My father died five years ago, my mother eight,' he explained. 'Life hasn't been quite the same since. I don't know what's happened to bring you to this point but we all carry on as best as we can.'

'Exactly!' I agreed, hopeful we'd reached an understanding. 'Please don't say anything about me?'

'Don't worry, I want no part of your game,' he said with a weak smile. 'But my silence comes with a price. You'll have to let me take you to dinner one night.'

'You are a master of mixed signals,' I said, exasperated. 'One minute you say such mean things to me and the next you're saving my butt and asking me out.'

'I could say the same about you,' he said, looking miffed.

'I'm easy to understand,' I replied. 'I know what I want.'

'I'm sure you do. Though I doubt that Vlad Mihailov is your man.'

I was taken aback. 'You know Vlad?'

'No,' he said flatly. 'I've never met him, but I've heard of him. He lives in London.'

'Yes, I know,' I said. 'He told me that.'

'He's not for you,' he said sharply. I was taken aback and offended at the same time.

'Who are you to determine if a man is right for me or not?' I snapped.

'Quite right,' he agreed sourly. 'But let's just say he's of dubious character and you'd be best to stay as far away from him as possible. He's not the sort to trifle with, especially not the kind of game you're playing.'

With that, he disappeared into the men's room, leaving me no choice but to hope I could trust him.

* * *

I returned to the table and gave my full attention to Vlad; there was still time to foist him onto Tatiana. But each attempt to start a chat between them was met with frosty glares and one-word answers. Even Fawn's southern charms were lost on them. It was a disaster. To make things more awkward, Griff came back and ignored me the rest of the evening. Nor could I engage Scott in proper conversation without Tatiana tossing in her two cents. We passed an entire tedious hour this way until, unable to take it anymore, Scott stood up and put an end to the charade.

'I see a client of mine,' he announced and gestured to a short, bald man at the bar. 'Tonight's been delightful but I need to mingle.'

He smiled and walked off with the pouty Tatiana slinking after him. Then it was Griff's turn.

'I'm also going to circulate a bit,' he said, still not bothering to look at me. I made a face behind his back as he strode away. We were obviously destined to clash. I was determined not to give a fig if he was angry or disillusioned. He had no right to be either and had no claim on me. I rolled my eyes at Fawn. But I should have known she wasn't going to give up that easily.

'What a lovely girl that Tatiana is,' Fawn said with a smile. I gave her a puzzled look but she shook her head. 'Vlad, don't you think Tatiana is one of the most beautiful creatures you've ever laid your eyes on?'

'No,' he snapped. 'Slovenian girls are whores. That whole country is filth.'

Fawn and I flinched in disgust.

'I like women, not girls,' he continued sternly. 'Young ones talk too much. Kate, she is woman.' I felt his hand on my leg.

'I have to go to the ladies' again,' I announced and stood up. 'All that wine.'

I darted off. It was useless. Our plan had totally backfired. He was still into *me*. Why did I have to find the one rich man who didn't want to date a cheerleader, but who I wanted nothing to do with? Classic romance dilemma; you always want the man you can't have, and you never want the man that wants you. Turning forty hadn't changed a thing.

*   *   *

The ladies' room was vast. It had two sections: there were the cubicles in one area and there was a 'parlor' in another; separating them was a mirrored foyer. The parlor was furnished with upholstered benches strategically placed in front of large mirrors and marble counters that were stocked with perfumes and hand creams. A female attendant stood guard, ready to squirt lotion or offer you a tissue at a moment's notice. At the far corner of the parlor was a chaise, or fainting couch, complete with wingback chair at its side for amateur psychiatrists to dispense advice. As we all know, the ladies' room is where broken hearts are revealed and soothed; that the Polo Bar addressed this fact of life by an isolated space to save face made me think that the Swiss really did know how to run everything like clockwork.

I sat down on one of the pink stools to reapply my lipstick and had just unsnapped the lid when I heard the unmistakable sound of crying. I looked around. The attendant stood like a sentry, indifferent to the sobs—no doubt she'd seen and heard plenty before. But to me, the crying was like a siren call and I went to investigate. I saw that the farthest cubicle door was shut tight. As I inched closer, the crying grew louder. Whoever was in there was sobbing her heart out.

'Are you okay in there?' I called out.

The only answer was more sobbing.

'Do you need me to get someone for you?' I offered. Still nothing.

'I'm going to leave now,' I said, raising my voice so she could hear me above her tears. I was about to walk away when the door opened. I felt my jaw drop and my eyes widen, not knowing where to look or what to say for the woman who had been weeping so mournfully was Tatiana. She marched past, her face streaked with mascara, and proceeded to wash her face at the sink.

'What's wrong?' I asked, half expecting her to say something rude. She straightened her posture so she stood tall and proud. Here it comes, I thought, the bitchy comeback. But instead she broke down.

Just then the door burst open and a group of women trotted in, chattering loudly. I grabbed Tatiana by the hand and led her to the chaise.

'Sit here a moment,' I said and, grabbing a box of tissues, sat beside her. I expected her to stop crying. But Tatiana didn't stop crying. Whatever was the matter was serious and I began to feel sorry for her. The fact that Tatiana had always been rude to me and also happened to have the man I wanted naturally made me hate her. But right now, she was just a wounded kid.

'Did something happen?' I tried again.

She looked up at me. All mascara and eyeliner had long vanished, her face was clean and her eyes were red. I had to admit that she was a very pretty girl. I could see why Scott found her so appealing, there was an innocence and vulnerability about her that was compelling.

'Scott broke up with me,' she blurted suddenly and collapsed into sobs again. I perked up.

'When?'

'Before the evening started,' she explained. 'He let me come because I was so upset.'

'What? Why?' I asked. I may have felt sorry for her, but if Scott was now single, I wanted to know.

'I thought he liked another woman,' she sobbed. 'You, maybe. He always goes on about how elegant and smart you are.'

'Really?' I said with a broad smile and quickly returned to a concerned look. 'I'm sure he doesn't think of me that way.'

'You are right,' she said. My heart sank. 'I hacked into his e-mail expecting to find love notes. But there was nothing.'

I knew he hadn't e-mailed me but clearly he thought about me enough to tell Tatiana. Maybe there was hope.

I took a deep breath. 'Oh, Tatiana, the problem with spying on your man is that whatever you find you have no one to blame but yourself,' I explained maturely.

'I guess so. He lost his temper.'

'And now he doesn't trust you?'

She nodded. 'He said I was ridiculous. He was a one-woman man and I should trust him. But I love him!' she shrieked suddenly and burst into tears again. I rubbed her back. That she was actually in love with Scott was a complication that I hadn't counted on.

'I didn't know you loved him,' I said gently. 'I thought you wanted him because he was rich.'

She stopped crying again. 'I do love him. And yes, I need a rich man because I don't want to live in Slovenia anymore. My family is very poor, I didn't have money to go to university because I had to work to support my mother. And I don't even like my mother.'

'I don't get on with my mother, either,' I said

210

sympathetically, thinking of Iris back home in Park Slope with Ann.

'I was raised by my grandmother,' Tatiana explained. Now it was my turn to sit up straight. I never imagined I'd have anything in common with this girl and now she had my sympathy. 'My grandmother lives in a one-bedroom apartment with my mother. I worked at a medical office but didn't make enough money, so I became a waitress at a very expensive restaurant and then I met Scott. I need to marry a rich man, and then I will take care of my grandmother.'

Tatiana suddenly impressed me. She had come to the conclusion twenty years before I had that the solution to her problems was to marry a rich man, to do whatever she had to do to help her family. She should move to New York and hit the clubs with Tina and Arianna. I thought of my article, how I was supposed to be figuring out how to help women like her find a husband to take care of them. But she stood in my way and I wasn't sure that I wanted to give her any advice. She kept crying so pitifully . . .

'Have you ever seen *Pride and Prejudice*?' I asked, giving in to my good side.

She looked up at me and nodded. 'With Keira Knightley? I love that movie.'

I rolled my eyes. 'Yes, there is that one, too. But it's nothing compared to the 1995 television miniseries with Colin Firth.'

She shrugged. 'I don't know him. Who did he play?'

The horror. 'Mr. Darcy, of course! I suppose every generation gets the *Pride and Prejudice* it deserves,' I said huffily. 'But my point is that

211

Elizabeth was always a lady even when she was suspicious of Darcy. And it turned out her accusations and assumptions of his motives were wrong. Chances are you're wrong about Scott. Now you have to make amends and behave like a lady if you want to hang on to him.'

I paused before uttering my final bit of advice, words that were hard to say. 'You'd better get back out there and apologize to him,' I ordered.

'He won't accept it,' she said, her eyes filling up once more. 'He hasn't spoken to me all night.'

'Beg him, then,' I instructed. 'He's your chance to be happy, and to help your grandmother.'

At that moment, Fawn burst through the door with a panicked look on her face. 'There you are! Your Russian bear is frothing at the mouth,' she said excitedly but then stopped dead when she saw Tatiana. 'What goes on here?'

'Tatiana and Scott broke up,' I explained. Tatiana stood up and, straightening her dress, glided across the room to the vanity. 'It appears that our brief intimacy is over,' I whispered.

Fawn was grinning ear to ear. 'So now that Scott is a free man, you have to make your move.'

'Oh, Fawn, I can't just sweep in there. Look at her.' I gestured to Tatiana, who was reapplying makeup to her red and swollen eyes. 'She's heartbroken.'

Fawn raised her eyebrows at me. I shrugged.

'You've been after him for how long?' she asked.

'Not that long,' I said.

As we headed to the door I glanced once more at Tatiana. She looked up in the mirror and for a few seconds our eyes met. I waited for a show of warmth, anything that said we had crossed the line

212

from rivals to friendship, but her expression was blank as she returned to her mascara. It was all I needed. I had a feeling that Scott could be made to forgive her. But I wasn't going to let that happen without a fight.

'I don't see him,' I said to Fawn on our way back to Vlad.

She looked around the room, then stopped the maître d'. 'Have you seen Mr. Madewell?'

'Monsieur left about ten minutes ago,' he answered and dashed off toward the lineup of people waiting to get in.

'Damn,' I said loudly. Truth was, I didn't want to go back to Vlad. There was only one man who would do and that was Scott Madewell. And now he was free.

It was then that I spotted Griff at the bar settling his tab. I asked Fawn to give me a moment and walking up behind Griff, I tapped him on the shoulder. He wheeled around to face me.

'If it isn't the robber bride,' he said coolly.

I winced a little but ignored his remark.

'You have something in your hair,' he said, lifting his hand to my head. As he did so I turned my face to see what he was plucking at and my lips grazed his arm. That alarm went off inside again, *ding, ding, ding,* clearly my body enjoyed his touch more than I wanted it to, which set off alarms of a different kind. I couldn't be attracted to Griff, could I?

'It looks like a feather,' he said and held the white piece of fluff up so I could see it. He smiled. 'You can trust me.'

I was suddenly speechless but couldn't take my eyes off him. Another second or two of intense

213

staring and he'd kiss me, I could feel it, and what's more, I wanted it.

'There you are.' Vlad had found me. Fawn was right behind him. I was far more disappointed at the interruption than I expected.

'Where have you been?' he demanded, completely ignoring Griff.

'Poor thing,' Fawn jumped in. 'She was feeling terribly faint. Luckily she didn't fall on the marble and get concussed.'

Vlad looked from Fawn to me. I feigned weakness and nodded.

'You okay now?' he said, softening a little.

'Yes, much better, thank you.'

'Then go get your coat,' he ordered. 'We go for nightcap.'

I was not going anywhere with him.

'Honestly, Vlad, I don't want a nightcap. I just want to go back to my room.'

Vlad grabbed my elbow and yanked me. My eyes widened in panic. I wasn't expecting him to be so aggressive.

'I said nightcap,' he snapped.

'I don't think you understood the lady,' said Griff suddenly.

'What did you say?' Vlad growled.

Fawn and I stood wide-eyed. I was suddenly afraid for Griff. Vlad was big and angry, and worse, sexually frustrated.

But Griff stepped forward and took me by the arm. 'Kate, give me your ticket and we'll go and get your coat.'

'Who do you think you are?' Vlad stamped his foot.

'A friend,' Griff answered calmly. 'You heard

214

Fawn,' he continued. 'Kate is unwell, she doesn't want a nightcap.'

'I don't,' I said quivering.

Vlad stood steaming like a villain in a cold war movie but Griff was unaffected.

'Good night, Mr. Mihailov,' Griff said smoothly and led me away, Fawn trotting behind us. After we got our coats, Griff escorted us to the hotel. We walked in silence; the crisp night air was so refreshing after the stale ambience of the Polo Bar, but my mind was far noisier, running through the events of the evening. I knew that I was unmistakably attracted to Griff. It wasn't just his showdown with Vlad—though his sudden display of manliness was very appealing—and sure, his looks had grown on me. But he was also kind, generous, and thoughtful. I was drawn to him because he took care of me. Geez, I tried to shake the thought free. I must be reacting to the disastrous night. That was it, I was vulnerable and Griff had saved me. I convinced myself the feeling was temporary.

'Can you make it to your rooms on your own?' he asked once we'd reached the hotel lobby. 'I'm not staying here. Too rich for my blood.'

'Yes, thank you,' Fawn said and grabbed my elbow.

'Are you free for lunch tomorrow?' he asked me suddenly. 'Before the polo?'

I felt Fawn squeezing me as a signal, and I was glad to have her there, otherwise who knows what might happen.

'No thank you,' I said firmly. 'I already have plans.'

'Fair enough,' he said and marched off. When he was gone Fawn applauded me.

215

'Good girl,' she grinned. 'It's hard to turn down an invitation from a handsome man.'

'Handsome will only get you so far,' I said blithely.

'Honey, I couldn't have said it better myself,' she agreed. 'It's too bad, though. He seems to have so many other qualities.'

'It's not quality I'm after,' I said. 'It's quantity.'

25

Cowbell

I know he dislikes me as much as I do him.

—Pride and Prejudice

Just when I thought Vlad was out of my life forever, a huge bouquet of roses arrived with my breakfast along with a handwritten note and two tickets to the VIP enclosure for the polo. The note said, 'Dear Kate, my apologies for seeming impolite last night. Allow me to make it up to you with these tickets for you and your friend. Yours, Vlad Mihailov.'

The man couldn't take a hint. The old-fashioned scheme to withhold sex obviously worked. Vlad was clearly determined to seduce me. There was little for me to do about it now. I would have to be civil with Vlad. But Fawn had already seen to it that we had VIP tickets so I decided if I saw Griff again, I would give them to him. He had helped me last night, it was the least I could do. He was still such a puzzle. I had texted Emma for advice, insight, anything, but she wasn't getting back to me.

'Look, I don't know how to tell you this, but your Dear Jane Austen advice dispenser worked a little too well. Scott is back with Tatiana.' Fawn delivered the bad news as we walked toward the field of machine-groomed snow that was set for the polo tournament. She had abandoned her yellow puffy jacket for her mink, while I made do with my black fitted outfit from the first day.

My heart sank. By then we had reached the tent, and sure enough, the first two people I saw were Tatiana and Scott arm in arm, champagne in hand next to a faux forest of potted pine trees. I stood and watched as they chatted and giggled like a high school couple. Tatiana caught me staring and raised her glass to me. I smiled and turned away, grabbing a glass of bubbly from a passing waiter's tray and found a seat by the ring while Fawn mingled with the players. I was stupid to give Tatiana advice. I should have been meaner and bitchier and sent her packing back to Slovenia. Instead, she had Scott and the best I could do was Vlad the Cad. As I sat there I noticed that stacked on the small cocktail table beside me mixed in with polo programs were more brochures for Penwick Manor. Clearly Griff didn't need my complimentary VIP pass. I picked one up and gazed at the elegant mansion on the cover. Now that was a life I could envision. I imagined driving up the long, winding gravel driveway in some cute convertible and being swept up in the arms of . . .

'You made it to your room all right, I see?'

It was Griff. Again, I felt my heart flutter and I smiled, expecting another flirtatious exchange to pick up where we left off at the bar, but his smile quickly turned to a scowl when he saw the Penwick brochure in my hand.

'I see you've developed taste in bed and breakfasts,' he stated matter-of-factly.

It was obvious from his tone the attraction wasn't mutual, which was for the best. He was as far from Scott as I could get and that wouldn't do. 'Why didn't you give *me* one of these in Palm Beach?' I asked.

'I didn't think you'd have use for it,' he admitted.

'Why is that?' I asked, even though I knew the answer—I wasn't rich enough to afford to stay there.

'I would have thought concrete and glass were more to your taste,' he said, surprising me a little. 'You come across as strictly a city girl.'

'Well, you're wrong.' I smiled. 'I love country manors. And besides, Penwick is very Jane Austen. And make fun if you like, but I'm an Austen addict.'

'I'm glad you like it,' he said, seeming to soften. 'And if Austen is what you're after, the private library at Penwick has a collection of first editions.'

'Really? I'd love to see them!' I said excitedly.

'I'm afraid they are off limits to guests,' he said solemnly. 'But I could get permission.' He hesitated as though struggling for what to say next. 'From the owner, Mr. Penwick, to show them. That is, if you ever come to stay.'

'I'll keep that in mind,' I said. 'Your boss must be very snooty to keep historic books away from the public.'

'I would agree with you,' Griff responded with a nod. 'The worst sort of snob. And he doesn't pay well, either.'

218

'That's a crime, then,' I said. 'Maybe you should look for work someplace else.'

'I don't know,' he answered. 'I've practically grown up there.'

'Then you must really love it,' I said, more than a little envious. I missed my home. I even missed Scarsdale, and wondered if I could endure an unsatisfying job if it meant I could keep my life intact. The truth was simple—if I'd had the option to keep my family home I would have made do scrubbing floors or delivering pizza. But thanks to my mother's gambling debts I never had the option. So here I was in St. Moritz living out some ridiculous charade. Scarsdale was far away, a past life. I touched Griff's arm, 'I'd like to see Penwick one day.'

I'll never know how Griff was to respond because our conversation was cut short when Fawn showed up with Scott and Tatiana in tow. Tatiana wore bright skintight red jeans tucked into black suede thigh-high boots and oversize sunglasses. She was definitely a glamour girl and against the stark whiteness of the snow she resembled a cartoon character, like Jessica Rabbit, or a blow-up doll.

'Can we join your merry group?' asked Scott. I quickly blinked my eyes dry. 'Tatiana said she wanted to sit close to Kate.'

'How nice,' Fawn said and gave me a look.

And there we sat in a nice, friendly tight-knit group, which grew that much tighter when Griff and Vlad came and sat down with me in between. I could feel the tension between him and Griff and I suddenly couldn't wait for the polo to begin.

'What is going on there?' Scott asked and got to his feet. The whole tent became restless and began

219

to chatter and point to the left side of the field. I strained to look and was shocked to see a farmer leading a cow across the snowy field toward us.

'What on earth?' I said.

'Who would bring a cow to a polo tournament?' Scott asked with a snort.

'Me,' Vlad said suddenly. We all looked to him for explanation.

'It's your cow?' I asked, thoroughly confused. By then the farmer, dressed in overalls, a winter coat, and hat had paraded his cow past the crowd and stopped directly in front of us. Vlad began talking to him in Russian. It was all very comical, until both men abruptly stopped talking and turned their attention to me.

'This is Boris,' Vlad explained. 'I told you of my cousin in Wales? The one with cattle?'

I nodded slowly, not sure I liked where this was going.

'Boris is my cousin's wife's brother-in-law's nephew. He quit his job at a bank in Geneva to run a dairy farm just outside St. Moritz.'

'Really?' I asked, perplexed.

'Everyone has a dream.' Vlad shrugged. 'Boris wanted the pastoral life. But he doesn't know what he's doing.'

'Lady Kate,' Boris said and removed his hat and bowed.

By now a small crowd nearest our part of the tent had gathered to watch.

'His cow is sick,' Vlad explained. 'But the village vet ran off last week with the mayor's daughter so I told Boris that you had your own herd of cattle and could help him. Can you tell him what is wrong with the cow?'

My eyes widened in horror. 'I'm not a vet!' I exclaimed.

'Boris knows this, but he is desperate. She is his best milk cow.'

I looked at Fawn for help but she shook her head. Griff was trying to stifle a laugh.

'Go on, Kate,' Scott said. 'The poor farmer needs your expertise.'

'Yes, do,' added Griff. 'We'd all like to see how *you* examine a cow.'

I shot him a scathing look, but it was no use, I had no choice but to climb off my seat and step onto the field. I could feel all eyes on me. I tried to act like I knew what I was doing by slowly walking around the animal, nodding and trying to look thoughtful. As unlikely as it may seem, I did notice some things. For instance, she was a very fat cow and her distended belly was hanging quite low and her udder was huge, swollen even.

'When was the last time you milked her?' I asked with authority.

'She won't let me near her anymore,' Boris said, sounding rejected and sad.

When I moved around to her head she looked up at me with her big brown sad eyes. Poor girl, she did seem uncomfortable. But to be sure I walked toward her tail end and without thinking put my hand on her butt. She snorted and tried to kick me. I jumped back but quickly regained my composure. This was one moody cow. Another clue.

'How is her appetite?'

'Eating everything in sight,' Boris said.

That was it! I'd seen it all before. The swollen udder, the round low belly, the big appetite, and the mood swings.

221

'She's pregnant,' I announced triumphantly.

But Boris and Vlad burst out laughing. Scott and the others looked from them to me, puzzled, as if this was a joke that they weren't in on.

'That is impossible,' Vlad said. 'Boris only has one steer and he is kept in another pasture with a five-foot fence between them.'

By now the others were looking at me doubtfully and Griff, rather rudely, was busy on his cell phone.

'Believe me, I've known plenty of pregnant cows in my life,' I said expertly, thinking of Claire, Ellie, and the Monster Mamas. 'And many women, I mean cows, they'll stop at nothing to get it, including jumping over a five-foot fence,' I continued, recounting the hoops of fire many women went through to get pregnant.

'You must prove it,' Vlad said sternly. 'Boris has an exam glove.'

'An exam glove?' I asked fearfully.

Boris produced an elbow-length latex glove from his pocket and held it up.

'Eeew,' Fawn shrieked. 'It's a cow condom.'

'It's for doing internal examinations,' Griff explained, still on his cell phone.

'I don't need to examine the cow,' I said firmly, hoping Boris and Vlad would be satisfied.

'You must examine your own Highland cattle,' Tatiana piped up, unhelpfully.

I scanned the sea of anxious faces. Fawn shook her head, but I knew what must be done.

'Give me the glove,' I said and wondered how far I was going to have to take this. Adding to the confusion, officials with the polo tournament were bustling about, trying to figure out how to end the spectacle. One wave from Vlad, however, and they were silenced. I pulled and yanked the latex glove over my right hand and arm and stepped to the back end of the cow just as a tall, blond man carrying a large suitcase ran over.

'Did someone call a vet?' he said.

'Yes!' I shouted in relief, even though I didn't have a clue who had called him. 'Am I glad to see you.'

'I called,' Griff said, stepping forward. 'We have a sick cow.'

'I'm Dr. McKee, I'm with the polo tournament,' the vet explained. 'But I've treated bovines before. What's wrong?'

'She says the cow is pregnant,' Vlad said, referring to me.

'This is a portable ultrasound machine,' Dr. McKee explained. 'We'll soon find out.'

We all stood around silently as the vet ran the wand over the cow's stomach and waited for his prognosis. I tried to look at Griff but his eyes wouldn't meet mine. I was surprised that he'd rescued me—yet again—from what could have been a very messy situation, but he didn't seem to want my attention or thanks.

'She's right,' the vet announced. 'This cow is pregnant.'

I took a deep breath and was surprised when the crowd applauded me.

'Thank you,' Boris said and bowed to me once more.

'You'd better take her home,' the vet told the farmer. 'The polo is set to start any minute.'

Vlad kissed me on the cheeks in true Russian fashion, Scott patted me on the back, Fawn got me another drink; I had saved the day. But I for one

223

was never so happy to see a horse as when the polo teams galloped onto the snow.

* * *

Polo in St. Moritz proved much more fun than it had in Palm Beach, the snow meant I had no fears of dust or manure landing on me. Scott kept his promise from the night before and spent a great deal of time explaining the rules to me. Tatiana didn't approve but I didn't give a damn. I loved how Scott treated me. He was such a gentleman, always charming, witty, and courteous. For the first time I had his full attention and I rose to the occasion and behaved every inch the aristocrat, completely ignoring Tatiana's presence.

Even Vlad's mood had improved and he managed to make Fawn laugh more than once. The day was ending much better than it had begun until Scott held up a Penwick Manor brochure.

'You know I've always wanted to stay at Penwick,' Scott said to Griff.

'You've heard of Penwick?' I asked, surprised.

'Of course, it's one of the oldest estates in England, and one of the few that still belong to the original family,' he said. 'Right, Griff?'

'Yes, the Penwicks have been there for centuries,' he said firmly.

'I'm surprised I haven't read about it,' I said. 'I read tons of British fashion magazines, including the travel sections.'

'It's not a trendy place,' Griff explained. 'It's hardly ever in the press.'

'Your clients would appreciate that,' Scott confirmed. Clearly, Penwick was even grander than

I assumed.

Griff changed the subject and Scott continued to describe the events on the field to me. During halftime as I headed to the bar to get more champagne, I dropped my handbag on the ground beside all those potted pine trees. It didn't just drop, mind you, it flew, upside down and open it went, scattering its contents everywhere. Lipsticks, odd change, hair bands, even my wallet lost its grip and lay spread-eagled in one of the pots. As I kneeled down to pick up my things I overheard Griff and Scott on the other side of the trees. Their conversation seemed to be wrapping up, but I heard this bit:

'So please don't say anything,' Griff said. My ears pricked up immediately. 'I prefer certain aspects of my life to remain private.'

'Your secret is safe with me,' Scott said warmly. 'Besides, it's not obvious with you. Some men you can tell a mile away, but you're very subtle.'

'It's important to me.'

Scott patted Griff's shoulder and chuckled. 'Don't worry, I won't out you.'

My eyes widened. I was dumbfounded. Secret? Out him? Those words meant only one thing where I came from. Griff was gay. At first I felt foolish not to have guessed earlier. After all, I worked with so many gay men in fashion and let's face it, he had a fey quality about him. But what was worse, I was disappointed, which was even more foolish. Then I remembered his repeated attempts to ask me out. Was that a ploy to avoid detection? But why? Or like the dozens of gay men in New York, did he just want to be my gay best friend? I had to tell Fawn.

'I don't believe it,' she said afterward. 'Though I suppose it's hard to tell with Englishmen. They almost always seem gay; they're so effeminate.'

'I don't understand why he kept trying to get me to go out with him,' I remarked, feeling the wave of disappointment again.

I sat completely perplexed throughout the rest of the polo. How could I not see he was gay? I also tried not to notice Scott and Tatiana groping each other. Fawn seemed content to drink champagne, oblivious to everything around her.

I watched Vlad hoot and holler when the game was in play. At least something got him excited. Maybe I should give him another chance. He was handsome and rich and technically that's all that mattered.

'I'm going to try talking to Vlad again,' I whispered to Fawn.

'After that cow episode, he should be proposing!' She laughed. I cleared my throat.

'So Vlad, what is it you love about polo?'

'Shush! I'm watching game!' he snapped.

I looked at Fawn as she stifled a laugh.

'Are all rich men mean like Vlad?' I remarked to her quietly.

'Successful men usually are,' Fawn said. 'You have to be ruthless to make that kind of money.'

'Good show!' Griff shouted and clapped when one of the teams scored. I rolled my eyes. The fact that he was gay seemed obvious now. And he sure wasn't ruthless.

'Unless you inherit it,' Fawn added.

When the polo game was over the tent cleared out fast. Scott and Tatiana disappeared without a word, which left me crestfallen. So much for making progress. Griff explained that he had to go to the stables. Vlad, however, was still hovering nearby, talking on his cell phone.

'You'd better say good-bye to Vlad,' Fawn said as we packed up, too. 'I think he's leaving St. Moritz.'

I took a deep breath. 'Do I care?' I asked. Fawn gave me a look.

'Up to you,' she said. 'But at the very least if you're going to walk away from billions of dollars, do so politely.'

Sometimes Fawn's southern ways irritated me. Why make a bad situation more awkward? But I did as I was told. When he saw me coming he quickly got off the phone.

'Fawn says you're leaving?' I said and forced a smile.

'I leave tomorrow,' he said firmly.

'Tomorrow!' I gasped, trying to act disappointed, but it was no use.

'It is my wife's birthday tomorrow,' he said without expression. 'I must go now, I have to buy gift. But here is my card, call me and we can still know each other.' At that, he walked away leaving me standing there holding his card and feeling like I'd been hit by a cement truck. Wife! He had tried hard to seduce me and all the while he had a wife at home. Was no one who they seemed? Griff was gay. Vlad was married.

One thing was for sure, I'd had enough of St. Moritz. It was done. My journey was over. All I had to do was fly home and write it up. I had spent almost my last dime chasing Scott and all I got for my trouble was a big fat nothing. At least the five thousand dollars for the article would help. Even

Ann's blue sofa didn't seem so bad. My sister had e-mailed me to say her trip to Chicago had been a disappointment. No big orders, just some vague interest from some specialty food shops. We had both come up empty-handed in our quest for gold. Unlike me, she wasn't giving up. Apparently there was another similar foodie event in Texas, called the SXSW Food Show, that she was going to in another week. Maybe if I got back in time I could make the drive with her.

I looked out onto the empty polo field. All that remained were hoof prints that would soon be covered by fresh snow, as if they'd never existed. Kind of how I felt. I lowered my head and walked slowly out of the tent.

When I got to the entrance the winning team was spraying champagne over one another. Scott was mixed up in it; he obviously knew some of the riders and was practically soaking wet, but judging by his jubilant expression there was nowhere else he'd rather be. I felt wistful as I watched him. At least he was for real. He caught my eye and smiled.

'Kate,' he shouted and waved me over. 'Did you enjoy the game?'

'I did, Scott, I did,' I said, stopping for a moment. 'Where are you off to next?'

'Me? London,' he said. 'There's a major art fair next week and I'm shopping for investors.'

'I'm sure you and Tatiana will have a great time,' I said graciously.

'She's not coming with me,' Scott said and gave me what I chose to consider a knowing smile. 'She's going home to Slovenia for a bit.'

All of a sudden I couldn't stop myself from grinning. Scott would be alone in London? No

228

Tatiana to compete with?

'That really is too bad,' I said, feigning disappointment. In a flash, my mind was made up. I didn't know *how* exactly, but there was no doubt *where* I was going next. Ann wouldn't be the only sister with a Plan B. 'What a coincidence! I'm going to London, too. You must tell me where the art fair is. I love art exhibits. In fact, I need some pieces for my estate.'

'Then you must come to the opening,' he said cheerfully and fished a card out of his pocket. 'Call me when you land.'

'I certainly will.' I smiled. As I moved away I saw Tatiana glaring at me in the corner. She'd heard everything but I didn't care. Two could play at this sugar daddy game.

*   *   *

When I told Fawn Vlad was married she was flabbergasted. I was sitting on an armchair across from the full-length mirrored closet as she packed up to leave.

'He's worse than that,' she said cryptically. 'Look at this story in the *Herald Tribune*.'

The story was about Russian billionaires and where some of them got their money. There were several paparazzi-type photos and one of them was of Vlad. According to the article he was a suspected gangster, a Russian mobster to be exact, with a penchant for arms dealing.

'Christ, no wonder he scared me!' I said, aghast. 'I'm no gangster's moll, that's for sure.'

'I feel just awful for encouraging you to be with him,' Fawn apologized.

229

'It's not your fault,' I said, feeling nauseous at how close I was to an illegal arms dealer.

As I stared at the paper a thought raced to the front of my mind. 'Griff must have known who he was.'

'Why would Griff know?'

'He said Vlad wasn't for me and was dubious,' I explained. Griff had been watching out for me, all right; maybe next time I'd listen to him.

It was our final morning at Badrutt's Palace and Fawn was as fed up with St. Moritz as I was. Fawn had decided she needed to be where the weather was warm and the men hot, so she was off to Rome. But as much fun as Italy sounded I knew I had to go to England. While there was even the teensiest chance of Scott and I falling for each other I had to try. Ann's blue sofa would be there in another week or another month, Scott would be alone and in my proximity for only a brief time. I thought of what Marianne would say when she learned I was still on this crusade. 'I don't know who you are anymore' were the words I imagined her saying with the signature disapproving scowl she normally reserved for staff at the magazine. I looked in the full-length mirror. The woman in the reflection looked like me. I suppose looks can be deceiving because Marianne had a point, I wasn't acting like the old Kate. Then again, the old Kate existed in another time, before life went to hell. The new Kate had to get her life back and for the first time it felt as though everything was on track for that to happen.

'I'm going to London,' I said suddenly.

'London?' she asked. 'I thought you were going

home.'

Then I told her about my talk with Scott.

'You must go,' she agreed. 'This is your chance. Go to that art opening. Make Scott fall in love with you.'

'I can change my plane ticket to London instead of New York,' I said.

'Don't worry about that,' she said dismissively. 'I'll take you there in Mona.'

'That's too generous,' I said and meant it. 'It would be different if you were going their yourself.'

'That's what money is for,' she said with a smile. 'I'm taking you there and that's that.'

* * *

An hour later our things were being packed into an airport limo. Another few minutes and we would have been off but Griff appeared, carrying an old beat-up suitcase. Cripes, he really was an atypical gay man.

'Kate,' he called to me. 'I'm glad I caught up with you. I wanted to say good-bye. Going back to America?'

'No, I'm going to London,' I said.

'Really?' he said, surprised. 'Are you staying with Emma and Clive?'

'Yes,' I said, even though I still hadn't received a response from Emma to any of my texts.

He proceeded to scribble something down on a scrap of hotel stationery. 'It's my mobile number. In case we can all get together one night.'

'Thanks,' I said and scrunched it into a ball and stuffed it inside my coat pocket where it would probably wind up in a washing machine one day.

231

'Maybe we can get together, if there's time, but I'm going there to meet Scott,' I explained. 'We're going to an art fair.'

'Yes, I know the fair,' he said and bit his lip. 'Lots of arts events next week. How about dinner one night in London?'

I sighed. 'Why not, since it doesn't really count,' I said flatly.

'I don't follow you,' he said suspiciously.

He kept standing there waiting for an answer. I had to say *something*.

'Griff, I overheard your conversation with Scott yesterday at the polo,' I confessed. 'And I want you to know your secret is safe with me.'

He looked at me askance but I continued. 'It's okay, I won't tell anyone.'

'That's very kind of you,' he said cautiously. 'But you were the only one I was trying to hide it from.'

'Me? Why?'

'I didn't want you to treat me differently,' he said vaguely.

'Why would I do that?' I said defensively. Then added, 'Though to be honest, I was surprised at first, but I have to admit you do have a certain air about you.'

'I do?' he said skeptically.

'But you shouldn't hide your true self,' I continued earnestly. 'Maybe it's different in England, but where I come from there are tons of men like you.'

'Really?' he said disbelieving. 'I didn't think your country allowed it.'

'Are you kidding?' I said with a start. 'We have a whole day dedicated to them. In New York we throw a parade and everything.'

232

Griff looked at me in shock.

'I know we started out on the wrong foot,' I continued, trying to be supportive and to avoid the word 'gay.' 'But I'm surprised given the *kind* of man you are that you don't dress better.'

'Not that again,' he said with a roll of the eyes.

'I know, I know, sorry,' I said.

'You're forgiven, I think,' he said reluctantly. 'Are you *sure* you heard what I said to Scott?'

'Yes,' I nodded gravely. 'I'm glad we cleared it up. See, we can be friends, probably easier now than before.'

'Kate!' Fawn shouted as she climbed into the backseat. I smiled one last time at Griff and then slid in beside Fawn and shut the door.

*   *   *

As Mona touched down at London Luton airport I was overcome with emotion. I had come to rely on Fawn and the thought of being without her made me feel very alone again. If I could still cry I would have.

'I'm going to miss you,' I said sadly.

'Hush, hush,' she said and hugged me. 'I'm only a text message away. Give me the blow by blows and I'll see you through it.'

'Maybe I should come to Italy with you after all,' I said hopefully, but she wouldn't hear of it.

'Scott is here alone, go get him,' she said.

'I need some parting advice,' I pleaded. 'A tip, anything.'

Fawn contemplated this for a moment and then beamed at me as though she'd just discovered electricity. 'Prove you can fit into his life. Become

233

indispensable to him. Make him realize that you're the one thing he's missing.'

I clenched my jaw. 'How do I do that?'

Fawn shrugged her shoulders. 'You'll figure it out. Think about him and what he needs and what Tatiana couldn't give him. It will come to you.' She smiled encouragingly. 'You'll do just fine.'

I walked down the steps onto the tarmac. The air was damp and a heavy fog hung like a canopy, lending an aura of mystery to this next step in my quest. I thought of my grandmother. She hadn't found love or fortune, just a recycled marriage filled with artificial roses. Here I was decades later, trying to fulfill my dream of a better life. I wasn't convinced it would end any better than hers had. I sat on my suitcase near a chain-link fence and watched Mona soar away to Italy. I'm not sure how long I sat there but eventually a steward came and asked me to move. There was only one place for me to go. After making my way through customs I left the terminal and hopped into a black cab and headed to Notting Hill.

26

Art Lover

We have all a better guide in ourselves,
if we would attend to it, than any other
person can be.

—*Mansfield Park*

Now, you, may have wondered what became of my
friend Emma and her man, Clive. Since St. Moritz,
Emma had been MIA. My texts had all gone
unanswered. As the cab pulled up outside her home
the mystery was partially solved by the shocking
sight of a **for sale** sign stuck on the front of it. I was
even more surprised to find Clive answering the
door on a Monday morning.

'Hey, Kate!' he said, happily enough. 'Why didn't
you tell us you were coming?'

'I tried,' I said. 'But Emma never responded to
my texts.'

'Oh yes, she, er, lost her iPhone,' he explained.

'Are you selling? Why?' I asked innocently but
noticed his face clouding over.

'Things have changed a bit,' he answered flatly.

Then Emma appeared in the hallway. 'Kate!' she
shouted and ran into my arms. 'How are you? What
a great surprise.'

This was the reception I had hoped for.

Clive carried my suitcases up to the spare room
and we settled down for tea. While the house
looked the same and my friends seemed genuinely

happy to see me, there was definitely tension in the air. Eventually when Clive left to pick up some milk, I asked Emma directly and she wasted no time filling me in.

'We've lost everything. Clive's job, the money,' she said forlornly. 'He's broke, we're broke. It was all an illusion, Kate; we were rich on paper but not where it mattered. My music doesn't pay much, as you know. I can't even afford my iPhone, had to give it up. I'm strictly a pay-as-you-go girl now.'

'I'm so sorry, Emma,' I said. At least now I understood why she'd disappeared so suddenly. I looked around the room at all the pristine furniture and rugs; it would be tough to give up such elegant surroundings. 'Your beautiful house!'

'Is being repossessed,' she said, tearing up.

'What? I saw the for sale sign . . .'

She shook her head. 'It didn't sell in time. This is our last week here. Next Saturday we're having a repossession party to say good-bye, so in a sense, your timing is perfect.'

'Should you really have a repo party?'

'Why in bloody hell not?' She grinned. 'If the house was never really ours, then I don't have to feel really and truly sad, so why not have a sendoff?'

'What are you going to do? Where will you go?'

'Can you keep a secret?'

I nodded.

'I'm pregnant.'

'Oh my God, how wonderful!' I said and hugged her. 'This is what you wanted.'

'Yes, but the timing is off, isn't it?' she said through a forced smile. 'Babies can be expensive. But we're moving down to Dorset to live with Clive's mum. She has a good-size house there, so

236

there we shall go until we can afford our own place again.' For a moment Emma became grave and serious, but then a grin erupted on her face and the old Emma was back. 'So tell me all about you! What on earth were you doing in St. Moritz? And what really happened with Griff?'

We had consumed a pot of tea and a platter of scones and clotted cream by the time I got to the part where I boarded a plane for London. She looked at me aghast.

'Bloody hell, you have had an adventure!' She laughed.

I could tell that my antics from Palm Beach to St. Moritz had cheered her, at least temporarily, and we were giggling like old times. Then she became serious again.

'Kate, darling, your masquerade may have fooled the Americans, maybe even this Russian bloke, but you can't be calling yourself 'lady' here. The English frown on that sort of thing unless, you know, you're a real lady.'

'Technically I am a real lady,' I insisted. She raised an eyebrow and gave me a look that said I was only kidding myself. 'Emma, really, who will notice?' I asked firmly. 'You can't pick up a magazine or a newspaper in this town without lady this or baroness that splashed across the pages, there must be hundreds; what's one more lady in their midst? Besides, it's not like anyone checks this sort of thing.'

'Very well,' she said with a slight shake of her head. 'Just be careful. Does anyone else know about your 'estate'?'

'Just my friend Fawn. Oh, and Griff.'

'Griff?' she gasped. 'You told him? You two

became fast friends?'

'Don't think 'friends' is the right word,' I admitted and filled her in, though deciding at the last second to omit the gay part, just in case they didn't know, either, and besides, I told Griff I could keep a secret.

'He is a bit broody, I think he likes to keep people at arm's length, though he's harmless. But honestly, Kate, are you sure marrying for money is really a solution?'

I nodded. 'What choice do I have? And when you meet Scott, if you meet him, you'll understand. We have a real connection. The fact that he's wealthy, well, it would really help me.'

She nodded and patted her stomach. 'Well, better to do it now before you end up like me, barefoot and pregnant with an unemployed man.'

'But you love Clive,' I said.

'I do.' She smiled. 'I really do.'

*   *   *

Three days later I was at the London Art Fair and completely out of my element. Scott had left me a ticket at the front gate and I was to meet him in one of the makeshift galleries somewhere. The space was enormous, more like a convention hall than any art fair I'd seen. I know nothing about collecting art, so I wasn't sure how this was going to go. On the one hand, I could admit my ignorance and acquiesce to Scott's valuable opinion, which he would probably like. But I couldn't buy anything. I decided it best to hate everything in the place to avoid any awkward moments.

I walked around trying to find the Gallery Blume

238

that was written on the ticket. I had dressed as artsy as I could and went for the beatnik look with a black cashmere turtleneck sweater and black wool pants with high-heel boots and it was a good choice; nearly everyone was in black.

Halfway down one aisle of exhibits there was a rectangular sign with Gallery Blume written in Day-Glo orange. I gave my ticket to a waif-with-attitude-plus-clipboard and she granted me entrance into the room. There was Scott, holding court as always, surrounded by people I didn't know, no familiar faces from either Palm Beach or St. Moritz. The man knew a lot of people.

I had given Fawn's advice lots of thought, as she knew I would. How to make myself indispensable and a seamless part of his life was a tough call. He had everything he wanted and then some. So I focused on what I had that Tatiana didn't. My maturity, grace, and confidence, even if I had to fake those occasionally, were benefits to a man in his position. And I was *Lady* Kate; that had to count for something. I had a plan to execute; all I needed was the right entry point, and that depended on Scott.

Studying the sullen faces and drab fashion sense of the crowd in the gallery, I felt confident that I could lend an air of sex to the room and swanned around, making a show of casually touring the exhibit, waiting for Scott to notice me. The sculptures were all life-size human forms with ragged edges and grotesque facial expressions. According to the exhibition notes the artist was depicting people at the precise moment of death during a biological terrorist attack. These would be easy to reject.

'Kate!' Scott called out as he came to greet me.

'So glad you made it!'

He kissed each of my cheeks and put his arm around my shoulder. This was a hopeful start.

'So glad you invited me,' I said and pointed to the sculpture. 'Though I hate to say it, these aren't what I had in mind.'

'Yes, awful, aren't they?' he said with a dismissive sniff. 'If you're not in a hurry, I just have to finish chatting up some old clients and then I can play tour guide. People are so frightened about their investments they want constant reassurance.'

That was my sign to launch the plan.

'If you like I can talk to them,' I smiled sweetly.

He looked at me with an expression that said, 'You? What could you say about finance?' 'I can talk up the work you do and how great you are with money, all that stuff,' I explained quickly.

He still seemed doubtful.

'Speaking in general terms,' I continued. 'Just to be supportive.'

'You'd do that?' he asked. 'Be my wing man, so to speak?'

'Of course!'

He pondered this for a moment. Then an invincible smile unfurled across his face; it was an expression that was hard to read but I said nothing. There was no backing out now.

'That would be lovely,' he said and held out his arm. 'Allow me.'

I smiled happily and followed him over to a group of people who had gathered around a tray of champagne.

'I'd like you all to meet my latest client, Lady Katharine Billington Shaw,' he announced.

'Happy to meet all of you. But please do call me

240

Kate,' I said, taken aback by his telling everyone I was a client. I had to go along now and smiled glowingly. 'Scott is such a gifted financier, I'm thrilled to know he's taking care of me.'

I looked at Scott and he nodded and smiled. I had become very good at being Lady Kate.

*   *   *

That was how I found myself seated in an upscale restaurant, opposite Scott, sipping a glass of Veuve. My little plan had gone well. I made it sound as though the only person who could guide millions through the recession was Scott. Then he would toss in a few specifics and I would nod in agreement, even though I hadn't the faintest idea what he was saying. We volleyed back and forth until I was convinced his real clients were breathing a collective sigh of relief that their lives were in his hands. Scott was grateful. He told me as much.

'You're something else,' he gushed. 'Now if you really want me to handle your money, I will do so happily and I won't charge you a thing to set it up.'

'That's so generous of you, but I wouldn't want to put you out,' I said evasively and tried to think of a legitimate reason why I had to turn down his offer. Other than the obvious, that I was broke.

'No pressure,' Scott said kindly. 'Let me know.'

'I will,' I said, relieved. 'My family has a long history with the advisor we use currently, so I'd have to figure a few things out.'

He nodded as if he understood and I politely changed the subject. There was one thing I was dying to know, his side of the Tatiana tale. He

241

needed little encouragement and he told me how he had caught Tatiana rifling through his e-mail and the fight that had ensued and that she had apologized and he begrudgingly accepted in order to make his appearance at the polo tournament.

'I really wanted to watch the game in peace,' he confided.

I didn't let on that I knew the whole story but gave him all the sympathy and indignation that such an admission deserved. Though I must admit I began to feel a little sorry for Tatiana. I imagined her cold and shivering in some tiny apartment in Slovenia, cursing herself for having blown it with a man like Scott. For his part he seemed much more into me than I had ever imagined. He commented on how he'd found me attractive way back in Palm Beach and we had a laugh over my falling into the manure. He admitted that he was secretly thrilled when he spotted me on the tarmac in St. Moritz.

I was, of course, ecstatic by this amazing turn of events. I began to relax and enjoy his attention. After all, the scene was perfect: glamorous location, great lighting, champagne, and an abundantly charming billionaire.

'There's a big art event, a charity thing, at the Serpentine Gallery on Friday,' he said with a billion-dollar smile. 'Would you be my guest?'

'I'd love to!' I said, a bit more shrilly than I intended.

*   *   *

'But I need something new to wear!' I exclaimed to Emma. The party was in two days and I was desperate. As much as I loved my Chanel, Scott had seen me in it twice. And besides, I didn't want understated glamour, I wanted out-and-out sexy. We were sitting on the bed in her spare room, going through my wardrobe, when she came across my dog-eared copy of *Pride and Prejudice*, which she picked up. It brought a smile to her face.

'Kate, you have to read modern fiction at some point.'

I looked at the tattered paperback in her hand. How I loved that book. I shook my head. 'I haven't been able to read it since my grandmother died,' I admitted. 'I just carry it with me like a lucky charm.'

'A talisman against falling in love with unworthy men?' Emma grinned.

I giggled. 'Let me show you the article I'm working on,' I added, and pulled out my notebook and handed it to her.

'Jane Austen tips to marry a rich man? What rot!' She laughed. 'Is this what your plan involves? Copying *P and P*?'

'It's a foolproof plan that's worked for centuries. The trick is I have to play both roles now, Mrs. Bennet, the meddling mother in search of a man of good fortune for her daughter, and Elizabeth, who will only be tempted into matrimony by a great love. Scott fits the bill!'

'Are you in love with him, then?' she asked.

I contemplated this. 'I'm definitely on the way to love.' I smiled.

This seemed to satisfy her. I kept looking at my dresses and eventually threw my hands up in the air in defeat.

'I know where we can look,' she said and grabbed her purse.

That was how we ended up at Selfridges. At first

the enormous showroom floor oozed potential with racks upon racks of designer gowns. But after two hours of trying on inappropriate and unflattering dresses I was exhausted. We had eliminated dozens as 'too slutty,' or 'too frumpy,' or my least favorite, 'too young.'

'I have to compete with twenty-five-year-old blondes in hot pink,' I said, dismayed.

'You're gorgeous and mature,' Emma consoled me. I hated the word 'mature,' such a fake way of saying 'old.' 'You don't look forty, no one will think you're a day over thirty-two.'

'I hope not!'

'Try this one!' shrieked Emma. She had been the huntress on the sales floor all morning and threw a frothy black number that consisted of two layers of chiffon, and not much else, over the change-room door. I shimmied into it and opened the door. Emma whistled.

'That's the stuff,' she said with a firm nod.

I stood in front of a three-way mirror. It looked gorgeous and fit in all the right places, it had a plunging neckline that showed the appropriate amount of cleavage, was nipped in at the waist, and had a skirt that swung if I twirled, not that I planned to twirl, but it was an option. It was the right dress. Sexy but not over-the-top sexy, it was still a classic—and it came with a classic price tag. I stared at the tag. The money from my London perfume story had finally come in and I had slapped it down on my Visa. There was just enough room to cover the dress but I would have to forego new shoes.

'I need to look the part,' I said confidently. 'You have to spend money to make money.'

Emma looked at the price tag and whistled. 'He better be worth it,' she said with a raised eyebrow.

'He is,' I answered, a bit defensively. 'Billions, in fact.'

'I suppose you could always return it the next day,' Emma suggested as we headed to the till.

'That's a possibility, isn't it?' I said. Emma shook her head.

'I was joking,' she said.

'I never joke about clothes or money,' I replied.

My new dress snug inside its garment bag, we headed to the escalator.

'See, Emma, I do rich well,' I announced triumphantly and held my garment bag up high.

'Don't we all,' she said.

27

An Exhibition

No one can be really esteemed accomplished who does not possess a certain something in her air, and manner of walking, the tone of her voice, her address and expressions.

—*Pride and Prejudice*

Emma had poured me a vodka tonic to settle my nerves. This was a big night and I didn't want to mess it up. I was sitting alone on the edge of my bed, poised for battle, when the doorbell rang.

'He's here!' Clive called up from downstairs. 'Or

245

at least his driver is at the door.'

I leapt up and switched on the ceiling light to get a final look in the full-length mirror. What I saw made me shriek. Why hadn't I noticed before now?

'Are you coming down or shall I tell him to go without you?' joked Clive.

'Emma!' I shrieked louder this time. 'I need you!'

I heard her run up the stairs.

'What is it, Kate?' she asked, panic-stricken.

I nodded at my reflection. 'The dress,' I breathed. 'It's see-through!'

Kate gasped. 'Bloody hell,' she said and moved toward me for a closer look. After a full 360-degree inspection she called down to Clive, 'Tell the driver to give her ten.'

'What am I going to do? I'm practically naked!' I bit my lip. 'I was going for class, not trash!'

I wanted to blame Emma because she'd picked the gown, but in truth neither of us had noticed how transparent it was. The dressing room had been dimly lit and about two foot square.

'What am I going to do?' I said anxiously.

'Let me think,' Emma said, her finger tapping her left nostril. 'The thong doesn't help. Have you tried tights?'

'Good idea,' I said and dashed into my suitcase for the one pair of tights I had that were black and opaque. I quickly slid them on over my thong and stood in front of the mirror triumphantly. Emma frowned and shook her head. 'They won't do. Too old lady. Looks like you're wearing support hose, especially in those open-toed shoes.'

I grimaced. She was right.

'Do you have boy briefs?' she asked.

'I just bought a package of black cotton ones

246

from M and S today,' I said and ripped open the plastic bag. Emma waited as I removed the tights and thong and pulled them on.

'There, much better,' she announced. I looked in the mirror; it looked like I was wearing a 1950s bikini bottom underneath.

'You think?' I asked, still unsure. There was a knock at the door. It was Clive. He stuck his head in. 'What's all the fuss?'

'You can see through my dress!' I said anxiously.

'Is that all?' he said, annoyed. 'Your rich bloke won't wait forever.'

Emma waved him off. 'Thankfully your nipples don't show through your bra,' she said with relief.

'Hang on a minute,' Clive said and lowered the dimmer switch until the ceiling light glowed instead of blared and miraculously my underwear disappeared, or rather, my dress became opaque.

'See, all better,' he said, a tad patronizing. 'Trust me, the lights will be dim at the gallery and no one will see your pants.'

'He's right,' Emma confirmed. 'I hadn't thought of that, these types of events are almost always pitch black.'

I stared at my reflection. The dress did look good. Who would have guessed that so much in life depended on flattering light—the lines on my face, and now the lines on my ass.

'Thank you,' I gushed. 'You saved my life.'

'Hardly.' He rolled his eyes and clambered down the stairs. I supposed my hysteria was irritating to Clive. He had lost everything while I had become uncontrollably self-absorbed. But I had lost everything, too. And this was my one option to get it all back. I vowed that if I married

247

Scott I would make sure that Clive and Emma were well taken care of.

*   *   *

Clive was right. The lighting at the Serpentine Gallery was designed to illuminate works of art, not undergarments. As I toured the exhibition on Scott's arm and sipped champagne, I felt confident and sexy, even as hoards of younger women paraded around the room. Scott was attentive, gracious, and thoughtful as he explained the artist's work to me, which I needed, since I didn't know squat about art. After we completed the full circuit I was relieved to enter the main reception area where the food stations and bar was located.

It was here that the party was in full swing and I got to see Scott in action. He seemed to know everybody, or everybody knew him, and for the next hour I was caught up in a swirl of introductions and cocktail chatter. Of course, it's these very situations where I shine brightest and determined to demonstrate the advantages a forty-year-old woman brings to the social table, I turned it on. I was charming. Sophisticated. Witty. And my charm, sophistication, and wit were increased each time he introduced me as Lady Katharine and each time I smiled graciously and told people to call me Kate. It created intimacy but people treated me with obvious deference and I liked it. They were his friends and acquaintances, mostly business and arts luminaries, and though I knew little of either, as a journalist I'm not shy, so asking them intelligent questions about what they did and what brought them to the exhibit was a snap. Scott had given me enough background on the art to wing it and with each conversation I amassed more opinion to pass off as my own for the next person and so on until I could come across as a bit of an expert. It was like conducting an interview. In fact, I could have written a review of the show if I'd needed to.

Better still, as we moved about the room and flitted from chat to chat, I sensed Scott watching and studying me as though he was weighing the benefits of a woman like me versus a girl like Tatiana. At least I hoped so for it seemed obvious that his friends liked me and that I belonged in his social sphere. He didn't say anything, of course, but he seemed pleased and would rub my back and I would squeeze his arm for emphasis if I felt it was appropriate. I wanted him to see us as a team. And as luck would have it, I got my chance to prove once and for all that a savvy financier like Scott needed a woman on his arm who could impress potential investors.

A balding man with gold-rimmed glasses approached us; he was tall and very thin and had a long pointy nose. If his tux had been pink he would have easily passed for a flamingo. He explained that an old friend had recommended Scott to him but they hadn't met until now. The mutual friend was discussed in that 'how is so-and-so' way that men have, but I knew that Flamingo Man wanted to get down to business and it didn't take long for him to ask Scott how his clients were faring in the recession. Now it was my turn to be impressed. Scott had a quiet confidence and reassuring ease with which he answered the man's questions. Still, Flamingo Man wasn't entirely convinced that he should trust anyone with his investments during

249

such a bad economy. Then he added, almost as an afterthought, that he was the UK CEO for a cosmetics company, one of the biggest, and that was my signal to act.

'I used to be a beauty editor,' I spoke up suddenly. Flamingo Man turned his beady bird eyes my way. 'I love your products. In fact, I was very impressed with how your company decided to increase advertising when your competitors shriveled up. Women love to buy cosmetics and it's reassuring that even in this economic climate we can count on your makeup to keep us looking pretty, even if we don't always feel that way.'

By then Flamingo Man was transfixed and we had a lovely chat about the ups and downs of the beauty business and how lipstick sales increased in a recession. It was clear I knew far more about his particular business than Scott. But Scott, to his credit, wasn't in the least threatened; in fact, he stood and listened and even put his arm around me as though bringing home the point that we were together. By the end of our conversation Flamingo Man asked for Scott's card and mine, too. I didn't have any but took the risk of saying, 'Scott knows how to reach me.'

'She's a keeper,' Flamingo Man said to Scott as he shook our hands.

'I have a feeling she's not going far,' Scott said to him. I was elated.

But the Flamingo Man had exhausted me and I was desperate for another drink. Scott stepped out for a cigar and I had a self-congratulatory moment with champagne and a platter of prawns. I was relieved that the evening had turned out so well. I had to be making progress with Scott; he'd be blind not to see how much more appropriate I was than Tatiana, and that a polished, classy woman was even sexier than a buxom, blonde twenty-one-year-old. Okay, I may be kidding myself there, but I was an asset to him. The thought made me giddy.

Then out of nowhere I spied Griff across the room. I couldn't believe it. Why was he suddenly everywhere I turned? He had said something about arts events but this was ridiculous. I gnawed on a prawn, absentmindedly double dipping the shellfish into the cocktail sauce until one of the staffers gave me a dirty look and removed the sauce altogether. I had bitten into another prawn, pinched its tail and sucked out the flesh, when Griff finally saw me. He raised his glass. I sighed and pushed my way to the bar.

'Pink champagne, please,' I ordered.

As the bartender filled a flute with rosé Veuve, Griff appeared at my side. At least he was wearing a proper tuxedo and had combed his hair.

'What brings you here?' he asked me, as though I didn't have the right to be there.

'I could ask you the same thing,' I said. 'I'm surprised they let you out of the B and B so often.'

'I'm on holiday.' He laughed. 'And I like art. We're trying to be friends, remember? Let me buy you a drink.'

'It's an open bar.'

'Precisely.' He smiled, then looked me up and down, examining every detail, or so it seemed. 'Makes you a cheap date.'

'It just so happens I'm on a date,' I corrected him. 'Scott brought me.'

His expression turned serious, which unnerved me.

'So, you managed to bump off Tatiana?' he asked dryly. 'That poor Slovenian girl sent back to her homeland to work in the salt mines.'

'I did no such thing,' I said defensively. 'It's not my fault Scott lost interest in her and besides, she was too young for him.'

'And you're not?' he asked. 'He must be at least fifteen years older than you, I'd even say closer to twenty.'

'Age is only a number,' I said dismissively.

'As is the amount on his bank balance,' said Griff slyly. 'But unlike age, the larger the better.'

'Don't judge me, Griff,' I said staunchly. 'I'm sorry I ever told you anything. Besides, I think we're falling in love, so there.'

'Love, eh?' he said with a raised eyebrow. 'As honorable as all that?'

'Don't you believe in love, Griff?' I challenged with my best flirtatious smile.

'What else is there to believe in?' he said seriously.

His answer surprised me. I was so accustomed to his sardonic tone. 'Then we're both hopeless romantics. Who would have guessed?' I said and touched his arm. Once again, the sensation it aroused was startling. He looked down at my hand on his sleeve, but I couldn't read his expression at all. Our eyes locked and we remained that way for several seconds.

'That's quite the dress,' he said, changing the subject and slowly looking me up and down.

'What's that supposed to mean?' I said, breaking out of my haze. I realized I was standing beneath one of the few spotlights in the room and stepped away, but he followed.

252

'It's rather insubstantial,' he retorted.

'You don't like it?' I said, worried that people could see through it after all.

'I didn't say I didn't like it,' he replied. 'On the contrary, it's very eye-catching.'

The moment we'd shared evaporated and feeling suddenly insecure I snapped at him. 'I hate to tell you this, Griff, but for a gay man your taste is all in your mouth.'

I expected a bitchy comeback; instead, he stood stalk straight and gasped. 'A *what*?' he said, clearly astonished.

I felt horrible for outing him like this and quickly scanned the room. No one could have heard me. I lowered my voice. 'I'm sorry, I said I would keep your secret and I will. You're just so infuriating.'

'I'm not gay!' he blurted a little too loudly. 'I'm English!'

'It's okay, Griff, I don't care,' I insisted, trying to soothe him. He really was a closet case. 'You don't have to deny it.'

'Where on earth did you get that idea?' he practically shouted.

'I heard you tell Scott,' I explained impatiently. 'You told him to keep it a secret ... he said he wouldn't out you.'

'That's not what I told him,' he stammered.

'Yes it is,' I insisted again.

'You heard me say I was gay?'

'Well, not exactly,' I admitted. 'But what else would be such a big deal? Not that being gay is a big deal, but you know what I mean.'

'Well, you assumed wrong,' he snapped.

'So, you're not gay?' I asked, still not sure I could believe him. 'Then?'

253

'Then what?' he asked and glared at me.

'Then when you wanted to have dinner with me?'

'Go on.'

'It was a date?'

He exhaled in frustration. 'Yes, it was a bloody date. Or it would have been.'

'You really wanted to go out with me?' It was my turn to stammer.

'Yes. Despite you insulting my taste, impersonating an aristocrat, and chasing after Scott and Vlad and whoever else I may have missed . . .'

I flinched a little.

'And yet,' he continued without cracking even the slightest smile. 'There's something about you, Kate. Something I feel like I want to know.'

I was dumbfounded. 'I don't know what to say,' I sputtered, not able to meet his gaze. My reaction, or lack of one, seemed to irritate him.

'I have to get a drink,' he announced and stormed off.

Before I could go after him Scott had returned. 'Is that Griff you chased away?'

'Yes,' I answered, feeling horrible for what I'd done. 'I mean no, I didn't chase him away. I offended him without really meaning to.'

'He's the sensitive, poetic type,' Scott said with a smile.

'What secret did he tell you to keep?' I asked bluntly. 'In Switzerland I overheard you both talking and he asked you not to tell anyone.'

Scott pondered this for a moment as though he couldn't recall any such conversation. 'Oh that,' he said and I perked up. 'I can't tell you, Kate. He asked me not to and a man doesn't tell another man's secrets. That's for women to do.'

254

I felt my shoulders slump.

For the rest of the night I kept an eye out for Griff to apologize. But I also wanted to continue our talk. He had to know that despite being attracted to him, I could never be with him. I had to keep my sights set on one man. Scott. And by midnight he had determined our night was over, I was exhausted and relieved to go. Maybe Emma was right, being a lady in London was more than I could handle. Then it got worse.

As we left the gallery we were greeted by a slew of press photographers who happily snapped away as if we were celebrities. I stood arm in arm with Scott, trying to shield my eyes from the flashbulbs.

'That's enough,' Scott announced and taking my arm, walked through the horde toward his idling limo. I heard one of the shooters call out, 'Excuse me, miss, can I get your name? I'm from the *Daily Mail*.'

'Don't you know, man? That's Lady Kate.'

I strained against the flashes and saw Flamingo Man, the cosmetics executive, wink at me approvingly.

The photographer jotted it down. But what did it matter? I was nobody to the British press.

Luckily, once inside the safety of the limo, I began to relax and all thoughts of Griff faded—I was finally alone with Scott. Something romantic was bound to happen. But I remembered Fawn's rule: withhold sex. I wasn't convinced her rule should be applied to Scott. Any chance to move the relationship forward I would take. And the evening was ending in the right direction. As we drove through the city he played travel guide and pointed out the sights, and I leaned on him and

255

he put his arm around me. I looked up at him as he spoke, ignoring the passing scenery. He was handsome, but, and maybe this was because it was late; he looked older than he had in Switzerland or in Florida. He was probably just tired. Damn Griff for pointing out that Scott was so much older than I was. I refused to think about it.

But suddenly all I could think about was what sex would be like with a sixty-year-old man. Probably great; after all, he had decades of experience. Yes, I would assume amazing sex was ahead for me. But I wasn't going to find out anytime soon, and I didn't need Fawn's rule to prevent it. When the limo stopped we weren't at Scott's hotel as I'd assumed, we were in front of Emma and Clive's town house.

'Here you are,' Scott said. 'Thanks for being my guest.'

At first I just sat there motionless, unsure how to react. Was he being a gentleman, or didn't find me attractive after all, or worse, did he think I was too old for him! It's one thing to have a no-sex rule but it was quite another not to be asked.

'It's so early,' I suggested feebly, wanting to make a move. 'Did you want to go someplace for a drink?'

'Not tonight; it's been a long day and it's past my bedtime,' he said gently and gave me a hug. A hug! Then, as if sensing my disappointment, he added, 'Are you free for dinner tomorrow?'

'Yes, that would be lovely.' I smiled at last and stepped out of the car into the damp night alone. A dinner date was nice but I would have preferred a kiss good night. As I slowly climbed up the front steps of the town house in my wasted effort, aka too expensive outfit, I watched the limo pull away.

He didn't even wait to make sure I got inside. I slumped into the house. All the lights were off. I crawled into bed and lay awake most of the night until sleep eventually won out.

* * *

'Oh my God!' Emma squealed as she stared at her laptop. We were having breakfast when she shouted at me, 'Kate, you're in the *Daily Mail*!'

Clive ran to the computer. 'Bloody hell!'

'What is it?' I asked and nervously stood over their shoulders to take a peek. My eyes widened in horror. It was from last night's gala. Scott had been cropped out of the photo; it was just me and my boy briefs on full display, illuminated by dozens of flashbulbs. I looked practically naked and not dissimilar from some of the Z-list celebrities who had also made the page. I felt sick. And if my skin and undies weren't enough, the caption read, 'Lady Kate dares to bare more than most.'

'I want to die,' I said and flopped onto the sofa.

Clive burst out laughing. 'Well, you certainly know how to make an entrance into London society,' he said.

Emma had her hand cupped over her mouth. 'You didn't go around telling people you were Lady Kate, did you?'

'Maybe,' I admitted.

There was no denying that everyone in England would think there was a Lady Kate.

'I guess we really will have to call you "lady."' Emma chuckled.

'What if the reporter snoops around to see who Lady Kate is?' I asked, suddenly worried. 'Scott

257

thinks I really am an aristocrat.'

'That is a problem,' Emma agreed.

'Just say you're a budding pop singer and it's a stage name,' Clive suggested. 'Ha!' I said with a fake laugh. 'A pop singer using a fake title like "lady So-and-So"? That would never fly!'

Clive shrugged.

'The evening went downhill as soon as I saw your friend, Griff Saunderson,' I said accusingly.

'Oh, was Griff there?' Clive asked innocently.

'Yes,' I said tartly. 'We had a fight. I told him I knew he was gay and—'

Clive spit coffee everywhere. 'He's not gay!'

Emma burst out laughing. 'What makes you think that?'

'I thought I heard him admit it to someone,' I said sheepishly.

'You can't have. I mean, he's no ladies man,' Clive explained. 'But he's as straight as a poker. Just never met the right girl to marry. I've met several of his exes, though, and trust me, they were all real women.'

'Apparently I heard wrong. Griff was offended,' I said, cringing as I recalled the conversation.

'Don't worry, it's an easy mistake to make. It is hard to tell with boys who went to their school,' Emma said as Clive shot her a look. 'Joking, darling!'

Clive shook his head in disbelief and Emma kept chuckling.

'Turns out he's been trying to get me to go out with him. On a date,' I admitted.

The exchanged looks made me wonder if this wasn't news to them.

'Has he said anything about me?' I wondered.

258

Clive shook his head. 'He wouldn't. Strong, silent type.'

I rolled my eyes.

'Do you want to go out with him?' Emma asked with a raised eyebrow.

I had pondered this all morning but there was only one answer. 'No,' I said with authority. 'I admit I find him attractive. But I can't let myself be distracted from Scott. He's the man I'm meant to be with.'

'Because he's rich?' Emma said derisively.

'It doesn't hurt,' I said, trying to make it a joke. No one laughed.

'Don't worry, Kate,' Clive said. 'Griff will be at our party tonight. You can get a second look at him before you decide once and for all to kick him to the curb.'

Then it hit me. The repossession party was tonight and I had made plans for dinner with Scott.

'You okay?' Emma asked, seeing the look of panic on my face.

'Scott invited me to dinner tonight. I forgot about your party.'

Clive said nothing, choosing to busy himself with cleaning the espresso machine. Emma looked at him and then back to me.

'You can bring Scott to the party,' she said thoughtfully. Again, Clive was silent.

'That would be wonderful. Thanks,' I said gratefully. 'Can we come here after our dinner? I need to have some alone time with him.'

Clive banged a pot in the sink. Emma glared at him.

'Of course,' she said with a weak smile. 'After your dinner.'

259

'Let me call and ask him,' I offered and dashed upstairs for some privacy. The call was brief—he didn't appreciate the humor of a repossession party but if that's what I wanted to do, he was in. I hung up, pleased that I could uphold both obligations. I came downstairs to tell Clive and Emma the good news but paused when I heard what sounded like arguing.

'She's just a bit much,' Clive said angrily. 'You never told me that Kate was such a shallow, inconsiderate little bitch! I mean "*Lady* Kate," what the fuck is that about?'

I gasped. They were fighting about me.

'She isn't like that, you hardly know her,' Emma defended. 'She's been through hell. Losing her grandmother, her house, her job. She's struggling to find herself.'

'Well, she can take her bloody midlife crisis or whatever it is out of our home,' he snapped. 'Trotting out some billionaire to our repossession party! Bloody insensitive. And you're pregnant, why can't she see that her escapades have been a drain on you? It's all Kate, Kate, Kate! Or rather, Lady Kate!'

I felt wretched. But Clive was right. It was the slap in the face I needed. I hadn't given much thought to their situation, or anyone else's, since I began this marrying well journey. I had to do better. I coughed loudly and entered the kitchen. They straightened their posture and got busy cleaning, but I couldn't let it drop.

'Clive,' I began. He stopped his fussing and looked at me. 'I'm sorry I've been a drain on you and Emma. I hadn't realized.'

Emma stood up and rushed to hug me. 'I'm so

260

sorry you heard that. He didn't mean it, did you, Clive?'

Clive shrugged and hesitated before saying, 'No, I'm just under stress.'

I looked into Emma's eyes. She was a dear old friend and we'd been through lots together, even if we hadn't lived in the same country for more than a decade. She was in as much of a bind as I was. Doubly so, when I considered the baby. She was stressing out for two now. She needed me, her friend, to help her through her ordeal.

'I have an idea,' I began.

A few moments later I was back in my room. I picked up my mobile and called Scott, and he answered on the first ring.

'Look, there's been a slight change of plan . . .

28

Repossession

You would never think of marrying a man like that just to secure your own comfort?

—Pride and Prejudice

If my friends had wanted to make a show of their newfound poverty they had outdone themselves. And there I was, having canceled my dinner plan with Scott to help my friends prep the house, standing alongside Emma and Clive and admiring our handiwork. We had 'decorated' for the occasion. Gone were the pristine white rugs and sofas, gone was the home theater system, gone was the pricey espresso maker Clive had been cleaning that morning, and in their places were folding chairs and milk crates, a boombox and CDs from the 1980s and 1990s, and Styrofoam cups for beer and wine with Ritz crackers laden with cheese spread and gherkins. Where the light fixtures had been, bare bulbs and exposed wires hung, casting the normally artfully lighted space in gloom.

'You really didn't have to cancel your dinner for us,' Emma said and put her arm around me, which meant she was glad I had done just that.

'Are you kidding? I know only too well what it feels like to lose your home, remember? Besides, this was much more fun than dinner at the Wolesley or whatever the place was called,' I said happily. 'I just wish there was more I could do to help.'

Clive and Emma exchanged knowing looks. 'Ah, the Wolesley is one of the most glamorous restaurants in London. Teeming with celebs,' Clive pointed out.

I shrugged. 'Scott said he'd drop by here. It's better this way. I can help you guys with the party. Anyway, it makes me look mysterious and not desperate.'

'Ah yes, very wise thinking, *Mrs. Bennet*,' Emma said and we both burst out laughing.

'I'm just thinking of darling Elizabeth,' I said in a fit of laughter.

'You girls are too much.' Clive grinned.

As it turned out, Clive was right. We were too much—at least for a man of Scott's stature. He arrived with the party in full swing and seemed unimpressed by our decorating.

'Your friends have quite the sense of humor,'

Scott commented wryly. I gulped. Clive was across the room opening a bottle of wine, I waved at him. He galloped over and stuck his hand out for Scott. He was stupid-drunk.

'Is this the man of the hour?' he slurred. 'Scott, I'm Clive. Kate has told us much about you.' Clive winked at me. 'Welcome to what was once my home.'

Scott shook his hand good-naturedly and wasn't squeamish when Clive handed him a Styrofoam cup.

'You want red or white?' Clive asked with a grin. 'Now that we're poor we no longer distinguish between cabernet and shiraz or pinot grigio and sauvignon blanc. It's just color codes.'

'Red will do fine.' Scott smiled politely.

'White for me,' I said and searched the room for Emma. I found her standing by the living-room wall where the plasma television once hung with a box in her hand.

'I want you to meet Emma,' I said and, grabbing Scott's hand, led the way through the crowd. As we got closer I saw what she was up to. She and a handful of revelers had each chosen a large magic marker from the box and were drawing graffiti on the walls. I stood in shock. Emma spotted me and laughed.

'Don't look so scared, Kate.' She laughed, then nudged me. 'If the bank is going to take the house, they can bloody well take the autographed copy!'

Clive dashed over to us and grabbed a black marker to scrawl his name illegibly in all directions.

'Woohoo!' he shouted gleefully as he wrote in huge strokes. 'I haven't had this much fun since I made that one-point-six-million bonus in 2005.'

I looked at Scott to see how he was taking my friends' rash behavior. He stood stock-still and sipped his wine and shifted uncomfortably from foot to foot. What must he be thinking? He was still successful and had been good with his money. Why had I brought him here to witness Clive and Emma's downfall?

'I'm going upstairs to grab my handbag,' I whispered in his ear. 'Then we can go somewhere else, if you'd like.'

He nodded gravely. 'Yes, let's do that.'

I left him and was navigating the sea of drunken partygoers to the foot of the staircase when I felt someone grab my arm. Of course it was Griff. I kept walking up the steps, but he followed me.

'I was hoping I'd find you here,' he said with surprising warmth. 'Emma told me you turned down your date with Scott to help her clear the house. That was nice of you.'

'She's one of my best friends,' I said. 'Of course she matters more than a date.'

'Of course.' He nodded. 'Look, I want to apologize.'

'I should apologize to you,' I said, cutting him off. 'I'm sorry I offended you last night.'

'Don't worry. Though I must admit that you looked rather fetching in the *Daily Mail*,' he went on.

'Thanks, I guess?' I said, shaking my head.

'Tabloids usually only run shots of famous people, not . . .'

'Not nobodies like me?' I said, annoyed, and stood with my arms folded, one step above him.

'That's not exactly what I meant. But in general, yes, I thought they would overlook you, but I should

264

have known that you're not the sort of woman that one overlooks.'

'That's generous, coming from you,' I said and allowed a hint of a smile to creep across my face.

'I mean you're a walking calamity, half the time falling into manure or picking up Russians mobsters . . .'

My smile quickly vanished and my expression turned to stone. 'Quit while you're ahead, Griff,' I said and marched to my bedroom door. 'Charm is dangerous in a man like you.'

'And one more thing,' he said and followed me.

'Yes?' But before I could say another word he grabbed me and kissed me. *Ding, ding, ding,* the alarm went off inside my body once more. I squirmed but he kept kissing me and I stopped fighting it. It felt perfect.

'I'm not gay,' he said playfully as he pulled away and leapt down the stairs.

'You don't have to prove it!' I shouted after him but I could feel my lips curl into a wide smile.

I went to my room and sat on my bed. I couldn't stop smiling. Now what? On the one hand, how dare he grab me like that! Why did he care if I thought he was gay? Even if he was a good kisser, what difference did it make to him or me? The only man who should kiss me was Scott. On the other hand, there was no denying there was a connection between us, no matter how unlikely that seemed. When I thought of how recently he'd entered my life I was amazed at how we had become close, in an odd and antagonistic way, but close nonetheless. I shoved all of my valuables into the closet and locked it. By the time I came back downstairs I noticed that Griff and Clive were huddled together conspiratorially. Wanting to avoid another encounter I sought out Emma for my good-bye. By this point she was in the kitchen spreading peanut butter on cheese crackers.

'Pregnancy craving?' I asked and put my arms around her. 'I hate to leave so early but Scott wants to go.'

She nodded and licked the knife clean. 'Are we past his bedtime?' she said, then looked aghast. 'Sorry, I didn't mean anything by it.'

I waved her off. 'Don't worry.' I grinned, hoping to soften the fact that I was making such a quick exit. 'I'll be back later.'

I found Scott, who was hovering by the front door. We jumped into his limo and peeled away.

'That was quite the party,' he said and smiled politely. I smiled back but I was tired of smiling, of being polite, and of rules. I threw my arms around Scott and kissed him because I wanted to and because I needed to erase the taste of Griff from my mouth. And I'm pleased to say he kissed back.

To hell with rule number one. Two hours later I was lying in Scott's hotel bed with a newfound knowledge of what sex with a sixty-year-old was like—more spa treatment than earth shaking. To my disappointment, unlike those close encounters back in Florida and Switzerland, there had been a total lack of *ding, ding, ding* alarm bells. Clearly Griff's kiss had shaken me up. But who needed hot? I couldn't have everything. Even I knew that. I got out of bed and took my BlackBerry into the washroom and sent Fawn a text message.

'We did it. Sorry, I know I broke the rule.'

I didn't have to wait long for an answer.

'Honey, if you want my help, you have to listen

to me. Oh well, we'll do damage control tomorrow. I'm pleasantly occupied at the moment.'

This last bit made me giggle, and even though it was very late, I decided on giving her one final bit of pertinent information.

'And btw, Griff's not gay.'

Sure enough, she responded in seconds.

'I'm afraid to ask how you found out.'

'I have my ways.'

'Careful, Kate. He's just the sort of man to mess up your plan.'

'Never fear. I can take care of Griff Saunderson.'

And then I turned off my BlackBerry and went to bed, not quite so sure I could take care of Griff.

29

A Very Short Engagement

In nine cases out of ten, a woman had better show more affection than she feels ... he may never do more than like her, if she does not help him on.

—Pride and Prejudice

I woke up to a gentle kiss on my cheek from Scott and rolled over as he tossed me a bathrobe.

'My Lady,' he said with a charming smile. With his salt-and-pepper hair tousled, he looked sexy and young again. 'Care for breakfast? I've ordered up a bunch of things off the menu.'

I followed him into the living area and spread

out on the tray set for two were pancakes, sausage, fried eggs, and toast. If I kept this up I would gain thirty pounds. We chatted as we ate and he read *The Financial Times*, handing me the fashion pages.

'Scott,' I began, determined to do my own form of damage control. He folded his paper and looked at me thoughtfully. 'Last night was wonderful. But I want you to know I don't behave that way as a rule.'

He surprised me by laughing. 'Are you saying I mean more to you than my groom, Bernardo?'

Oh shit. I squirmed a little and felt my face turn red.

'I'm teasing, Kate,' he said. 'I also don't jump into bed with every woman I meet.'

I nodded and smiled like a fool. Maybe I did need Fawn to be my Cyrano. 'What I'm trying to say is I'm looking for something long-term,' I continued. 'I realize we've only spent one night together so this may sound ridiculous, but you should know what I want. If you don't want the same thing, then that's fine, too, but tell me.'

I followed up with a swig of coffee. He rubbed his lips together and placed his knife and fork on his plate.

'I'm glad you told me,' he said. 'I'm not looking for a fling, either. Tatiana was enough and you've shown me I need more from a relationship than a sexy young thing.'

I squirmed some more. How old did he think I was? I was still nearly twenty years younger. I bit my tongue, now was not the time to be feisty.

'You're a mature and elegant woman, Kate,' he said as I bristled further at the word 'mature.' 'I look forward to getting to know you better. In fact, I was thinking. Why don't you move in here with

268

me?'

'Really?' I asked, stunned. His suite at the Langham Hotel was exquisite and spacious. 'Are you sure?'

'Sorry if I shocked or offended you,' he said quickly.

I recovered as fast as I could. 'No, I wasn't offended at all. Just surprised, it's so quick.'

'It would only be for a few weeks until I'm done with all my business in London,' he explained. 'After seeing your friends' place last night I think it may be a good idea and if we don't like each other after a day or two, that's that. Besides, I get lonely.'

'I'd love to,' I said, forcing myself to relax, as if moving in with a man after one night was the most natural thing in the world. 'I'll get my things after breakfast.'

*　　　*　　　*

'I'm impressed,' Fawn wrote in her text response to my update. 'Just make sure you're not just his date while he's in London and he dumps you before heading back to America.'

I hadn't thought of that. Never mind; I'd worry about that later.

As I stepped into Emma's house the state of the place shocked me. The wannabe graffiti artists had found inspiration and all the main floor walls were covered with gruesome stick figures performing lewd acts. Garbage was strewn everywhere and whatever wine wasn't consumed appeared to have been poured on the floor, judging by the sticky mess I couldn't avoid stepping in. The party had obviously continued well into the morning as I

269.

climbed over passed-out revelers. I made it to my room and nervously opened the door, unsure what to expect. Sure enough, there was someone asleep on my bed. I flipped on the light and the body stirred and rolled over. It was Griff.

'Not you again,' I said, trying to sound exasperated even though my stomach fluttered from excitement.

He sat up, his hair jutting out in all directions, and rubbed his eyes.

'Kate?' he said, sounding bewildered. 'This is your room?'

'It is,' I said bluntly, trying to hide any tone of being glad to see him from my voice. 'Now if you'll excuse me, I have to pack.' I don't know why I was hesitant to tell him the truth about Scott. It was ridiculous.

'Pack? Where are you off to?' he asked as he got up and stumbled to the doorway.

'If you must know,' I said, pausing, not wanting to spoil the flirtation I'd only just begun to enjoy. 'I'm moving to Scott's hotel for the time being. We're becoming involved.'

He pursed his lips and ran his hand through his mop of hair. 'Congratulations then,' he said coolly. 'Love triumphs once more. When is the happy day?'

'Don't be so mean,' I said quietly. 'We may very well fall in love and get married.'

'Look, Kate,' he said and put his hand on my shoulder and off went those damn alarms again. 'I don't want to be mean. I'm glad you're getting what you want. You deserve it.'

I looked at him expecting a snarky comment to follow. When none came I relaxed and forced a smile. 'Thank you.'

'I just hope it makes you happy,' he continued. 'Being with a man just for his wallet.'

'I knew you couldn't let things be nice and polite,' I said accusingly. How quickly we could revert back to enemies. 'Scott is a great man and I like him. That he happens to have money is icing on the cake.'

'We both know you wouldn't be with a man his age unless he had money,' he said pointedly.

'Is that so? And who would I be with? You?' I said icily.

'You might,' he snapped.

'I wouldn't be with you if you paid me,' I said with a sniff.

'Apparently that's what it takes,' he retorted.

I threw whatever I had in my hands at his head but he was too fast and bolted out the door. I slammed it behind him and furiously stuffed my clothes into suitcases and shopping bags. When I came back downstairs there was no sign of Griff, but Emma was sitting on the floor nursing a cup of coffee. I sat down beside her.

'I've got news,' I said. She was half-awake as I told her about moving to the hotel.

'That's great,' she said with a weak smile. 'I hope you know what you're doing. Not that I do. You'll have to visit us in Dorset.'

'I will and I'll bring Scott with me,' I said, liking that it was so easy to speak of us as a real couple.

'You know Penwick Manor is near where we'll be living,' she said, hoping to pique my interest. 'You can stay there.'

'I couldn't!' I insisted, not letting on about Griff's kiss or the fight we'd just had, or worse, my inexplicable attraction to the man. 'It would be awkward having Griff wait on me and Scott.'

'I see your point,' she agreed.

It was sad leaving her in that house but as she pointed out, they were going to pack up what was left and drive to Dorset. I was very relieved to be back at the hotel and was greeted enthusiastically, if not lovingly, by Scott.

'I've made a list for you,' he said and handed me a printed page. I looked at it and was confused.

'This looks like a schedule,' I said and pored over the list of times with names beside them.

'It is,' he answered and began to put on his jacket.

'Whose?' I asked.

'Yours,' he said with a grin. 'And mine.'

I smiled at him. Clearly, we were going to spend a lot of time together and I was happy with that, but I had no idea who any of the people were.

'Are all these people friends?'

'Some yes,' he said. 'Mostly they're business associates and their wives.' He rolled his eyes. 'We made such a good team last night, I really like the idea of our spending more time together.'

'We do make a good team,' I agreed. 'But time alone might be more fun.'

'Unfortunately, my whole purpose of being in London is business and these engagements were prearranged,' he explained. 'I can't cancel them. If you come, we get to see each other. Besides, I like that I can bring you places. Tatiana didn't always go over well, especially with wives.' He made a face.

'Your wish is my command.' I laughed. Not that I had a choice. Still, it pleased me that he had noticed my abilities last night. Of course his clients' wives didn't take to Tatiana; all they saw were two large breasts aiming for their husbands' wallets. I was no threat to them; I didn't want married men. But there was a slight problem.

'My only concern is my clothes,' I said, trying to sound cheerful. 'I packed for skiing in St. Moritz, not socializing in London. I have a few things, but looking at this calendar I hope you like some of my pencil skirts because you'll be seeing them a whole lot.'

He pondered this for a moment and said brightly, 'Can't you go shopping?'

I scrunched up my face and shook my head. I had arrived at the point of no escape and no excuse. I had to come clean, or at least almost clean.

'The truth is, Scott,' I began carefully and sat down on the gold velvet sofa and patted the cushion beside me for him to sit, which he did. 'When my grandmother died, money wasn't part of the inheritance.'

He nodded slowly, digesting this new information. I shifted nervously on the sofa, not sure how he'd take this.

'I don't mind wearing the same outfits,' I offered. 'Just as long as you don't mind.'

He kissed me gently, reassuringly. 'Don't fret, Kate,' he said kindly. 'It's nothing to be ashamed of, there are lots of noble families like yours in this very situation. Let me take you shopping. We can go tomorrow.'

'I'm not sure I'm comfortable with that,' I said slyly, so as not to appear too excited by the prospect of shopping with a billionaire.

'Don't argue,' he said. 'Now get changed, we

273

have an afternoon tea to get to.'

The next week flew by in a series of lunches and dinners with different couples. Mostly it was endless talk about the recession, which thoroughly bored me as it would anyone who had already lost everything. But I was just as determined to please Scott as I was at the Serpentine arts gala and was charming and effusive toward him and his guests.

In between his so-called business socials we went shopping. He took me to the best department stores—Harrods, Selfridges, Harvey Nicks—but he also gave me the credit card tour of the flagship boutiques: Louis Vuitton, Gucci, Prada, and Hermès. I'm not going to lie. Being able to pick what you want and not care about the price tag was an experience I could get very used to. But I didn't go crazy; I just picked up one or two things I really liked. I didn't want to come across as greedy. Even when I tried to pay for things, which wasn't often, Scott never let me.

'Money is vulgar,' he said. 'Women shouldn't touch it.'

I liked his way of thinking.

When we were alone he was warm and romantic. Sex was still gentle and nice, though not too frequent. I wanted to fall in love with him and I wanted him to fall in love with me, yet despite all the positives there was something that seemed to hold both of us back. I decided that I just needed to be patient. Love would come. For his part, I couldn't put my finger on it, but he seemed detached, as if his mind was somewhere else or with someone else. It was a worry that had one solution: Fawn.

'I think he might still be in love with Tatiana,' I called her when I was alone.

'Gosh, I can't imagine he is. Not after what she did, spying on his e-mails,' she said. 'Have you checked for yourself?'

'Fawn! I don't spy on people. That's an invasion of privacy,' I shot back. Her suggestion made me laugh. Fight fire with fire, I suppose.

'Suit yourself. It's probably your imagination anyway. You're probably too clingy,' she advised. 'Pull back!'

'Pull back? I was just getting somewhere!' I said.

'I know what I'm doing! Play hard to get. Now I must dash.'

She hung up before I could remind her that I'd already slept with the man and was staying in his hotel room. 'Hard to get' doesn't work when the chase is over. I sighed. This required thought. I paced back and forth, trying to imagine what would pass for playing hard to get in my situation. What did Scott want that I could stop giving so easily? It wasn't sex. It wasn't money. Then it hit me, of course! I knew what to do. I crossed through the suite to the den where Scott was working on his computer. We had plans that evening with yet another power couple.

'Scott,' I said calmly. 'I'm going to have to cancel on you tonight.'

He wheeled around in his chair with an alarmed look on his face. 'Why?'

'I have things to do,' I said vaguely and turned and walked away and counted. One. Two. Three. And sure enough the sound of his footsteps coming after me followed.

'Kate,' he said and turned me around and kissed me. 'Are you not feeling well?'

'I'm perfect,' I said and pecked him on the cheek. 'Enjoy yourself.'

'Okay,' he said slowly. I could feel his eyes watching me as I walked into our bedroom and shut the door.

* * *

The next day I got up and was out of the hotel before he was awake. I strolled along the Thames and sat on a park bench reading a magazine before coming back around noon. He was at his desk but hurried over when he heard me.

'Are you all right?' he asked and sat me down on the sofa.

'Yes, fine,' I said and smiled again.

'Did I do something wrong?'

'Not at all,' I said breezily.

'Are you sure? If I've offended you or something—'

'Scott, relax, I'm fine. I was feeling a little claustrophobic, that's all.'

He seemed taken aback by this. 'I've crowded you too much.' He nodded. 'Forcing you to socialize with a bunch of bores. I'm sorry, Kate. It's just that I could never bring Tatiana anywhere and with you, it's so easy to mix business with pleasure.'

I perked up at this, then remembered my hard-to-get act.

'I'm very independent, Scott,' I said solemnly.

'Yes, I know you are.' He smiled. 'I'll tell you what. Let's cancel tonight's dinner and let's just you and me do something romantic.'

'Hmmm. Like what?'

'Room service.'

That was just the beginning. Fawn knew her stuff. The more I pulled away the closer Scott wanted to be. And as much as I wanted to bring up Tatiana I resisted. I couldn't let my insecurity show; that's what did her in. And believe it or not, I didn't check his computer when he left me alone. I wasn't going to stoop to her level, either. It was too risky.

From then on and for the next three weeks, Scott wined and dined me like I've never been wined and dined before. We were inseparable. We went to the theater, the opera, and yet more charity balls. I was having fun for the first time in months. I was developing real feelings for him and I hoped he felt the same for me. But try as I might, it wasn't love I felt, not yet, but it was enough to make me think love was still possible one day. The only fly in the ointment was a confused e-mail from Marianne. Despite being on maternity leave, her travel editor had sent her a flurry of angry e-mails from Badrutt's Palace. I had neglected to file any stories on the hotel and naturally, the hotel's owners and Helga, the PR girl, were upset. It's not that I didn't want to write about the hotel, it's just that I'd been so busy with life in London that I'd forgotten and now it had blown up in my face. If I'd filed on time, then Marianne would never have found out that I'd lied to the hotel about my assignment. Fortunately, websites always need content, so she agreed to let me write the stories, as long as she didn't have to pay me. Which was fine with me since Scott seemed well equipped to support me. Still, I felt bad and had sent a very apologetic e-mail to her and the travel editor. I'd hardly been in touch with Marianne or Brandon since Christmas when I ignored their advice and spent my last dime on a flight to Switzerland. I was a bad friend. I'd have to make it up to them somehow.

*   *   *

It was the last week of February. London was its usual gray self and I was out on my daily solitary walk. I found it useful to maintain my air of independence and aloofness whenever possible and had taken to walking alone each morning. It had been a month since I'd come to London. I had managed to become Scott's girlfriend but not much else. The word 'love' was never uttered by either of us, not even once. This could go on forever. I was living a sort of suspended life, an ongoing vacation, which, despite deriving some pleasure from it, mostly I had a lingering sense of unease. And it didn't offer me any security, no home and no future. Ann's blue sofa, unemployment, and my mother's nonstop bingo habit were still perilously close to becoming permanent fixtures unless something changed. Fawn had been harder and harder to reach. I was convinced she'd met a man, but she denied it. But now was an emergency and I called her once more.

'Fawn,' I said anxiously. 'I've been dying to talk to you.'

'Sorry, Kate darling,' she purred. 'I've had my hands full. What's happening?'

I told her and she hemmed and hawed. 'I don't know how to take it to the next level,' I said desperately. 'How do I make him propose?'

'There's only one way,' she said knowingly. 'It will require you risk everything.'

'Yes,' I said cautiously. 'Just tell me.'

278

'Leave him.'

When I got to the suite, I found Scott poring over a floor plan.

'What is that?' I asked.

'Come take a look,' he said.

I looked at the plan. It was an apartment, an enormous one with five bedrooms, each with a fireplace, an oversize kitchen and dining area, and an extremely large media room.

'It's a palace,' I said.

'It used to be,' he remarked with a wink and handed me a brochure with colored interior photos. 'But the family has to sell it. Foreclosure. I want to snap it up.'

The apartment was stunning, with high ceilings and tons of windows.

'Poor them, lucky you,' I said, feeling sad at another family losing their home.

'I hope you like it,' he said.

'Yes, it's gorgeous,' I said.

'Good, because I've just bought it.' He smiled.

'Congratulations,' I said. It was now or never to launch Fawn's plan and I cleared my throat. 'I have to pack.'

'Pack?' he said, and gave me a puzzled look.

'I'm going back to New York,' I said and walked toward the closet and began to pull my clothes off the rack, carefully choosing what was actually mine. 'I can't do this anymore.'

'Do what?' he said and stood leaning on the threshold.

'I can't be like Tatiana,' I said and gave him a look to convey I meant it. 'I've enjoyed our time together, but I have a life. I can't just be your trophy girlfriend. I want more.'

279

He didn't say anything for a long time and just stood watching me pack.

'I have an appointment, to close the sale on the flat,' he said quickly. 'Don't go until I'm back. Promise?'

I nodded and kept shoving my wardrobe into my suitcase. I had finished packing and sat on the edge of our bed, holding my old plane ticket home and wondering why I'd ever listened to Fawn. Then at last Scott returned. He smiled when he saw me perched on the bed ready to leave.

'You are a fast packer,' he remarked and sat down beside me.

'You were gone a long time,' I said.

'Was I?' he asked. 'I suppose I was. But I'm very selective and that takes time.'

'What do you mean?' I asked, feeling myself shake with nerves. I didn't want to go home to Ann's apartment. I wanted to stay here. Maybe I should backpedal and tell him I was overreacting and that I could handle being his girlfriend. But before I could speak he pulled something from his pocket; it was a dark blue velvet box.

'Will you marry me, Kate?' he said earnestly.

I took the box from his hand and opened it. Inside was a gorgeous square-cut diamond ring.

'I can't believe this,' I said, completely stunned. I had envisioned this moment for months but never imagined it would happen. How could Fawn have known? I stared at the ring.

'Is that all the answer I'm going to get?' he joked. 'I know this is fast, maybe you want to think about it a bit . . .'

'Yes, I mean no, I mean yes; yes, I will marry you,' I shrieked and threw my arms around him.

280

To hell with cool and aloof. Despite proposing, he still didn't say he loved me but that didn't seem to matter. We just basked in the whole thrill of the moment and the realization that we both got what we wanted, or at least a large portion of it.

And that was how I came to be engaged to Scott Madewell. My friends said it couldn't be done but I had done it.

* * *

'And so you own a flat in London?' Fawn asked, perched on the edge of her seat. We were having tea at Claridges, she'd flown up from Italy the moment I called with my news.

'Not yet, he's finalizing all the paperwork after the wedding,' I explained. 'But that's not all, once we're married I'll be getting my own stock portfolio.'

I sat back in the chair, exhausted by it all. I had come very far, very fast, and I was overwhelmed.

'Have you told him you're not really a titled aristocrat yet?' she asked darkly.

'No, and don't you, either,' I teased, but meant it.

'I would never!' she said, acting insulted. 'But what are you going to do? You have to tell him.'

'I will, in time,' I said, then added gravely, 'At least he knows the truth about my financial situation.'

'You okay?' Fawn asked, seeing the gloom fall across my face.

'I don't know . . .' I began, then hesitated.

'Go on,' she encouraged.

'Well, it all happened so fast with Scott,' I said cautiously. 'It seemed almost too easy. Obviously,

281

you helped. But do men, especially rich ones, really pop the question to someone they barely know? And without mentioning a prenup?'

Fawn waved my worries away with both hands. 'Don't let that concern you. He's a very successful businessman, he's used to getting what he wants when he wants it. He decided you're to be his next wife and when a man like Scott Madewell makes a decision, he acts on it. Besides, it wasn't that easy. Remember, I was there, you had to slay a Slovenian dragon.'

'That's not all, Fawn,' I admitted. 'He's never said he loves me.'

Fawn chewed on this briefly. 'Do you love him?'

I breathed in deeply. 'The truth? Not really.' I spoke slowly as though my honesty was physically painful. 'I like him. We enjoy each other's company. But it's not the big whirlwind romance that I thought would finally lead me down the aisle.' I hung my head in embarrassment and picked at my plate.

'Don't worry, he loves you,' she said and put her hand over mine. I looked up at her and she smiled. 'And you love him in your way. You've been through a lot this past year. You're not yourself, you've said so many times. But you wouldn't marry a man who couldn't make you happy. It will be all right.'

'Thanks, Fawn,' I said with a smile. 'I needed that.'

'When's the wedding?' she asked. 'I hope I'm invited.'

'Of course you are,' I reassured her. 'The wedding is in six weeks. I know that's coming up quickly, but we don't want to wait.'

282

Fawn nodded as if she understood perfectly.

'Can I bring a date?' she asked with a sly grin.

'Of course you can!' I said enthusiastically. 'Who is he?'

'I have someone in mind,' she said. 'I'm heading back to Italy tomorrow.'

'Italian men can be dangerous,' I teased her.

'Never you mind,' she said. 'I've seen *The Roman Spring of Mrs. Stone* and it's nothing like that.'

I hadn't seen the movie, but I had a feeling I didn't want to know.

'I can finish my article, too,' I said triumphantly. 'Not that I need the money, but it will be a nice swan song from my journalism career.'

'It will make for fascinating reading,' she said with a grin. 'Legions of American women will see you as an inspiration and rich men the world over will be running for cover!'

'They can run but they can't hide,' I joked, wondering if what happened to me could really happen to anyone else. I thought back to Jennifer's friends, Tina and Arianna, and wondered how their quest for a rich husband was going. How amusing it was if at forty, I'd beaten them to the punch. Then I thought about the future. How I could help Ann out, give her real backing for her company. I could pay off my mother's debts. I could even buy my home back. I could, but as I allowed the thought to settle in my mind, I knew that I could never live there again. The memories were too painful. It was time to move on.

'Your grandmother would be very proud of you,' Fawn added sweetly.

'Yes,' I said, feeling a choke of sadness. 'All she ever wanted was for me to be happy.' I forced a

283

smile. I had achieved my goal but I was still waiting for the happiness part.

*   *   *

Planning a wedding in six months would be a challenge, six weeks was insane, even when you have loads of money. Location was the hardest to come up with and everywhere in town was taken. We were contemplating an island elopement when Scott said he had a brainwave.

'Let's hold the wedding at that estate,' he said as I felt the blood drain from my heart. 'Where that chap Griff works.'

'Penwick Manor?' I scoffed, hoping to change his mind. 'It's in the country, people would have to travel.'

'It's a lot closer than St. Barts, and it's posh enough,' he pointed out. 'Besides, I liked him and a wedding party would give the place an influx of cash.'

I admitted that was true. One look at Griff was enough to know that business wasn't booming. I did love the look of the place. But I didn't want my wedding to be the scene of any social awkwardness and I hadn't told Scott about Griff kissing me. Not that I should. It was one kiss and a few flirtatious conversations. I was overreacting.

'Let me call and see if they have rooms,' I offered.

'Here's the card Griff gave me.' Scott tossed the card out of his wallet. Seeing Griff's name in print made me flush. Such a simple card: **griffith saunderson, penwick manor** and a phone number. Not even a website; no wonder business was bad.

I dialed the number, then felt my stomach lurch when the phone rang at the other end. What if he answered? We hadn't exactly parted on glowing terms. But it was an older woman who took the call. Penwick Manor was available for our dates. She seemed thrilled we were coming. Times must be tough. She made a point of saying the family would be away for an extended period so we'd have most of the place to ourselves. Still, I felt I had to ask the obvious.

'Will Griff Saunderson be there?'

'Let me check my calendar,' she said and put me on hold. I bit my lip nervously. 'No, dear. He's off then, too. It will just be me and the gardener.'

I felt my shoulders collapse with relief. I would have some time alone at Penwick to prepare. Should Griff return before my wedding, I'd be strong enough to cope.

BOOK 3

AUSTEN'S POWER

30

Taken Aback

A young farmer, whether on horseback or
on foot, is the very last sort of person to
raise my curiosity.

—*Emma*

I left for Penwick Manor a few weeks before the
wedding. Poor Scott was stuck in London on
business, so I had to tackle the arrangements solo.
Fawn was arriving on the weekend and Emma and
Clive were meeting me tomorrow.

To be honest, I was thankful to be alone for a
bit because it gave me time to take it all in. That I
was about to be married after a life of avoiding it
was enough of a shocker, but the reality that I was
getting married to a man I hardly knew also sunk
in. This was a fact that hadn't escaped Ann when
I'd telephoned to invite her and tell her all about
Scott and my hope that our financial situation
would be resolved soon.

'Who is Scott Madewell?' she had asked me.
'And what do you know about him?'

That she Google him had been the wrong
suggestion; a gazillion Internet hits, press clippings,
nor an imposing résumé didn't impress practical
Ann.

'I don't care that he's rich, only that he's good
to you,' Ann insisted in her older sister tone. 'Why
don't you bring him here first? Why the hurry to

marry?'

'Because we wants to,' I said, offering no further explanation. The hasty marriage was Scott's idea. He insisted he couldn't wait that long for me to be his wife. He was so generous, too, giving me his credit card to book flights for my friends and family. Who couldn't see how much he loved me? But Ann wasn't cooperating.

'You'll meet him soon,' I offered hopefully. 'We're having a prewedding party the night before, so you can meet before the ceremony. Say you'll come.'

'What about Mom?' Ann asked pointedly.

I bridled at the suggestion. Iris was one of the main reasons I was in this mess. Besides, she would only embarrass me by seeking out the closest casino or bingo hall. I knew from Ann that nothing had changed on that front, and her attempts to stop Iris from gambling weren't successful. The one government program had been a washout because Iris had only been to half the classes. We were still thousands of dollars away from bailing her out from debt and from getting her the help she needed. I didn't want my mother to be a reason for Scott to back out of the marriage. It was too risky.

'I'm not inviting her,' I said plainly. 'I'm still so hurt about the house and part of me is afraid she'll mess things up somehow.' I waited for Ann to say she understood and sympathized, but she didn't.

'Then I can't make it,' she said coldly. 'I'm not leaving Mom alone.'

'She'll be fine,' I answered, feeling the sarcasm rise in my throat. 'She can go to bingo every day for a week.'

My tactless joke was greeted by silence, then, 'I don't think so.'

'Ann!' I pleaded. 'I want you here. It's my wedding!'

There was a long pause, which gave me hope, but Ann's voice, when it came, was cool. 'Sorry, Kate,' she said firmly. 'It would hurt her too much if I went and she wasn't invited. She's just happy you've found a man you love enough to finally get married. I will tell her that you couldn't afford to fly us over.'

'That's rubbish!' I snapped. 'I can afford whatever I want now! And that includes helping to finance your sauce thing.'

'That's nice of you to offer, but I don't need your money,' she said pointedly. I recoiled at her shutting me down so sharply.

'It went that well in Austin?' I asked, trying to sound upbeat. 'Did you sell your soul at the Texas food fair?'

'You could say that,' Ann answered vaguely. 'I'll let you know when I've got real news.'

'I hope so!' I said, but felt deflated. Why was Ann's sauce such a secret all of a sudden? So she sold a few jars, big deal. It used to be all she'd talk about. She must be angry with me. 'I'll e-mail you the wedding photos!' I added with false enthusiasm.

'Do that,' she said. 'Congratulations. I hope we get to meet him soon. Good-bye.'

The dial tone hit me in the head like an anvil. I was stunned, but was quickly jolted back to reality when the car hit a pothole. The chauffeur had turned off the main road and was driving down a long gravel drive that cut a swath through an enormous wood. I rolled down my window to have a better look, but what I saw didn't exactly instill confidence and joy. The forest had a ghostly appearance, as if the thousands of leafless twigs bowing and blowing in the wind were vast fingers of aged bone trying to ensnare the car. Everywhere I turned I saw only gray and brown, not the green of England I had dreamed of. I sank into the backseat. Emma had promised that the countryside would be in full bloom by my wedding day. But now the gloomy scenery brought back my conversation with Ann. She was stubborn. I was right not to invite Iris. She was never a real mother to me, she had gambled our home away, she would embarrass me and never be able to pull off being anything more than a poor relation. I would help Iris once I was married. Why couldn't Ann understand that?

At least Marianne and Brandon had accepted the invitation. The flight to London would be Thomas's first plane ride. I had arranged a local girl to act as nanny during the wedding. He was nearly four months now, big enough for me to hold. I had explained to the housekeeper that I'd be baking lasagna for our first dinner together—I had to live down that barbecue sauce debacle—and with Emma pregnant it seemed fitting. Brandon was coming alone, and declined to say why Lucy wouldn't be joining him, which made me wonder if he'd finally given her the boot.

'Penwick Manor is coming up on the right, miss,' the driver announced.

I slid over to the open window and stuck my head out again. Sure enough, as we rounded the final bend, the house came into view. Despite the bleak weather, the house stood as elegantly and stately as the photos in the brochure. I beamed at the sight of it. Now this was more like what I had in mind to launch my new life.

Built of blondish brick, it had columns and balustrades that stood like sentries and loads of ivy climbed to the roof and across the walls like an invading army. Its second floor was festooned with balconies and French doors. It was grand, all right, but as the car drew nearer, the same veil of melancholy that first picked up our scent in the woods blew down from the overcast sky as though it were a living thing and wrapped itself around the house. I shrugged off the sense of foreboding. My wedding would make Penwick a happier place.

The limo driver unpacked the trunk of the car as I climbed the stone steps to the front door and looked for the bell. But I needn't have bothered. The towering door creaked open and in its enormous frame a small elderly woman stood smiling at me, her bright eyes welcoming. She looked so much like my grandmother that I caught my breath and stood motionless, my high heels frozen to the stone.

'Hello. Lady Katharine, is it?' the woman asked warmly.

I nodded self-consciously.

'Come in, love, and make yourself at home,' she said and walked inside. I followed her, still struck by the resemblance. 'Your man can bring the luggage in while I show you around. I hope the drive up from town wasn't too hurried.'

She turned to me, waiting for my answer. I shook my head. She gave me a puzzled look, as if I might be dim-witted or something.

'Glad to hear it. Those townspeople are always in a hurry, it's enough to make you want to ban them from the countryside,' she said, smiling.

293

'Oooh, where are my manners? My name is Doris. I'm the housekeeper. We've spoken on the phone. If you need anything, you ask for me. Here are your keys.'

'Thank you,' I answered, relieved to find my voice once more, and took the keys from her. There I stood, my eyes sweeping the vast foyer and grand staircase that was once opulent perfection but had become worn with age; there was cracked plaster on the walls, wood trim that was splitting, and the white-and-black checkerboard floor was noticeably scuffed. It surprised me that Penwick was still considered a luxury destination for the wealthy types who preferred seclusion. Maybe that was the appeal—rich people could take less bling and even less opulence if it came with total privacy. Still, despite its flaws, it exuded a warmth that immediately made me feel at home. I couldn't believe I was actually here in the house Griff took care of every day. My stomach suddenly fluttered at the thought of him. What if I'd been given wrong information when I'd made the reservation and we ran into each other? Or what if his plans had changed? Who was away from their workplace for more than a month? I wanted to ask but I also wanted to be subtle. I cleared my throat and tried to sound nonchalant. 'Doris, are the Penwicks still away?'

She acted puzzled; it must be her age, I thought. 'Oh my, yes, the Penwicks, yes, indeed they are,' she said with a firm nod.

'And Griff Saunderson?' I said, asking the question I really needed answering.

'Everyone is gone, Mr. Saunderson, too,' she said and looked at me as though I must be hard of hearing. 'Left this morning. He's gone for the whole month at least, maybe longer, back to town I think, though I know he don't like it much there.'

I was able to breathe again. I smiled for real this time. 'Penwick is beautiful. I can't wait to get the full tour.'

'And that you shall have,' Doris said with a firm nod and walked down the hallway.

'The entire house is open to you and your fiancé; everything, that is, but the private rooms of the family.'

I nodded and followed Doris upstairs. Despite the well-worn foyer the rest of the house was exquisite. Now I saw why Penwick kept attracting a well-heeled clientele, clearly more effort went into the rooms and not in making a good first impression. It was everything that I had imagined. Little wonder Griff wanted to stay working here no matter how awful the money or the family was. There were enough bedrooms for most of our guests. The rest, mainly business associates of Scott's, were to stay in neighboring inns. But there was also a ballroom, a great room, a library, morning room, and breakfast room, each with an enormous stone fireplace. It looked like something out of a movie. I was desperate to share it, and the one person in the world who would have appreciated it as I did was my grandmother. A rush of sadness swept over me. I had done a fair job these past few months barring her from my thoughts as much as I could. It was too painful to think of her. But I knew if she were here she would be so proud of me, marrying a man who could give me a place like this. I think she would have liked Scott. I was almost certain of it.

We had come full circle and I was back in the entranceway, my suitcases expertly piled up by the driver. I looked down the hall, opposite from where we'd been, and saw a set of enormous mahogany doors.

'Doris, what's behind those?' I asked.

'That's the family wing of the house,' she said with a nod, then gave me a warning glare. 'Guests always want to go where they aren't allowed. Curiosity is a powerful thing.'

'Don't worry, Doris.' I smiled reassuringly. 'I won't try a midnight break-in.'

With a look that said she didn't quite believe me, she shouted down the hall, 'Herbert!' A man, slightly younger and more spry than Doris, entered from a backroom. Not exactly a uniformed bellhop, he looked more like a gardener. His hands and fingernails were dirty and he wore overalls.

'Herbert will take your bags,' Doris said by way of an order.

I was taken aback. The words 'you're not serious?' slipped out of my mouth.

'Don't worry, we're hardy types in Dorset.' She smiled. 'He's used to it.'

Hardy or not, I felt guilty about letting an old man carry my luggage, so I grabbed what I could and climbed up behind him. Neither Herbert nor Doris stopped me from pitching in and I got the feeling that Penwick Manor was a bit more than they could handle. Maybe Griff should have found a replacement for himself while he was away this long. I'd never thought of him as selfish before, but clearly he needed to think of others a bit more.

Herbert was clearly the strong silent type. When we got to my room and I tried to tip him, he refused

296

with a shake of the head and a wave of his hand. After he'd left, I went to my window and sat down at the window seat. The clouds had lifted and for the first time in days, rays of sunlight peaked through. Just the hint of sunshine gave the grounds a more welcoming glow. I could swear that there were buds on those ghostly tree branches after all.

I looked at my watch. It was just past noon. What to do with the rest of my day? I wasn't meeting the caterers until early evening. I looked at the pile of suitcases and decided to unpack. As I unzipped my brand-new Louis Vuitton duffel (a gift from Scott), *Pride and Prejudice* fell out and landed on the rug with a soft thud. It fell open on the scene where Elizabeth traipses through the mud to see her sister at Netherfield, causing quite the scandal within the Bingley family, but also causing Mr. Darcy to fall in love with her. I smiled and put the book away. That's what the afternoon's sudden sunshine called for, a walk, or a ramble, as the English called it.

I changed into more practical clothes, a black turtleneck, dark jeans, black Burberry trench (again, thank you, Scott), and black Hunter wellies and headed toward the garden. Sure enough, there was Herbert bent over a shrub doing whatever shrubs needed done to them.

'Herbert,' I called out. 'I want to go for a walk in the grounds. Is there a path I should follow?'

He stood scratching his head and looked up at the sky, before finally pointing me toward a wooden gate.

'Go past the stables and you'll see a footpath into the woods. It leads to the meadowlands,' he said with a toothless grin. 'It's a bit slippery underfoot, so be careful. Looks like it might rain again.'

'I shall be,' I said, feeling very Austen-esque in tone, if not outfit.

After crossing through an orchard I reached the stable yard. There wasn't a soul around, but there were horses aplenty. Several poked their heads over their stall doors, and still more were outside in the grass paddocks. I wished I wasn't so afraid because they seemed to want me to pay attention to them. Griff must be down here all the time when he was working. Penwick seemed like a lot for three people to manage. The Penwick family probably didn't lift a finger to help, either. Maybe Scott should buy the property and then there would be changes. I would see that the estate was run like clockwork.

It was still cold out but I was determined to enjoy the brisk March weather. I picked my way down a narrow path in the woods that was covered by stumps and roots until the trail abruptly ended at a tall fence on the edge of a meadow. I could see over the fence to another footpath and supposed that you were expected to climb the fence to continue. I grabbed hold of the top rail and was about to pull myself over when I noticed a small wooden stile to the left. Much easier! I hopped down from the fence and put my right foot on the top step. I must have moved too quickly as my left foot was no sooner off the ground than the right slipped off the icy step and I catapulted through the air. My legs did the splits as my lower back smacked the stile before I landed in a heap on the other side of the fence. As I lay on the damp ground, I felt my back muscles yanked in different directions. The intense pain made me dizzy and I tried taking deep breaths to calm down. I managed to reach in my pocket to call for help but after fumbling around I discovered that I had left my cell phone in my room. How long would it be before Doris noticed I was gone? Would Herbert remember where he sent me?

After what seemed an eternity, I tried to roll over, hoping to grab hold of the fence to heave myself up, but it was no use. The pain was too much and each attempt to reach the fence was met with searing agony. I screamed out in pain and lay there, my heart racing. Then, just when I thought it couldn't get worse, as Herbert had foreseen, it started to rain. Softly at first, but within seconds the skies opened up and torrents of water soaked me through to the bone. I tried once more to get up, but my back went into spasms and I fell back down. Again, I screamed out in pain, only this time someone heard me.

'Hello? Are you okay?' a man shouted in the distance.

'I'm here. I've fallen and can't get up!' I shouted back, unable to lift my head up to see who it was.

What came next can best be described as my worst nightmare. As I lay on the ground the earth beneath me started to pound in a distinct three-beat rhythm—*boom, boom, boom. Boom, boom, boom. Boom, boom, boom.* Then I saw it: a big, black horse galloping across the meadow toward me. This was it. I was going to die. The monster would trample me until I was pulp. I closed my eyes and held my breath. But the pounding stopped suddenly and realizing I wasn't pulp, I opened my eyes and squinted through the rain. The horse was a few feet away, quietly grazing, as its rider ran to my side. He wore a green raincoat and some sort of peaked hat. I strained to make him out, but my vision was blurred from the rain and smeared mascara. As he

299

got closer, I thought I recognized him and wiped my eyes to get a clearer view. It couldn't be . . . But when the man crouched at my side I knew I wasn't seeing things.

'Griff!' I said, clearly dismayed. 'What are you doing here?'

'Kate?' he said, equally shocked.

We remained in our respective positions, like some kind of bizarre tableau, until finally I couldn't take the silence and the rain any longer.

'You weren't supposed to be here,' I explained breathlessly. 'I asked; Doris said you were gone. I'd have never have come here if I'd known.'

'I was supposed to leave today but decided on a final ride before driving to London,' he explained. 'But I can see I'll have to delay it. What happened to you?'

'I fell off that stile thing and hurt my back.'

'I see,' he said as rain dripped off his hat and onto my forehead. 'Can you put your arms around my neck?'

I thought back to our kiss and hesitated.

Griff smiled as if sensing my reticence. 'Don't be afraid,' he said smugly and extended his hand. 'I won't try and kiss you this time. You're not really my type.'

'Very funny,' I scoffed. 'Fine. I will grab you by the neck.'

'Good girl,' he said cheerfully. 'Just don't strangle me.'

Not until I'm safely at Penwick, I thought. I put my arms around his neck and he slowly hoisted me to my feet, but as soon as he let go my knees buckled and I grasped on to him. He caught me and held me tightly to his chest and there we stood, like marionettes waiting for the puppeteer.

'You're awfully wet,' I said stupidly. The rain was letting up but we were both soaked through.

'It's raining.'

'I'm freezing,' I said faintly and began to shake from the cold and the pain. I felt like vomiting. That's what I needed, to puke all over Griff. Still, I must have looked pathetic because he was suddenly very caring and nice.

'I know a shortcut to Penwick, but we'll have to take my horse,' he said matter-of-factly.

'I can't, I'm terrified of horses!' I shrieked.

'You're not going to ride him!' he barked. 'I will lead him behind me. You can walk and use me as support.'

He leaned me up against the fence post as he retrieved his horse. The cold rain had dampened the animal's warm coat so that steam poured off its flanks and its nostrils flared red. I'd never seen anything more frightening.

'He's harmless, I assure you,' Griff said as he approached with the beast. 'His name is Fred. He's a very docile Friesian stallion.'

'Can't I just wait here?' I said, shaking.

'No,' he said flatly. 'You're hurt, wet, and cold. Now, just shut up and let me rescue you. Put your arm around my neck and I'll hold on to your waist.'

I shook my head.

'You're not going to cry, are you?' he said with a roll of his eyes.

'I don't cry,' I said firmly.

He gripped me by the waist and I leaned on him. Fred walked on the other side of Griff, but I kept a close eye on him just in case.

'So, Scott is making an honest woman out

301

of you?' he said after we'd taken a few steps in uncomfortable silence.

'Yes,' I answered through gritted teeth. 'He's not here yet. I came ahead to make arrangements. He's going to try and come on weekends. You don't have to leave on our account.'

'I have no desire to see you marry the poor bloke, but thanks,' he said flatly.

'Fine,' I snapped. 'You sound jealous!'

'Don't be ridiculous!'

After we'd gone a bit farther he spoke again.

'Are you happy,' he asked. 'Now that you're set for life?'

'Yes,' I said resenting his tone.

'So why don't you cry?'

'What?' I asked. Talk about a non sequitur.

'You said you didn't cry. Why?'

I stared down at the ground, watching my black wellies tread the sodden grass. How did I want to answer that? I can't cry? That I haven't cried since my grandmother's funeral and the house was lost? I shook my head and forced a smile.

'I'll never tell.' I grinned, but then my foot snagged on one of those twisty roots and I screamed in pain again.

'Okay, that's it,' he said impatiently. 'How much do you weigh?'

'I beg your pardon?'

He looked me up and down. 'Nine and a half stone?'

I glared at him. 'What is that in pounds?'

'About one thirty-five.'

'I'm no such thing! I'm only a hundred and twenty pounds, thank you very much,' I snapped.

'Even better,' he said and tossed Fred's reins

over his shoulder. 'Now, grab on.'

'What are you doing?'

'I'm going to bloody well carry you,' he snapped.

'You aren't strong enough,' I snapped back.

'Aren't I?' With that he leaned down and scooped me up into his arms. 'Light as a bloody feather. Comfortable?'

'Not really,' I said huffily. The positioning left much to be desired but it was easier than walking or standing, not that I would admit it to Griff.

'We'll get you to Penwick, My Lady,' he said sarcastically. 'Even if it kills me.'

I wanted to say something equally sarcastic in retaliation but didn't have the strength. I felt faint and dizzy again. All I wanted was to lie down and be warm.

31

On the Mend

I'm not romantic, you know. I never was. I
ask only a comfortable home.

—*Pride and Prejudice*

I was so relieved to finally see Penwick poking through the gloom. But we must have been quite the sight as Herbert rushed over without letting go of his spade and took Fred. I could feel Griff staggering beneath the weight of me. It was true, I did weigh one hundred thirty-five pounds. Actually, it was closer to one hundred forty pounds, depending on the day, but I was never going to admit it. The front door was within reach but I was dismayed when he turned and went toward the back of the manor.

'Servants entrance?' I asked with mock derision. 'I am a guest, you know.'

'But I am not,' he answered flatly. 'And this is the fastest way to the kitchen.'

'Kitchen? I've had lunch, thank you.'

'Don't be daft. You're soaked through. There's always heat on in the kitchen.'

We burst through the door and he dropped me on a Victorian chaise. 'Ouch! Jesus!' I yelped.

'I meant that to be gentler,' he said.

'Well, you failed,' I answered icily. We both stared at each other in silence, unsure of what to do next.

'Thank you for rescuing me,' I said as warmly as I could.

'You should probably get out of those clothes,' he said uncomfortably.

I slid up into a quasi-seated position. 'I think I can handle that on my own.'

'Quite right,' he answered. 'I will go find Doris. She may be able to help.'

Doris was helpful. She brought me a thick terry robe and some slippers and led the way to the great room, both of us stooped and shuffling, where Herbert had lighted the giant stone fireplace. Two wingback chairs and an overstuffed velvet sofa were strategically placed for maximum warmth near the fire.

'Thanks, Doris,' I said softly. 'Can I get changed in here?'

'Of course,' she said. 'Do you need help?'

I did, but was too shy for that sort of help. 'I'll manage, thanks.'

After the door closed, I tried to remove my wellies but the pain was too much. I shook off my coat and peeled my long turtleneck from my back and arms. I had just slid out of my bra when there was a knock and the door swung open. I quickly clutched the bathrobe to my breasts.

It was Griff. Seeing my state of undress, he averted his eyes. 'Pardon me, I didn't realize you were . . . I thought Doris was in here.'

'You're supposed to knock first, then wait for an answer.' I glared at him. 'You don't just barge in like you own the place! Now turn around so I can get into my robe.'

He did as he was told. I saw that he was carrying an armful of towels.

'What are those?'

'Hot towels. I had them sitting on the Aga for you,' he said loudly, as though with his back to me I couldn't hear him. 'May I turn around now?'

'Yes,' I said and couldn't help smiling. 'That was very nice of you.'

He turned and handed me the towels and, seeing my expression, he smiled also. Then we both giggled like schoolchildren.

'I suppose I should turn around again so you can wrap yourself up?'

'I think that would be a good idea,' I said. After he turned, I removed the robe and wrapped myself in one of the towels. It was as soothing as a cup of tea. But with my jeans and boots still stuck to my skin, true comfort eluded me. There was only one solution.

'Griff,' I said imploringly. 'Can you please pull

305

off my boots? I can't do it on my own and I can't get warm with these soaking wet jeans on.'

He slowly turned and walked toward me. The fire crackled loudly. I shivered and my lower lip began to tremble from the damp chill that had penetrated my bones, but also from an unexpected nervousness. My reaction startled me. I had forced Griff from my mind weeks ago, but he was stirring things up that I had thought were buried for good.

'You'd best hang on to the chair,' he directed. I grabbed the chair and slowly, carefully, he twisted and pulled until each boot was off.

'Are you all right to take off your jeans?' he asked.

I nodded. He went to leave.

'Don't go,' I said, startled by the urgency in my voice. 'Just in case I need you,' I quickly added.

'I'll keep my back to you once again,' he said and didn't take another step.

I somehow managed to slither out of my wet jeans, which was no easy feat. Once they were off, I grabbed the remaining towel and wrapped it around my naked body. I should have slipped back into the robe immediately but instead I found myself uttering the words: 'You can turn around now.'

He did as he was told. I stood there and smiled, wearing only a towel, my hair wet and not a stitch of makeup on. It was his turn to be frozen to the ground. I didn't understand why I was behaving this way. I was engaged to Scott. Griff had taken care of me. I was grateful for that. Maybe that was what I was feeling; gratitude, that must be it.

'Thank you for the towels,' I said. 'When I was little my grandmother would warm towels in the oven and wrap us up in them after our bath.'

'I think you should try the dressing gown, too,' he offered and held it up for me. 'I won't look.'

He shut his eyes. I let the towels drop to the floor so that he knew I was naked. But as I stepped into the bathrobe my back went into spasms again and I yelped in pain before falling backward. I clung on to the chair while managing to wrap the robe around myself so he couldn't glimpse my naked body. He opened his eyes and rushed over to ease me into the chair.

'Thank you,' I said through the pain. If I had been attempting a seduction it would have been a laughable effort.

'You need some muscle relaxants,' he offered. 'I'll ring our local GP and see what he can offer you.'

'That would be great.' I forced a smile. 'I can't exactly walk down the aisle like this.'

'We have walking sticks,' he said. 'Quite nice ones.'

'Thanks, but I'll pass.' I grinned. Then I paused. 'No really, Griff, thank you.'

'Helping a damsel in distress, especially one who is paying to be here, is part of my job.'

I nodded slowly, not appreciating the implication that I had bought his kindness. 'So, you're heading out to London now?' I asked, fighting off a feeling of disappointment.

'It's too late for today.' He smiled. 'I may go tomorrow. But I'll check in on you later, if you like.'

'I'd like that,' I stammered. 'Oh, can you please ask Doris to get my cell phone? It's on the dresser in my room.'

When he'd left I felt a twinge of regret. How

307

ridiculous! I was merely reacting to the pain and was thankful that Griff was there when I needed him. There was nothing more to it. I had to stop thinking of Griffith Saunderson and call Scott to tell him what happened.

* * *

'If I'd known he was here I wouldn't have come,' I told Clive and Emma. They had driven up as planned the following day. I had told them all about my accident and my rescue.

'Bollocks,' Emma teased. 'You've been obsessed with Jane Austen all your life. This is your dream location and you know it. Though in this weather it looks more like Manderley than Pemberley.'

We all nodded in agreement.

'Besides, what does it matter if Griff is at your wedding?'

'It doesn't really,' I said vaguely. Though the truth was it did matter. It mattered very much to me that my attraction to Griff had only intensified since I'd been at Penwick. But I wasn't about to confess it to anyone.

* * *

After our visit, I took one of the walking sticks that Griff had left for me and went for a stroll. The doctor had prescribed drugs and they had taken the edge off the pain, but he had warned that it would take a couple of weeks for me to be one hundred percent. It was no wonder I was in a foul mood. But it wasn't only my pain, or impending wedding that had me irritated. It was also my fiancé. Scott

308

had been sympathetic but hadn't offered to drop whatever wheeling and dealing he was doing to help me or see that I was in one piece.

'You'll be fine,' he had said. 'Take the meds and a martini, while you're at it. That will kill the pain!' He had laughed. I had not.

As I ambled along, I was so deep in thought that I found myself in the stable yard without realizing I'd been walking in its direction.

'Hello there,' Griff called out. 'Nice to see you up and about.'

'Thank you,' I said and hobbled over. He was saddling up a horse. It snorted and I took a step back.

'You really are afraid of horses,' he said with a look of astonishment.

'Petrified,' I admitted. 'They hate me.'

'Horses don't hate anyone,' he said and led the animal past me and into a riding ring. I limped after him and leaned on the railing. 'They are the noblest creatures,' he said earnestly. 'You know where you stand with them.'

'Yes, at least twenty paces back,' I joked. He didn't laugh. He seemed disappointed and I didn't want to disappoint him. I didn't like him thinking less of me. 'What do you like about them?'

'Aside from their strength of character and physical beauty?' He smiled. 'I like that they trust me enough to let me ride them. That they work with me and we create harmony, a partnership, a relationship of mutual respect.'

'Sounds nice,' I admitted.

Griff tightened the girth and ran the stirrups down, then looked at me with a sly grin. 'Why don't you try it?'

309

I shook my head. 'No way, I'm already crippled.'

'Ah, but you see, it's great therapy for a sore back,' he said.

'I don't believe you,' I answered. 'I have a starring role in my wedding. I can't take the risk.'

'Sounds like you can't risk not riding,' he said and led the horse toward a wooden step in the center of the ring. 'You sit on this horse every day and just walk around and it will loosen your back and undo all those knots.'

'Are you serious?' I asked desperately.

'I will hold the reins the entire time. You don't have to be afraid,' he said convincingly. 'I'll take care of you.'

I was no horse, so trusting a man didn't come easily to me. But I had to try something. I took a deep breath and stepped into the ring, walking slowly toward the horse with my cane. The horse looked askance at the walking stick and I stopped.

'Does he think I have a weapon?' I asked nervously.

'Horses aren't used to seeing a person with three legs,' Griff said cheerfully. 'That's what it looks like to them.'

I smiled and walked closer, but as I got within reach I felt my legs shake with fear. 'I can't,' I stammered. 'I'm too afraid.'

Griff stepped toward me and took my hand. His skin was soft but his touch was strong, masculine. He held my hand the final steps until we were standing beside it.

'You just need confidence,' he said soothingly. 'Horses know when you're nervous and they can take advantage.'

'That's not very reassuring,' I snapped.

'Shush. I'm talking,' he snapped back. 'If you behave in a calm, assertive manner they will have confidence in you and respect you. It's no different to how you behave with people.'

'I can be assertive,' I said sulkily.

'Yes, I know,' he said. 'But can you be calm and confident?'

'I *am* confident!' I said and yanked my hand from his.

'Really?' he said unsmiling. 'You strike me as a beautiful woman who lacks confidence and instead relies on sarcasm and fashionable clothes to give you the appearance of it.'

I stood there, anger and frustration welling up inside, unsure of what to say, no doubt because on some level I knew he was right.

'You're forty years old,' he continued. 'It's time you overcame your fears.'

'You really are something,' I said and was about to make a brisk exit when my walking stick snagged on a rock and I tripped. Once again, Griff was there to catch me. He held me, folded over his arm like a sack of grain. It was the closest I'd come to crying since my grandmother had died. The pain, the pressure of the wedding, and the humiliation of my horse phobia were overwhelming. I managed to stand again and tried to shove him away but he held on firmly. I thumped his chest with my fist. 'Who are you to suggest I'm insecure?' I said angrily.

'Come on, Kate,' he said gently and relaxed his grip. 'I wasn't trying to offend you.'

'Weren't you?' I snapped as I stood on my own again.

'It's just that you're like a jigsaw puzzle with its pieces scattered about,' he went on. 'I've tried to put it all together but some vital piece is missing. I can't make you out at all.'

'I'm easy to figure out,' I retaliated. 'An open book.'

'If the book is a mystery, then I'd agree.' He smiled. 'Accept my apology for my boorish behavior?'

'Are you really angry that I'm marrying Scott?' I asked bluntly.

'It's not my business,' he said and looked away.

'That's true. But you did kiss me,' I pointed out.

'I remember,' he said dryly. 'Water under the bridge. Your life. Your marriage. As long as you love him, then I'm happy for you.'

I bit my lip. Griff was the last person I'd confess the truth to—that despite my best efforts, I still wasn't in love with my future husband. Instead, I gestured to the horse.

'What's his name?'

'Ratina,' he said. 'He's a she.'

I inched toward the mare and held out my hand. Ratina stretched her neck out so that her muzzle touched my fingers. I yanked my hand back and yelped. Ratina shook her head and pawed the ground. I sighed. So much for bravery.

'Give me your hand,' Griff said. He covered my hand with his as you would a child's and we stroked the mare's neck. It was silky smooth but I could feel the taut muscles beneath her coat. She was the color of dark chocolate, with a black mane and tail and a white star on her face and three white socks with small black polka dots on them that Griff said were called ermines.

'She must be some sort of horse princess to have ermine.' I laughed and stroked the horse on my own. Ratina turned her neck and watched me. Feeling braver, I stroked her face and muzzle again. It was like velvet. She lifted her head high so that her nostrils brushed my cheek and I felt the warm air against my skin as she exhaled.

'Blow gently into her nostril,' Griff instructed me.

'Are you kidding me?' I said, aghast at the suggestion.

'They like it,' he explained and stepped to the other side and blew into her nostril. The horse lifted her head and placed her nose next to his. He blew again and this time she blew back. I tried the same thing and Ratina leaned closer to me and exhaled again. The warm air on my cheek was sensual.

'I've never air-kissed a horse before,' I joked.

'Ratina is more sincere than the people at those dreadful parties,' he said, smiling.

'You're probably right,' I agreed. We both stood there, so close, just Ratina between us. I looked at Griff and smiled.

'Okay, so now you know Ratina isn't going to eat you, will you get on?' he said, interrupting our intimacy, probably for the better.

I nodded. He helped me up on the wooden steps, which were called a mounting block. Ratina stood patiently as I swung my leg over. At first I leaned forward, clinging to her neck, but slowly I propped myself up. Griff adjusted the stirrups and told me how to sit and hold the reins, then took a long rope and clipped it to the bridle so that he had complete control.

'Okay, now just relax.'

He led the horse forward and I was immediately

thrown back and forth in the saddle with each step.

'Whoa!' I called out, but Griff and the horse ignored me. Ratina's walk took getting used to. She was a large horse and her strides covered a lot of ground. My hips rocked back and forth and while it hurt, it was a pain that felt good. I could feel the muscles deep inside loosening.

'This does feel good,' I confessed.

'Glad to hear it,' Griff answered and kept walking. After about fifteen minutes, he halted Ratina at the mounting block.

'Is my quarter up?' I teased.

'I have work to do, Lady Kate.' He smiled.

My expression darkened and I dismounted. For the first couple of steps my back felt like Jell-O, but it was definitely better.

'Again tomorrow?' he suggested.

'Absolutely!' I said enthusiastically. 'Have you changed your mind about London?'

'I've decided to stick around for a few more days. I have loads of work to do,' he explained.

'Please don't go on my account,' I said. If he could stand it, so could I.

*   *   *

The next few weeks were spent with the caterer, wedding planner, seamstress, florist, you name it. Emma was an immense help and I was thankful to have a real friend with me. I had kept up with my daily riding exercise and also learned to groom. I discovered that I loved brushing Ratina, it was quality time with her and I felt we bonded. Being with the horse gave me a sense of peace and tranquility that my normal routine in the city had

314

never given me. Perhaps I had a country girl in me somewhere. Griff was patient and attentive but horses were all we spoke about. We never discussed the wedding again. Anytime I mentioned Scott he would go silent or change the subject. I was just happy to be friends once again, even if the flirtation had vanished. The more time we spent together, the more I came to like him, really like him. He wasn't aloof or cold, he was kind, funny, and sincere. He knew about many things that seemed to go along with his job on the estate—groundskeeping, animal husbandry, even accounting. And eventually he began to ask me about my work, the beauty babble I wrote, publishing, and even fashion. We seemed to realize at once that we could learn much from each other. Yet we also shared common interests that I would never had guessed, like our passion for old movies. The odd night he'd venture into the house and watch a DVD with me. We always sat on opposite sides of the immense sage green sofa. That we were growing close couldn't be denied. It didn't help that it had been almost a month and I hadn't laid eyes on Scott. He kept making excuses each weekend as to why he couldn't leave London. At first it bothered me. But as weeks passed, I found it bothered me less and less. Griff never asked where Scott was.

But now it was mere days before the wedding and there was a big prewedding party planned for Friday night. Scott would be here soon and when he came I'd lose Griff. Not that I really 'had' him, for despite all our time together I learned little more about him, other than he lived in a flat above the stable. I knew his parents were gone and he had two siblings. Otherwise, he avoided speaking about

315

personal matters. On several occasions he joined Emma, Clive, and me at the pub. It was here, at the local, as they called it, that I got a glimpse of Griff as just a regular guy. He and Clive told silly boarding school stories and tales of Oxford, many beginning with being drunk. Then his eyes glazed over whenever the conversation turned to my wedding.

'He's just a bloke,' Emma explained in the pub's loo. 'All men tune out wedding talk. It bores the hell out of them.'

'I suppose,' I acquiesced. 'I just can't tell what he's thinking half the time. I know he doesn't approve of my marrying Scott.'

Emma stopped applying her lipstick and stared at me in the mirror.

'What?' I asked.

'Why would you give a damn what Griff thinks?' she asked with a raised eyebrow. 'Are you in love with him?'

'Don't be ridiculous!' I gasped. 'Why would you say such nonsense?'

'Oh, I don't know,' she paused for effect. 'You have been spending a lot of time with him. He got you to ride a horse, for Christ's sake. He's obviously had an influence on you.'

I shrugged. 'He's fixed my back. Look at me now. I don't even need a cane. Horses are great therapy.'

'Aha,' she said with a wink.

'I'm serious,' I insisted. 'I could write a health story for *Haute* about it.' I rummaged in my handbag for my compact and as I did, I could feel Emma scrutinizing me. She clearly had something on her mind. Sure enough, within seconds she spoke.

316

'You don't love Scott,' she asked carefully. 'Do you?'

I pressed powder onto my nose in firm dabs and checked my teeth for lipstick stains.

'I will,' I answered at last. 'He's a good man. I *will* love him.'

'Oh, Kate,' Emma said softly. 'Don't do it. Call it off. You can't marry a man you don't love.'

'Bollocks, as you say in this country!' I answered, snapping the compact shut and zipping up my makeup bag. 'Marrying Scott is the smartest move I've ever made. Women once *only* married for security, affection was a bonus. And I have both. My Jane Austen guide works!'

'We don't live in bloody Jane Austen's time,' Emma barked. 'I know you've been working on this article and all that, but women can make their own fortune and buy their own house and marry for love, and only for love. You got lucky.'

'Luck had nothing to do with it. My plan worked and other women like me can do it, too,' I said. 'Besides, I'm forty, it's too late to make my fortune. I squandered my youth on dead-end jobs. Hell, I wasn't even a *real* beauty editor, just an *acting* one. A *pretend* anything is pathetic unless you're twelve.'

'You mean like a *pretend* aristocrat, *Lady* Kate?' she interjected meanly.

I'd never fought with Emma before. But her comment struck a nerve, so, hurt and angry, I lashed out at her.

'Look at you, you married for love and what do you have to show for it?' I snapped. 'You're a struggling film composer with no money, no home, a baby on the way, living cooped up with your mother-in-law. No thanks.'

317

As soon as the words were out of my mouth I wanted to yank them back. But it was too late. Emma's eyes were filled with tears.

'That's not fair,' she cried angrily. 'It was the recession that did this. Clive will make money again and we will have a home!'

'Emma! I'm sorry!' I said desperately as she stormed out of the loo.

I chased after her but she had already grabbed her coat and Clive.

'We're leaving,' she said to Griff without looking at me.

'Emma, please, I said I was sorry,' I pleaded.

'You *will* be sorry one day,' she scolded me. 'But it's your funeral. Oops, I mean wedding.'

She walked away with Clive on her heels, leaving me standing there like the fool I was.

Griff coughed.

'I'm a bitch,' I announced and sat down at the table.

'Let me guess, you opened your mouth and all your charm fell out?' he asked dryly.

'I should go,' I answered with a forced smile. 'Fawn arrives tomorrow morning and Brandon and Marianne get here in the afternoon.'

'And what about the groom?'

I looked at him, shocked. It was the first time in weeks he'd mentioned Scott.

'Your husband-to-be?'

'I know who you meant. He comes Friday morning; we have the whole day to ourselves before the party.'

'You must really miss him,' he said flatly.

'Of course,' I said and put on my coat.

But as I walked along the lane to Penwick,

Emma's and Griff's words haunted me. I hadn't seen Scott in weeks and I didn't miss him. But I'd been so busy with the wedding plans, and the accident, and recovering and all that, how could I?

32

BFF

How despicably have I acted! I, who have prided myself on my discernment! I, who have valued myself on my abilities!

—Pride and Prejudice

I was never much of an athlete, so when I borrowed Doris's green Pashley bicycle, its wicker basket loaded down with home-baked muffins, I had underestimated the fitness level required to cycle into the village. The lanes were bumpy and full of stones and crevices, making steering a challenge. I arrived at the small stone house panting and sweaty.

'You look frightful,' Emma said and stood squarely in the doorway with no intent of inviting me in.

'I'm out of shape,' I said and smiled, hoping she'd warm up. She didn't.

'What do you want, Kate?'

'Your forgiveness,' I said plainly. 'I was a total cow last night. I had no business insulting you or Clive. I'm sorry. I wish I could take those words back.'

Emma nodded. 'I can't say the same thing. I do

believe you're making a mistake marrying Scott.'

'I know you do,' I said. 'But I have to do what's right for me and for my family. At least you and Clive have his mom's cottage. I have nothing. Being homeless is worse than being alone or poor. Scott will give me a home and in turn I can give Iris and Ann a home.

'And I want you there, I need you there, with me, when I marry him,' I said more pitifully than I'd intended. 'Scott is a good man and I do care for him. Not every romance can have the passion you and Clive have.'

Emma smiled at this and glanced over my shoulder at the Pashley. 'What's in the basket?'

I grinned. I could always count on Emma's appetite.

'Only homemade strawberry muffins,' I responded and retrieved them from the bicycle. Doris had baked them for me that morning after I'd told her I needed them to make up with Emma. 'Your favorite.'

She raised an eyebrow and smirked. 'You do know the right buttons to push, don't you? Okay, come in. But bring all the muffins.'

I laughed and followed her inside.

*   *   *

An hour later I was once again an overheated mess as I cycled back up to Penwick's front door. I was just in time to see a dove gray Rolls-Royce pull up. Only one person would hire *that* car.

'Darling!' Fawn squealed when she saw me. 'Look what a country girl you've become! Cycling about like a mad thing and not giving a hoot about

your hair! Did you get the gown finished in time?'
I laughed at her comments about my appearance
and as I moved in for a hug, I noticed straightaway
that she looked fabulous. Clearly, Italy agreed with
her. She was back in fighting form in a pale gray
sheath dress that Jackie Kennedy would have killed
for. Her hair had been cut into a crisp but stylish
shoulder-length bob. She looked modern and sexy.

'I did,' I said gleefully. 'In oyster, just as you
suggested. Vera Wang had the perfect bias-cut
gown. You'll love it and I love your hair!'

'Thank you, dear. I needed a change. As for your
gown, oyster is much nicer than cream, especially
with your complexion,' she said as we walked arm
in arm up the master staircase. 'White just won't do
at your age.'

'Thanks a lot,' I said playfully.

'Oh, hush,' she continued. 'You're lucky you can
still get away with a dress; if I don't hurry, at my
next wedding I'll have to make do with separates.
Now pour me a drink.'

'It's ten in the morning!' I exclaimed.

'Fine, fine,' she waved me off. 'Make it a
mimosa. Is that "morning" enough for you?'

'Fawn!' a man's voice called out and we turned
on the steps as a small, slightly built man with a
swarthy complexion strided toward us. I gave Fawn
a look.

'Marco!' she called out. 'Come meet Kate. Isn't he
darling?' she said to me.

Marco kissed my hand and smiled. He was short
but perfectly proportioned. He looked to be in his
thirties and wore a very expensive-looking navy
pinstripe suit. I wondered if it was new.

'Nice to meet you,' I said.

321

'Marco, go check us in with that lovely lady over there,' Fawn said and pointed to Doris, who was seated at an ancient desk with the register. Once he was out of earshot, Fawn grabbed my arm and told me everything.

'Marco is Italian,' she breathed.

'Yes, I guessed that.' I laughed.

'He exports coffee,' she said. 'He runs his own business. He's not rich but he does all right. And I just love his sense of style! European men know how to dress, when we met he was wearing a lavender suit.'

'The suit he's wearing now is very nice, too,' I agreed, impressed that Marco bought his own clothes. 'And you don't need rich.'

'Ain't that the truth? And what I do need he gives me plenty.'

'Too much information!' I shrieked.

'Don't worry, I won't give you the gory details.' She smiled. 'But what's the point of all my money if I can't fall for any man I please. Men like Scott can't have all the fun.'

I gave her a look that said she was treading on thin ice.

'Sorry.' She grinned.

Mimosas in hand and giggling like schoolgirls, we toured the house as Marco went to their room to unpack. I knew the house by heart, but I wanted Fawn to see the grounds, so we took our drinks and hoofed it through the gardens, eventually, and what was now second nature for me, winding up at the stable. There was no sign of Griff, but I lingered near the horses, petting Ratina as she hung her head over her stall door, waiting, but he never appeared.

322

'Since when do you like hanging out with horses?' Fawn said impatiently. 'It's damp and smelly out here.'

I kicked at the dirt and bit my lip, unsure how to tell her the truth; after all, she was bound to have an opinion.

'I forgot to tell you,' I hesitated. 'Griff is here, he postponed his trip to London.'

Fawn looked as if she might implode. 'You haven't . . .'

'God no! I'm engaged,' I blurted. 'We're just friends.'

She looked at me suspiciously. 'Not with benefits, I hope.'

'None.'

'I don't like it, Kate,' she said and squinted at me as if trying to read my mind. 'You've been attracted to that scoundrel since day one.'

'Not day one,' I corrected. 'I didn't like him at all when I first laid eyes on him.'

'Even worse!' she countered. 'Tension like that is bound to explode.'

'Let's drop it,' I said. 'Everything is fine. Besides, he doesn't feel that way about me. Apparently I'm not his type.'

She pursed her lips at this new information and shook her head. 'It was much easier when you thought he was gay,' she said.

'Time to refresh our drinks,' I announced. 'Follow me.' I gave Ratina a pat and headed back to the house with Fawn in silent pursuit.

* * *

That afternoon Brandon and Marianne arrived,

323

with Thomas in tow. As excited as I was, I was also nervous about seeing them, knowing how crazy they thought my life had become. But it was just like old times.

'Congratulations,' Marianne said and hugged me.

'You look every inch the lady who lunches.' Brandon grinned and kissed me on each cheek.

'Can I hold him?' I asked Marianne as I squatted down to Thomas, smiling from his carrier.

'I thought you hated holding babies,' she said as she picked him up and handed him to me.

'Thomas is different, he's yours.' I smiled and held the baby. He was cute, all right, though he looked far more like Frank than Marianne. Not that I would ever tell her.

'I know, he's got Frank's face.' She grinned sourly.

'Well, Frank is handsome,' I said and tried to balance Thomas in my arms but he was starting to fidget. Marianne looked around the foyer, eyeing the space. To prepare for the wedding extra cleaning staff had swept in over the past few days and Penwick was looking more spiffy.

'I have to hand it to you, when you research a story you really research it,' she said. 'Have you finished it yet? You still owe the magazine a finished draft end of this month. We're counting on it.'

By now Thomas had wiggled so much in my arms I was grasping him around his tummy, which he didn't seem to mind all that much. Marianne scowled, though, and grabbed him from me.

'And you'll have it. Is that your way of saying you approve?' I asked tentatively.

324

'I just want you to be happy,' she answered and put her hand on my arm. 'I admit I thought your idea to marry a man just because he was rich was a great idea—for a *story*. But in reality? But if Scott makes your life complete, then who am I to judge?'

'Nonsense,' Brandon cut in. 'Of course she's judgmental; she's Marianne, she's perfect!'

Marianne slugged him with her handbag and all three of us burst out laughing. Brandon could always be counted on to break up an awkward moment.

'It's wonderful, Lady Kate,' Brandon continued.

'That's me,' I said quickly. 'And this is my estate!'

'Nice digs,' he joked. 'This is some place. I'd love to shoot a film here. Can we check it out?'

Again I gave the tour. Emma had loaned me a stroller that she'd bought used in the village and I pushed Thomas along as we walked. And once again, no Griff. 'This is frustrating,' I said. 'I wanted you to meet Griff Saunderson, he's the manager of Penwick and he trains all the horses I showed you. You'd love him.'

'Would we?' Marianne asked with a raised eyebrow. 'As much as we're going to love Scott?'

'Of course not!' I smiled. 'You will meet my fiancé tomorrow. Tonight, we're having dinner in. You're going to enjoy Fawn, Emma, and Clive.'

'Yes, you've talked a lot about this Fawn, she sounds special, all right,' Marianne said severely. I knew there was a risk they wouldn't like each other. I knew on some level that Marianne held Fawn responsible for everything that had happened to me. Fawn might find Marianne aloof and prudish. Oh well, they only had to endure each other's company for the weekend.

As we strolled back to the house, I enquired after the magazine, Brandon's latest epic commercial, and, finally, Lucy.

'So, did you break up?' I asked.

He shook his head. 'What makes you ask that?'

'Only that I offered to fly her over and you refused the invite,' I explained. 'What other reason could there be?'

'She's pregnant,' he said and beamed proudly. 'But it's a high-risk pregnancy, the doctor said she can't fly.'

I was stunned. Brandon was going to be a father? I never thought it would happen, certainly not with Lucy.

'Say something, Kate,' Marianne admonished me.

'Congratulations!' I shouted, feeling guilty about not saying it sooner. 'Sorry, I'm in shock! Hope she's okay?'

'Baby and mother are both doing well,' he said. 'Just a no-fly zone.'

'Why didn't you tell me?' I chastised him.

'I didn't want to steal your thunder,' he said. 'This is your big weekend, after all.'

'Yes it is,' I agreed with a laugh.

*　　　*　　　*

I should have been happy; after, all I had everything I wanted. Yet as I sat through an elaborate dinner that Doris had prepared, accompanied, I might add proudly, by two steaming lasagnas baked to perfection by me (without barbecue sauce), surrounded by my closest friends, I felt lonely and sad. I told myself I was missing Scott; if he were

326

here I'd be joyful, bright, and full of energy. But he wasn't here, and I was none of those things. Still determined to appear the happy bride, I tried harder to focus on the dinner conversation to take my mind off my melancholy.

Brandon, Marianne, Clive, Emma, and Fawn had never been in the same room before and it was amazing how they all seemed to get on. Even Marco managed to speak enough English to tell us a funny story about a coffee farm in Africa. In fact, given my state of mind, it was fortunate that the conversation continued without me. They were so fascinated with one another's careers and children and upcoming children that they didn't seem to notice I'd stopped talking.

The night would have continued this way if Griff hadn't strolled into the room unannounced. For the first time since I'd been at Penwick, he wasn't in riding or work clothes, but a dark purple fitted shirt, flat-front black trousers, and patent leather shoes. Shockingly, there was only one word to describe him: stylish. His usually unkempt black hair that I'd grown to like glistened beneath the light of the chandelier and as he stood leaning on the back of an empty chair I noticed that his hands were clean of stable dirt.

'You must be Scott!' Marianne exclaimed with a huge smile and gave me an approving look. 'Kate, your man is a day early! He must love you!'

'Everybody, this is Griffith Saunderson. Griff,' I said in a rush and leapt up to intervene before Marianne went in for a hug and kiss. 'This is a surprise,' I told him but he wouldn't meet my eyes.

'I decided to make sure our guests were settled in.' He smiled cordially. 'And to say hello to Emma

327

and Clive.'

His voice, his expression, his entire demeanor was dark and broody. Not at all like he'd been during the past several weeks. I could only imagine what caused the change because it had changed something in me, too: with my friends here and Scott arriving tomorrow, the wedding was really happening. In two days, I'd be Mrs. Scott Madewell. No longer free to spend hours strolling across Penwick, gabbing about movies and books as Griff taught me things about plants and animals. I felt anxious all of a sudden. I wasn't sure how to handle this new Griff and Kate.

'You know everyone here except Marianne, Brandon, and Marco,' I said through gritted teeth.

'Pleased to meet you,' Griff said quietly and shook their hands.

'So nice to see you again,' Fawn said politely before shooting a warning glare at me. 'There's an empty seat beside me, Griff.' She patted the vacant chair that was farthest from me, obviously determined to keep us as far away from each other as possible. She needn't have bothered; Griff barely looked in my direction. Clearly he was showing me how things between us must be from now on.

'So, you work here?' Marianne asked brightly.

'Yes,' Griff said. 'Hasn't Kate told you? I'm a glorified stable hand.'

'Charming way to earn a living, I'm sure,' Fawn said. 'Keeps you out of trouble.'

'Until Kate showed up, it did,' he said slyly. Fawn looked horrified and made another face at me. I rolled my eyes at her. And even though he spoke my name, he wouldn't so much as glance at me. Then again, why should he be attentive to me? I

328

was marrying another man in two days.

'I want to propose a toast,' Fawn announced suddenly and held up her glass. 'Here's to Kate, who has single-handedly proven that Jane Austen, though long dead, knew a thing or two about snagging a rich husband. And by that, I mean Scott,' she said as her eyes darted from Griff to me.

'What about Austen?' Griff asked Fawn.

'It's a story my magazine assigned Kate months ago,' Marianne explained, a little drunkenly, I might add. 'Our features editor Jennifer had this crazy idea that women could use the same tactics that Austen's characters used to make a good marriage. Kate has been obsessed with those novels her whole life so she was the perfect writer for it. And now look at her! Kate's our modern-day Austen. She set out to make a wise match and played her cards right and here we are.' Marianne grinned widely, then stuck her fork into the leftover lasagna.

Griff said nothing and I felt the urgent need to make light of the subject.

'Jane Austen did create the blueprint for marrying well.' I laughed awkwardly.

'Yes, but in reality she died a spinster,' Griff said, twirling his glass of wine on the table.

'Lighten up, Griff,' Marianne said through her mouthful of lasagna. 'Here's to Kate having her cake and eating it, too! This is delicious.' Marianne continued to dig at her plate. 'And not just the food, but the whole thing. In fact, I could get used to having a rich best friend.'

Everyone laughed but Griff and me. I forced a smile but as the conversation turned to money and being rich, I began to get a bad taste in my mouth.

I gulped my champagne, desperate for it to relax me. The bubbles swirled and popped on my tongue like fireworks, little explosions to take the edge off, I could almost feel the stress lessen with each burst. Then he spoke.

'You've all known the bride-to-be for some time,' began Griff, addressing the room with an authoritative tone I'd not heard from him before. I glanced around the table fearfully; all eyes were transfixed on him. 'So, tell me then: just *who* is Kate? Describe her to me, each of you.'

Silence greeted his direction. I stared at him until finally our eyes met. Neither of us gave away an ounce of emotion but I had never felt more self-conscious in my life.

'Why would you want to know about me?' I practically squeaked.

'I want to know who you are,' he answered firmly. Moments before he wouldn't look at me; now his gaze was so unwavering it forced me to look away.

'To know me is to love me,' I teased, unsure where to look. Still, his eyes never left me.

'Consider me warned,' he said, then turned his attention to the other end of the table. 'Marianne, why don't you start?'

I knew I should rescue my friends from Griff's game, but it was no use. My friends, once recovered from his provocation, took up the challenge with gusto.

'Oooh, this is better than truth or dare,' Marianne said and clapped her hands together. 'Let's start with her fashion sense. She's very into the whole retro 1940s look. Pencil skirts, sweaters, dresses, and heels. Kate very rarely wears trousers or jeans. She's a bit formal that way.'

'I know much of this already,' he said, as though disappointed. 'Would you say she's old-fashioned?'

'Classic,' Brandon countered. 'Kate is a classic.'

'Kate is a true Anglophile,' Brandon continued. 'And not just Austen, but music, movies, you name it. She's a sucker for an accent like yours. In fact, you're lucky she met Scott first. I would have thought you were more her type.'

'Brandon!' I scolded.

'I think what Kate is trying to say is that I'm definitely *not* her type,' Griff corrected him, then turned his ice blue eyes on me once again. 'Nor is she mine. We are merely good friends.'

Fawn coughed. I swallowed hard.

'Yes, good friends,' I agreed and smiled, but he didn't smile back. If I didn't know better, I'd think he was angry with me.

'Kate thinks the fight scene between Colin Firth and Hugh Grant in *Bridget Jones's Diary* is porn,' Marianne said suddenly.

At this everyone laughed, even me.

'They're both so sexy!' I giggled. 'You never know which one to cheer for.'

'She never wanted to get married,' Emma chimed in. 'That's so shocking to us all, that we're here for Kate's *wedding*.'

'She's always been independent,' Brandon added. 'To a fault.'

'That *is* interesting,' Griff said.

'Her father walked out when she was little,' Marianne volunteered. I shot her a scathing look. She grimaced back and continued. 'Her mother never recovered, Kate and her sister, Ann, have had to be the grown-ups. Except for her dear grandmother, of course. Since she died, Kate had to find inventive ways of supporting them all, hence the Austen story for the magazine and of course, Scott.' Marianne took a big chug of wine and looked away from my glare. Why did she feel so compelled to out me in this manner? I could feel Griff staring but I couldn't look at him.

'My grandmother and mother had such unhappy marriages that I didn't want to make the same mistake,' I admitted. 'They couldn't count on any man. I suppose I take after them.'

'Except Scott, of course,' Griff said. 'You can count on him. He must be an exceptional man to change your mind on marriage.'

'Exceptionally rich!' Fawn giggled. But everyone else was silent. I stared down at my plate, thoroughly uncomfortable.

Then Griff took a deep breath and leaned back in his chair. 'Your friends would have me think you're shallow and superficial,' he said coolly.

'She's not!' Marianne leapt to my defense. 'She's extremely loyal. And she looks after everybody, her family and even me. She doesn't even want children, yet she's made sure Thomas has a nanny and all the gear necessary to keep him, and me, happy while we're here.'

'And that makes her thoughtful and considerate,' added Brandon.

'She loves deeply,' Emma said firmly. 'Even unconditionally.'

'Though she's extremely single-minded,' Marianne tossed in half-jokingly. 'Asks for advice but never takes it.'

Griff nodded and silence fell across the room once more.

'Then Scott is a lucky man,' he said at last and sipped his champagne. 'I hope one day to be as fortunate in my choice of wife.'

I glared at him, knowing he was being sarcastic.

'I'm sure you'll meet a lovely country girl to help you run this place for the owners,' Fawn added. It was his turn to glare. Thankfully, Marianne stood up and raised her glass.

'You once asked us if it was too late to marry well,' Marianne said to me with a smile. I felt a pang of horror at what was coming next and made sure not to look at Griff. 'I think we know the answer to your question. Here's to forty and it never being too late, or a woman too old, to have it all!'

More cheers and clinking. I forced myself to laugh along with everyone else but I saw that Griff wasn't laughing. Once again, his eyes wouldn't meet mine.

'I hate to change the subject,' Fawn said brightly.

'Please do,' I begged.

'What are you wearing to your party tomorrow night?'

'There is only one dress that suits the occasion,' I said confidently.

'The Chanel.' Marianne nodded. 'Of course.'

'We can't wait to meet Scott!' Brandon said.

Griff stood up so abruptly his chair went crashing to the floor. He picked it up awkwardly before clearing his throat.

'I have to go check on the horses,' he announced. 'Good night, everyone.'

'Oh, don't leave,' Emma pleaded. 'You just got here.'

'Never come between a man and his work,' Fawn

countered, her own agenda in play. 'If he has to leave, he has to leave.'

'Have a lovely evening,' he said politely.

I gazed at him, expecting, hoping, for some knowing look to be exchanged between us. But there was nothing.

'Will we see you tomorrow night?' Marianne asked. 'At the party or at the wedding on Saturday?'

'I'm going to London on Saturday morning,' he answered and walked out the door.

When he was gone, there was a collective sigh of relief. Then again, it might only have been mine.

'What a strange dude,' Brandon exclaimed.

'He's very handsome,' Marianne said with a smirk. 'And he works here?'

'He's the manager,' Clive said, speaking for the first time in ages.

'My, my,' Marianne joked. 'It's a good thing you're engaged, Kate. Otherwise, you'd have a tough time turning your back on that one.'

'I quite agree,' Fawn chimed in. 'Keep him away until you're married.'

'Don't be ridiculous, Kate hates horses and he's not rich,' Brandon said with a sniff.

Emma coughed. 'I've had too much champagne,' she explained. 'I really shouldn't have any. The baby and all that.'

'One glass now and then won't hurt,' Marianne said calmly.

And then what always happens when women of a certain age are pregnant happened again, the conversation went from my upcoming nuptials and the mysterious Griff Saunderson to baby talk. This time even Brandon joined in. I didn't mind, really. In fact, I was pleased for all of them. It was nice to see people I loved get what they wanted. I only hoped it was the same for me. I was getting married the day after tomorrow and I had only one man on my mind and it wasn't Scott.

*   *   *

I had consumed too much champagne. I knew this because whenever I drink too much I wake up in the middle of the night and can't go back to sleep. That was how I found myself, clad in my nightgown and robe, descending the staircase at 3:00 a.m. I wanted to heat up some milk, even though I detested the taste, as it had been proven to work on more than one occasion. But as I reached the landing, I noticed a light coming from under the mahogany doors to the private wing of the house. The family must have returned home—I was dying to meet a Penwick. I pictured the patriarch, a man in his eighties, rotund and bald, sipping brandy and smoking a pipe, seated in a leather club chair. I tiptoed over and pressed my ear to the door and clasped my fingers around the handle. The doors were heavy and as much as I wanted to pry one open, I daren't.

'What do you think you're doing?'

I nearly screamed. It was Griff.

'You scared me to death!' I began to speak, then quickly brought my voice down to a whisper.

'Answer me,' he persisted. 'Why are you down here?'

He looked me up and down so intently that I drew my robe tighter.

'I couldn't sleep,' I explained and smoothed my hair. 'I came down to get some warm milk.'

He grimaced. I shrugged.

335

'Why are *you* here?' I asked, not wanting to be the only person caught someplace they didn't belong.

He stiffened. 'I sometimes sleep in a spare room beside the kitchen,' he explained.

'I saw the light under the door,' I pointed out, hoping to draw him in. 'Mr. Penwick must be back from London.'

'The light is on a timer,' he said as if I were stupid not to know this. 'It comes on during the night to fool intruders like you.'

My heart sank a little.

'Fine, I'll go to bed,' I said and began to climb the stairs. 'But aren't those Jane Austen first editions in there somewhere?'

'I'd forgotten you knew about them. Now stop being nosy,' he said sharply, the niceness ending as quickly as it had began. 'Be a good little girl and go to bed. Santa will be here in the morning.'

I shot him a dirty look and found I couldn't contain the words any longer. 'Why do you hate me all of a sudden?'

He bristled at this and stood watching me. Feeling brave, I stared back.

'I don't hate you,' he answered finally. 'I never want you to think that.'

I nodded, relieved. 'You've been so terse with me since my friends arrived. You say we're good friends, then tonight and just now you ...' My voice trailed off and I waited for him to finish my sentence. He did.

'Am being unkind?' He smiled. 'I'm sorry if you thought I was angry with you. I'm just not comfortable making nice with strangers.'

I nodded. If I thought about it, he was reverting

336

back to how he'd behaved when I met him. I supposed it didn't have anything to do with his feelings for me. But I still wanted to ask him if he was jealous. I wanted him to admit he was attracted to me without having to admit it myself. But it was all too late. I'd played enough games and I'd won—I was marrying my billionaire. I walked up the stairs, painfully aware that he was still standing at the bottom, watching me.

33

Baby Talk

An engaged woman is always more
agreeable than a disengaged. She is
satisfied with herself. Her cares are over,
and she feels that she may exert all her
powers of pleasing without suspicion.

—*Mansfield Park*

The early morning sun beamed through the double-glazed windowpanes that lined the upstairs hallway. As I glided down the long hall from my bedroom, I carefully placed each high-heeled step along the oriental runner. Silence was vital because I didn't want to wake the others. There was no need for a welcome committee—they would see him soon enough. When I reached the grand staircase, I felt as though I was in a trance. Not surprising, when you consider I tossed and turned all night, reliving the dinner party as well as my 3:00 a.m.

337

conversation with Griff. I blinked several times to try and focus my vision, as well as my mind, but it was no use. There was no antidote to Griff consuming my thoughts. Exhaustion had found its victim and only a Lorazepam and a nap would cure it.

As I reached the landing, I heard the unmistakable sound of car tires crunching on the gravel drive. I flung open the ancient door and ran down the stone steps and into Scott's arms, suddenly very awake and smiling from ear to ear. It was a relief to be so happy to see him and he held me tightly, happily. I clasped my hand in his like a schoolgirl and led him up the stone steps.

'Did you miss me?' he asked as we entered the house. 'I'm sorry I've not been around. I can't believe it's been over a month!'

'You're rotten to have abandoned me like this!' I answered and put my arm around him. 'But I kept busy. Don't you love this place?'

He looked about the entranceway and shrugged. 'As long as you do, that's all that matters.'

My heart sank, but I forced a smile. 'I do like it. It's very *me*.'

He slapped my behind. 'Now, show me to our room.'

'*Your* room,' I corrected him. 'We aren't sharing until after the wedding!'

'Old-fashioned, are we?' He smiled as we climbed the stairs.

'Classic,' I corrected, then felt a shiver run through me. I had to find a way to shake last night from my thoughts.

As soon as we'd dropped off his bags, I gave Scott the tour of Penwick. I was proud of how

338

much of an expert I'd become. It was also a chance to feel close to him again. Our brief time apart had muddled things, but seeing him and touching him gave me back the confidence I had that our marriage was the right decision. The doubts that had arisen over the past few weeks slowly retreated. Until, that is, we finished up our tour at the stables. I knew he'd like to see them, owning polo ponies as he did. But when we got there I was startled to find Griff mucking out stalls. He had always managed to disappear when I'd brought the others. The sight of him made me feel all mixed-up again. It was a state of mind I had to suppress and I willed any thought of attraction from my mind, concentrating on squeezing Scott's hand. As soon as Griff saw us, he put his pitchfork down and, wiping his hands on his jeans, held out his hand to Scott.

'Scott, welcome to Penwick,' he said with some effort at warmth. 'Congratulations on your wedding.'

'Thank you,' Scott said and squeezed my shoulders. 'I've made a wise choice, don't you agree?'

Griff stared at me and for a moment I was afraid of what he'd say, but he smiled politely. 'Yes, very wise.'

'You're welcome to join us for the wedding, you know,' Scott said.

'He has to be in London,' I jumped in.

'Kate's right. I'm wanted elsewhere,' Griff said and looked at me in a way that made me sad.

Scott nodded, then conversation turned to the upcoming polo season, which left me out of the loop entirely. I noticed Ratina poke her head over

339

her stall. I went over to her, then gestured to Scott to follow me.

'This is the horse I've been riding,' I said proudly, stroking her muzzle. 'Her name is Ratina.'

Griff smiled at us. 'She's a good mare.'

Scott ran his eyes up and down the horse. 'What is she?'

'She's a Hanoverian,' Griff said. 'Had two great foals. She was quite the jumper in her day, too.'

'Isn't she pretty?' I asked Scott.

'Sure, nice enough,' he said, as if he were bored. 'Now, let's leave Griff to his work.' He nodded to Griff and walked off toward the house. But I was annoyed. Scott could at least pretend to be interested in what I'd been doing while he was in London working.

'Shouldn't you follow your fiancé?' Griff said matter-of-factly.

'I'll do as I like,' I snapped, then realized I was taking out my frustration on the wrong man.

'That you will,' Griff snapped back and marched away toward the barn, leaving me standing there alone. I looked at Scott, off in the distance, seemingly unaware that I wasn't with him, and back at the barn where Griff had vanished. I stamped my foot hard on the ground. Ratina threw her head back in protest.

'Sorry, girl,' I said and stroked her face. 'It's not about you. But I'm beginning to wonder *who* it is about.'

*   *   *

Fortunately, the rest of the day went more smoothly. Fawn, Emma, and Clive got reacquainted

340

with Scott while Marianne, Brandon, and Marco were introduced to him. We lunched in the morning room and had a lot of laughs. Scott regaled everyone with zany stories of polo in Dubai and sailing off the Ivory Coast. I insisted he tell them more about his charity work in Malaysia and this impressed them all quite a bit. But by 2:00 p.m. he announced that he had work to do and would need to be holed up in his room for a few hours, so after a swift kiss on my head he was gone.

Marianne took me aside and said very graciously, 'Maybe I was wrong to be so critical.'

'Were you being critical?' I teased.

'Oh, stop it. I just want to say that Scott is handsome and charming; I'd imagine you'd be with him even if he wasn't a billionaire.' She smiled. And I, of course, smiled back as if she were correct, although deep down I could sense the cracks were beginning to widen.

It was just the three of us, Marianne, Emma, and me, Thomas asleep in his stroller. Fawn had decided to go into the village with Marco in search of antiques. Clive had offered to drive Brandon around the countryside to point out famous sites that had been used for filming. Naturally, when left to our own devices, the three of us headed straight to my room and began to inspect my new wardrobe, courtesy of Scott.

'Oooh, I'm loving your spoils of romantic war. This is Lanvin!' Marianne gushed and pulled an emerald green dress off its hanger and held it up in front of her. 'Can I try it on?'

'Of course!' I laughed. 'It will be like old times.' Recalling our former habit of invading department stores and trying on designer clothes we couldn't

341

possibly afford, I explained this to Emma. She wasn't obsessed with fashion like Marianne and I were.

'That sounds fun but kind of depressing,' she said. 'I can't even window-shop. It makes me sad to look at things I can't have.'

Marianne shrugged and began to strip down as Emma examined my new set of Louis Vuitton luggage. 'You've got everything but the steamer trunk,' she exclaimed.

'It's coming next week,' I confessed sheepishly.

She nodded. This must be so difficult for her, I thought. Mere months ago she had plenty of money and beautiful things and now she had very little.

'Sorry, I shouldn't be so obnoxious about my stuff.' I waved my hands across my closet. 'I'm being insensitive again.'

She shook her head dismissively. 'I never went in for designer clothes, as you know,' she said with a wry grin and indicated her trademark jeans. 'I'm perfectly fine with what I have—Clive and this baby.' She patted her tummy, even though she wasn't showing yet. 'In fact, I'm very happy.'

I smiled gratefully to her. Emma always liked things to be simple. I wish I had more of that quality in me.

'I can't zip it up!' Marianne moaned in frustration. 'I haven't lost all the baby weight.'

'You look great,' I said and helped her out of the Lanvin.

'We used be able to wear each other's clothes,' she fumed to Emma. 'And now look at me. This will happen to you, too!'

'I'm not worried,' Emma said sweetly.

Marianne stepped into the closet and examined

342

every item and every label like the fashion editor she was. 'Tell me, does Scott have a brother?' she asked. 'I think I could learn to be a rich wife, too.'

'I think Frank would be upset if I set you up.' I laughed, assuming she was teasing. She wasn't.

'Frank is a good man. But we can barely afford our co-op,' she said ominously. 'We make okay money, it's true. But we want Thomas to go to a private school and you know what that costs in Manhattan.'

Emma and I nodded, even though neither of us knew.

'Just promise me when you're back in New York you'll take me shopping with you! If I can't be rich, the next best thing is a rich best friend,' Marianne said with a wink. 'I can shop vicariously, and if Kate wants to treat me to the odd thing, then that's fine, too.' Marianne rested her arm on me and laughed as if to say she was kidding, only I don't think she was. I knew money would change things and it can change people, but I thought that by marrying Scott the only person who would be altered would be me.

'Thomas!' Marianne shrieked suddenly. Emma and I whirled around, expecting that he had fallen out of the stroller and was knocked unconscious. Instead, he was sitting there happily gnawing on the leather strap of my LV envelope handbag. 'You can't chew Louis Vuitton!' She pried the strap from his mouth, but he began to wail like the world was ending.

'It's okay,' I said hoping to calm her down. 'It's just a purse.'

'Just a purse! It's expensive,' she cried and tried to settle Thomas. 'I wasn't paying enough attention. I think he ruined it.'

343

I examined the strap; it was gooey and a bit gummed down, but otherwise okay.

'It's fine; besides, Scott can buy me another one,' I said to lighten the mood. 'It's not as if I've saved up for months to buy it.'

Then it hit me. All the beautiful clothes and accessories I had in my possession didn't have any special meaning for me. They had all been bought by Scott. He had given me so much, but none of it felt like it belonged to me. I was overcome by the realization that there was something to be said for earning your own life of luxury, even if luxury meant different things for different women. The freedom I've always craved and managed to have in one way or another was luxury to me. I had avoided being married or taking a full-time job so I could be in control of my life, be independent, and not rely on anyone. And now I had sold that freedom to Scott. I shook my head, staggered by what I was thinking. What a terrible way to look at my marriage!

'I'm going to take Thomas for a walk,' I announced with a note of anxiety in my voice that I couldn't hide. I needed to get away to clear my head. 'You stay here and play dress-up.'

As I was leaving, I heard Marianne rummage in the closet.

'Emma, try this on,' she instructed, holding up a plum chiffon dress. 'You're still skinny, for now.'

*   *   *

I was thankful for the escape and pushed Thomas along Penwick's now familiar footpaths. What had gotten into me all of a sudden? It must be wedding jitters. I was getting what I wanted. I would be rich and be married to a wonderful man. I could do amazing things with his money. I would be a philanthropist and help people. It wouldn't all be shopping. And yet, and yet . . .

We ended up at the stables and I picked Thomas up from his stroller and held him so he could meet Ratina. She stuck her nose out above her stall door and I took the little boy's hand and gently stroked her muzzle. He laughed and tried to reach out again. Ratina was extremely patient and held still for him to pet her. Thomas giggled once more and I laughed, too, and kissed his buttery-smooth cheek. He really was a sweet baby.

'You'd make a great mother.' It was Griff. He had been watching us.

'I don't think so,' I said shyly.

'Why not?' he asked, puzzled.

'I don't know,' I said and realized I didn't have a real reason. 'I like to travel and be free to do what I want. A baby needs stability.'

Griff pondered this for a moment and then said, 'Maybe that's because what you're missing is a reason to be still.'

Thomas squeezed my finger and I smiled. 'I don't normally hold babies, or baby-sit,' I admitted. 'But he's Marianne's and he feels like family to me.' I realized then how much I missed Ann and wished she were here. Part of me also missed Iris and now regretted my decision not to include her. It was for the best, I reminded myself. Soon she would know the reason for my detachment.

'Life can be quiet, Kate,' Griff said and stroked Thomas's head. 'Love doesn't have to be explosive twenty-four/seven. If you'd slow down long enough, you might be happy.'

I ignored his comment as there was no proper response, and was content to watch as Thomas stroked Ratina once again and giggled even more. We both laughed.

'He's a natural horseman.' Griff smiled.

I kissed the baby's head. 'I'd better get him back to his mother,' I said and put him back in the stroller.

'Before you go, I need to know one thing,' Griff said with an abrupt note of seriousness. I stopped and waited. 'I can't stop thinking about the dinner conversation last night. This whole charade of yours, chasing after Scott, pretending to be a lady, is all for an article?'

I felt my shoulders slump. It did sound bad the way he said it. 'It started off that way,' I admitted, forcing myself to look at him. 'I was just going to write a story, but then I realized I could do it. I could be like Elizabeth Bennet and fall for the wealthy man and marry him and have it all and I did. And I needed to.'

'What do you mean, "needed to"? I know you've told me you're broke, but this seems extreme.'

'It's complicated,' I said and fussed over Thomas to distract myself. 'And I never wanted to tell you about the article because you're English—Austen belongs to England. I didn't think you'd like an American co-opting one of your literary stars.'

'Austen belongs to everyone,' he corrected me. 'Though I admit it wouldn't be something an English girl would likely attempt. You Americans take a lot of, shall we say, creative license?'

I bristled at this. 'It's a fun idea; loads of girls back home would benefit from a better

346

understanding of what it means to make a good marriage and—'

'Yes, yes, I get it. So, you fell in love with Scott and the article is—'

'Not written yet,' I said, choosing to ignore the fact that I wasn't in love with my fiancé. 'I guess I'll finish it after the wedding. Not that I need the money now.' I smiled faintly.

'What does your fiancé think of your writing a self-help guide with him as one of the case studies?' he smirked.

My stomach lurched.

'He doesn't know yet, so please don't tell him!'

'He doesn't know?' He grunted.

'It hasn't come up, but I will tell him. I'll let him read the first draft and if there's anything in it he's uncomfortable with, then I'll edit it out,' I said rapidly, thinking on my feet. 'He'll find it amusing, I'm sure.'

'You appear to have it all worked out. But if I were him, I'd want no part in a Jane Austen Marriage Manual,' he said icily.

Good title, I thought, filing it away. But he wasn't finished.

'Though you should know that Elizabeth Bennet was not so calculating in her choice of husband,' he added.

'I have to go get dressed for the party,' I said and pushed the stroller and Thomas away. So much for my escape.

34

It's My Party

And I have nothing to regret ... nothing
but my own folly.

—Sense and Sensibility

I once again slipped into my Chanel dress, now as
comforting as an old slipper, a very expensive old
slipper. I stood in front of a gilt-edged mirror and
examined my reflection. The dress was as elegant as
ever, but something was missing, and I knew what. I
picked up the pearl necklace that Ann had given me
at Christmas and did up the clasp. There. Perfect. I
was ready for anything.

A knock on my door told me that it was time.
Sure enough, Scott stood on the threshold in his
bespoke tuxedo and held out his arm for me.

'Darling,' he grinned.

I swallowed hard and forced a smile. I was
suddenly afraid to leave my room. Nothing seemed
real—it was as though I were an imposter about to
be unmasked, which wasn't too far from the truth.
Scott gently kissed my forehead as if he understood.

'Don't worry,' he said softly. 'You're with me.'

I smiled up at him and tried to relax as we
descended the staircase and entered the ballroom.
My eyes widened at the room's altered appearance.
It had been given the wedding planner treatment;
everywhere were flowers and ribbons in my
colors of blush pink and white. Peonies and roses

practically leapt out of vases and urns. Candelabras lit the entire ballroom, their flames emitting warmth in all directions. The room was packed with people. I scanned the crowd for familiar faces and realized that I had only my small entourage—none of whom were visible at the moment—and that the rest belonged to Scott.

'You invited a ton of people,' I said with panic.

'Don't be shy, you've met most of them, they're mainly business associates,' he explained nonchalantly as he paraded me through the sea of middle-aged men and women. He was right, most of the people I had met before over endless lunches and dinners and they greeted us enthusiastically. There was lots of 'Kate, we're so happy you met Scott . . .' and 'Scott needed a wife with a touch of class,' or my very favorite, 'You're such an improvement on that Slovenian girl, thank God he didn't marry *her*.' It wasn't long before my nerves faded and my confidence returned. I was about to become a permanent member of Team Madewell and I had to enjoy it. But as I stood surrounded by well-wishing strangers, I wondered if Scott's crowd would consume my life as it had done in London. The thought made me want to be with my friends—people who knew me, the real me. I politely excused myself and went in search of my gang, who weren't exactly tough to locate. All I had to do was find the bar.

'You look gorgeous,' Brandon said and kissed me gently on the lips.

Clive shook his head and gestured to Scott. 'Does he ever stop working?'

'I was surprised he'd invited so many people,' I admitted, and seeing Scott scan the room for me, ducked behind my friends to avoid detection. 'All clients and financial types.'

'That's not the only type he invited,' Fawn scoffed and pointed to a far corner. I turned around and my jaw dropped.

'Tatiana!' I said in disbelief.

'Who is she?' Marianne asked. 'And *what* is she wearing?'

'That's his ex,' I said stiffly. Tatiana was wearing the shortest minidress I'd ever seen, and worse it also had a plunging neckline. '*Tsk, tsk,*' Marianne said in her best fashion editor voice. 'You should never show that much leg *and* that much boob at the same time.'

'Yes,' agreed Emma. 'One or the other, never both.'

But Clive, Brandon, and Marco couldn't stop staring. Clearly, they weren't offended by Tatiana's crime of fashion. Emma eventually stepped on Clive's toe.

'Why would he invite her?' I asked, puzzled and angry.

'Don't look now,' Fawn advised. 'But she's coming this way.'

Sure enough, Tatiana was moving toward us, swaying her hips and running her hands through her hair like she was in a music video.

'She's going to knock someone over swinging those hips like that,' Brandon said with a gulp.

'Pick your tongue up off the floor,' Marianne snapped.

Then we were face-to-face.

'Hello, Kate,' Tatiana purred. 'Congratulations.'

'Hello, Tatiana,' I said with fake warmth. 'So nice of you to make it.'

'So nice of you to invite me,' she said.

The girl had nerve.

'I didn't,' I said honestly and tried to sound snooty.

She looked surprised. 'But Scott said you wanted me here,' she said, dismayed. 'I would not have come otherwise.'

No one knew where to look, least of all me.

'Well, you're here now,' Fawn said, smiling. 'What are you drinking?' With that, she escorted Tatiana out of my field of vision and to the bar.

'That bastard!' I seethed. 'Why would he invite her and not ask me first?'

'She looks harmless,' Clive piped up.

We women rolled our eyes. 'She looks many things and harmless isn't one of them,' I said.

'Are you going to say anything to Scott?' Emma asked.

My mind raced over the past month. Who knew what he had been up to in London? All those weekends he was too busy to visit me? All this time I was feeling guilty about Griff and he'd been spending time with Tatiana or at least talking to her enough to invite her to my wedding.

I spotted Scott in a small circle of people, puffing on a cigar.

'I'll be right back,' I said staunchly and marched over to him. 'Can I speak with you a moment?'

'My fiancée needs me,' he said, grinning at his friends.

Once we were out of earshot, I whispered angrily, 'What were you thinking, inviting Tatiana?'

'She's a friend,' he said with feigned seriousness. 'Besides, I thought you liked her.'

'She doesn't belong at my wedding,' I insisted.

351

'It's my wedding, too,' he reminded me coldly. 'She called me when she got back from Slovenia, poor kid, she doesn't know many people in England, so I invited her. Big deal.'

I was fuming but it was clear that I wasn't going to get any real answers. Not now. Just then Marianne interrupted, trying to stop the situation from getting worse.

'Excuse me,' she said politely. 'Brandon has taken over DJ duties and he'd like you two to dance.'

We looked over and saw that Brandon had indeed taken up the post at the DJ table. He waved as the old jazz standard 'A Sunday Kind of Love' came over the speaker system. Scott rolled his eyes.

'I don't dance,' he said firmly and smiled. 'Now, I have to get back to those people. I handle millions of their dollars and they deserve a little face-to-face time.'

'But what about me?' I stammered. 'Don't I deserve it?'

'They have real concerns about their financial statements,' he said angrily, implying my concerns weren't real. 'It's my responsibility to ease their stress.' Then he walked away leaving me there to fume; this was our first fight and I wasn't winning. I became aware that I was standing there like a fool but I didn't know what to do next—run after him or run away from him? I felt a hand on my shoulder. 'Marianne, I need to be alone,' I began but a man's voice cut me off.

'May I have this dance?'

I turned to find Griff standing in front of me wearing a tuxedo.

'I have to get another drink.' Marianne smiled

352

and scurried off.

I stared at him in disbelief. I hadn't expected him to show up, let alone ask me to dance.

'I thought you'd be in London by now,' I stammered.

'Tomorrow,' he said.

'But don't you have to pack?' I asked stupidly.

'I'm not a fashion plate like you are, remember? Or so you keep saying.' He smiled. His hair, though slicked back, still managed to fall across one eye. There was something wild about his appearance that unnerved me: something dangerous and glamorous at the same time. 'The song will be over before you answer me.'

'Yes, I'd love to.' I smiled reluctantly.

'A Sunday Kind of Love' is without a doubt one of my favorite songs of all time. Brandon wasn't holding back. I looked over to see if he knew it wasn't Scott he was inspiring. Brandon nodded and grinned. He knew, all right. I should explain that 'A Sunday Kind of Love' is a romantic ballad that I'm sure was the 1940s equivalent to 'Stairway to Heaven,' with lyrics that were impossible to ignore. The words spoke of a love that went beyond one night and that first blush of romance, a love that endured beyond Saturday date night and into the reality of Sunday.

As the song played I was suddenly all nerves and self-consciousness and couldn't bear to look at Griff, so instead I buried my head in his shoulder, which didn't help because it reminded me how good it felt to be this close to him. I tried to distract myself by being thankful he didn't smell like the barn, but it was no use. Then the song ended. As the music faded, I worked up the nerve to look at

353

Griff. He gazed back and the corners of his lips curled up ever so slightly into a smile. Both of us stood there, motionless and speechless, but still holding on to each other. I knew he wanted to kiss me, and worse, I wanted to kiss him. The fight with Scott was affecting my judgment. Any concern about what we might do vanished very quickly. Remember what I said about Brandon's talent for breaking up awkward moments? Out blasted Tony Bennett singing 'Rags to Riches,' all about love making you feel rich, like a millionaire. That did it. Griff and I leapt apart as if we were on fire.

'I have to get back to my friends,' I blurted out awkwardly and practically ran away. I needed a drink and fast. Oh God, no matter how much I'd tried to deny it, I was still attracted to Griff. I grabbed a glass of champagne and drank it like water. What was I going to do? Loads of people repressed feelings for one person in order to marry another, I was sure of it. I couldn't think of Griff, not now, not ever. Scott would take care of me. He didn't still love Tatiana. She was just a friend. I was being petty. I repeated the above over and over as I drank and drank.

The party continued and I was quite drunk as I circulated among the guests, avoiding Tatiana. I had watched Griff sitting next to Clive and Emma. He was no mingler. I supposed that was expected, they were his only true friends in the room. I slumped onto a sofa next to the rest of my group and sighed heavily.

'I think you've had enough,' Brandon said and pulled a half-empty glass from my hand.

'They call it a cup of courage,' I slurred.

'You have enough courage by now,' Fawn added.

Before I could protest any further, the

unmistakable sound of silverware clinking crystal reverberated around the room. The crowd parted and in the center was Scott, a cigar in one hand, a champagne flute in the other. He had brought the room to silence.

'Go to him,' Fawn said and gently pushed me forward. Everyone's eyes were on me as I walked toward him. The loud echo my heels made on the hardwood made me quicken my pace awkwardly.

'There you are,' Scott called out and grabbed me by the waist so that I was practically in his lap. The smoke was too much for me and I swatted it away.

'She's not a fan of my cigars! But you'll have to get used to them, sweetheart!' He laughed, and the crowd laughed uncomfortably. It was obvious he was drunk, even more than I was. I'd never seen him like this and I didn't like it. 'But when true love happens, what's there to complain about?'

He clutched me to him and kissed me hard on the lips. The crowd applauded awkwardly. I couldn't breathe, his grip was so tight, and the smoke so powerful, I could feel myself struggling to get free. At last he let me go and I stumbled, teetering on my heels. I wiped my mouth as subtly as I could and as I did I spotted Griff, not six feet away, staring at me with an expression I couldn't put my finger on. Was it pity?

'To my fiancée,' Scott said triumphantly and raised his glass, but as he did so the cigar dropped from his hand and fell toward me. I tried to catch it. But my reflexes were too slow and I missed. The cigar struck my thigh and instantly burned through my dress and singed my flesh. I gasped, but it wasn't because of physical pain. It was the hole in my Chanel dress that caused the agony.

355

The room went deathly silent. I quickly brushed off the ashes but it was no use—seared through the fabric was a hole the size of a quarter. I stared at it in disbelief. I looked up at Scott. He was still grinning. My whole body shaking, I ran my hand over the hole and poked my finger inside. I could feel skin. The cigar had burned through the wool and right through the silk lining. My Chanel dress was ruined. The dress *my grandmother* had bought me. The dress we had fought over, and made up over, and that I treasured dearly because it reminded me of her. Now it was destroyed. I stood like a statue, not knowing what I should do next, when all of a sudden I sniffled, once, then again. It was as though I was struck by a sudden head cold. Another sniffle. Then I knew I was crying, tears were streaming down my face, salty and hot. They ran into my mouth and down my neck. I hadn't cried in months and now I couldn't stop. Scott's voice boomed, cutting through the silence.

'Don't be silly, my dear,' he said with a laugh. 'It's just a dress. We can buy you a new one.'

That did it. I began to sob uncontrollably. 'My grandmother bought me this dress,' I cried. 'It can't be replaced.'

'You're over reacting!' he snapped and grabbed my arm again and whispered angrily. 'Stop behaving like a child. You're embarrassing me.'

He had never spoken to me like that before. I wanted to snatch my arm away but I didn't have to; someone else had my arm and was pulling me free. I watched Scott shrug in defeat and turned and saw Griff leading me away and then the ballroom door closed behind me.

'Put your arms around my neck,' Griff said

356

gently, just as he had after my accident. I did as I was told, only this time I did it without objection. He lifted me up and carried me down the long hallway, past the great room and morning room and dining room until we were in the entranceway. But we didn't stop there, nor did he carry me upstairs to my room. Instead, he kept walking until we reached the mahogany doors. He put me down and, taking a key from his pocket, opened the lock. The huge door creaked open, revealing an enormous library with floor-to-ceiling built-in bookcases, oriental rugs, leather armchairs, and a ruby red fainting couch.

'I thought we weren't allowed in here,' I said through tears. 'I don't want to get you into trouble.'

Griff didn't answer. He led me to the sofa and there I sat and watched as he locked us in, then went to a sideboard where there were glasses and decanters and poured two glasses of wine before taking up residence in one of the leather club chairs opposite me.

'Drink this,' he said and handed me a glass. 'It will do you good.'

I nodded and sipped. It was a full-bodied cabernet; its strong taste warmed me up. We sat in uneasy silence. Where was Brandon when I needed him? Even though my tears had dried, I didn't know what to say, so I turned my attention to the room. It was spectacular, more so than any other in the house. But I was struck mostly by the color of the walls. They were a dusty pinkish grey; it was soothing in an all too familiar way.

'My bedroom was painted a similar color,' I explained. 'It was called . . .'

'Smoked Trout,' Griff finished my sentence.

357

'This room has been this color for nearly three hundred years. Farrow and Ball took samples for their reproduction.'

I looked at him in disbelief. 'Are you serious?'

'Englishmen don't joke about heritage paint.' He grinned.

'Wow, I knew Penwick was important.' I smiled then laughed. 'Obviously more important than the name of a paint.'

He smiled graciously and beckoned me to follow him to the bookcase, where he grabbed a very old volume and placed it in my hands.

'First edition of *Pride and Prejudice*, as promised.' He smiled.

I gasped. I couldn't believe it. I carefully opened the cover and read the date of publication—1813— and clutched it to my chest.

'Not so fast,' he teased. 'It doesn't leave the room.'

I smiled innocently.

'You can visit it anytime,' he said. 'Read it in this room, if you like.'

'Is this the library where Mr. Penwick reads?' I asked and sat back down with the first edition on my lap. 'When he's here, that is.'

Griff sighed in exasperation.

'There is no Mr. Penwick,' he said bluntly.

'There isn't?' I was confused. 'Doris said the family still lived here, in these rooms, when there wasn't an annoying wedding going on.'

'She's right,' he said with a mixture of seriousness and anxiety in his voice, as if he didn't want to tell me something but knew he had to. 'The eldest son lives here mostly, the others only occasionally. But the name isn't Penwick. That's the name of the

358

estate.'

'You told me the family was Penwick,' I said, confused.

'I made it up,' he said with a guilty look on his face.

'Why would you do that?' I asked.

'Privacy, I guess,' he said simply. 'The name of English estates isn't always the same as the family name.'

'I knew that,' I said, trying not to sound foolish. Then holding the book up for added emphasis, 'I mean, Mr. Darcy lived in Pemberley, not Darcy Manor. Oh God!' I stared at Griff. He took a deep breath. Oh God, why hadn't I thought of it before? 'What is the name of the family who lives here?' I asked even though I knew the answer.

'Saunderson,' he said and smiled sheepishly.

I blinked several times, letting this development sink in. 'You mean?' I stumbled over the words. 'You're the, the, the . . . ?'

'Yes, to answer your almost question. I'm the heir of the estate.' He stood up and held his hand out for me to take. 'The Eleventh Earl of Penwick, at your service.'

I placed my hand in his and he bowed and kissed it. I laughed.

'I can't believe it.' I giggled. 'Am I the only one who didn't know?'

'It seems that way,' he said. 'That was the secret I asked Scott to keep. And obviously he's a man of his word.'

'Oh, fuck,' I swore, suddenly horrified. 'I said you were gay!'

'I know,' he said wryly.

'Well, we both know that rumor didn't catch

359

on,' I said. 'I still can't believe it. Not even Clive or Emma said a thing. Wait until Fawn finds out.'

'Yes, Fawn may approve of me now.'

I smiled. No doubt he was right about that; a real aristocrat would make her bend the rules a bit.

'Though I don't fit into your scheme. You see, the Saunderson family may own Penwick, but we are without a fortune. Quite nearly broke, I'm afraid. When my father died I inherited the title and Penwick and all its debt. My younger brother works in the City, and my sister is a jewelry designer. I run this place as a tourist trap.'

I was stunned. 'You must do well hosting weddings and things,' I said hopefully.

He shook his head. 'We manage to make ends meet, but you've seen the state of things. Penwick needs to make much more money to maintain it, never mind renovate it.'

'So all this time when I've been pretending to have money and pass myself off as Lady Kate, you've pretended not to be Earl of Penwick?'

'People treat you differently when you have a title,' he said with a smile. 'I never much cared for special treatment. And just so you know, one of the keys to behaving like you're from old money is never to talk about money.'

'Gotcha,' I said and felt my face flush. 'Were you afraid I'd chase after you if I knew who you were?' I asked, knowing the answer.

'Yes, and for all the wrong reasons,' he admitted. 'I didn't want it to be because you thought I was rich, which I'm not.'

I nodded. Thinking, sadly, he had a point. I looked down at my dress, at the hole in the skirt, and a wave of sadness hit me again. He saw my

360

expression and put his hand over mine.

'Doris might be able to mend it,' he said softly and studied me as if I were a painting. 'She's a wonder at invisible mending.'

I sat quietly, still fingering the hole, remembering when I'd bought it and all the years it had hung unworn in my closet. Strange, it was one of the longest relationships I'd ever had.

'Tell me about your dress,' he said gently.

'My grandmother bought it for me,' I began. 'She died a few months ago.' I drew in a deep breath, feeling another crying fit coming on. 'She was like a mother to me. I miss her.'

And cry I did, and through my tears I told Griff everything, including how my mother's gambling had cost me my home. He listened and when I was done he brought me a box of tissues. I blew my nose and wiped my eyes. I was sure I looked frightful.

'So, that's why you're marrying Scott?' he asked. 'It wasn't just a lark.'

I nodded.

'You're grief stricken,' he said sympathetically. 'Now I understand.'

'Why does everyone say that?' I snapped, fed up with everyone telling me why I felt as I did.

'Because it's true,' he explained. 'It's not a sign of weakness, you know. Losing the person you loved most in the world isn't a cold that works through your system.'

'I just want to feel normal again,' I said simply. 'I want to be happy.'

As if that were a cue, Griff took my hand and pulled me up out of the chair toward him. I closed my eyes and felt his soft but firm lips on mine and we kissed, a lot, and I didn't try to stop him. As

361

our kissing became more and more passionate he lifted me up and pinned me against the bookcase. I opened my eyes briefly; we were smack up against the entire volume of Jane Austen's first editions. I giggled and kissed him harder.

Then suddenly, he stopped.

'What's wrong?' I asked.

'We should break the news to Scott that you're not marrying him,' he said.

'I'm not?' I answered and pushed myself free.

'Kate,' Griff said with a smile. 'It's obvious; we're in love.'

I was stunned that the words came so easily to him. 'In love?' I repeated, astounded.

He looked at me, puzzled and disappointed. 'Are you saying you don't feel the same way?'

'I don't know,' I said. The overwhelming thing I felt was confusion. 'I've avoided you for months. Half the time we seem to dislike each other, the other half—'

'That is true,' he admitted and reached out to touch me but I pulled away.

'The wedding, the guests,' I stammered. 'It's too much.'

'You can't stand there and suggest you're going to marry him tomorrow?'

I stood stock still. I didn't know what I was doing, or feeling. The conflict welled up so vehemently I wanted to scream. Somewhere deep down my intuition was searching for its voice but the struggle against the months of single-minded plotting ensured it remained silent.

'I've come this far.'

'Kate, I've seen boatloads of gold-digging women in my time. I've even had a few take a swipe at me

362

just to get their hands on my title,' he said bluntly. 'You're not one of them.'

'Are you so sure about that?' I spoke in a strained voice. 'You don't understand what marrying Scott means to me. You couldn't, you have Penwick; even if you're not rich, you've grown up knowing who you are, who your family is and knowing that no matter what this is your home.

'Marrying for money isn't all about buying things, Griff. You know what having money means? Independence. When I'm rich I don't have to rely on anyone for anything. Who cares if Scott divorces me in a year? I'll be free and able to live how I want and no one will be able to hurt me again.'

He recoiled at my words. 'There's nothing wrong with relying on people,' he argued. 'You can rely on me, on your friends, your family . . .'

'Family? You mean my father who ran off, or my mother who gambled away my home? No thank you, I'll rely on me. I have to go,' I said firmly. 'Scott will be wondering where I am. I owe him an apology.'

'You're not who I thought you were,' Griff said sadly.

'Tonight I'm Lady Kate,' I answered. 'Tomorrow I'll be Kate Madewell.'

Not waiting for a response, I walked out and closed the heavy door behind me as though it were a secret passage to a place that didn't exist in the real world, or at least not in mine.

* * *

I should have raced around Penwick desperately seeking Scott but that's not what happened. It

363

was as though the hole in my dress had released months of pent-up emotions, and the realization of what I was doing and Griff's words had shaken me to the core. I was in no condition to see Scott. What I needed was time alone to think things through. Slowly I climbed the staircase, then inched along the hall, dragging my feet to my room. Once locked safely behind its door, I perched on top of the window seat and sat there, staring blankly at the damask curtains. When some time had passed, and no right answer had come, I couldn't delay any longer and I called him. Within seconds I heard the familiar cell phone ring and peered through the curtains and down onto the terrace, where we were to be married. There was Scott, standing alone as he reached into his pocket.

'Where are you?' he said grimly, staring off into the dark woods.

'I'm in my room,' I answered and gazed down at him. He made for a lonely figure, stranded on the stone slabs, whispering into the night air. 'I'm so sorry. I wish I had a better explanation, but the champagne, the crowd, my dress, I just had a meltdown.' He stood breathing into the phone, completely unaware he was being watched and paced back and forth as if contemplating jumping off the terrace, which was ridiculous since the stone steps were probably less than two feet high. I waited, wanting him to get angry, waiting for the wrath I deserved. But instead, he was calm.

'Are you all right now?' he asked.

'I'm fine. Can you forgive me?' I responded warily, feeling the tears that had vanished for months return all too easily tonight. 'I still want to marry you.' I thought my voice sounded unconvincing and again, I watched for his reaction.

'Okay then,' he said. 'Do you want me to come see you now?'

Relief swept over me and I forced a smile, even though he couldn't see it, I wanted him to sense it. 'No, that can't happen. It's after midnight and it's bad luck for the groom to see the bride before the wedding.'

'Kate, don't be superstitious,' he said.

I flinched a little. I needed to take advantage of superstitions, no matter how I hated them.

'I'm not superstitious, I just want tomorrow to be perfect,' I pleaded and traced his silhouette on the glass with my finger. Before he answered, a shadow crept across the terrace and he turned and extended his hand toward it. Like a panther on the hunt, Tatiana strolled sinuously across the stone. She took his hand and in one stride she was in his arms and stroking his face as though he were a wounded child. I couldn't pry my eyes away, yet as I watched I only felt numb where jealous rage should be.

'I'll see you at the altar,' I said coolly.

He hung up without another word. I stared down at them as they strolled away like lovers and returned into the belly of the house. If I listened carefully I would probably hear their footsteps coming to his room. I went to the door and pressed my ear on the keyhole like a vaudevillian actor in a detective skit. And there they were, faint footsteps marching toward my door. I braced myself, expecting the thump of Scott's size-thirteen brogues, followed by the patter of Tatiana's paws, I mean platforms, to pass swiftly by when there was a bang on my door. I leapt upright.

'Kate? Are you there?'

It was Marianne. I took a deep breath and opened the door a crack. Marianne, Fawn, Emma, and the others were gathered outside my room.

'Are you okay? We were worried sick,' Fawn said breathlessly.

Seeing their alarmed faces, I softened my lips into a smile. 'Look, I had my freakout. I'm fine now. But what I really need is my beauty sleep.'

'Have you seen Scott?' Fawn asked, I thought with a hint of suspicion. 'Is he here with you?'

'He's in his room,' I said dismissively, half expecting him and Tatiana to hoof it by us any moment. 'We made up. The wedding is still on but I'm going to bed. Good night and I'm sorry you were all so worried.'

I shut the door on their anxious faces and raced over to the window in case Scott had returned, but the terrace was as empty as a vacant parking lot. I hoped none of my friends would find them together. A few moments later I heard another set of footsteps and ran to the keyhole in time to see Scott walking alone to his room, turn his key, and close the door behind him. He must have put Tatiana into a cab. With bewildered relief, I flopped on my bed and stared up at the ceiling in the dark. It was going to be a long night.

35

Family Fortune

> But when a young lady is to be a heroine.... Something must and will happen to throw a hero in her way.
>
> —*Northanger Abbey*

The first time I encountered heartbreak was the night my father left. I was four and have only the slightest memory of Iris's hysterical wails in the darkness as my grandmother tried to soothe me to sleep. The second, I remember more vividly. It was after Ann's first boyfriend broke up with her. It was late and far beyond the bedtime of a twelve-year-old like me, but as I soon discovered there is nothing quiet or still about a teenage girl's broken heart. When Ann came home, sobbing, stomping, and slamming about, she woke us all. Bleary-eyed, I wandered into the living room and sat on the floor as Nana and Iris consoled Ann and railed against the injustice of her being dumped.

'Peter is a fool to listen to his parents,' Nana said critically. 'You're every bit as good as they are.'

As Ann cried, the story flowed with the tears that Peter had been told to break up with her because his family didn't approve of the relationship. His father was a very successful real estate developer who owned shopping malls and condo towers and preferred his son to date girls from the local private school.

As I listened, half-asleep, to the drama unfold, it never occurred to me that Ann would probably have her heart broken many more times in the course of her life. All the fuss convinced me that this was a once in a lifetime event.

But that night stood out for another reason. Ignoring me as I slumped on the floor, my head on a sofa cushion, my grandmother told Ann about a man named Mitchell.

They had met during the Great Depression at a neighborhood cafe. My grandmother worked across the street in a dress shop and once a week, as a treat, she'd sit at the counter and order coffee and a sandwich. Mitchell was from some industrial city like Pittsburgh. He was in New York visiting a cousin and he asked Nana out the first time he saw her. He took her to a movie, even picked her up in a convertible that belonged to a relative. My grandmother still lived at home with her mother and stepfather, who were very strict, and she lied to them about where she was going and who she was going with. 'Mitch was a sweet boy,' she told us. 'We went out together for weeks. He'd pick me up after work and we'd walk in the park, or go to the movies, even went out dancing once or twice. But then he was to go back home.' She got a sad look on her face and her lip trembled, only slightly, and she continued. 'Our last night together he asked me to marry him.' At this, I sat up and rubbed my eyes hard to stay awake.

'Our plan was simple. He would return in two

weeks and meet me at the train station, we'd get married at city hall, and I'd go home to Pittsburgh with him.'

I blinked some more; the thought that I might have been born in Pittsburgh scared me. It sounded so far away.

Nana rocked gently on the edge of the sofa and wrapped her bathrobe tightly around her waist. 'My stepfather found the one letter Mitch had written me, giving the date and time of the train. My mother was livid. Mitch worked in a factory, see, and that wouldn't do. Pittsburgh was full of steel factories and no daughter of hers would marry a laborer. She spent her life on the sales floor at Bloomingdale's and wanted me to have what she didn't. Only a lawyer or doctor for me.'

My grandmother stopped her rocking and her eyes turned brazen, as though it were still within her power to defy her mother. 'They tore up the letter and wouldn't let me contact him or meet him. Of course I'd memorized the date, so I knew when he was supposed to be on that platform. But so did my mother. She made me stay in that house all day and all night. And Mitch . . .' her voice trailed off into memory.

'He just waited there,' Ann finished her sentence. 'He probably thought you'd changed your mind.'

'I still picture him waiting, endlessly checking his watch, heartbroken that I never came. Then again maybe he didn't show up, either. I never knew because I never had the courage to contact him afterward,' Nana said. 'I certainly didn't have the courage to stand up to my mother. Mitch was good enough for me. You're good enough for Peter.

369

Parents shouldn't meddle. He'll regret listening to his mother, mark my words.'

We all sat in silence, contemplating the future regret of Peter, a boy I'd only seen half a dozen times and I thought had greasy hair, when out of the quiet came my mother's voice.

'The good news is that your grandmother met Grandpa,' Iris said. 'If she had run off with Mitch then I wouldn't have been born and none of you would be here.'

My grandmother nodded and smiled, putting her hand on Iris's knee. I thought about this for a moment and shook my head. 'We would,' I disagreed. 'We'd just be living in Pittsburgh.'

*   *   *

Dawn arrived and it was my wedding day. The skies opened up and sheets of rain and hail pelted the stone terrace where the ceremony was to take place, a bad sign if ever there was one. I had sat up most of the night watching the storm gather, feeling trapped in my room like my grandmother on the day she was to meet Mitch at the train station. What if he had been her one great love and she'd let him go, only to make a life with a man she didn't love who gave her artificial roses instead of real passion. I was desperate for my grandmother's advice; she would know what to do. But she was dead and I was alone. For the first time since I'd arrived at Penwick I wanted to call home. I wanted my family, what was left of us, to pull me away from here and ground me. I supposed I was reacting from last night's outburst. But it was too early to call Iris and Ann. Besides, how could they help? My intuition would have to do and do quickly for I was running out of time. But Lady Kate was still battling against plain old Kate's gut instinct.

At noon I could be a rich man's spoiled bride. I could be financially secure. I could have a home, or several. Yet what stood out above all was that Scott never said he loved me, or I him. I tried to remember any instance where we'd spoken the words but it was as though I thought I remembered it rather than it actually happening.

On the other hand Griff did tell me how he felt. His assertion that we were in love and that I wasn't the type of girl to marry for money played over and over in my mind, like an annoying jingle you can't get out of your head.

There was a knock at the door. It was Griff, I was sure of it. I raced to the vanity and, confirming that my hair and makeup was perfect, I flounced to the door.

'If you're here to change my mind,' I snapped as I opened it to the puzzled faces of Marianne and Emma.

'Should we?' Marianne asked and marched past me. They were dressed in their bridesmaid gowns, which I had left up to them to choose. Each wore pink but Marianne's was a sleeveless, floor-length gown with a high neck, while Emma's was a miniskirt with long sleeves and an empire waist in case she suddenly started to show.

'I thought you were someone else,' I said with a light laugh.

'Evidently,' Marianne answered. 'The ceremony's been moved to the ballroom as you wanted.'

'Change your mind about what?' Emma asked.

'My hair,' I said, thinking quickly. 'Up or down?'

371

'Definitely up,' Emma said.

'I like it down,' disagreed Marianne.

'Well, if you two can't agree, how can you expect me to decide?' I said, laughing, and more than a little bit relieved to have so easily diverted attention from my earlier slip. 'I wish I knew what Griff preferred.'

'Griff?' Emma said, intrigued. 'Why do you care how Griff likes your hair?'

'I didn't say "Griff,"' I answered, and felt my face flush.

'Yes you did,' Marianne shot back. 'You clearly said Griff.'

'Well, I meant Scott, obviously.' I laughed artificially and rolled my eyes, as though the error had been theirs, but they continued to eye me suspiciously.

'Well, now that you're mentioned him, what happened last night?' Marianne asked pointedly.

I shook my head but I was suddenly very warm. Then there was another knock on my door and I nearly jumped out of my skin.

'I have to get that,' I said urgently.

'Maybe it's Griff come to tell you how to do your hair,' Marianne said sarcastically. 'You know I did wonder if he was gay . . .'

'He's not!' I shouted.

But when I opened the door it was Fawn, dressed in a long yellow gown, her hair teased as big as a daytime soap opera star.

'Is this where the party is?' she joked and sashayed past me, but she immediately picked up on the tension in the room. 'What gives?' she asked. 'You all look positively guilty.'

'What do you say, Kate,' Marianne started again.

372

'Should you feel guilty?'

I didn't know how to answer when I noticed Emma staring at her nails as if she had plenty to say.

'Emma, have you spoken to Griff?' I said accusingly. She looked up and smiled awkwardly.

'Clive did,' she said nervously.

'So, what happened?' demanded Marianne, turning her attention to poor Emma, who was feeling the pressure.

'Nothing!' I snapped at Marianne.

'What did Clive say happened?' my best friend pushed.

'Nothing,' Emma agreed sheepishly.

'See!' I said and marched to my closet and grabbed my wedding gown. 'It's time to get dressed.'

'This is intriguing.' Fawn sat down beside Emma, putting her hand on her knee for encouragement. 'What is that phrase the preacher says at weddings? "If anyone has any just cause why these two people should not be married"? If you know a reason, Emma, be a good girl and tell us.'

I was livid. 'Fawn, you of all people! Emma, you don't have to say anything, there's nothing to say,' I steamed, ready to boot the whole lot of them from my room as I began to slip into my dress.

'Tell the truth, Emma,' Marianne pleaded. As a fashion editor she knew how to drag gossip from anyone. All she had to do was ask and Emma was ready to cave.

'Griff doesn't want you to marry Scott,' she blurted. 'And neither do I.'

By this point my dress was half on, but hearing Emma's words I panicked and somehow managed

373

to become stuck. Trapped inside the sheath of oyster silk I couldn't breathe or see and my earlier flush of embarrassment was now an inferno.

'Get this off of me!' I shouted and twirled around blindly until the others yanked the dress off, nearly sending me backward into the closet. I stood there panting in my underwear, my hair in a state, perspiration breaking out on my forehead. 'Really? What else did the Earl of Penwick say about me?'

'Earl of Penwick?' Fawn asked with a snort.

'Oh, yes,' I said and marched over to Emma. 'Go on, tell them. If you want to gossip, give the full story.'

Emma, suddenly indignant, rolled her eyes at me and shrugged. 'Griff owns Penwick Manor, it's been in his family for ages.'

'He's a real earl?' Marianne asked in shock.

'Lordy!' Fawn practically shouted.

'Exactly,' I answered, finally cooling off. 'And did he kiss and tell, too?'

'You kissed?' Emma's eyes grew wide. 'How was it?'

I flicked my hair back defiantly, 'It was good. And for your information it wasn't the first time.'

'That does it,' Marianne said flatly. 'You can't marry Scott now.'

'Because I *kissed* another man?'

'Because you're in love with Griff,' Marianne corrected me. 'It's obvious.'

'No it isn't.'

'Yes it is,' Emma agreed.

'No it's not,' I repeated.

'You're not denying it,' Marianne pointed out.

That stopped me in my tracks. Suddenly I had nothing to say.

'I knew it.' Fawn shook her head as though I'd let her down. 'You've had a thing for him from the beginning. What did I keep telling you? If you wanted to marry money, you had to avoid Griff.'

I grimaced. She was right. I couldn't deny it. I didn't love Scott. I was in love with Griff. Exhaling loudly, I slid my back down the wall until I sat on the floor, propped up against the wall.

'You're right,' I confessed. 'I love him.'

'Thank God!' Marianne cracked, but then, seeing the troubled expression on my face she softened. 'I knew you couldn't marry a man for his money.'

'I only said I loved Griff, I didn't say I wasn't marrying Scott,' I reminded her and ignored the disapproving glare that followed. 'I need to marry a rich man and Griff isn't rich.'

'Maybe not,' Fawn said softly, 'but Penwick Manor isn't exactly a pile of rubble.'

'He's barely holding on to it,' Emma interjected somberly. 'He's got nothing compared to Scott.'

Fawn pursed her lips at this unwelcome piece of news. Marianne shrugged as if Emma had only said that Griff was short or had bad teeth or anything else that could be easily overlooked.

'You can't marry Scott when you're in love with Griff,' she stated firmly, as if it were a done deal.

'But I can,' I said equally firm, trying to shake my doubts away like dandruff. 'All I have to do is throw on this wedding dress and walk down the stairs into the ballroom and say 'I do.' It's simple; a trained chimp could do it.'

'You're not a chimp,' said Marianne, as though it needed affirmation.

'I'll marry Scott for a year, get the money I need, divorce him, and then be with Griff,' I said, pleased

375

with this compromise, then turned to Fawn as if seeking her permission. 'Right, Fawn?'

Emma and Marianne also turned to her with the full weight of their disapproval bearing down heavily. A regular woman would bow to the peer pressure and agree with them, even if she didn't, but not my Fawn. She knew how these matters were dealt with. Fawn smiled confidently. I smiled back.

'Kate, darling,' Fawn began, her smile still intact. 'This isn't one of your contract jobs. You may have been an acting beauty editor your whole life, but you can't be an acting wife.'

Marianne looked relieved. But I started to tremble. All at once I became very confused, and my stomach felt like it would turn against me any second. 'What are you saying?' I begged Fawn, overcome and exasperated. 'You're my mentor. You got me here, this is what we planned and we did it.' I forced a smiled but felt tears fill my eyes. 'This is everything I wanted, I can't turn back now. Can I?'

She looked at me and I saw tears well up in her eyes, too. She quickly brushed them away and, hitching her yellow gown up above her knees, sat down on the floor beside me.

'Oh, honey,' she said gently. 'I can't tell you what to do. Only you know what's right, what's in your heart.'

'My heart? This isn't about my heart! Love doesn't conquer all. I need money desperately. I want my life back and I need to take care of my family. No one but me can do it, I can't rely on anyone else,' I explained. But as I spoke the words, I realized I had relied on someone. I'd relied on Griff. He had been there to catch me every time I

376

fell, literally and figuratively.

'Darlin',' Fawn spoke and put her hand on my bare knee. 'You've got to rely on people. I know you're hurting because of all the bad things that have happened to you, but in order to live, truly live, you've got to feel pain, you've got to trust, and you've got to love.'

I looked in her eyes, letting her words sink in, when there was a loud bang on the door and we all jumped.

'Ladies, it's almost time. You've got fifteen minutes,' Clive bellowed.

My friends turned to me, waiting for my decision. I couldn't breathe. I looked past them and out the window where the clouds were as gray and threatening as they had been that first day at Penwick when I'd fallen and Griff had found me and carried me home, or rather to his home. As the rain pelted the glass I knew what to do; it was as clear to me as the rainwater that ran down the windowpane.

'I can't marry Scott,' I said shakily. 'I'm only going to be with a man if I love him.'

'Welcome back, Kate!' Marianne exclaimed and gave Emma a high-five. I giggled at the absurdity of my current predicament. Then I stared at the door. 'Now what?' I asked stupidly.

'I think you need to talk to the groom,' Marianne said.

'I'll ask Clive to fetch him,' Emma offered and went out the door.

'You did right,' Fawn said and squeezed my knee. 'I'm proud of you.'

'Better get dressed,' Marianne suggested.

I was still holding my wedding gown when Scott

377

knocked on the door.

'He sure doesn't waste any time,' Fawn observed dryly.

'It's me, Kate.' His voice sounded impatient. He would be so angry in a few moments.

'Hurry up,' Fawn said and tossed the wedding gown over my head.

'I can't wear this!' I protested but she had already pulled it over me.

'You don't have time to change,' she insisted. 'Besides, you've got to wear it once.'

Scott barely acknowledged Fawn and Marianne as they stalked past him and out the door. He stood like a statue and glared at me.

'Well?' he asked sternly. 'What's the matter now?'

I hesitated. I knew what I wanted to say, but I didn't like that it was going to hurt him. I took a deep breath. 'I can't marry you,' I blurted at once and didn't stop. With the worst of it out of my mouth, for the next several minutes Scott listened to me admit that I didn't love him and that I wasn't going to marry him, even though I had come very close to doing just that for his money. I told him that at one point I had genuinely believed we'd come to love each other, but I could see that it wasn't possible. As I talked I was struck by how calm he was about it all. Unemotional, even. There was no show of anger, but there was no passionate protest, either. He merely leaned against the window watching me with his arms crossed like he was observing a game of chess.

'You're taking it well,' I said when I finished my speech. 'I guess you didn't love me, either.' I'm not going to lie. The fact that his demeanor was so cool

378

and unaffected irritated the hell out of me.

'Kate, let's be grown-ups,' he said finally. 'We don't love each other, big deal. That's for kids like Tatiana to believe in. We have to be realistic. I need you in my life, you're a great asset.'

I blanched at being called an asset. 'I want more than that,' I sniffed.

'You can have whatever you want,' he said turning on the charm. 'Marry me today and if you don't like it in a year or two we can get a divorce.'

'No, Scott,' I said confidently. 'I don't want to be your acting wife and my heart isn't for sale, not anymore. I'm sorry.'

I thought how strange it was that after months of desperately trying to be close to this man, now that everything was out in the open I didn't want to be anywhere near him. I wanted nothing more than for him to leave, which I expected him to do. Instead, he grabbed me by the shoulders, poised as if to shake me, and so close I could smell last night's cigar.

'Look, Kate, I'm desperate,' he said, not loosening his grasp. 'I didn't want to tell you before we were married, but business is bad.'

'What do you mean, "bad"?' I asked and shook myself free of his clench. His eyes had a wild look about them, like a caged animal. It frightened me.

'I've lost money. Lots of it,' he spoke rapidly. 'And my clients are worried that I've done something wrong. I've tried to adjust their financial statements so that they wouldn't be suspicious, so they wouldn't worry. But Kate, people are circling me like vultures and threatening to call the police.'

'Oh God,' I said, afraid to even say what I was thinking. 'You didn't steal from them, did you?'

He started to pace back and forth, not looking

379

me in the eye. 'I didn't steal anything, I moved it,' he said angrily. 'Most people don't understand the types of funds I manage. It's complicated stuff.'

'That sounds like an understatement,' I said awkwardly. Then a sudden chill swept over me and it was as though the shiver that followed made the events of the past few weeks fall into place. 'What did you mean when you said I was an asset to you?' I asked him, but I already knew the answer. All those wealthy men and women we were cozying up to in London weren't just troubled by the recession, they were troubled by Scott, and he was trying to assuage their fears and using me to do it.

'Kate, I need you,' he pleaded and stopped his pacing. He looked at me and once more his lips turned up into that charming smile that I had craved to shine on me for so long. 'I need a wife on my arm who will make me look like a good, honest man. Someone that people can trust. I'll make it worth your while; that London flat can be in your name. Same for my New York apartment.'

'Sounds like you're afraid, Scott,' I said, my voice shaking. 'Are you in that kind of trouble?'

'I might be,' he admitted.

I was too stunned to speak. The whirlwind romance, the quick proposal, the even quicker wedding—I wasn't such a gifted gold digger, after all. In fact, I'd been outplayed. Scott was far cleverer than Bernardo had been. I shook my head. 'I can't.'

'Kate, I know all about you,' he said in a tone that suggested I wasn't going to like what he was about to say. 'I know you're just a nothing girl from Scarsdale. I know your estate is one square foot of dirt. I looked it up. Loch Broom Highland Estates

380

is a joke.'

Yup, didn't like it one bit. 'When did you find out?' I asked, trying to maintain my dignity, knowing there was no point denying it.

'In Palm Beach,' he admitted.

'As early as that?' I was stunned.

'Afraid so. Your slip-up about croquet, and that little Scottish Colonel What's His Name, MacKay. It wasn't hard to figure out your scheme, just a few Google searches.'

I looked down at my engagement ring, talk about a joke, and twisted it off my finger. 'You might need this,' I said and handed it to him.

'But none of that matters,' he continued, holding the ring in his hand, prepared to put it back on my finger. 'You impressed me with your talent for invention, you're a believable person. No one would ever think you capable of lying. And the fact that you can pass yourself off as a lady, hell, it's a smart ruse, I'll give you that. I know what it's like. Do you really think I built anything for charity in Malaysia? I made that up! Never been. Never want to.'

I was stunned. 'So, all you really needed was to transfer your assets and hide your money. I was your backup plan,' I said flatly. My mind went back to that night in St. Moritz, when Tatiana was sobbing in the bathroom because Scott found her searching his e-mail. 'What really happened with Tatiana?'

'I couldn't trust her, I wasn't sure what she'd read on my computer, what she may have uncovered,' he admitted sourly. 'Besides, she's not as smart as you, or as good an actress. I'm asking, begging, Kate. I'm afraid the law may be closing in on me. I have to take care of things.'

I felt sorry for him. Really, I did. He was in a much worse state than I was and all this time he was putting on an act to rival my Lady Kate of Loch Broom. It seemed that neither of us was happy with our lives. We were chasing and chasing some abstract happiness, but were never within reach of it, not even close. It was all make believe.

'I suppose this makes us con artists,' I said slowly and felt the sting of the words on my tongue. 'I never thought of it before but that's what we are. But not anymore, I'm done.' I slowly turned and walked toward the door, not bothering to look back. Scott never loved me. Yet he was willing to marry me to save his money. How alike we were. How vile. But there was still time for me to alter the ending to my Jane Austen dream turned nightmare, or so I hoped.

'You're walking away from billions!' he called out.

'Good-bye, Scott,' I said. 'Good luck.'

36

Lottery Winner

It isn't what we say or think that defines
us, but what we do.

—*Sense and Sensibility*

This is where my story began. I walk stealthily down
the unending hallway and down the grand staircase.
I could hear the crowd in the ballroom; someone
would have made an announcement by now. I slink
past the doors, not wanting to be seen, when out of
the corner of my eye I catch a flash of color.

'Hello, Kate,' said Doris, catching me slink.

I turn to see her decked out in a pastel pink suit
suitable for the wedding; shame it wasn't going to
serve its purpose.

'Change your mind?' she asks simply.

I nod. 'Do you know where Griff is?' I ask slowly,
not wanting to give it away.

'You missed him,' she answers, and I feel my
heart fall to my knees. 'He's gone to London.'

I remember that had been the plan.

'Although he never leaves for town without a
final ride on Fred,' she says and winks at me.

By the time I reach the front door I'm almost
running. I sprint outside and run barefoot along
the garden paths. The rain is still coming down in
torrents, making my satin gown cling to parts of
me that shouldn't be seen in polite company, but I
don't care. Instead, I bolt through the garden gate

and down the path to the stables. I reach it just in time to see Griff and Fred canter through the gate and disappear into the next field. I shout after him but it's no use, he's gone.

I pause and take another look back at Penwick Manor. I think of the guests inside. I could go back. There's still time. I can dry my dress. Redo my hair. I could take Scott's ill-gotten money and live the life. Instead, I merely stand there out of breath, soaking wet, and feeling hopeless when Ratina nickers at me. I smile. Within seconds I have her tacked up and at the mounting block. She stands patiently as I hike up my gown and swing onto the saddle. But as soon as I am mounted I realize that all I'd ever done was walk around, usually with Griff leading me. He had never taught me to trot, let alone gallop. My childhood ride from hell floods back but I shake it off. This is different. This is a matter of life and love. I lean forward and speak softly in Ratina's ear.

'I need to catch that man,' I whisper. 'He's riding a very handsome stud. One for me, one for you; do we have a deal?'

She turns her head and looks at me as if she understands. I kick her gently with my bare heels and she takes off like a shot. I am completely out of control and desperately clinging to her neck when I spot Griff and Fred ahead of us. They are far away, maybe too far. Then, as though sensing my urgency, Ratina whinnies loudly and within seconds Fred answers. I watch as Griff and Fred pull up and pray that Ratina will stop when she reaches them. Fortunately she immediately slows down when she sees them stop and we slowly walk toward

384

them. I must be a sight. My dress is now practically transparent and I can barely see through all the hair that is stuck to my face. But despite my appearance, Griff doesn't seem all that surprised to see me.

'Hello,' he says calmly, as though a wet woman in an overly revealing dress riding a horse was the most common thing in the world.

'Hi,' I say back. 'Going for a ride?'

'Yes, I was.'

'Good. We'd like to join you.'

Griff urges Fred into a walk and Ratina follows without any direction from me.

'Aren't you otherwise engaged?' he asks after we walk a few strides.

'I had a change of plans,' I admit and stare straight ahead.

He stops Fred and Ratina pulls up beside him. Griff looks at me as if waiting for more.

'And a change of heart,' I continue more seriously, this time looking him in the eye. 'You were right. I can't marry Scott. I don't love him. And I don't love money as much as I thought I did. I want to stay here, at Penwick, if you'll have me, Lord Saunderson, or whatever I should say.'

I bow my head as I imagine one did to aristocrats. Griff raises an eyebrow but the warm smile I expect doesn't appear.

'I'm not the bloody king,' he says solemnly and grabs Ratina's reins, removing his raincoat and putting it over my shoulders. 'That's better.'

I am dumbfounded. I admit a gooey happy ending all tied in a perfect bow is too much to ask but a little bit of romance was due. Or so I think.

'That's all there is to it, then?' Griff asks as he kicks his horse forward, his hand still gripping

Ratina's reins, leading her along beside him as though giving me a pony ride. 'You jilt Scott at the altar and assume I'll run into your arms, grateful you've come to your bloody senses at last?'

Kind of. I don't know what to say now. I feel my stomach knot up with each stride.

'I thought you loved me,' I blurt. 'Last night—'

'Last night,' he answers, cutting me off and once again yanking us to a stop. His expression isn't anger exactly, but if I'm not mistaken, it is grave disappointment. I imagine in me. 'You were determined to marry Scott for his money. He was the answer to your problems. I was merely a distraction. You may have slept on it last night but so did I. I don't want to be with a girl who shows such lack of character and judgment. I believed in you, Kate, even when I saw you chasing after that man in Switzerland. I thought you would realize what a fool you were. Despite all your pretenses of being Lady Kate, your behavior has been anything but ladylike.'

I flinch at his words.

'I do realize I was a fool!' I snap defensively. 'And I love you.'

We sit there not speaking. The only sound is an occasional snort from one of the horses. I won't take my eyes off him and, for once, it is he who refuses to meet my gaze. I begin to get very cold. We have remained here long enough that the rain has penetrated his coat and I shiver. This at least gets his attention.

'Let's take you back.' He speaks calmly and leads us down the roadway to Penwick. His expression seems to soften and gives me hope. 'But it's too late for us. We're not a romantic film or an Austen novel.' False hope, as it turns out, despite his voice finally returning to the soft warmth I've grown to love. 'There isn't going to be a happy ending. You should go home, back to America.'

I don't know what to do or what to say. Ratina falls a few steps behind Fred and with Griff's back to me I begin to cry. With the rain falling in torrents no one would ever know that I am heartbroken.

*   *   *

My friends help me pack. We are a solemn bunch. I have never seen Emma, Marianne, and Fawn so quiet. I have, of course, filled them in on every word, there were so few, that Griff had said to me. They listened but said little. What is there to say? That it's all my own doing? That my blind determination to marry for money has cost me a fine man? I know the answers and don't need to be told, just as I know that the Austenisms 'good prospect' and 'eligible match' mean something different than they once did. Griff is right. I am a fool.

'Get a load of those two,' Marianne says and gestures for us to come to the window. We all peek out just as Scott and Tatiana are piling their luggage into the back of the limo. He takes her hand and kisses it as he helps her into the backseat.

'That didn't take him long,' Fawn says with a huff.

'They deserve each other,' I say with a shrug and go back to packing. I really don't care anymore about either of them.

Fawn offers to fly me home on Mona tonight. She won't take no for an answer, though I admit I don't try very hard to decline. Marianne and

Brandon will fly home with us. At least in front of them I can have a meltdown.

'I will file my story to Jennifer by Monday,' I say finally, in a weak attempt at humor at my own expense.

'Don't worry,' Marianne says softly. 'Leave it for a bit. We can hold the publication date until next issue.'

'Don't be silly,' I snap. 'The June issue is all about weddings! And I've dumped my billionaire, remember? And the man I love, the poor Lord of the Manor, has dumped me. If nothing else I need to file the story so you can pay me!'

Then I laugh. No one else does.

'Besides,' I continue brashly. 'I know the ending. I have my answer.'

'What was the question?' Emma asks reluctantly as she folds my ruined wedding gown in the flattering shade of oyster, though now with watermarks, into my suitcase. I cross the room, yank it out, and throw it into the trash bin, much to the shock of my friends.

'At forty years of age, is it too late to marry for money?' I repeat the words that launched my quest. 'And the answer is yes, it is. I'm old enough to know better.'

37

Hell's Kitchen

Friendship is certainly the finest balm for
the pangs of disappointed love.

—Northanger Abbey

I stand outside and stare up at Ann's window for a
long time. It is just past noon on Sunday and despite
the comforts of Mona, I didn't sleep much on the
flight home. Marianne and Brandon have deposited
me here in the taxi, but I haven't worked up the nerve
to knock on the door. What will Ann and Iris say to
me? Last they knew I was marrying a billionaire and
all our problems would be over. Here I am, flat broke
with a Louis Vuitton suitcase and no husband. The
term 'spinster' suddenly seems completely apt. At
least I can always sell the suitcase.

'Are you lost?' a male voice calls out to me. I
turn to see its origin and watch as a man in his late
forties step out of an SUV. He is dressed casually
but elegantly. Clearly, he is a man who knows the
meaning of weekend wear, even if he does look as
though he'd stepped out of a J.Crew catalogue. He
isn't handsome exactly, but attractive in a preppy,
middle-aged, soft chin and even softer midriff way.

'No, I'm waiting for someone,' I lie.

He nods and begins to walk up the path to the
building. I suppose he knows someone there, as
well. But he hesitates at the door, turns, and walks
back to me. I straighten my posture defensively, not

389

sure what he is up to. Then he smiles warmly as if we are long-lost friends.

'You're Kate, aren't you?' he says happily and extends his hand.

'Yes,' I admit reluctantly and shake his hand. 'Have we met?'

He shakes his head. 'I've seen your photo.'

My mind races to where he may have seen my picture and the horror of the sheer dress in the *Daily Mail* floods back. Before I can say another word he continues speaking cheerfully.

'Your sister, Ann, has a few photos in her place,' he answers. 'I have a good memory.'

'And you are?' I ask a bit sternly.

'I'm Doug,' he says. 'I'm Ann's boyfriend.'

I must look taken aback for he chuckles at this. 'You're not the only sister that's met a dashing stranger. At least I hope Ann finds me dashing.'

What the . . . ? Doug picks up my suitcase and, taking my elbow, leads me to the door and up the staircase. Ann has a boyfriend? Why hadn't she mentioned Doug in any of her e-mails or on the phone when we last spoke?

'Hey, Ann, I brought you a surprise,' Doug announces when we enter the apartment. I hear clanking in the kitchen; where else would Ann be, after all, and then the padding of footsteps.

'What kind of sur . . . Kate! You're home!' Ann shrieks happily and hugs me. She looks me up and down, then grabs my left hand excitedly. 'Where is it? Your wedding ring? Your husband?' she asks, then, looking me in the face, her expression turns from anticipation to confusion. 'What happened?'

'I think I'll see what's happening in the kitchen,' Doug says, excusing himself.

390

When he disappears into the kitchen I mouth 'who is he?' to Ann, but she shakes her head and mutters 'later.'

'Where's Mom?' I ask, not sure if I want to spill my guts to both of them at once. Ann, I can count on for sympathy, whereas my mother would no doubt resort to hysterics.

'She's out,' Ann answers furtively. 'Come sit down and tell me what happened.'

For the next while I can't stop talking except to cry. She gets all the details that had been missed in the sporadic e-mails I'd dispatched. But when I get to Griff and his complete rejection of me, I break down again.

'I failed completely,' I say tearfully. 'All I wanted to do was meet and marry a man of substance, a man who would take care of me and of us. I wanted to get our home back. I had that man but I couldn't do it. I couldn't marry for money and, oh Ann, how I tried! But then Griff lost all respect for me. I'm a complete Austen screwup!'

'Kate, you haven't failed,' Ann says kindly and rests her hand on my knee. 'You just got the point of Austen all turned upside down. What you love about those books is that the heroine finds love, not money. Elizabeth loves Darcy. Emma loves Knightley. Fanny loves Edward. You love Griff. If he's really Mr. Right, he'll come back.'

I shake my head. 'There's no such thing as Mr. Right,' I say indignantly. 'But Griff was right for me. I only wish I'd realized that before it was too late. I wish you'd met him.'

'Maybe I will, one day,' she offers hopefully.

I shrug. A loud clang sounds in the kitchen and Doug calls out, 'Oops! That was only an empty bowl. Nothing's broken!'

We both giggle, but the crash in the other room does bring up the point. I shake my head to clear the remaining cobwebs of Penwick from my mind and force a smile. 'Come clean, Ann, who is Doug? Tell me everything.'

And Ann does just that, while the man in question can be heard banging about in the kitchen. She can't stop talking except to laugh. As I listen I realize that I wasn't the only one who had a plan. Ann had indeed taken her sauces to the Chicago food fair and she had some interest from a few specialty food shops, but nothing to indicate she should give up her day job. But on the last day a man came to her booth and loved the sauce, all varieties of it. He loved it so much he stayed in her booth for over an hour. When it was time to close the booth he asked her to dinner. It was Doug. Douglas LaForce of South Carolina. He was an entrepreneur with an interest in gourmet cooking and was in Chicago on business, but had read about the food fair in the paper. Now you can imagine where this is going. Sure enough, Doug not only paid for dinner for two, he offered to help her build her sauce business because he had investment money and he could literally taste a winner. He set up meetings for Ann with grocery store chains, starting with Piggly Wiggly in the South, which proved the perfect fit for her barbeque sauces and marinades. Before she knew it she had orders to supply the entire South Carolina Piggly Wiggly chain with sauce and she had a boyfriend. And Doug LaForce of South Carolina was a very good prospect indeed. Not that Ann needed his prospects so much because now hers looked so good. They were in the process of renting a professional factory kitchen in order to keep up with demand and were about to post an ad for help when yours truly arrived.

'Will you do it?' Ann asks when her tale had been told. I'm no cook, and my interest in food resides solely in the eating category, but I need a job and, well, if the family's prospects lie in a gooey substance to spread over meat, then so be it.

'Can I at least get an apron from Chanel?' I joke.

The door opens and in walks my mother, Iris. She looks at me, as shocked as Ann had been. Since we exist in the land of awkward family moments our reunion went like this:

'You're here,' Iris announces, not moving an inch toward me and clutching her handbag as though I might snatch it away.

'I am,' I respond, not bothering to get up from the sofa.

'Why?' Iris asks.

'Mom, what kind of question is that?' Ann says wearily.

'Because I dumped my fiancé,' I answer in as blasé a manner as I can.

'Well, you know, we Shaw women never have good luck with men,' Iris says in her trademark way with words. 'It's the family curse.'

I sigh. Then Doug walks in and sees the three of us staring at one another. He is carrying a tray with three champagne flutes full of pink bubbly.

'I thought Kate's surprise homecoming needed celebrating,' he says and gives each of us a glass.

'Don't you want a glass?' Ann asks, but Doug has grabbed his coat and is kissing her on the cheek.

'When I get back,' he says wisely. 'I think the

393

three of you have lots to catch up on.' He squeezes Iris's shoulder reassuringly on the way out. It is a gesture of kindness that surprises me.

'He seems like a nice guy,' I say when he leaves. 'And I don't mean that in a bland way.'

'Ann is lucky,' Iris says and takes off her coat and sits down in between Ann and me on the sofa. 'Or I should say, Doug is lucky.'

We clink our flutes and sip the champagne. With my lack of sleep and jet lag it doesn't take more than a few sips to get the requisite buzz and with it comes a sigh of relief that I am home. As awkward, dysfunctional, and moody as the three of us are, it feels like home, minus one very important person, my grandmother.

'Doug will need luck,' I say with a smirk. 'If he's going to spend any great amount of time with our family.'

We all laugh and as we do my eyes rest on a photograph of my grandmother that was taken years before I was born. It is one of my favorites. She's in a pencil skirt and fitted jacket and had a mink stole wrapped around her shoulders, very glamorous.

'How old was Nana in that shot?' I ask and point to it.

'I don't know,' Ann answers and furrows her brow as though trying to guess.

'She was your age,' Iris says with authority.

I keep staring at the photo. My grandmother died at ninety-three. When this photo was taken she still had fifty-three years of life. That was a long time, long enough to make changes. Who knew how long I'd live but I have good genes. A woman can do a lot in fifty-three years.

I've been home one week and I'm sitting across the desk from Jennifer. She has in her hands the hard copy of my article.

' "The Jane Austen Marriage Manual," great title,' she says. I only nod and think back to Griff's disapproving tone when he'd said it and the memory instantly darkens my mood. 'I love it,' Jennifer continues with her signature crooked smile that is more of a smirk. 'Especially the stable boy bit.'

'Thank you,' I answer, hoping her approval will get me a rush on the check.

'But in the end your advice is Austen only works if you fall in love with the object of your desire.'

'That's correct,' I answer simply. There is no way I will change the ending.

'You may be right. Remember Tina?' she asks.

How can I forget? Tina is one of the most ruthless gold diggers I'd ever met. She could give Tatiana a run for her money, pun intended. I nod.

'She fell head over heels in love with an auto mechanic and has moved with him to Minnesota.' Jennifer says all this with a wrinkled nose, as if she smells something rotten.

'Good for her,' I say, though I'm loathe to admit that Tina is smarter than me.

'So, your article is bang-on,' she continues. 'It will be a big hit, I can tell. But what about your personal ending? You don't really say . . . no Darcy, no Knightley for you?'

'I'm still looking,' I say vaguely. She agrees to rush my payment and I stand up to leave.

'Why are you in a hurry?' she asks. 'I love what you did and I have loads of other freelance articles for you to write.'

I don't bother to sit down. I smile and say, 'I'm taking a break from writing.'

She looks aghast, as if I've slapped her. 'What are you going to do?'

'I'm joining the family business,' I answer as gamely as I can.

38

Ever After

If I could but know his heart, everything would become easy.

—*Sense and Sensibility*

Six Months Later

They say time heals all wounds. And nothing makes time stretch like working twelve hours in a steamy kitchen slicing, dicing, and stirring five different types of special sauce. In six months of kitchen duty, my wound hasn't healed nearly enough for me to say I am over him. By him, I mean Griff. I still think of him daily, often alone at night when I crawl into bed on my sister's pullout sofa, but also when I am stirring that bubbling brownish red goo. There is something meditative about the process and involuntarily my thoughts drift back to Penwick, to my days riding

396

Ratina, and my conversations with Griff. How just a few weeks can impact a life! For despite months of chasing Scott I think little of him now, but Griff is an ache that pounds sharply in my chest.

Speaking of Scott, he was arrested for fraud and embezzlement, but not until after he had married Tatiana. According to Fawn, who knew many of the people who lost money, Tatiana admitted she had understood all the e-mails she'd read that night in St. Moritz and after they were married she wisely convinced him to put a lot of his assets solely in her name so that when he was arrested, his property confiscated and his bank accounts frozen, she had already accumulated millions of her own. Now she was filing for divorce. It was perhaps the cleverest of all bank heists. Scott had underestimated her.

To think that could have been me. But Tatiana's money still belongs to other people and I am no thief. Making sauce is making money the honest way and that is just fine.

Doug and Ann had grown the company enough to employ Iris, as well, and to get her some much-needed counseling. She goes to classes, or sessions I suppose you'd call them, twice a week, including Sundays. We refer to it as her 'Sunday school.' I am living rent free with Ann until all my searching for a rich husband debt is paid off. Life is all right. I am managing.

I would have carried on like this until one day it comes in the mail—an invitation to Clive and Emma's baby's christening. They had a son they named Jonathan. Clive got another job at a bank but it's at a branch in Dorset, not London. They are still living with his mother for now, but Emma assures me that the extra pair of hands is helpful with the baby. I want to go. I want to bake her a lasagna and help. And it isn't just a regular invite; Emma asked me to be Jonathan's godmother. It is a huge honor and I want to accept but I don't have the money to fly back to England. The thought that Griff will be invited to the christening also gives me pause. I'm not ready to see him again.

'You have to go back,' Ann insists when I tell her about it.

'I can't, it's too expensive,' I say.

'I'll pay for you,' Ann offers and a wide smile comes across her face.

'No, you can't do that,' I say and wave my hand. 'You're just starting a business.'

'I have capital,' Ann corrects me, her smile growing even wider. 'In fact, we can all go. It's a research trip, Doug and I can meet with Waitrose or Marks and Spencer, even bring Mom with us.'

My eyes stare at her in disbelief. 'I've always wanted to go to England,' she continues. 'We could use a family holiday and besides, isn't the christening awfully close to your birthday?'

She has me there. My forty-first birthday is two weeks after the christening. A year after our grandmother died.

'I'll arrange everything,' she says gleefully. 'Now, you call Emma and tell her you're going to be the godmother. Do it.'

*   *   *

'Holy shit, it *is* like an Austen novel!' Ann exclaims from the back of the rental car as Doug slowly cruises past Penwick. I had tried to dissuade my family from spying on Griff this way, but they just stuck me in the backseat and said they would act lost if anyone came out of the house. No one did. But we are down the drive and on the road to the village church before I can breathe again.

'Will your Griff be at the church?' Iris asks.

'He's not "my Griff,"' I correct her harshly. 'Never was.'

'I'm sure it will be a large party,' Ann says reassuringly. 'You will hardly see him unless you want to.'

That is the trouble, I think sullenly. Part of me does want to see him, even though I know he despises me. My thoughts run back to his cruel words that I behaved in an unladylike manner. Even though I know he's right, I want to prove to him that he is also wrong and that the real, plain Kate is ladylike and no fool.

We find the church and park the car. There seems to be quite a crowd gathering. Ann is right. It will be a big party, which means that Griff sightings will be few and far between. I leave my family to find seats as I go to find the private church room where Emma told me to meet her. But before I take even a few steps, my name comes loud and clear across the parking lot and it comes with a southern drawl.

'Lady Kate!'

I turn to see Fawn running toward me on her signature dove gray kitten heels. We throw our arms around each other.

'I haven't been called that in a very long time,' I comment wistfully.

'Darlin,' I just can't get used to you being regular ol' Kate!' Fawn beams. 'You'll always be a lady to me.'

'I'm so glad Emma invited you.' I smile at the irony of her words. If only Griff could hear her!

'She's a doll!' Fawn grins. 'And since I've moved to Europe to be with Marco, I haven't had a chance to see you, so this is perfect.'

We walk toward the church arm-in-arm and catch up on things beyond what we've shared in e-mails since my ill-fated wedding day. We find the private room and knock.

'I'm sure Emma would love to say hello,' I say to Fawn as we walk into the room.

'Kate!' Emma shouts and runs over. We clutch each other tightly, but I notice as Emma squeezes me that Fawn is staring awkwardly at the ground, which isn't like her. I pull gently away from Emma and touch Fawn's arm.

'What's wrong, Fawn? You look like you've seen a ghost,' I say, half joking.

'Oh, yes,' Emma says knowingly. 'I wanted to tell you about it sooner. Griff is to be Jonathan's godfather.'

I look up and there he is, standing across the room, holding the baby in his arms as Clive chats to the priest. He hasn't seen me yet, but from Fawn's reaction, she had seen him the moment we entered the room.

'That's just charming,' Fawn says to Emma with a big smile.

'Does he know I'm here?' I ask nervously, wondering how long it will take for him to notice me.

'He does now,' Fawn says and points. My eyes follow her gesture and I find myself staring into those giant blue eyes again.

'Is this the godmother?' the priest asks jovially.

Emma leads me toward him and we shake hands as though meeting for the first time. 'Have you met Griffith Saunderson? He's to be your partner in this.'

Griff barely ekes out a smile as he shakes my hand. Feeling his touch again, I am torn between wanting to pull him toward me and kiss him and slapping him across his handsome face for hurting me.

'We have met,' I respond.

'Indeed,' Griff answers, then proceeds to turn away and follow the priest and the others into the church. The priest's words, 'he's to be your partner in this,' echo in my head as the ceremony begins and I perform the rituals required of any good godmother.

Throughout I keep wishing for Griff to make any gesture of warmth, a smile, a knowing look, but he blatantly ignores me.

Before I know it, I am in the church garden and drinking a Pimm's. Fawn hit it off with Ann, Doug, and Iris and is situated beneath a giant chestnut tree discussing the food business, Marco's coffee and Ann's sauces. I take my drink and stand off alone, watching Emma and Clive introducing their son to the guests.

'They look happy, don't they?' a voice asks. I don't bother to turn around. I know Griff is right behind me.

'They deserve to be happy,' I say, desperate to keep any whiff of nerves out of my voice. 'We all do.'

'And have you figured out the key to your happiness, Kate?' he asks.

If only he knew. But I give him the answer that

401

matters most to me.

'Family,' I answer and move my gaze to Iris, Ann, Doug, and Fawn under the tree chatting merrily. 'And friends.'

'Ah, but what about love?' he asks. He is so close I can feel his breath on the back of my neck and I shiver.

'Family and friends are love,' I answer, still refusing to turn around. How dare he talk to me like this? There had been no e-mails, no text messages, not a word for six months and now he is behaving like an intimate friend?

'Yes, but surely you need more than friends and family to be truly happy; what about romance?'

That does it. I whirl around ready to tell him off when he grabs me and kisses me. I am too shocked to resist and as he continues to kiss me, his arms wrap around my waist and I lean into him. I wonder if everyone is watching but I realize I don't care. When we pull away he gently touches my cheek. My eyes close against his fingers and I smile as the tears come but stop short of falling.

'What are you doing?' I manage to blurt out.

'I'm not sure, to be honest,' he says quietly. 'What would you like me to do?'

'Don't play with me,' I snap suddenly and turn and walk away from him.

'Kate, stop!' he shouts. I notice that quite a few guests, including my clan, witnessed the kiss and now the brief chase. 'Come with me for a drive.'

'I don't think so,' I say in a muffled voice. 'Why should I?'

'Because I'm asking nicely,' he retorts and smiles for the first time that day. 'And because I love you.'

I feel my eyes widen and my jaw go slack. Maybe

402

this is jet lag and I am going to wake up and still be on the flight to Heathrow.

'I should never have let you go,' he continues breathlessly. 'I've thought about you constantly. And Emma, well, she's kept me informed. I know you've been working with your sister and that's wonderful. It's great you're building such a life for yourself back home. But Emma said you still had feelings for me, too.'

I shoot Emma a scathing look of betrayal but she was busy cooing over Jonathan with some lady in a shocking pink outfit wearing two different shoes.

'You said I lacked character and judgment. And that I was no lady,' I remind him.

'I cringe when I think of how I behaved and what I said,' he answers passionately. 'But it was my ego talking. When you said you were still going to marry Scott I was jealous and hurt. I was a fool and not a gentleman. Can you forgive me?'

'I'm not sure.'

'I love you very much and know you were in a desperate state and were doing what you thought was right, even though it was a half-baked scheme,' he pleads. 'If I could take back those words, dear Kate.'

I look into his eyes, so big and blue, they are a beacon to me.

'Will you have me?' Griff asks.

I wait just long enough to make him squirm; not enough to be cruel, but enough to make him wonder. I have fantasized about this moment for months, whether stirring sauce or lying awake on the sofa, and yet the reality of it far exceeds my dream. There is only one possible answer for me to give him. I smile and nod. He grins widely and

403

kisses me again.

'Then let's go home,' he says.

*   *   *

It's two weeks after the christening and I'm on my hands and knees, scrubbing at the scuffmarks on the white-and-black floor in the entranceway. I'm living the fairy tale only it's the reverse Jane Austen story, where I become a scullery maid instead of a wealthy wife. I have no idea where Griff and I will end up. I'm still not sure about marriage. Neither is he. We are going to live together and see what develops. What we both know is that we're in love. Unconventional has been a sort of code my whole life and I see no reason to stop it now.

I work at the house all day helping Doris and Herbert keep it clean. There are many improvements to be made and I have this idea of opening a spa on the estate. I'm going to London to meet editors at the fashion magazines so I can flex my beauty editor muscles and drum up buzz. It makes sense. Penwick is a relaxing place when you're not marrying the wrong man or passing yourself off as someone you're not.

I look up from my scrubbing and see Griff come toward me. He was out riding. I ride nearly every day now, too. It's great exercise. He sees me give him the look. The look that says 'don't even think about crossing my clean floor in your dirty riding boots,' and he retreats to the mudroom. I smile.

I'm finished with the floor and it's time to change. We have a party at Penwick tonight. My forty-first birthday is today and as usual, I'm not the least traumatized by turning another year older. In

404

fact, despite my harrowing debut, I'm okay with the forties—in fact, I'm perfectly fine with forty-one.

Ann, Doug, and Iris are still here, as are Fawn and Marco, Emma and Clive, and in a final feat of sisterly love and indulgence and a large order from Waitrose, so are Brandon, Lucy, and their daughter, Stella, and Marianne, Frank, and Thomas. Sauce sells. If only my grandmother could see me now. She would have loved Penwick and Griff. I like to think she is watching and smiling. I have the great estate I always wanted, albeit with a debt load to match, but we're working on that. As I climb the great staircase, the opening line of *Pride and Prejudice* plays in my mind. 'It is a truth universally acknowledged, that a single man in possession of a good fortune must be in want of a wife.' And as I begun my story with my own twist on those words, I'm going to end my story with this variation, 'It is also a truth universally acknowledged, that a woman of forty who is in want of love, needs to follow her heart and when she finds the right man, rich or poor, that is fortune enough for her.'

Acknowledgments

I wouldn't have completed this novel if it hadn't been for the encouragement of my early readers and 'critics'; Kate Mayberry, whose first name I borrowed for the main character and who spurred me on to make it as funny as possible; Athena McKenzie, Vivian Vassos, Arlene Stacey, Suzanne Boyd, Meredyth Young, Victoria Winter and Jamie Reid for providing support and insight.

The novel would have remained a personal exercise, however, if it weren't for the invaluable judgment of my film rights agent Jerry Kalajian, who after reading the first draft gave spot-on notes and believed in me as a fiction writer. Then there is the incomparable Diana Beaumont, my dear friend, wise editor and superlative agent, who saw something in this story of mine and pushed me to get it right. And the glamorous Grainne Fox, who jumped on as co-agent and made it happen in North America. Huzzah, indeed!

I'd like to thank my fabulous editors, my own version of the 'three tenors', namely Isobel Akenhead from Hodder & Stoughton, Brenda Copeland from St. Martin's Press, and Jennifer Lambert from HarperCollins Canada, who believed in this book and willingly worked together across borders and time zones and made it so much better. And to everyone behind the scenes at all three publishing houses in London, New York and Toronto, some of whom I've met and others I know only by name, who gave their expertise in copy-editing, design, lay-out, marketing, sales, publicity and the digital universe, I say thank you, thank you! With a special thanks to Laura Chasen and Jane Warren—you both have been such a help.

I'd also like to thank Griffith Saunders for the use of his name as well as his parents Doug Saunders and Elizabeth Renzetti for also saying yes and for giving me a roof in London for my research trips.

And continuing gratitude to my family and my friends and colleagues at *Zoomer* Magazine, particularly Julie Matus, and my slew of 'horsey' friends and others who continue to cheer me on.

And finally, to Richard.

408